WITHOUT
SANCTION

Without Sanction

J.M. Roberts

Boston ♦ Alyson Publications, Inc.

AUTHOR'S NOTES

With the exception of Oscar Wilde, Mrs. Fiske, Harrison Fiske, Charles Frohman, and A.L. Erlanger, all other characters are fictional and are not intended to represent any persons living or dead.

The story of Minnie Maddern Fiske (1864–1932) and her courageous fight against the Theatre Trust may be found in *Mrs. Fiske and the American Theatre,* by Archie Binns (Crown Publishers, 1955).

Typeset and printed in the United States of America.

This is a paperback original from Alyson Publications, Inc.,
40 Plympton St., Boston, Mass. 02118.
Distributed in England by GMP Publishers,
P.O. Box 247, London N17 9QR, England.

This book is printed on acid-free, recycled paper.

First edition: April 1993

1   3   5   4   2

ISBN 1-55583-215-6

Special thanks to Larry L., whose friendship and encouragement mean so much, and thanks to the members of the Brother-to-Brother Book Club for their enthusiasm and willingness to comment on the manuscript. Thanks also to Timothy M., for reading the manuscript and thinking I'm brilliant.(I'm not, but don't tell Tim.)

A very special thank-you to Sasha Alyson, for taking a chance on an unknown, and to Karen Barber of Alyson Publications, whose cheerful voice and willingness to answer many really dumb questions were like the answer to a prayer.

Without the sanction of Society
without the sanction of the Church
without the sanction of God
I love you

The Phoenix

England, 1882–1895

1

"P a's coming 'ome, ain't 'e," Jonathan said in an edgy, frightened voice. He turned anxious brown eyes upon his brother.

Harry Rourke did not answer or acknowledge his twin's fearful words. There was no need to. Nor did he have time. His sharp gaze was searching for an easy-to-pick pocket in the crowd trying to board the Margate steamer.

The breeze riffled Harry's blond hair down over his forehead and into dark eyes that were hard, the eyes of a man beset by devils though he was only a few days past his thirteenth birthday. Beyond and around the brothers, families of father, mother, and several children plus their baggage streamed toward the steamer boats waiting to take them on a two-day holiday.

Directly in front of Harry, like a gift from the god of thieves, a stout man with wife and a dozen children, stopped and bent over to pick up the youngest of the brood. When he bent, his coat pocket gaped open. Harry's fingers were clever butterflies as they dipped in and removed the man's purse without his being aware of it. Quickly Harry handed it to his brother and, giving the man a light blow on his pocket, ran away.

The man jerked upright, checked his pocket, and shouted, "Stop him! Stop him! Thief! Thief!"

Laughing, Harry ducked into alleys and jumped fences, without effort eluding the fat man and the half dozen men who joined in the chase. In the meantime, Jonathan walked slowly away from the scene, the purse inside his shirt, heavy against his thin body. He passed unnoticed through the holiday crowd until he had reached the appointed place, an abandoned bottle shop. Harry was there waiting for him. Jonathan handed him the purse and he seemed pleased with what was in it. Harry glanced at his brother, a smaller and frailer version of himself. Jonathan was pale and shivering.

"What's wrong?" Harry asked.

"I thought I saw Pa."

"He wouldn't have been down there, Jon. You look all in. Sit down and rest. Anyway, Pa's not due back for another week."

"'E's comin' today, 'Arry. I know 'e is."

Harry did not ask Jonathan how he knew. Jonathan knew the same way he did. They knew because Ma had stopped smiling and joking with her friends. At every real or imagined bit of "back-talk" her hands were quick to slap whichever son was closer. She drank more spirits and made Harry, not her favorite of the boys, spend hours on his hands and knees scrubbing the bare, drafty floors of their rickety shack. Never mind that the floors were never even swept while Pa was gone to sea. In the past few days she had become more and more silent and tense, pacing the floor and a dozen times a day stepping outside to look for him.

"You don't know he's coming for certain," Harry said flatly. He moved a pile of debris that hid a rotten floorboard in a corner. Lifting the board aside he dug into the dirt for a bottle found in the building the first time they'd gone there. There was money in the bottle. Harry rolled up most of the money from the man's purse, put it in the bottle, reburied it, and hid the spot again. Then he sat down beside Jonathan on an upturned crate.

"Soon we'll have enough money to leave here, Jon. We'll never have to see him again. I hate him."

Jonathan's forehead wrinkled. "You mustn't say that, 'Arry. The missionary man says it's wrong to 'ate anybody."

Harry's full-lipped mouth twisted. "Let him live with the old man for a while. Let him get beat. See what he'd say then."

He glanced down at his right hand and the crooked little finger. Pa had bent it so far back one day it had snapped with the sound of a stick cracking. The bones had knit crooked; the finger looked like a badly made hook and was all but useless. Though there were scars, most of the strap-marks on his back and arse and legs had healed. There would be fresh ones before Pa left again.

He did not tell Jonathan what he had overheard Ma say to a friend one day. She'd said it with a laugh but he knew she meant it. "Wisht I knew for sure who fathered those brats. If I knew for sure, I'd leave Tom for good and dump 'em on their real pa. I'm too young and pretty t'live like this."

Harry didn't care that they would be bastards if that was true. He hoped it was. He'd rather be the bastard of that black-spittin' chimney sweep on the corner or even of the Devil Himself than Tom Rourke's son.

Maybe their real pa was one of the "pretty soldier-lads," as she called them, who came into the Sextant Public House where she served tables while Tom was at sea. They came home with her often, the soldier boys. Her sons heard them tell her how beautiful she was, with her yellow hair and dark eyes. Those were the nights when Harry and Jonathan could hear sounds from the other side of the threadbare blanket that walled off half the single room, sounds that frightened Jonathan but which sent crazy feelings through Harry's body and mind.

Harry got up. "Are you rested? Come along then. Let's go back." He rumpled the hair that was a match for his own. "Let's race."

It was an unequal contest, for Harry always outran Jonathan in the crooked, cobbled streets. He was laughing and panting upon the sagging step of the shack that leaned against its neighbor when Jonathan ran up and flopped down beside him. "Someday I'll be bigger and faster than you."

Harry grinned at this other half of himself. "I'm twenty minutes older. You'll never catch up."

In Harry's eyes Jonathan was exactly like himself in looks. To others the differences were obvious. It were as though Harry's perfect features had been skewed a little when applied to Jonathan, as if his body had been cheated of Harry's vitality and strength, as if Harry's sharp mind had been dulled when given to Jonathan. And in the back of his mind Harry knew that Jonathan needed protecting from things both physical and mental, a task he had set himself when he was running and Jonathan just learning to walk.

He saw his brother stiffen and sit up. He peered in the direction Jonathan was looking and saw a very tall, brawny man trudging down the dark, narrow street, a duffel bag over one shoulder, brass buttons glinting. He had the distinctive rolling gait of a sailor.

"It's him." Harry scrambled to his feet. "I'm going away for a little while."

Jonathan clutched his sleeve. "Don't go, 'Arry. I don't want to be the only one 'ere."

"Oh, don't fret. Nothing's going to happen tonight. You know he's always nice the first night or so."

"Then why go?"

"Because I hate him. I don't want to have to speak to him just now. If 'tweren't for you I'd run away now. Today. Maybe we should both run away."

Jonathan shook his head. "We can't leave Ma."

It was on Harry's tongue to retort, "She'd leave us quick enough had she anywhere to go," but he didn't say it. Aloud he said, "I'll be back before he misses me. He don't never remember which of us is which anyways."

Harry did not go aimlessly through the neighborhood of dingy shanties and sooty little shops. He had a destination. He did not even stop to talk to Spitter and Toad when they called to him to come see the dead cat Toad stole from a ragpicker. He just waved at them and ran on his way to a street that, to the outside observer, was little better than what he had left, but which to Harry was another world. On this street was a magical place: the Royal Lion Theatre.

❐

He had discovered the theatre by accident one night a year earlier when he was running away from his father's fists. Frightened, angry, rebellious, blood bubbling from his cut tongue and dripping from his jaw, he had stumbled through the open doorway and stopped in confusion.

A group of people in strange clothes were standing upon a platform. There was a peculiar smell in the room. There were a lot of benches, like the church he'd once nipped into to pinch the poor-box, a chalice, and a crucifix. He had turned to go, when one of the women left the platform and caught his arm.

"You poor baby," she'd said. "What happened to you?"

He had stared at her. She was soft and clean and pretty and she spoke in a very strange way. A large man had gotten loud and angry that he had interrupted something called a "dress rehearsal," but the woman had spoken sharply to the man and he had stopped complaining. Her name was Lizbet and she became his best friend second only to Jonathan.

Lizbet was one of the owners of the small theatre, as well as its ingenue. She hired Harry to carry water and run errands and shine shoes and brush costumes. Though to most people the Lion would have been nothing but a run-down old ale-house with delusions of grandeur and the actors laughable amateurs, to Harry Rourke it was a place of magic. In the theatre anybody could become someone else altogether.

Harry loved everything about the theatre, from the actors like Lizbet and Roger, the juvenile lead, to the smells of makeup and old costumes and dust. Even the spiders in the corners had a certain theatrical charm for him though he hated spiders anywhere else. He liked to pretend they were some other kind of creature – in costume and stage makeup. Lizbet had laughed at his fancy.

"What are they really, then, when they take off the costume?"

He looked at her, grinned, and said, "Pigs."

When she discovered he had never been to school and did not even know his alphabet, she put her hands on her hips and said, "Well, my fine lad, we'll see about that!"

"I don't want t'go t'school," he said sullenly, and sidled toward the door. She grabbed him and would not let him go until he promised to let her teach him how to read.

The lessons came at rehearsals, between scenes, and at other odd times when he showed up. She forced him to put the *h*'s on his words and refused to acknowledge anything he said that was not said the way it should be. She taught him to say "Please" and "Thank you" and "Yes, sir" and "Madam." It was a new world. Once he began learning, he became starved for it and soaked up everything she taught him. She bragged about his quickness and eagerness to learn. She trimmed his hair and found used clothes to fit his rapidly growing body.

His reading primer was whatever play script happened to be lying around at the time. Harry could not share his newfound friends, his reading, or the theatre with Jonathan, even though Jonathan plagued him to tell where he went. He feared that Jonathan would let it slip to Ma and there would be an end to it. When Harry thought about never seeing the theatre again, he became almost sick.

Lizbet watched him one day as he sat on the floor in the light streaming through a backstage window, a book in his hand, his head bent over it, the sunlight turning his hair to a halo of gold. "Harry," she said softly. He looked up and smiled. "Harry, I don't think you have any idea how beautiful you are."

He shrugged off the compliment and went back to reading. She was nice, but barmy in the crumpet. He couldn't be all that special since there was another who looked just like him. Besides, he wanted to look like his idol, Roger, with his sideburns, mustache, and shiny, pomaded black hair.

◻

Harry arrived at the theatre to find no one there but Lizbet. She smiled, as she always did when she saw him. "Hello, Harry. I've nothing for you to do at this moment. Why don't you practice your reading? There's a script over there."

He picked it up and retired to a corner where he struggled to read the current script. His concentration was intense, but he heard his name mentioned. He kept his eyes on the script in case they looked over, but he listened to what they said.

"I wish we could use Harry as Young Christopher," said Lizbet.

"I wish we could use anyone else for Young Christopher," groaned Roger. "Toby is terrible. He has ten lines and he gets half of them wrong. Not to mention that he's growing so tall he doesn't look the part anymore. Harry—" The boy looked up and Roger tossed him a coin. "Be a good lad and go get a bucket of beer."

Harry almost blurted out, "Why don't you just tell the director to put me in instead of Toby?" He stifled the impulse. Even in his short time with the theatre he knew that The Director was next to God and could not be told what to do.

"Kid – the beer?" Roger reminded him.

Harry tugged at the bill of his soft cap and darted off, proud at being entrusted with such an important task. And there would be a shilling in it for him when he returned. As his feet churned toward Frenchie's Pub, his thoughts revolved around the too-tall Toby.

Toby Augustus, too, was thirteen years old, though he was a head taller than Harry. He and Harry had hated each other on sight with the same intensity with which Lizbet's cat Tiger Lily hated Mr. Wittenmeyer's bulldog. Harry had known for months that sooner or later he would have to fight Toby. Harry was a good fighter, a dirty fighter, but Toby was taller and fifteen pounds heavier. Until now Harry had never had a reason to risk getting beaten up. Now he had a reason.

He had seen the play so many times, he knew all of Toby's lines. He knew the cues and the exits. And Roger and Lizbet both wanted him instead of Toby. The solution seemed simple: get rid of Toby.

On the way back from the saloon, Harry went over his plan. Arriving there, he gave the bucket to Roger and went out behind the theatre. Toby was there, boldly smoking a thick black cigar as he tormented a starving puppy by holding a bit of fish in front of it then snatching the food away. Harry scooped up the puppy and dared Toby to do something about it.

"Gimme back the dog, Mistress Mary," Toby ordered. "Pretty Mistress Mary–Harry Quite Contrary. I've heard Lizbet go on and on about you. Enough to make me puke."

"Just lookin' at you is enough to make me puke," Harry retorted.

"Oh, yeah?"

"Yeah."

"What d'you know? I'm an actor and you're some drunkard's brat who can't even talk good English. Everybody knows that."

Harry put the puppy down and it wandered away. "I want to go on in your place," he said. "I know your lines better than you do."

"Is that so?"

"I'll make a wager with you. Winner goes on tonight."

"What wager?"

"Whichever of us can stay in the yard with Mr. Wittenmeyer's bulldog for five minutes is the winner."

"You're crazy. That dog's a killer."

"Scared!"

"Am not."

"Are so. If you wasn't you'd do it." Harry was counting on the fact that Toby was a bigger fool than he was.

"Okay, Mary-Harry, come on. I'll show you."

Swaggering, Toby led the way to the enclosure where the night watchman's dog was kept inside a stout, locked shed. They could hear the big dog hurling itself against the door. People said the dog was mad, but since he had been the same for a long time Harry doubted it. He was just mean. Like Toby.

Harry went over his plan again. If his timing was off or if the dog did something unexpected, he could be chewed to ribbons while Toby laughed his head off. The boys went inside the enclosure. Harry, last in, left the gate ajar as Toby lifted the bar on the shed door.

The dog hit the door and burst to freedom as Harry threw open the gate. While Toby was staring at him, open-mouthed, Harry shoved him into the shed and dropped the bar.

From inside Toby pounded on the door and yelled, "Let me out! Let me out! You son of a whore, let me out!"

Whistling, Harry went back to the theatre. There was an hour before curtain. No one would be going near the shed now.

For the next hour he was kept busy running here and there for the cast members, doing whatever he was asked to do. His stomach cramped with nervousness, waiting for The Moment.

The stage manager hurried past asking for the dozenth time, "Where's Toby? Anyone seen the little bugger?"

From out front came the sound of stomping feet. The crowd was what Roger called "riff-raff" and did not take kindly to delays.

Harry said loudly, "Mr. Jones—"

"Not now, not now. Damn it all, where is—"

"Mr. Jones, I know all of Toby's lines."

Jones stared at him, then shoved him into the arms of the wardrobe mistress. "Fix him up as Christopher. If Toby doesn't get back in two minutes the kid goes on."

Harry's heart raced. His first role. He suffered the ministrations of the wardrobe mistress, who hastily took in the pants Toby wore and stuffed rags into the shoes. With a dab of makeup and a lick with a hairbrush, she pronounced him ready. He waited in the wings, dancing with excitement, repeating the lines over and over to himself.

His cue came and he rushed on stage. "Mrs. Waring's coming and she's got—" He stopped, stricken, no further words coming. He was suddenly terrified of the huge men beyond the gas footlights.

"'—blood in her eye,'" whispered the prompter.

"—and she's got mud in her eye!" Harry cried.

The audience burst into howls of laughter. Harry was transfixed. It was supposed to be a funny scene but this was the first time anyone had ever laughed.

Afterward, when makeup and costumes were being taken off, men on one side of a curtain and women on the other, they talked back and forth.

"Did anyone ever see Toby?" asked Lizbet, her voice coming over the curtain.

"Not me," said someone and there was a chorus of voices in answer.

Harry was stripping off Toby's costume and shoes. There were blisters on his heels.

"Hey, kid, what are you doing over here on this side?" asked a man who was pulling off a fake beard. "Women and children on the other side."

Harry glared at him. "I ain't a child. I'm an actor now."

Everyone laughed. The man drawled, "Well, listen to Mr. Irving."

Roger chuckled and rumpled Harry's hair. "That's right, Harry, you're an actor. Ignore him."

"You did a swell job for a newcomer," put in another actor. "Saved that bloody scene."

Harry glowed. But then everyone left the theatre and he was alone.

Tonight he wanted to run home and share it all with Jonathan. But he couldn't, not while the old man was there. But — how could he not share it? It had been torture keeping it a secret all this time. After all, he had few secrets from Jonathan and Jonathan had none from him.

Harry hugged his excitement to himself. He had been on the stage. He would be on the stage again. "Listen to Mr. Irving" had been said in jest. Harry meant it to come true. B'God he would be better than Mr. Irving, than all of the Mr. Irvings in the whole world. Kings and queens and dukes – everyone would come see Harry Rourke!

It was well past midnight when he arrived home. As he reached for the doorknob he heard his father's loud, gruff voice from inside. He heard his mother give the strained laugh that was always the sound for the first night or so that his father was home. A minute later the door opened and Jonathan came out, a bemused look on his face. He had a small box in his hand.

"Jon!" Harry whispered. "I'm home."

"I didn't think you'd be away so long."

"I got something to tell you–"

"Look, 'Arry." Jonathan held out the small box. It was enameled and contained candy. "It came all the way from America."

"'Druther eat frogs than eat something he brought."

Jonathan shrugged and ate the candy. "Where've you been?" he asked with his mouth full.

"Can you keep a secret?"

Jonathan spit in his hand and crossed his heart.

Harry told him everything, his words falling over each other. Jonathan watched him with wide eyes. "But what if Pa finds out?" he asked.

"Don't care. I'll do it anyway."

"He – he'll beat you."

"He'll beat me anyway so I might's well get beat for something important."

He spoke with defiant bravado. Inside he quivered, knowing his brother was right. Jonathan was beaten less often because Harry drew the lightning of Pa's temper, often deliberately. Yes, he was afraid. But he couldn't let Jonathan know it.

He changed the subject. "Anything to eat?"

Jonathan nodded, disappeared under the porch, and surfaced with a wedge of cheese and a thick slice of bread wrapped together in a dirty rag. "I hid these for you."

Harry hadn't known how hungry he was until he started wolfing the food taken from Jonathan's grimy hands.

They perched on the warped front step and talked quietly. The door opened and Tom Rourke stood there.

"Well, well, look who's decided to get his arse home. Where you been, Jonathan?"

Harry stood up. "Jonathan was here. I'm Harry." He was surprised to discover he now came up to his father's Adam's apple. The realization electrified him. Soon he would be big enough to teach the old man a lesson when he got mean!

"I said where you been, boy."

Harry drew out the coins Lizbet had given him for the night's performance. "Working," he said with pride.

Before he could protest the coins disappeared into his father's pocket. The protest died on his tongue. Those few coins were not worth the beating he would get.

❏

Harry lay half-awake on the cot he shared with Jonathan. On the other side of the curtain Ma and Pa groaned and slurped and made the bed creak. One afternoon the last time Pa was home, Harry had stood on an upturned bucket and peeked in the window. He could not get rid of the images of what he had seen that day. His ma and pa naked on the bed, her underneath him, her legs spread. But it was his father's big, furry body that had held him hypnotized. There had been something about the muscles working in his pa's hips that had made the breath stop in his throat. He'd had this same feeling before, many times, and he thought about his own growing body.

Soon, he thought. Soon there would be big muscles in his chest and arms, and a man's thing where now there were only a few paltry inches that his mother, seeing him naked a few weeks ago, had laughingly called a "nubbin."

His musing turned to the two men he had seen not long ago in the Turkish bath where he had worked for two days cleaning floors, picking up wet towels, running errands. The red-haired man's towel had been wrapped apronlike around him. The other man carried his towel. Harry been astonished by the length of what dangled between the man's legs. He had been unable to wrench his eyes away.

While he had gaped at the man's cock his own had gotten hard. It had happened before, of course, when he wanked off alone or with Toad and Spitter, but this was different. He wished he could sneak a peek at it; it felt enormous.

The dark-haired man noticed the hard little bulge that appeared in the towel-boy's pants. He snickered. "What are you looking at, boy? Haven't you ever seen a real man's Hanging Johnny before? What d'you think, hey? Want to touch it? It's good luck if you do." He had grabbed Harry's hand and put it on his "Hanging Johnny." Harry gasped when it began to grow beneath his fingers.

The red-haired man said, "Oh, come on, Edmund. Leave the boy alone. Save it for Madame Boudinot's girls."

"I'm just getting warmed up, Andrew. Anyway, I don't hear the brat objecting. Do you?" The dark-haired man had grinned at Harry. "Like magic, isn't it, boy. Hanging Johnny becomes Standing Jack." Keeping his hand over Harry's, he moved Harry's hand up and down the shaft. Harry felt faint from the pressure inside him.

"Boy, you have natural talent." Without warning the dark-haired man put his free hand on Harry's shoulder and forced him to his knees, holding him there. Harry was too surprised to resist. Then the man clamped Harry's head in a viselike grip.

Alarmed, Harry struggled against the strong hands. "Hey, let me go, mister—"

"Come along, you little nelly," the man demanded, "I'll give you a shilling if you just open that pretty mouth of yours—"

The redheaded man hissed, "Edmund — someone's coming!"

Abruptly the dark-haired man shoved Harry away from him with such force that he tumbled backward on the wet floor.

"You dirty little bugger!" he shouted. "You keep your filthy hands to yourself." Then he had hastily knotted his towel around his waist and nodded at an older man who had just come in. "Good evening, Vicar." He cast a disdainful look at Harry, who was picking himself up off the slippery floor. "You have to watch the help here these days," the man said. "River rats! No education, no breeding, no morals. Why, one's own body is not safe! You would not believe what he just tried to do."

The vicar glared at Harry. "One can well imagine. One would be justified in calling a constable," he said. "One should be able to go into a public facility without being molested by vagabonds."

The red-haired man said in a low voice to Harry, "You'd better leave. Quick, now."

When Harry went to work the next day he discovered he had been sacked because of his public indecency. He was not even paid for the two days he worked. That made him angry.

And he had been angry with the man for making him do something and then turning on him. And yet he knew he liked what he had been made to do and would do it again given the opportunity. Afterward he was tormented by wondering what would have happened if the vicar had not come in, if he had done what the man wanted.

Thinking of it now, there in the darkness, he grew hot all over and Standing Jack was rigid and aching. He stroked himself the way he had stroked the man, almost at once gasped softly, and shuddered in release. He lay there dreamy-eyed for a while. Then he reached beneath the bed for the rag he kept hidden there for this purpose and cleaned the stickiness off the old sheet.

Ready for sleep, he turned toward Jonathan. Jonathan, he thought, was lucky; he didn't think about such things. Within moments he was deeply asleep, one arm over Jonathan, his lips against Jonathan's hair. They often slept like this, sometimes with Jonathan's arms around him. They had done so since infancy.

❐

During the week Tom Rourke was home the boys avoided him as much as possible, for whenever his eyes lighted on them a curse was followed by a blow. Harry got the brunt of them, though Jonathan came in for his share. Seeing Jonathan's lips bloodied, seeing the abject terror in his eyes whenever Pa looked at him made Harry hate the old man even more.

The night before Tom Rourke left for sea again, he got drunker than usual. Harry "looked at him" in a way that infuriated him. He knocked the boy down, and beat him with the cracked leather strap until his threadbare shirt was striped with blood.

Harry lay in bed all the next day, hurting too much to move, wishing he could cry. But he couldn't. He was almost a man; he could not cry. Not in front of Jonathan. But he didn't know how much more he could take. He remembered that Toad had a gun he had found. It was an old cap-and-ball and it was rusty, but maybe he would get it from him and kill the old fool.

Before he could do more than think about it, Rourke shipped out and would be gone for months. Good riddance.

A few days later as he and Jonathan wandered among the people in the teeming, crowded streets he said through clenched teeth, "I hope a typhoon blows Pa away. I hope his ship sinks and sharks eat him."

Jonathan said halfheartedly, "You oughtn't say that, the mission lady says. She says it's wrong to hate your own pa. She says we have to honor our pa and our ma."

As real as if he were still nearby, the big, brawny man loomed up in Harry's mind – hands like hams, brass buttons gleaming on his dark coat, thick black beard barely hiding the red mouth that bellowed hatred. Honor *him?* Then a new idea struck, one that pleased him no end.

"He's not our pa," he said. "He's the Devil. We're supposed to hate the Devil, ain't we?"

Jonathan looked puzzled but could not counter the argument.

With Tom Rourke's departure Harry went back to the theatre. Lizbet greeted him with concern for his bruises, scolded him for locking Toby up in the shed, and then offered to let him play Young Christopher for the final week of the run.

"Well, what about Toby?" he asked cautiously. He couldn't fool the bigger boy twice, and this time he'd get the worst of it.

"Toby stole from the ticket box this morning. He's not around anymore." She smiled. "So will you?"

"Yes, ma'am!"

"And would you like to play William in *The Bridge Crossing?* It's about a crippled boy. I think you could do it. I think you would have the audience awash in tears."

"Oh, yes, *ma'am!*"

"But you'll have to work much harder on your reading."

In the new play, poor crippled William saves his home from the villainous banker, rescues his widowed mother from the clutches of the villainous riverboat captain, then takes a fever and almost dies, only to be visited by an angel in the nick of time who restores both his life and his limbs. "Because," says the angel in the last scene, "you have been virtuous and brave, the things every boy should try to be, because only from such boys do virtuous and brave men come, because of these Christian virtues I say to you: Arise, William, and walk." Whereupon William not only arises and walks, but dances a hornpipe as well.

The hornpipe had been Harry's idea and he did it without first asking the director. It brought down the house. The director was ready to maim Harry and then replace him, but Lizbet said firmly, "It stays in. Let's add music to it." So it was that the actor portraying the poor but honest shoemaker who loves the widow from afar found himself blowing a mouth organ in the last act.

The play gave Harry another idea. "Jon!" he said to his brother, "we'll work together. We'll make lots of money."

The next day he sneaked Rourke's extra coat, unbeknownst to his mother. They begged a ride from a riverman who was sweet on Ma.

"Where we goin', 'Arry?" Jonathan asked, frightened.

"Oh, Jon, there's places in this City we ain't ever seen, places where people have all kinds of money. My friends at the theatre told me. You just do what I say and we'll be rich."

They left the boat downriver and soon found themselves in a part of town that had them both looking around open-mouthed.

The streets were wide, the shop windows clean. The children they saw wore no patches and they looked scrubbed to the point of pain. People hurried past wearing fine clothes, the men with derbies and the ladies with bustles and big hats or umbrellas. Behind the shining glass windows were things they had never imagined. They stood fascinated outside a toy shop and watched, noses against the glass, as toys moved as if they were alive. Jonathan loved a mechanical clownish figure dressed in a gaudy uniform. Then Harry roused himself and poked Jonathan. "Come on into the alley and sit down. Look sad's cat shit."

He draped the coat over Jonathan's shoulder, arms inside, and buttoned it, leaving the sleeves dangling. "Now," he said, "all you have to do is sit there on the sidewalk and look unhappy. I'll do the rest."

Jonathan sat huddled at Harry's feet, his face averted.

Harry called up the accent he was working so hard to discard. "Please, mister," he pleaded, holding out his cap, his eyes filled with tears, his lips trembling. "Me brother ain't got no arms – and he can't talk neither. And our pa died of consumption and Ma and the babe just was called to Heaven yestidy and we ain't got no 'ome no more ... 'Elp us, won't yer? God'll reward yer, mister..."

If it was a lady who stopped she would almost always look first into Harry's face and then at Jonathan and back at Harry. Harry would give forth a brave, quivering smile that called up the deep dimple in his left cheek. The power of that dimple was a mystery to him, but he knew it existed.

The lady would say softly, "You poor darling children. How dreadful." The ladies always got tearful before dropping coins into the hat.

At the end of the day they had enough money to go back to the toy store. Harry marched up to the clerk and bought a mechanical clown like the one in the window and had enough left for a shared kidney-pie and sour ale, with a small addition to the fund in the bottle.

"Here," he said, handing the toy to Jonathan.

His brother could not even speak; it had never occurred to him that he would own such a wonderful thing. He cradled it in his arms.

"See?" said Harry. "I told you acting would make us rich."

"You're a wonder, 'Arry," his brother choked.

Embarrassed but pleased, Harry punched his brother's arm. "Ain't I?" he said. "Ain't I just?"

2

Harry tried not to show his excitement as Lizbet, still wearing her wings as the Good Angel, introduced him to a "real theatre man," as she had described him to Harry. Still in makeup and costume for the character of William, Harry held out his hand to the gentleman.

Harry had never seen a man dressed quite the way this one was. His keen eye took in the diamond on the man's finger, the diamond stickpin in his cravat, and the ruffles on his shirt bosom and cuffs. With a touch of contempt Harry thought the gentleman looked like a regular nancy-man. A moment later the thought was forgotten. It didn't matter what the man looked like: he was "real theatre."

"So this is the young fellow you've told me so much about? How do you do, Mr. Rourke. I am Xavier St. Denys."

"Yes, sir, she told me. She said you're real theatre. Are you?"

The gentleman laughed. "In a sense. I've never acted, but I do love fine plays and good performances. Elizabeth has mentioned you in several letters to me. She believes you have talent and could amount to something in the theatre if you were aimed in the right direction. After all, even the best of arrows must be well aimed. You do have talent, Mr. Rourke. And your comeliness would certainly be no hindrance."

For a moment he puzzled over "Elizabeth"; nobody ever called her that. And he didn't know what "comely" meant and the remark about the arrow made little sense, but since Lizbet was smiling it must be good. He smiled his biggest smile. "Thank you, sir."

The gentleman reached into the breast pocket of his coat and gave Harry a small card. "Perhaps when you are grown and decide that acting shall be your profession, you might come see me."

Harry gazed at the card.

Xavier P. St. Denys
Entrepreneur

Then the gentleman was gone, leaving him almost giddy with his first meeting with Real Theatre. "Did you hear, Lizbet? He said he'd help me! And what's an enter– an entre– that word?"

She pronounced it for him. "It's a man who invests in things and takes risks in business. Mr. St. Denys is very successful. And very rich." She hugged him. "Oh, Harry, I don't want to lose you but you deserve better than we can give you. I'll work with you day and night and get you ready. Then you can go audition for him and do it up right."

"Audition?" He was astounded. "Why should I audition?"

She laughed. "Oh, Harry, you know so little. You're far and away the very, very best this company has, but we're not very good. Mr. St. Denys owns a theatre here in the City, and he helps me pay expenses here or we'd have to close."

"A theatre? He owns a theatre? Then why aren't we playing there?"

"Good heavens, that theatre is very professional. Rich people go there, and titled people. We are not as accomplished as all that. And that's all right. I love owning my own place and being able to act in my own plays." She brushed back his hair. "But you ... you have something special inside. Great actors have this – a kind of power."

"I still don't see why I have to audition."

Her eyebrows lifted. "Oh, my. Is my sweet Harry developing conceit? Darling, you have enormous talent. You don't have the training you need. If you can convince him beyond doubt that you have what it takes, he will sponsor you. You must work and make sure he will."

Harry returned home downcast. Talent? Well, he knew he had that. But ... no training? What had he been doing for six months of his life there at the Royal Lion? Wasn't that training?

But when he was telling it all to Jonathan in their hiding place in the warehouse, there was no room in his heart for anything but excitement.

"I'll be famous, Jonathan. I'll – we'll – go to America." He put an arm around his brother's shoulders, noticing with a little shock that Jonathan seemed frailer than he had, and he could now see the top of Jonathan's head. It was almost like he was growing and Jonathan wasn't. "And because you're my brother – my *twin* – you'll be famous too. People will mistake you for me, maybe."

Jonathan's smile was wistful. "Ain't nobody never done that yet. You're ever so much 'andsomer and smarter."

"That's not so, Jon. It's just those extra twenty minutes. You'll catch up. See if you don't." But what Jonathan said was true and he knew it. Sometimes he felt guilty because he was glad he was handsome and smart. Sometimes, to make up for the guilt, he pretended to himself that he was Jonathan.

❒

For two months more their lives did not change except that Jonathan was left home oftener since Harry was at the theatre. Jonathan did not complain and Harry himself did not stop to think about it, caught up as he was in his new life.

When Rourke returned before he was expected, everything was turned topsy-turvy. This time there was no brief period of pleasantness. He was drunk when he walked in the door that morning. He brought no gifts from strange faraway places like Seattle or New York or China. He brought nothing but sullen silence broken by outbursts of rage.

Harry was torn between not wanting to leave Jonathan there with him and not wanting to miss a day at the theatre. He begged Jonathan to come with him.

Jonathan shook his head. "You go, 'Arry. It's for you and I'm glad. I'll be all right."

That night Rourke and his wife had a fight that broke a table and several dishes and discolored both of her eyes. Harry came home to find Jonathan cowering in the corner in terror, Ma crying hysterically, Pa gone to a pub.

Harry calmed Jonathan and they went to bed. Still Rourke did not come. Harry was still awake when he heard the door creak. He sat up, fearing it was his pa. Instead he saw his mother's silhouette. She was wearing a hat and carrying a case. He stole from the bed, pulled on his pants, and followed her outside.

"Ma – where are you going?"

She spun about. "'Arry – you scared me. I'm goin' away. I can't stay married to that man anymore. 'E ain't 'uman, 'e ain't."

He stared, bewildered. "Away? But can't we go too?"

"I got no money to take care of two boys. But you're almost a man grown now, 'Arry. You're almost fourteen!" She moved her arms toward him as if to hug him, then drew back. "Look after your brother, 'Arry. 'E ain't as strong as you."

She turned and went resolutely on her way. "Ma!" he cried. "Ma!" She did not turn again.

He wavered, wanting to run after her and demand she take them with her. But if Jonathan woke up and there was no one there he would get frightened.

He went inside. The future loomed large and frightening. He shivered at the idea of no one there but themselves and Pa. But there was hope. Maybe Pa was not at a pub after all. Maybe he'd left again for sea and was on a ship bound for someplace a million million miles away. He lay down beside Jonathan and wrapped his arms around him.

"Ma's gone," he said. Jonathan started to cry.

"We got each other," Harry whispered, his voice fierce. "We don't need anybody else. We got each other."

Rourke did not return the following morning. Jonathan sat with big scared eyes, expecting Harry to do something. So he tried his hand at fixing breakfast. The coffee was thin and bitter but the thick slices of hard bread dipped in it at least filled them up.

Rourke did not come back that night or the next morning. Harry breathed a sigh of relief; the old man had indeed gone away again. Harry ran to the theatre, to face an ultimatum by the director. Either he was going to perform or he was not and if it was the latter he'd better decide pretty bloody quick.

"Of course I'll perform," he retorted. "I'm an actor, ain't I?"

The director rolled his eyes heavenward. "God save me from juvenile Hamlets."

❐

Harry knew the minute he opened the door at home that Rourke had returned. He smelled gin. Careful not to slam the door or step on the creaky floorboard, he went in, softly calling, "Jon?"

He found Jonathan curled up in bed, shivering violently, his face and body almost too hot to touch, his eyes glassy, his face bruised.

"Jon, what's wrong? Do you need a doctor?" Neither of them had ever been to a doctor and he didn't know where to find one but if Jonathan needed one...

"No!" cried Jonathan. "No."

"But you're sick. I'll get Lizbet. She'll know what to do."

"No, please, no, 'Arry. Don't get nobody. Please." A tear rolled down his face. He pulled the blanket up tightly under his chin. "No doctor, 'Arry. Please."

Harry pulled back the blanket. Jonathan's thin arms as well as his face were purple with bruises and the slightest movement of his body made him whimper.

Harry had felt angry most of his life. Now for the first time he felt rage. "He came home, didn't he! He beat you, didn't he!" Harry slammed his fist against the wall and started toward the door. "Toad's got a gun and I'm goin' t'get it. I'm goin' t'blow the old man's—"

"Don't, 'Arry!" Jonathan cried. "Don't make things worse." He started to sob. "'E did awful things, 'Arry. 'E hurt me so bad. 'E said I wasn't no good, no better'n a woman is what 'e said, then 'e knocked me down and 'e – and 'e – Oh, 'Arry, I want t'die. Don't do nothin' to make 'im mad. Promise me you won't."

"I'll try," said Harry through clenched teeth.

"Promise me!"

"I – promise."

Just then Rourke lurched in and grabbed Harry's shirt. "Where's that slut you call mother? Eh? You know, don't you, you whore's get."

"No, I don't."

Rourke slapped him. "Of course you do. Little Mister Know-It-All. You and your airs, prancin' around like you're better'n me! You know everythin'. Where be your mother?"

"She's gone's all I know."

"Where'd she go?"

Fear made Harry's stomach twist and turn. *I won't show him that I'm scared I won't show him I'm scared—*

"I asked you where she is, you son of a poxy whore!"

"I don't know and if I did I wouldn't tell you." He was amazed when his father released him and grinned.

"Well. The bitch's whelp is growing up, is it? Does it think it's becomin' quite a man? Eh?" He directed a look of disgust at Jonathan, who had been watching, cringing, with tears on his face. "At least I have one son who's gonna be a man and not a damned cunt." Harry had never seen anything so evil as that smile. "Sit down, 'Arry. You and me got man-things to talk about."

Harry perched on the edge of one of the rickety chairs. His father stood over him with a full gin bottle. "Drink up, 'Arry. That's how real men do. Right out of the bottle."

Warily, never taking his eyes from the man, Harry took the bottle and downed the first swallow. At the theatre he often had beer and ale, but he wasn't prepared for the gin that sent water pouring from his eyes and fire burning all the way down to his stomach. He choked and tried to give the bottle to his father.

"Drink it like a man," Rourke demanded.

"I don't want to."

"I said drink it like a man."

"Go to hell."

Rourke stalked to the cot. He seized Jonathan and held him across his knees, his arm twisted behind his back. "Drink it down, boy. Or I'll snap his arm like a twig and it will be your fault."

Jonathan whimpered. Harry tilted the bottle up and drank. Nausea began heaving in his stomach. He lowered the bottle. Rourke pushed Jonathan's arm and he cried out.

"Like a twig, 'Arry," Rourke said with a grin. *"Snap!"*

Head spinning, stomach ready to burst from liquor and sickness, he drank some more. He couldn't see straight. The bottle was still half-full.

"Drink it!"

"'Arry — 'elp me–," Jonathan wailed.

Harry forced another swallow down. And another. Suddenly it all came back up in wave after wave. He leaned forward, sending it all over the floor. It splattered upon Rourke's shoes.

"Damn you!" Rourke bellowed. He leaped from the cot toward Harry. "You're a bloody swine! Okay, swine, wallow in your mess!" He clouted Harry across the back of the head, sending him tumbling from the chair to lie sprawled in his gin-reeking vomit. Rourke seized a handful of his hair and dragged his face back and forth through it, smearing it not only on his face but in his hair and on his shirt. Harry struggled, cursing and crying. Jonathan wailed. Rourke kicked Harry, rolling him over in the stinking puddle.

"Clean up this mess, you filthy little swine!" he ordered. "Got t'get this place ship-shape."

He let loose of his son. Crying from hatred and humiliation, Harry got to his knees, trying to find a dry place on his clothes where he could wipe his hands. Rourke shoved his foot against Harry's back, sending him flat on his belly in it again.

"Clean it up before you go to bed." He laughed, then lurched to his own bed and fell across it, mumbling, "One son's a cunt and the other's a swine." Soon he was asleep.

"I'll kill him," Harry sobbed. "I'll kill him. I'll kill him. I'll kill him."

From the bed, Jonathan said in a barely audible voice, "Don't say that, Harry. I wish I could help."

"Don't be a fool. You're sick. Go to sleep."

Jonathan nodded and closed his eyes.

By the light of the kerosene lamp Harry scrubbed the floor, several times running outside to vomit again. When the floor was clean he listened to make sure Pa was asleep and then took his other set of clothes, left the house, and slipped away to the river. There he swam and washed himself with a piece of lye soap he had stolen from the woman next door. Not until he felt clean from head to heels did he leave the cold water and go home.

Shivering, he crawled into bed with Jonathan, reaching out to him for warmth as he always did. But Jonathan did not smile in his sleep and put his arms around Harry's neck as he sometimes did. He did not murmur. He did not move.

"Jon?" he whispered. "Jon, are you all right?"

He felt his brother's face. It was cold. As if he were the one who had just come from the river.

"No," he whispered. He wanted to scream. But if he did Pa would take Jonathan away. He put his arms around his brother and held him throughout the night, too grief-stricken to cry. As soon as day came he'd get Lizbet. She'd know what to do.

❒

The theatre people took up a collection for a coffin and came to the funeral. Rourke stood alone on one side of the plain pine box. Harry stood on the other side with his friends. Lizbet had her arm around his shoulders. He still couldn't cry; he was too numb. He didn't know what had happened. Jonathan had been sick and feverish a lot of times after getting beaten by their pa, but he couldn't have died from it.

The service ended. Lizbet said, "Harry, you can come home with me if you like."

He shook his head. "Jonathan's things are still there."

So he returned to the small house with Rourke.

They ate supper in silence until Rourke said, "It ain't much of a loss, you know. He was a fairy. And now he'll rot in the earth and the worms will eat him." He chuckled and said in a sing-song, "Worms'll crawl in and worms'll crawl out and his eyes'll fall in and his—"

Harry's face went even whiter and twisted with grief and hatred.

"Stop it!" he howled. "Stop it!"

"...guts'll pop out—" Rourke roared with laughter.

"You killed him! You killed him! You bastard!"

Harry flung himself at his father, beating with his fists at the big sunburned face. His father hit him, sending him reeling against the wall. Harry scrambled to his feet and hurled himself again and again against that unmovable wall of flesh. Each assault was stopped with a blow to his face or his belly. His fist struck Rourke's nose and a stream of bright red spurted out.

Rourke seized the boy's wrists in one huge hand and hit him repeatedly across the face until blood ran in rivulets from his nose and mouth.

Harry's knees buckled and the only thing keeping him upright was the hand on his wrists. Still his hysterical young voice shrilled, "You killed him! You killed my brother!" He was still shrieking when everything went black.

❐

He woke an eternity later, crumpled on the floor. He struggled to his knees and then to his feet. The left side of his face felt wet; his fingers came away red. From the sound of heavy snoring Harry knew Pa was on the other side of the blanket. Harry stifled a moan of pain as he got to his feet and staggered to the kitchen table.

His mind was doing strange things. Objects revolved and melted into one another until nothing was left in his mind but his father's evil and the image of Jonathan's decaying body.

On the cluttered table he found his mother's fish knife. Bits of the last fish she had cut still clung to it and it smelled foul. Its blade was long and razor sharp.

On legs that threatened to give way, he went to where Rourke lay, his shirt unbuttoned. With both hands, Harry lifted the knife above his head and plunged it into the broad, black-furred chest. Blood bubbled out around the blade.

Rourke's eyes flew open in shock.

"Die, you bloody bastard," Harry gasped as he yanked the knife out and plunged it in again. Rourke tried to rise, then fell back and did not move.

Able to see nothing but blurs through his swollen lids as he crept through the shadows, hiding from the world, Harry made his painful way to the theatre and collapsed in the dressing room.

The next thing he knew, someone was raising him up. Pa! He cried out and struggled until he heard Lizbet say, "Harry, my poor darling, what happened? Did that monster—"

He stopped fighting and collapsed in her arms. "Pa killed Jonathan and I killed him and what am I going to do?" He clutched her sleeves, his teeth clicking together.

"Can you walk?"

He nodded and she helped him to his feet. "I'm taking you to my home. It isn't far."

In her small shabby parlor Lizbet listened as she treated the wounds on his face in silence, her own face ashen. "What a terrible, terrible thing...! I wish you had come here with your brother as soon as your mother left."

He could not let loose of his terror. "The Yard'll catch me! They'll hang me for killing him."

She held his icy hands in hers. "No, dear. They won't. I promise you. The Queen should give you a medal. You're safe here. No one knows you came here. You need to sleep."

"I – I can't—"

She gave him some medicine. "Laudanum," she said. "It will help you sleep."

He lay down on her settee. She threw a blanket over him and gently kissed his forehead. "My poor baby. That devil got what was coming to him. I only wish you had not been the one who had to do it."

Lizbet was jarred awake. Hurrying to the parlor she found Harry thrashing about, his head thrown back, his throat and jaw rigid. Lizbet wrapped her arms around him and held him.

"Pa's not dead!" he cried. "He's coming after me!" Over and over he said it, trying to tell her that he had seen the big man come into the room, the buttons on his coat gleaming. Gradually the violence stopped and, exhausted, he lay his head on her shoulder.

"It's all right, Harry. You're safe here. He can't hurt you, ever again. Hush, Harry. Hush."

She soothed him back to sleep and cursed the soul of Tom Rourke, wishing him into an everlasting hell hotter than any parson ever thought of.

Harry slept for almost forty-eight hours, and when he moved from the settee it was with slow, painful steps. His face was swollen and bruised. Deep bruises showed on his neck. Looking into the haggard, half-crazed young face, Lizbet said, "Harry, you know you can stay here forever if you like, but I think you need to get away. We don't want the police to find you."

His eyes filled. "My brother ... I was always going to run away and take him with me. I waited too long. I should've taken better care of him."

"You're naught but a child yourself. You did the best you could."

His eyes were haunted and he shook his head. "If I'd done the best I could, I'd be far away and Jon would be with me. Pa said Jon's being eaten by worms." He shuddered, remembering. "I saw a dead dog once that was rotten and its eyes were–" He gulped. "I'm scared. I don't want Jon to be like that."

She again put her arms around him and rocked him. "Oh, Harry, don't. Jon is in your heart and your mind and there he will always be young. He can't be hurt anymore, ever. Think of that, not the other. Hold him in your heart." After a while she smoothed back his tangled hair and looked into his eyes. "I must be away for most of the day. Stay here and rest. Don't answer the door. Don't talk to anyone, not even someone from the theatre."

He tried to sleep again after she was gone, but whenever he drifted across that border his father's distorted face, twisted with hatred, swam before his mind and his father's hands were raised to strike him. He crouched in a corner, clutching the fireplace poker. Lizbet found him there.

"Harry, I am going to take you to Mr. St. Denys. I have been to see him, and have told him what your circumstances are. He has agreed to help you."

He said nothing; he was too confused and too numb to think. She handed him some clothes. "There is blood on what you're wearing so I bought you these." He took them but did not even look at them.

Lizbet studied his battered face. "I hope that monster did not scar you."

Harry did not hear her. He could think of but one thing at that moment: Jonathan was dead. He would never see him again.

Tears slid down his cheeks and dripped from his chin.

3

Harry crowded closer to Lizbet as they boarded the train at Victoria Station. He had never seen a railroad train and the hugeness and the steam and noise were frightening. Panic brushed him; people were looking at them.

"Lizbet—," he whispered, "those people. They know what I did! They're staring at me—"

"No, they're not. See? Most of them are far too concerned with their own affairs to worry about us. Up you go." She glanced sideways at him. She had artfully applied stage makeup to the worst of his marks and hoped he could keep from rubbing it off before they reached their destination.

Inside the car he sat down beside her. She was talking about acting. He stopped listening. It didn't matter anyway. He didn't want to be a famous actor anymore. He just wanted his brother back alive. With a huge groan and creak the train began to move. He clutched the arms of the seat until his knuckles were white.

Too much had happened. He felt as if he were in someone else's body, looking through someone else's eyes. Sunk in misery, he did not even see the green beauty of the wooded hills and the valleys where cattle and sheep grazed, a world free of smoke and dinginess and noise. He saw nothing but his own fear and his imminent death by hanging.

❑

"Miss Crawford and friend to see Mr. St. Denys," Lizbet said to the butler who opened the great door of the brick-and-stone mansion.

The butler inclined his head. "Very good, madam. He is expecting you."

They entered a hall which led up a wide staircase worn with generations of passing feet, the smooth handrail darkened from the oils of gliding hands. The butler led them to a room with thousands of books on wooden shelves from floor to ceiling. Harry had not known there were that many books in the world. Many small tables and shelves displayed artifacts and statues. Habit took over. He reached for a small statue to slip into his coat.

The towering double doors opened and St. Denys strolled in. Harry froze, thinking in panic, *I ought to leave here. I ought to run for it—* Hastily he replaced the little figure he had been holding.

"I was just – looking–"

The man smiled. "Quite all right. That's what they are for."

Harry was still suspicious, but relaxed a little. He tried to take an interest in this man who, in one way or another, was the key to his future, according to Lizbet.

"Harry," St. Denys said gently, "Elizabeth told me of the loss of your brother. I am most sorry."

Harry tried to swallow the sudden lump in his throat. "Yes, sir. Thank you, sir. We was twins, you know. It was like he was part of me."

"I understand. Harry, I would like to invite you to stay here for a while, if you would like to. This place is large enough for twenty like you. I would be your guardian, so to speak, until other arrangements could be made."

The boy's back stiffened. "I won't be beholden to you, sir. If I stay I'll do something to earn my keep. I'll muck out the stables or–" He paused. He was good at nothing except picking pockets and playacting. He was stuck with the stables. "Whatever you need. But I ain't charity."

"I understand. There is plenty of time to discuss particulars. I warn you, if you stay here for even a few days I will make a gentleman of you. For whatever time you are here you will have a tutor and hard studies to make up for lost time."

"Yes, sir," he said, with a touch of rebellion in his voice.

"Xavier," said Lizbet, "I've been thinking ... Should he not take a different name for safety's sake? If the police should hold a warrant for him, even though he is miles from the City..." Her voice trailed off.

"I thought the same." St. Denys looked at the boy. "Harry, it must be your decision."

"No. I won't change my name. It's how Jon knew me. The missionary man says there's a heaven. I don't believe it but Jon did and if there is, he's there. If I change my name maybe he can't find me."

"It's for your own protection," said Lizbet. "We could choose a name Jon would recognize. A character from a play, perhaps."

"No."

"You need to make a new life," said St. Denys. "You need to start that new life with a new identity."

"No."

"Isn't there some character Jon would know?" asked Lizbet. Harry hesitated. "Young Christopher Smith. I told him about it."

"Then Christopher Smith you shall be until it's safe to be Harry Rourke again." St. Denys's tone was firm. "That is settled."

Harry looked from one to the other. Once again his decisions were taken from him. They meant to help him the best way they knew how, but the loss of his name was the loss of one strong tie to his brother. "All right," he said dully. "I'll be Christopher if you think it's best."

"Now, then, I would like to talk to Elizabeth awhile. I'll have Brady show you your room and then you may explore the house, the grounds, anything you like." He pulled a velvet rope and to Harry's amazement, the butler appeared as if by magic.

He once again followed the butler, this time up another flight of the stone stairs, down a hallway to a room as large as the small house he had always known.

"This is to be your room, sir." The butler indicated a velvet cord. "Ring if you require anything, sir."

Harry stifled nervous laughter. *"Sir"*? "Wait. How does that work? How do you know when it's pulled?"

The butler arched an eyebrow and said with the slightest touch of condescension, "It rings a bell in the servants' quarters, sir."

When the door closed behind the butler he lay down on the bed. It was incredibly soft. Jonathan would like it—

Jonathan! Just the thought of the name wrenched him inside like nothing else had ever done. He covered his eyes with his arm and fought the tears. Tears were for kids, not for somebody what had killed his own pa. He was a criminal hoping he would not be found out. He was not even Harry any longer. Christopher. Christopher. The name felt foreign.

He was almost a man. He shouldn't cry. But he did.

❏

Xavier St. Denys dressed like an effeminate dandy, but beneath the silk shirts and ruffles was a small-boned and muscular body. He had been born in this house, St. Denys Hill, son of an ancient family of easily changed alliances which miraculously moved from serving Plantagenets to serving Tudors without the loss of lands or heads.

Xavier had been disowned by his family for being involved at university with the one unforgivable vice. The young man with whom he had been found committing "a crime of gross indecency" found himself a wealthy virgin to marry with dizzying speed. He had become respectable, a Member of Parliament, and, Xavier knew, shared Wilde's pederastic taste for young telegraph boys, a taste Xavier could neither understand nor condone. Xavier himself had refused to either marry or repent. He was banned from England by his father and told he would be prosecuted if he returned.

He went to America without a penny, panned for gold and found nothing, won a gold mine in a poker game, made a huge fortune from it, and sold the mine at an enormous profit just months before the vein petered out. There followed a pistol duel with the new mine owner, who wound up dead with a bullet between his eyes. Canny investments, along with a good deal of luck, had made Xavier a very wealthy man. In the meantime, the St. Denys family had fallen on hard times. Taxes, social changes, these had all taken their toll. The Hill was in danger of becoming the property of the Queen.

Xavier returned to England and saved the family home. He expelled his father and let his mother stay there until she died. Now he had a grand home in England and another in California. He had everything he could desire save one. A son.

At Elizabeth's invitation he had gone to see the Rourke boy perform. Something had drawn him to the young actor he had seen at the small theatre. Yesterday morning she had come to him with that dreadful story, and instinct told him she did not know half of what went on in that house. The invitation had been instant. For a day or a week or a month or a year, he would have a son.

❏

The day passed, and then the week, the month, the year. Other years passed and still the boy fugitive stayed at St. Denys Hill. Bit by bit the name Harry Rourke receded in his memory. He became, even in his own mind, Christopher.

He'd never met anyone as grand or as educated as St. Denys, nor anyone with so many affectations, and few men who were as physical. St. Denys was a crack shot, and a superb horseman and fencer. He had ridden to the hounds as a boy. He told Christopher stories of riding into the American hills looking for wildcats.

"Someday I'll take you there," he said. "And we'll hunt wildcats together."

He educated Christopher in every phase of polite living, from how to handle a bewildering array of tableware, finger bowls, stemware, and napkins to how to fence and ride a horse like a gentleman.

He never seemed to be taken by surprise. Christopher had been in the library often, but not until he had been at the Hill a few months did he really look at the statues. And then he had stared in disbelief. Every one of them was of a man, stark naked and perfect in every detail. St. Denys caught him one day, examining the three-foot-tall statue that was the centerpiece of the collection.

"Do you like it?" he asked, not at all put off at catching him.

"It's, um, naked. They're all naked. Why?"

St. Denys smiled. "For many reasons, the most important of which is that they represent physical ideals of beauty. When you are older perhaps I'll tell you the other reasons."

"Why didn't the sculptors put clothes on 'em?"

"Partly because they didn't wish to, and an artist is allowed license other people are not. Mostly because fashions are often ugly and quickly grow boring. The human body is beautiful and unchangeable."

That was just one of those fancy sayings Christopher did not understand right away. He filed it away for later thought.

St. Denys provided tutors and mountains of books for Christopher, who found that he liked most of the learning, though he would have been more than happy to bypass geography and mathematics. Christopher did not know of the monthly conferences St. Denys held with his tutors, one of whom sang the praises of the boy's quick mind and imagination while the other despaired of ever teaching him to border the countries of Europe and Asia, name the most important products of Turkey, or do simple equations.

When Christopher's voice settled, St. Denys hired a voice master who was enthused by the quality and depth in one so young.

St. Denys himself was a fount of knowledge about everything from astrolabes to Xanthippe, and he loved telling stories to Christopher.

But most important, in Christopher's eyes, St. Denys loved the theatre. Almost daily he took Christopher to the Xavier Theatre, a small but elegant place in London. Christopher was put to work, to learn the trade from the ground up.

By the time Christopher was fifteen he had gotten splattered with paint from head to heels helping to paint flats; he had developed strong shoulders and arms working with the flyman to raise and lower scenery; he had smashed his right thumb with a hammer while driving nails into vignettes. He had developed monkeylike agility while clambering around high up in the fly loft. He had tasted the paste used in making *papier-mâché* rocks and fruit and other properties to be used on stage. He had been call boy, making certain the actors were ready for their entrances.

St. Denys hired an acting coach for him, a man named Wilson Humboldt, who had worked with Edmund Kean and though now an old man, still retained his fire and his passion for acting.

Humboldt worked with him on written plays of all kinds, from the lightest comedies to the darkest tragedies, and between the two of them they played both genders, every age, and every role.

From the first year St. Denys periodically stopped all lessons for two or three months and he and the boy would travel. "There is so much of life you have never seen," he said. "I intend that you shall see it while you can."

They went to Welsh mining towns and the Liverpool docks. They visited the Midlands and the Scottish Highlands, crossed over to Ireland. They explored the forests of Germany, the culture of France, the sunlit stones of Greece. Wherever they went, St. Denys told him history – of fierce Celts and Picts, of Richard the Lionhearted and Richard III, who, he said, was a tragic and misunderstood man. He told him about the Caesars, and about Alexander and Hadrian, Zeus and Hera. They visited Spain and Christopher discovered the guitar. St. Denys hired a Spanish guitarist to teach him how to play.

Wherever they went, St. Denys made him listen keenly to the language, dialect, and inflection and practice speaking that way until he could do a creditable imitation. They went to California, where Christopher discovered a hundred dialects, all called American.

Back home again, studies resumed.

Lizbet came to dine often. At some point he learned that Lizbet was his guardian's cousin. "We're both black sheep of the family," she said, laughing. "Xavier because of – well, reasons he'll have to tell you, and myself because I became an actress and as everyone knows, actresses are tarts and scarlet women." She laughed again. "But it's much more fun being thought a harlot than a lady."

❐

Without realizing he was doing it, St. Denys fell into the habit of calling the boy "Kit."

One night at dinner Christopher asked, "Why do you call me that?"

St. Denys looked puzzled. "I beg your pardon? Call you what?"

"Kit. You've called me that for quite a long while. So long I even think of myself that way half the time."

"Hm. I didn't know I was. Well, if there is a reason, it's because it fits you. Kit Carson. Kit Marlowe. Adventurous, sometimes reckless, rebellious." A frown of anxiety added another line to his forehead. "If you don't like it, I shall stop."

Christopher smiled. "I rather like it. It's mine, not just the name of a character in a play. I just wondered the reason for it, that's all."

So without effort, Harry who had become Christopher now became Kit.

❐

Though it had been not quite three years, he could sometimes forget he had not always lived here and been this man's friend. Despite the differences in their ages and backgrounds they got on very well and spent much time together.

As Kit moved into his late teens St. Denys increased the boy's exposure to culture. They went to concerts and operas now, and Kit could speak with a little insight about the composers and the singers. He expressed himself well, whether in his own words or those of a poet or playwright. He learned to dance with style, a fit partner for any young lady.

He was still awkward with a foil but was progressing rapidly. He rode his horse like a born gentleman.

Outwardly, his life was nearly perfect, given the empty place in his heart that Jonathan's death had left. But there were things warring inside him, things he knew he could never tell his guardian. The peculiar thoughts and feelings he had about men had gotten stronger. And often in the silence of night he had nightmares about

Pa. But these things he held to himself, believing if he did not speak of them they would go away.

◻

St. Denys had two circles of friends, and they did not mingle. The first group, who did not even know about the second, were those who came to soirees that glittered with jewels and filled the air with ladies' perfumes and the music of string quartets playing Mozart. Other times they came to picnics with two hundred guests, dining outside, served by servants, and eating from gold-bordered china beneath thousand-year-old oaks. At these events Kit, whether in evening dress or white flannels, was much made over by the ladies, who pronounced him a "heartbreaking young gentleman" and coyly told St. Denys to remember that they had daughters or nieces who would be wanting a husband in a few years.

For some reason his guardian did not explain, Kit was kept away from the other circle of friends. Annoyed at being excluded, Kit discovered he could crouch on a landing and look down into the Lesser Hall. He was puzzled that there never were any ladies at these parties, only men his guardian's age or younger, but none as young as he.

There was something intoxicating about the nearness of all those men, the rumble of their voices undiluted by the shriller sounds of female voices. He resented being kept away; he didn't understand the reason. The one time he asked, St. Denys had looked stern and said, "Because it is best." And then he had looked even sterner and asked, "And how, exactly, do you come to know about these gatherings?"

Trapped, Kit had to admit his spying.

St. Denys sighed. "Well, I won't have dishonesty in my house. Friday evening you may join us. But for an hour only."

Kit spent four days in eager anticipation.

That night he walked into the Lesser Hall to find thirty or so casually dressed men. The air was heady with the sounds of their voices and laughter, the smell of their pipes. He saw his guardian talking to a black-haired man; their heads were close together and his guardian laughed at something the man said. A tall fleshy man with brown hair parted in the center and hanging about his face was keeping the small group around him regaled with a story. He was the first to see Kit. He stopped talking and stared. When he did so, those around him had to see what he was staring at. And then St. Denys and the black-haired man looked at him. Kit's face was hot. Lizbet had been right when she said he did not realize how strikingly handsome he was; he assumed he must look a right fool for them to be gawking like that!

The man with the long brown hair drifted to him and took Kit's hand in his. "What a lovely lad you are, a dainty blossom among us old withered weeds. I didn't know Xavier had the good taste to have anyone like you."

Kit's mouth dropped open. He had never heard a man talk like this. "Lovely"? "Dainty blossom"? Was the fool talking about *him*? The fellow was lumpy and effeminate with a big moon-face. Kit extricated his hand from the damp grasp.

"I'm Oscar," the strange man said, "and I cast my heart at your feet and wish to lose my soul in the depths of your eyes."

Just then St. Denys shouldered between them and put his hand on Kit's shoulder. "Gentlemen," he said, with a baleful glare at the long-haired man, "this is Kit, my ward, and so far as I am concerned, he is my son. He is under my care and my protection. Do you take my meaning, gentlemen?"

The long-haired man smiled, showing bad teeth which he covered at once with a finger. "Oh, Xavier. We are not simpletons, you know. Of course we take your meaning." He winked at Kit, and Kit was more than ever convinced the man was a fool.

As if St. Denys's words had broken a spell the men resumed their conversations, though every now and again Kit would catch a pair of eyes looking in his direction. Bored, he left before his hour was up to go to the library to read.

The three-foot-tall statue, which St. Denys had told him was of a young man named Antinous, was his favorite. Sometimes he talked to that lifelike stone face. "I don't know what I expected," he said, "but they were just fusty old men, except for the one called Oscar. He was younger but a very peculiar chap."

He selected a book and sat down to read. He had had a long day at the theatre and fell asleep while reading, his right leg curled under him, his head tilted sideways against the wing of the chair. He dreamed, a threatening dream of brass buttons and–

Suddenly he was brought awake by a hand on his shoulder. Pa–! He gasped and leaped to his feet, almost falling as his numbed right leg almost buckled. The book tumbled to the floor.

He was caught before he fell. He found himself in the arms of the black-haired man who had been talking to St. Denys.

"I'm sorry," said the man. "I didn't mean to startle you. I was going to the w.c. and as I passed by I noticed the door was ajar and I caught a glimpse of you." He smiled. "I couldn't resist coming in. You looked like a Renoir martyr sleeping there."

Kit snorted. "If you'd called me a lovely blossom I'd have bloodied your nose."

The gentleman laughed. "That's not my style."

Kit pulled away from the steadying hands and tried to regain his dignity and ignore his pounding heart. "Do you always enter rooms to which you were not invited?"

Kit could not help noticing that the man's eyes were almost black, his lips were moist, and his teeth were white. "No. But I'm glad I did. I was hoping to meet you without Xavier's guarding you as if you were his virgin daughter."

"Well, I'm not," said Kit quickly. His mouth was so dry he could scarcely speak.

"Oh?" The question was asked with another laugh. "You're obviously not his daughter. Am I to understand that you're not a virgin either?"

"Think what you like."

"Ah..."

At that moment Kit realized the door was now closed. He stopped breathing as the man touched his cheek and kissed him. Kit murmured deep in his throat and leaned into the kiss, almost sick with physical need.

The man drew back. "Xavier would horsewhip me if he knew I kissed you. And God knows I want more than a kiss. Well, I'm not of a mind to be horsewhipped today. Good-bye, Kit. I'd better find the w.c. and then return to the party."

"Wait – who are you?"

"My name is Rawdon. Rawdon McPherson." He took a step away, then turned. "If I were you, I wouldn't tell our mutual friend that we met."

"Mightn't we meet again?" Kit asked in a kind of gasp. "Somewhere else?"

There was a little silence. "I don't know. You're very young."

"I'm sixteen, Mr. McPherson, I've lived many lives in those years. In some ways I'm much older than you are."

McPherson took a card from his coat inside pocket. "Put this in a safe place. If you really would like to get better acquainted away from our friend, come to the City if you can get away alone, ring me up on the telephone, and perhaps we might meet."

Kit nodded. McPherson abruptly seized Kit's face between his hands and kissed him again, this time with brutal demand. Kit responded with an urgency that equalled McPherson's and he thrust his body against McPherson.

McPherson drew back with a quizzical smile. "I see you are not as innocent as our friend believes. You know what our meeting would be, then, do you not?"

"Of course." Kit did not know, exactly, but he knew that instinct and his own heat would fill in what experience did not.

"Very well, then. So long as you know. I do not seduce innocent children. Do not mislay the card."

"I won't."

◻

Kit's sleep was troubled that night. He dreamed of Rawdon McPherson and, half-awake, he turned over on his stomach while he dreamed. The dream ended with heat-shivers and the inner melting that obliterated everything but itself. Gradually he slept again.

The dream shifted and his father's face, filled with hatred, covered with blood, was floating about him and hands were coming out of nowhere to strike him again and again and again while the brass buttons gleamed—

He sat up shaking, hugging his knees. Why wouldn't Pa stay dead! Damn him, oh, damn him!

He wanted Jonathan body's next to him, his breath warm against his cheek. He wanted someone next to him, coming between him and the horrible phantom of hatred. He sat up the rest of the night, a blanket wrapped around him.

A few days later Kit was startled to again encounter McPherson in the St. Denys library. Their eyes locked. Kit nearly dropped the book he had been carrying.

Rawdon took it from him, brushing Kit's fingers with his own. "What are you reading?" He glanced at the title and again into Kit's eyes. "Plays. I ought to have known. Our friend brags *ad nauseam* on your talent. He seems to think you are another Edwin Booth."

"I am."

"Ah, well. I never cared much for American actors, but he likes them. Our friend is going to be away for a fortnight. Did you know?"

"I know he has to leave tomorrow for Edinburgh on business."

"I'm to look after some things for him," said McPherson. "I'm to look after you as well."

Kit's heart and stomach lurched together to form a quivering lump of nerves. "Are you?" It was inane but he could think of no other response.

"I think I should stay here at the Hill, don't you? In order to keep you safe?" He grinned and traced the slight peak of Kit's left eyebrow with his forefinger. "Do you know where the Dower House is?"

The touch rattled Kit and he stammered, "Y-yes."

"Have you a key to it?"

"I c-can get it."

"Good. Tomorrow night, then. Ten o'clock. At the Dower House."

Kit did not sleep that night. He felt guilty, knowing he was going to betray the trust St. Denys put in him. But he was driven to go. Before dawn the next morning his guardian bade him farewell and left.

At the appointed time Kit slipped from the house and rode his gray filly to the Dower House, a stone cottage set against the backdrop of the forest that covered the western acres of the estate. In the olden days, according to St. Denys, when the eldest son took a wife the matriarch of the Hill had to take the Dower House for her lodging.

He unlocked the door and went in. Within minutes McPherson was there and took their horses to the small stable at the back, then returned. Kit turned the key in the ancient lock, securing it behind them. A charged silence fell. McPherson put his hand on the back of Kit's neck, kneading the taut flesh there and said, "So tense? Don't you want to go through with it?"

"Oh ... Christ...," Kit whispered, closing his eyes at the question and the touch of the warm hand on his neck. Then he said, "Let's be about it then." He lit a candelabra to light their way to one of the two bedrooms upstairs. Though no one was expected to stay there, the servants changed linens often, and aired and dusted the place. It could have been a pigsty for all Kit noticed at that moment.

They threw their clothes aside and fell upon the bed. To Kit's dismay his nervousness was going to ruin the entire adventure; his Hanging Johnny not only didn't become Standing Jack, it was closer to being Shriveled Willy. If McPherson laughed at him he knew he would die of humiliation.

McPherson did not laugh, but instead left the bedroom and after a few minutes returned with a dusty bottle of wine. "There's a wine cellar," he explained. "Xavier showed it to me once."

Kit felt another twinge of guilt at the name. But several swallows of the wine and he ceased to worry about it. Not drunk but tipsy, Kit let McPherson educate him. He gave himself entirely over to the erotic touches and the sensations of pain and breathtaking pleasure that shut out all thought.

◻

Pa hit him again and again, while Jonathan's rotting corpse was forced to watch—

Kit woke with a cry, sweat streaming from every pore. Where was Pa – for that matter, where was he? He reached out and recoiled as his hand encountered the warm, solid form beside him. But this was no phantom; this was flesh and blood. In his nightmare-dazed state he could not remember the man's name. The name did not matter. He got as close as he could. The man, still asleep, roused enough to put his arms around him. Kit's eyes closed. His pa would not dare come back now. He slept without waking again.

In the morning he looked uneasily at the mussed bed. He had not before considered the servants.

"They'll know," he said.

McPherson seemed amused. "I suppose they will. Does that bother you?"

"Suppose they tell?"

"They won't. No servant would jeopardize a secure position by doing that."

Over the next few days Kit wondered if what he felt for McPherson was what the ladies liked to call "falling in love." All he knew for certain was that his skin remembered McPherson's hands and mouth the way his brain remembered words.

Every morning those two weeks they met for breakfast, and every evening for dinner. Kit wondered how McPherson could just sit there cutting his meat, drinking his wine, talking of commonplace things while he, himself, could not stop thinking that in just a few hours they would be at the Dower House again.

The day came when McPherson said matter-of-factly, "You know it's all over now, do you not?"

Kit was stunned. He had not once thought this would stop. He had tried to think of ways it could continue even after his guardian was home.

"What are you talking about?"

"I mean all good things come to an end."

"I thought – there must be ways around–"

McPherson's face was pleasant; there was no indication in it of the hours of passion they had shared. "You are a beautiful boy, Kit. I'm fond of you, but not enough that I want to lose Xavier's friendship because of you. If this goes on, that is inevitable. I won't see you like this again. If we meet, it will be as strangers. Do you understand?"

Kit's voice shook with the sense of betrayal. "Damn you," he choked. "Damn you. I'll tell him everything."

McPherson laughed. "No, you won't. Good God, boy, I didn't drag you here. You threw yourself at me and I took advantage of it as any man would. If that makes me a cad, so be it."

For several weeks Kit replayed every minute, every word, trying to learn what went wrong. One night, out for a late ride across the estate, Kit stopped to walk his horse in the lush grass. McPherson's rejection still hurt. If only he had had the power to– He stopped at the thought.

"Power," he mused, stroking Jezebel's soft muzzle. "That's what is important, isn't it. Pa had power over me. And so did Lizbet and Papa St. Denys. And McPherson."

Everyone had power over him except himself. There had to be a solution to this question of power. Why did they have it? How did they get it? And how did they keep it? Someday he would find out. And when he did, he would be the one with the power.

❑

At night when the nightmares came he desperately missed Mc-Pherson, not for himself but for his warm, solid presence.

Kit had long ago found that calling up images of strong-looking men he had seen would help keep Pa away while he slept. But now that he had slept with a flesh-and-blood man the images did not work as well and the nightmares grew more frequent.

◻

St. Denys was called away to Edinburgh on business more often. Whenever he was gone Kit went into London alone, and there he found men to give his young body what it craved and his spirit what it needed, men who could keep the nightmares away.

For a while there was a stagehand named Hudson. And then an understudy named Albert. For a few nights there was a young man who drove an ale wagon. He was followed by a photographer with elegant hands and a tenor with melancholy eyes. Kit learned to live at ease with the deception.

◻

For three years Kit had done as St. Denys wished and had not pleaded to go on stage, though every play he saw as call boy or stagehand made him long to be in costume.

He was seventeen now, but his long legs and broad shoulders made him look older. Unexpectedly, the part of Mercutio fell open due to the choking death of the actor playing the part.

Full of hope, Kit spoke to St. Denys about it, giving him many solid reasons why he should play the part. St. Denys listened then said, "But Kit, the director wants James DeLong to take it."

"He's never seen me act. All he's ever seen me do is stagehand work."

"You're too young."

"DeLong is too old. He must be thirty! Please let me do it."

"It is not my decision. I'm not the director."

"Make him use me."

"Oh, Kit, you have a lot to learn. If I did that I would have a theatre with no directors, for no self-respecting director would work there."

Behind Kit's dark eyes were rebellious thoughts and a memory: Toby – tricked, and locked into the shed while he himself went on to triumph. What worked once would work again.

A week afterward, Kit was called to the library, where St. Denys waited with the director, a man named Shull. Shull looked angry and resentful.

St. Denys said, "Kit, Mr. Shull needs to speak with you. I shall leave you alone to talk."

Nervous, Kit balanced on the balls of his feet. Did Shull know about the note he had written to DeLong, threatening him with public exposure of a certain woman not his wife whom he kept in a fine apartment while his wife and five children lived in a shabby boardinghouse?

Shull ran his hand over his bald head. "Kit, do you know the lines for Mercutio? Mr. St. Denys tells me you do and suggests I try you. I admit, I am doing it because of his position, not because I am optimistic."

"Yes, sir."

"Very well. Audition for me."

He feigned surprise. "But, sir, what of Mr. DeLong?"

"He has withdrawn from the play altogether. With no bloody reason that he will give. Ill health, he says. He was healthy enough when we began rehearsal."

Kit said nothing. Shull waved his hand. "Begin. Do you need to look at a script for a few minutes?"

"No, sir. Where shall I begin?"

"Anywhere."

Kit was not nervous. He knew every line in the play. He could have been Romeo or Juliet, or the Nurse or Juliet's father with equal ease. He was caught up in it and did not even notice that Shull was sitting up straight with a rapt look on his face, nor did he notice that St. Denys had returned and was standing beside the door, glowing with pride.

When he was finished, Shull stood up slowly and said, "Report for rehearsal tomorrow at eight o'clock sharp."

When he was gone, Kit and St. Denys grinned at each other.

"I knew you could do it," his guardian said. Then he added, "I was so sure, I had the programs already printed." He gave one to Kit, who opened one to see his name in print. It did not say:

Mercutio .... Christopher Smith

It said:

Mercutio .... Kit St. Denys

"But there's a mistake. It says..."

"It's not a printing error. Kit, I – we've never discussed it and perhaps I should not have pursued the matter without your consent, but I have petitioned the Court to let me adopt you. It means falsifying certain records and paying a bribe, but it will be worth it to me. Your name shall be legally St. Denys. Do you approve, Kit?"

The boy was overwhelmed. Adopted. Made his son and heir in name and by law. "How could I not?" he asked. "There is no way I can thank you for all you've done for me."

"You will repay me many times over by growing up to be the man I know you can be. Set the world on fire with your talent. Never be false to that talent. Promise me."

"I promise." It was a nebulous promise, since he was not certain what it entailed, but he would somehow keep it.

That night he lay in his bed and looked up at the moonlit ceiling and imagined a theatre playbill pasted there, with a picture of himself and with his new name as lead, in large letters. He had once seen a picture of a legendary bird rising on wings of red-and-gold flames from the ashes of its own self. It was the Phoenix, Papa St. Denys had told him.

"That's what I am," he whispered. "A phoenix."

Harry Rourke and Christopher Smith were gone forever.

From their ashes rose Kit St. Denys.

4

The critics were cautiously impressed with the performance of young Kit St. Denys in the part of Mercutio. They all speculated that it augured well for a distinguished career in the theatre if he could learn to be more forceful in his actions.

"What do they mean by that?" he asked St. Denys.

St. Denys considered. "I can't speak for them, but in the case of two of them, at least, they think you should chew the scenery more."

Kit frowned. That kind of "emoting" did not feel natural to him, though his acting teacher assured him it was standard technique. He tried, making grand theatrical gestures and exaggerating every speech. The critics the next day ridiculed him. More than one went so far as to say his first performance had been a flash in the pan, and that he had been cast because he was the son of the theatre owner.

The director raked him over red-hot coals in front of the entire cast. "I am the director. You perform it the way I said or you will be replaced. Is that clear?"

Kit was humiliated but faced Shull without flinching. "Yes," he said. "It's clear."

Another example of undiluted power, he thought.

Following *Romeo and Juliet* he was cast in a comedy in which he played a young curate. He felt awkward doing a comedy and the critics pounced. Young St. Denys, son of the theatre owner, had seemed so full of promise in his first appearance but with *Miss Lovejoy's Revenge* that promise seemed to fade away; he was stilted and distinctly unfunny.

The criticisms stung. The play did not run long and the next was a tragedy, *The Stone*. This time he was not settling for supporting roles. He auditioned for the male lead. The director was new to the Xavier. He was from Ireland and the actors auditioning were all strangers to him. Kit gave his name to the director as James Johnson, and his age as twenty-one.

He won the role of Paul, a young man who commits a crime out of desperation and takes his life rather than face the law. The story itself was intensely personal to Kit. Sometimes it gave him chills, for he could not divorce himself from that always-lurking boy inside his skin, who had killed his own father.

This time the critics veered in the other direction. He was superb. The promise he had shown as Mercutio had returned with the brilliance of shining gold.

The play that followed *The Stone* was a drawing-room comedy by Sheridan. He knew he did not do as well in it. But the critics were even more complimentary than the last time.

At the age of eighteen he decided critics were fools and he would never again let them influence anything he did in the theatre. In a book, he had found a simple passage by an American: "Sink or swim, live or die, survive or perish I give my hand and my heart..."

This he took as his credo, his only religion. Daniel Webster was talking about a vote. Kit St. Denys applied it to the theatre, his life.

□

Though most of his time was taken up with the theatre, rehearsals, performances, and social events, as well as with the formal education that St. Denys insisted upon, Kit found ways to explore the secret side of his nature. St. Denys was away often on business and Kit used each opportunity to meet men. Each liaison confirmed his belief that this was what he wanted, that this was what he was. He did not understand it, but saw no reason to fight it.

In Kit's nineteenth year Rawdon McPherson briefly figured once more as a lover, but this time it was Kit who aggressively began it and who deliberately called an abrupt end to it. McPherson had looked shocked and had cried, "You can't do this to me!" Kit had laughed in his face. For the first time he was the one with the power.

In the day he was learning to use his new powers of intellect and talent; a night alone stripped him of power. The nightmares plagued him still, and as time passed they grew worse. Only the presence of another man could keep them away.

One night at the Three Chords, he met a handsome man of thirty. Such meetings were commonplace at the Three Chords.

There was something about Turner that made Kit a little uneasy, but not enough that he refused the invitation to Turner's house. Turner did not know who Kit was because he never gave his rightful name to the men he met casually.

Kit's nightmare came to life at Turner's house. He suspected that Turner put something in his wine, for he felt groggy and uncoordinated. Turner was a big man and though Kit was tall and strong, Turner was just as strong and undrugged. When Kit refused to let Turner tie and gag him Turner overpowered him, tied him, and brutally used him. When Turner let him go Kit made his way home, barely able to move.

He crept into the house unseen by anyone. He shook as he poured water into the basin from the pitcher, and as he washed his face he was washing away both blood and tears. "Never again," he choked. "Never again. Nobody will *ever* have power over me again! Never!"

But the only way he could be sure to avoid the nightmare was not to sleep. He walked the floor until he crumpled, exhausted, fully dressed, across the bed...

❒

Pa kicked him. "Ye little whore's brat!" he bellowed and kicked him again. "No better'n a woman!" Pa's big hands closed around his throat and squeezed, squeezed until he could feel the blood pouring from his eyes, could feel his head leaving his shoulders clutched in his pa's hairy-backed hands— "Join yer brother an' rot!" His head was flying, cartwheeling through space and Jon was there, or was it Jon, with peeling flesh—

Thrashing, screaming, Kit sat up in bed, his skin slick with sweat. His door opened and his manservant peered in, his face lighted from below by his candle.

"What is it, Mr. Kit? I heard you cryin' out."

Kit reached out imploringly. "Don't leave, Tomkins. Please—"

Tomkins drew near the bed. "Mr. Kit, your face ... what happened?"

Kit was confused. His father was not there – yet he hurt all over – his face was stiff– "Tomkins," he whispered. "I think I am going mad."

"Oh, no, sir. I'm sure not. Is there anything I can do, sir?"

Kit looked up into the slightly older man's face, his eyes wide and stark. "Sleep with me, Tomkins. I beg you. No one will know."

•56•

The candle quivered as if the hand holding it trembled a little. "Oh, I couldn't, sir, you bein' a gentleman and all. If Mr. St. Denys found out—"

"I beg you. I need someone."

Tomkins hesitated a moment longer, then blew out the candle, removed his shoes, and lay down on the bed with Kit.

"Put your arms around me," Kit whispered.

Tomkins did. Only when he could feel warmth and strength next to him did Kit go to sleep and not dream of his father.

Tomkins slept with him the next night and the night after that, holding him. On the fourth night Kit's bruises and hurts had eased far enough into memory that need stirred him again. Tomkins again lay with him and Kit put his hand on him and kissed him. Tomkins was willing. He submitted to Kit, without question.

It was a strange thing, Kit thought, to be the one in control. It was a feeling he liked.

❏

The next night Kit waited in vain for Tomkins to come to his room. When he did not, Kit got up, pulled on a dressing gown, and started toward the servants' quarters. He was startled when from the candle-lit semidarkness of his room St. Denys spoke his name.

"Kit. I would have a word with you."

Kit had not expected Papa St. Denys back for another day. He went into St. Denys's suite. His adoptive father was standing there, hands behind his back, waiting. St. Denys lit a candelabra and set it down close to Kit, throwing light on his face.

"Papa, welcome home. I did not know you had returned."

"Obviously." St. Denys stared at Kit. "How did you get those bruises?"

"I was thrown from a horse."

Without warning St. Denys slapped Kit. Hard. It stung.

Bewildered, Kit put his hand to his throbbing cheek. "Why did you do that?"

"Don't lie to me. Ever." St. Denys's face was taut with anger. "I came home last night and went to your room to tell you. I saw you in bed with that fool of a servant. From the look of your face, things must have gotten rather rough between you two! I kept myself busy today so I would not see you lest I give you the whipping you deserve."

Kit straightened. "Where is Tomkins?"

"That is none of your affair."

"He was my servant."

"I hired him. I sacked him. I sacked him without reference."

"You had no right to do that!"

"I had every right."

"It wasn't his fault. I made him do it."

"Then more fool you."

"I can't believe you would be so unjust!"

"Kit, because of certain things I did in my youth I lost everything. I will not let you fall into that same trap. I forbid you to pursue those evil tendencies any longer."

"You sleep with men."

There was a space of silence. Then, "You can't know that."

"I've known it for years."

"That is different. I am set in my ways and cannot change. And *I* do not sleep with my inferiors."

Anger made Kit rash. His lip curled. "Inferior? Superior? Does that not depend upon who is on top?"

His father's face went white to the lips. When he spoke, his voice was icy. "You were a gutter rat when I took you in. I thought I could make a gentleman of you. I was wrong. You will never be anything but a gutter rat."

Pain ripped through Kit. Nothing Rourke had ever done to him hurt him like those few words from the man he called Papa. He turned and walked out. He went to his room and packed his clothes, intending to take nothing except those things he had bought with his own earnings at the theatre. His hands hovered over the gold razor and brushes Papa St. Denys had given him on his last birthday. He carefully wrapped them and put them into the valise. He packed dress clothes. Papa had given those to him also but he would need them. He was still packing when St. Denys came into the room.

"Kit, I'm sorry. Forgive me."

Kit did not look up. "You're right. You'd have to be an alchemist to make a gentleman of me. I did come from the gutter. I suppose that is where I will die." He looked up, his jaw set. "But before that happens I will make sure the world hears of me. But don't worry. I won't embarrass the St. Denys name. I'll change names again. Why not? Rourke, Smith, St. Denys ... what difference does it make? A gutter rat by any name is still a gutter rat."

"You don't understand, Kit. Listen to me. If you are drawn to men it's my fault. I should never have exposed you to my friends."

Kit uttered a bark of laughter. "Papa, I've been drawn to men, as you put it, since I was very young. I assure you, you are not to blame."

"It's a sickness. I, Wilde, all the others, even you if what you say is true, we're very sick in the mind. Otherwise we would—"

Kit did not look at him, but continued packing. "You may be sick. I'm not."

St. Denys grabbed his arm and stopped it in midair over the valise. "Kit, you must listen to me. There are laws in this country that ... I never told you of them because I did not know there was a need. But men like myself can be sent to prison for life! Not long ago they could be burned at the stake or hanged. I'm circumspect. I am in no danger, or at least very little. But *you!* You're reckless! I know that about you if I don't know anything else. I don't want to see you in prison."

Kit's anger was fading. "Papa, don't worry so. I will not be sent to prison. And I'm not sick."

Very little was changed after that. Kit still did not let St. Denys know of his amours, nor did the older man want to know. St. Denys rehired Tomkins, but gave the butler orders to assign him duties that would keep him away from Kit.

It was three months later, following another journey to Edinburgh, that St. Denys came into Kit's room. Kit was reading a new script by lamplight. He looked up, smiled, and put aside the book.

St. Denys sat down across from him and for several minutes said nothing. "Kit, I have never told you how very much I love you."

"Of course you have. A thousand times in a thousand ways."

"I could not be prouder or love you more if I had sired you." Then to Kit's astonishment, he began to cry.

"Papa, what's wrong?"

St. Denys blotted his eyes and tried to stop the tears. "I'm very ill, Kit. I'm dying. I won't live to see you become a man."

Kit stared, and knelt slowly beside the chair, one hand on his father's hand, the other on his knee. "What?"

"I have a cancer in my head, Kit. The times I was in Edinburgh I was consulting an old friend who is a physician. He has suspected for some time but is now certain."

Kit made a helpless gesture. "But ... medicine? Surgery?"

"There is nothing anyone can do. I have perhaps six months to live. Perhaps less. I am ... in pain most of the time."

Guilt swept over Kit. He saw now that St. Denys looked thinner and his face was more lined. It was also slightly misshapen by a shallow bulge just above his left jaw. His father did look ill. And he had never noticed.

"Papa, there must be something that can be done. I do not accept your diagnosis. Let's go to America. Or Germany. France. Anywhere. Someplace, there is a doctor who will cure you."

St. Denys shook his head. "There is no help for me. But I've lived my life. It's you I fear for, Kit. When I am gone I am afraid you will harm yourself by your excesses. You are a passionate and intense boy. You will be a passionate and intense man. That is good for an actor—"

"To hell with acting!" he cried and got to his feet. "I'll quit, spend my time with you."

St. Denys smiled. "Oh, hush. See what I mean? Let me finish. Passion and intensity are good for an actor or an author or a painter, to a point. Beyond that point, passion and intensity can cause great harm." He took Kit's hand in his, locking their fingers together. "I just – don't want you to – do harm to yourself. Promise me."

"How can I promise such a thing? I don't know what the future holds."

"Then promise me this: As long as I have breath in my body, honor me and yourself by disowning the vice we seem to share. I am seeking peace with God. I advise you to do the same."

Kit swallowed. "I promise."

❐

Now, knowing what would soon happen, St. Denys spent hours each day teaching Kit about his business interests, primarily the theatre. It was only a negligible source of his income, but it was the one thing other than Kit that he loved. He taught Kit everything about being an owner and manager.

Kit insisted he wanted to stop performing in order to spend more time with him. St. Denys would not hear of it. "It is one of my great joys to watch you on stage," he said. "Don't deprive me of that."

Kit saw him failing almost daily and was unprepared for how soon he was unable to go to the theatre. He saw his father's face become misshapen, with the right side wrinkled and skeletal while the left side was pulled smooth and unlined by the tumor that bulged like a large, obscene bubble beneath the skin. He wore an eyepatch now; he could not close his left eyelid and his eye was dry and painful.

Why? thought Kit in grief-stricken rebellion, *Why can't he just die? Why does anyone have to suffer like this? Why?*

He wondered how far human skin could stretch without bursting, and had horrible dreams about it.

He arranged for the cast of *Rose's Heart* to do a performance in the Great Hall while St. Denys sat propped up on pillows to cushion his fleshless bones.

Soon afterward St. Denys stopped coming to the dining room for meals. Kit himself took the tray to the bedroom suite and dined with him there, though little food was eaten.

Kit furiously dismissed a gardener who whistled beneath the bedroom window, causing St. Denys to whimper in pain.

The dogs were gotten rid of. Their barking was agony to him.

Every moment of every day his moans could be heard. Sometimes they seemed to fill the house. Laudanum in ever-increasing doses did not help. Kit stood beside the bed by the hour, frantic to leave because he could not bear the suffering, and unwilling to leave because he might be needed.

One day when he went into the bedroom and spoke to St. Denys, his father started. He had not seen him; he was blind. Kit gently put his arms around the skeleton that had been a man and wept when St. Denys cried, "This is cruel – too cruel – if only I could still see you..."

Within two days his father could not hear.

The next day he died.

❐

Kit was bitterly surprised at the small number of mourners who came to the services and to the cemetery. His father had helped many people, had been a patron of all the arts, yet few bothered to stand in the rain beside his grave.

Then Kit wondered why he was surprised. Few of them had bothered coming to visit him during the last pain-filled months of his life.

He had been surprised by Rawdon McPherson's faithfulness in coming every day to visit for several hours. He was one of the pallbearers, as well. He seemed genuinely grief-stricken and when Kit, in a hard voice, asked him why, his answer astonished the boy.

"I loved him. I know you don't believe that. But I did. Xavier and I were lovers for many years. If we could have lived together without scandal, we would have."

"But you seduced me, knowing how he would feel about it if he knew."

McPherson's eyebrows lifted. "Which of us seduced the other is a matter of opinion. And that has nothing to do with what I felt for Xavier."

They were in the St. Denys library. Kit was exhausted. He had not rested for weeks. He had lost flesh and there were dark circles beneath his eyes.

McPherson said gently, "Kit, you need to get away from here. Xavier wanted you to devote yourself to acting. He believed, as do I, that you have a divine gift. You will never have to worry about money since everything he possessed goes to you."

Kit could not say anything. So he was now a very rich man.

He thought of his life before: the wooden shack and the sagging porch ... two barefoot boys cringing before their drunken pa ... the sounds of his mother and his pa going at it in bed, or of his mother and a "sweet young soldier boy" fucking behind the dividing blanket ... fear and pain at his pa's hands ... hatred from his pa's mouth .... brothers sharing a cot, comforting each other in bad times, laughing together in good times ... Jonathan dead beside him, taken from him forever.

Jonathan. Papa St. Denys. He had loved only two people and now he had lost them both.

Love hurt. It hurt a great deal.

He vowed he would never again let it have power to hurt him.

❐

London, 1890

Kit St. Denys, at twenty, played Hamlet each night to full houses in the Xavier. The critics found fault because his portrayal was not traditional. The purists complained about his elimination of the political statements with which Shakespeare had closed the play, and they were disturbed by his prowling Hamlet who simmered with violence just below the surface.

Kit smiled, shrugged, and threw away the reviews. When asked about them he laughed. "The people come, don't they?" he answered. "What other critics do I have to concern myself over?"

The people loved it. And loved him.

They waited in long queues for the cheap seats, and when the seats were filled they stood in the aisles.

Each curtain call brought a mixture of elation and sadness to Kit because Papa St. Denys was not there to see them.

Twelve weeks *Hamlet* played there, and always to a full house.

At twenty-one Kit came into his inheritance – the theatre, the money, everything. The dream he had hugged close to his heart for several years could now be made to come true: the formation of his own repertory company. The advertisement he placed in the trade papers in England, Canada, and America brought him fine talent from which to choose.

He formed the company from the ground up. He handpicked the costume designers and set designers, the actors, the general manager, the stage manager. He himself would be director, owner, and star. The St. Denys Repertory Company was born.

In the company of actors was a rangy man with a plain but engaging face, Francis Mulholland by name. Kind, easygoing, his talent as an actor was mediocre. But there was something about him that appealed to Kit and it was soon apparent that Francis Mulholland was enthralled by him. Maybe it would be nice for a change, thought Kit, to have a real lover.

For a while, Francis was part of his life in a way no one else had ever been. But before long, Kit realized he had no grand passion for Francis and Francis became a good friend, a useful actor in small roles, and a sometime bed partner – a situation Francis stoically accepted as better than never being with him at all.

❐

At first the people came only to see Kit. They returned to see him again but also because his crew was so talented. The sets were innovative, the costumes beautiful. "Spare no expense to make them the best," those craftsmen had been told.

Between the ages of twenty-two and twenty-five he became one of the most famous men in England. People recognized him in the streets. Women wrote love letters to him, offering to leave their fathers, husbands, or fiancés for him. They begged for a lock of his hair. They begged for pictures.

They begged.

He gave the letters to his secretary to answer.

When he wanted sport it was not with a woman. And it would never be with anyone who begged.

5

Six months after Harry Rourke had been brought howling in protest into his squalid world another baby boy was born, this one to a country physician and his wife in the heart of the beautiful Cotswold country. He was an unexpected child, coming ten years after his sister Agnes.

The physician, William Stuart, delivered his own child, though truth to tell his wife was so experienced at it she needed little help. This was her sixth child and second son and he was, she declared minutes after his birth, the handsomest of the litter.

William Stuart, a humorless man, rebuked his wife. "He is not a puppy, Mrs. Stuart. He is a child. I will thank you to remember that."

Mrs. Stuart wanted to name her son Patrick, after the patron saint of her native Ireland. Mr. Stuart was adamant that the name would be Nicholas, after his own father. He frowned dourly at his wife's stubborn clinging to her old Roman nonsense about saints, in spite of his conversion of her.

Sometimes he wondered what had drawn him to her, forgetting that before the first child she had been a pretty colleen with black hair and vivid blue eyes. In the intervening twenty-one years she had broadened, grayed, and become sharp-tongued. It did not occur to him that her sharp tongue might be dulled if he spent some of the money he earned from his practice, and some of the large sum of money bequeathed him by a grateful wealthy horse breeder for having saved the breeder's prize stallion from a fever.

Stuart was both physician and veterinarian, and though his formal training had been small, he had learned enough through his apprenticeship to his own father and had read enough and taught himself enough that he was famous in the county for his magic healing touch.

He held his new son in his arms and inspected him for any missing or deformed parts. He was pleased. He had no doubt that Nicholas would grow up, apprentice with him, follow in his footsteps, and take over the practice in the valley when the time came for him to lay down his medical bag.

❏

It was a strict upbringing little Nicholas had. His father, his mother, his four sisters and one brother were all Particular Baptists, and his father was a staunch member of the English Baptist Missionary Society. Only a particular number of souls were to be preserved on Judgment Day; William Stuart and his family were among the chosen. Every day began and ended with prayer and Bible reading. Nick often squirmed when his knees ached, and it earned him a swat on the ear from Agnes.

"But if her eyes are shut while she's praying," he complained to his father, "how does she know what I'm doing?"

"God sees," was his father's stern reply.

"Agnes is not God," Nick protested. His father cuffed him across the same ear.

Nick was a lively little boy who wanted to run barefoot in the lush grass in the summer, not sit for hours in the sweltering church with nothing more exciting to do than watch the fat fly which kept landing on Mr. Duckett's bald head. The three-hour church services on Sunday morning and the equally long services on Sunday night, in particular the two-hour sermons, were torture. If he yawned or dozed Agnes would dig her elbow into his ribs – she could not hit him in church – and then she would tattle on him as soon as they got home. Many Sundays ended with his buttocks stinging from a rigorous birching.

He retaliated by tying her high-buttoned boots together. Once he dumped an open fruit jar full of worms in her bed. Hearing her screams was worth the thrashing he got from his father.

They lived in the same small cottage in which Nick's father had been born. Until the three eldest married and left home, the family of eight almost burst through the light-colored stone walls but the patriarch refused to consider building another or enlarging the original structure.

"It was good enough for my parents and it's good enough for my children," William Stuart growled.

"But, Mr. Stuart," his wife would retort, "nine of your mother's children slept in the churchyard, not in the house. You were the only one who lived. Have you forgotten?"

He turned livid at such times. "Have you forgotten your place, Mrs. Stuart?" he shouted. "Show me in the scripture where it is written that a wife questions her husband."

On Nick's sixth birthday he made his first medical journey with his father and watched round-eyed as his father gelded Farmer Tucker's pigs. Their squeals of pain and the blood running down the pink little bellies frightened him but he bit his lip and said nothing until later.

"Why is it done?" he asked his father.

"So they have no desire to fornicate." And the mysterious glare he turned upon Nick seemed to say, "The same should be done with little boys." And he did not even know what fornicating was.

He went with his father often, making up his schoolwork with the village schoolmaster as tutor. He and his father rode in silence from village to village in the valley. He stood at his father's side, helping wherever his father directed, handing him instruments or water. He was nine when he assisted at the birth of a farm wife's baby.

Birth by now was nothing new to him; he had seen many calves and lambs born. But until now never a human infant.

He held it, slimy and covered with blood and mucus, while his father cut the umbilical cord. He gazed at the baby. It was the most wonderful thing he had ever seen. Eyes shining, he smiled at the mother. The woman later told her neighbors, "The little Stuart lad ... what a love he is. He delivered my baby and gave me such a beautiful smile it was like the sun coming out over Cleeve Cloud Hill. I named the baby for him."

William Stuart was thunderstruck when the story got to him a few weeks later that his nine-year-old son "had single-handed delivered Molly Oliver's baby." Nick laughed in delight. His father failed to see the humor.

Nick had few secrets from his father, but one he did have was his friendship with the son of the village ne'er-do-well. The father was a drunkard and the boy, Hugh, four years Nick's senior, was marked by the righteous to be headed down the same path.

Nick liked Hugh because he was funny and carefree and because his father would not approve. And the additional four years made Hugh seem very mature and wise. There was nothing Hugh did not know. On the rare occasions when Nick could escape from his father's keen eye or his sister's tale-telling, he roamed the countryside with Hugh, having adventures.

Hugh gave him his first cigar, swiped from Hugh's father. Nick decided cigars were not for him, ever. Hugh gave him his first taste of whiskey, another sin he decided was not for him since it made him vomit his breakfast.

When Nick was thirteen, the church and the village were rocked by scandal involving the sexton's daughter and Mr. Somers's farmhand. The young couple were brought before the congregation for discipline. Nick had seen other people disciplined before the congregation, but their sins had been of little interest to him. This couple was different. The girl was Angelica, and when he was little she had made a great pet of him at the socials after church. The young man was James, in Nick's eyes the most splendid creature in the world, with long legs and thick muscles in his chest and arms. Nick had loved to watch James, stripped to the waist or with his sweat-soaked shirt unbuttoned, fork the hay higher and faster and neater than anyone in the valley.

James and Angelica stood in front of the congregation for an hour, he with his face red, she with her face averted, her shoulders shaking from sobs while the minister and then Nick's father as elder harangued them about their sins.

The two young sinners then knelt while many long prayers were said over them. Nick lifted his head from his clasped hands. James's head was still erect; the tendons of his neck stood out like cords, and his stony face was full of hatred. Nick was shocked. Hatred in the church? He half expected lightning to burst through the roof. He lowered his head again and said a fervent prayer to God to forgive James and not destroy him with a lightning bolt. The prayer worked. James and Angelica walked separately from the church when the prayers were over at last. They were forbidden ever to speak to each other again.

The next day the village woke to the news that Angelica and James had run off together. Nick's father said harshly, "The Devil claims his own."

"Fornication" had been mentioned in every other sentence during the discipline, and beneath Nick's smoldering anger at the treatment of his friend Angelica ran a current of curiosity that would not be stilled: what was fornication? He knew it was written in the Bible many times and he had heard at least a million sermons dealing with it and it was the reason they castrated baby pigs, young horses, roosters, and bulls. It was something very serious and must be a great sin when indulged in by people. And every time he heard the word his desire increased to know what it meant.

He asked Agnes, by now a sour-faced spinster of twenty-three. She slapped his face and told their father. William Stuart's face turned red and he barked, "Let me not hear that word from you again until you are grown!"

Summer passed. Hard work, scripture readings, prayer. None of these things dulled his curiosity about the sin of James and Angelica. One afternoon his father was called out unexpectedly and did not take Nick with him. Nick, knowing this might not happen again for a long time, slipped from the house without telling his mother or his sister and ran to find Hugh.

At just past seventeen, Hugh was nearly a grown man. Nick was flattered that he would still hang about with someone like himself, who was so much younger. Hugh's position as almost-grown meant he would have the answer to Nick's question.

They left Hugh's house and struck off for the sloping green hills, and once there they picnicked on cheese and apples. Hugh just grinned when Nick asked where the cheese had come from. They lay on their backs and watched the clouds form into odd creatures. Nick was struck by how different their perceptions were. The cloud he thought looked like a castle Hugh insisted looked like a gunboat.

"I'm going to be a sailor," Hugh declared. "I'm going to join Old Queen Vic's navy."

Nick sighed. "I suppose I shall never leave here." He pushed himself up on one elbow. "Hugh, what's fornication?"

Hugh stopped chewing on his grass stem. "What's your old man say it is?"

"Well, I asked Agnes and she slapped me and then Father became angry and said I wasn't old enough to know."

"God, little Stuart, you've seen bulls servicing cows and stallions servicing mares and dogs servicing bitches. And what d'you think the pussies and tomcats are screechin' about in the night?"

"What of it? That's the way they continue the breed."

"So where do you think babies come from? Trees?"

Frostily Nick said, "Don't be an idiot. I've seen lots of babies born. I know where they come from."

"So how do you think they got in there?"

Nick's forehead furrowed as he peered down at Hugh. "You mean a man services his wife?" He had an appalling and immediately banished picture of his mother and father—

Hugh chuckled. "Yes, dear little fellow. It's called fucking. And..." Hugh's smile faded; he held Nick's eyes and Nick could not look away. There was something in Hugh's eyes that caused a tremor deep inside Nick. "And it ain't always a husband and wife. That's why your stupid church hung Angelica and James out to dry. They did it and they weren't married. And ... and sometimes it ain't even a man and a woman."

Nick's throat was so tight he could hardly breathe and his heart was pounding in his ears. He knew he should move away and he couldn't. Then Hugh's arms were around him, tightly, bringing his face down and Hugh's mouth was on his and Hugh was pulling Nick's entire body down to lie between his spread legs. Nick's eyes flew open when he felt his organ get hard, something that had never happened without his own secret and evil ministrations. He gasped when he felt against his own erection something as hard but much larger mounding Hugh's trousers.

His mind was not working when Hugh suddenly shoved him aside and scrambled to his feet, tugging at his own trousers. "Get your drawers down! Hurry!" Nick was struck dumb by what he saw as Hugh dropped his pants. Impatiently, Hugh fell to his knees, yanked at Nick's trousers, and pulled them down around his ankles. He fell upon him, gasping and rubbing against him. Nick shut his eyes tight, closing out all sensations except that in his groin where an intense, fiery pressure built up until he thought he would explode. And explode he did, letting out a raw moan just as Hugh also cried out with a curse, "Oh, Christ and all the saints—!" Hugh collapsed on top of him.

The explosion left Nick drained. Hugh's weight was squeezing the breath from him. He wondered dizzily what his father would say when they found him there, probably dead, underneath Hugh. He pushed Hugh off. Hugh sat up and exhaled. When he spoke his voice was unsteady.

"Well," he said, "now you know what fornication is. More or less."

Nick lay breathing heavily and looked at the clouds. "Hugh ... that was a mortal sin, wasn't it?" He was suddenly terrified that behind the cloud which looked like a sea dragon God was watching, readying a special pit for him in Hell.

Hugh brushed his hands through his hair. "It felt good, didn't it?"

"All sin feels good," sighed Nick. "That's why it's sin." The pleasure faded like a sunset. Embarrassment set in, even more powerful than the fear that God was watching. He was aware of being sticky and it was unpleasant.

There was a creek nearby and they bathed there, and Nick vigorously used a handful of grass to wash the evidence of his sin from his flat, hairless belly. Hugh suddenly grabbed him and ducked his head underwater. Nick surfaced spluttering.

Hugh laughed. "I met a sailor once," he said. "In Liverpool when my old man took me there. He taught me all kinds of things. I'll teach you more next time, now you're my sweetheart." He ducked him again and at the same time slipped his hand between Nick's legs.

Nick fought free and scrambled to the bank, his face scarlet. "There won't be a next time, Hugh! I'm not your – your sweetheart! I'm lucky God didn't strike me dead already." Trembling with his haste, he pulled his clothing on over his wet skin. "I'm never going to do that again. It was disgusting." Lying was a sin. But not to tell this particular lie would lead to bigger sins.

Hugh climbed out on the bank. "Oh, bollocks, Nick. The apple's off the tree now. You can't put it back. The sailor told me that some fellows like other fellows the way some fellows like girls and no one knows why. It's–"

"*I* know why. It's si–"

Hugh scowled. "If you say that word again, I'll smash you in the face." He grasped his member. "You like this, little Nick, and someday you'll admit it."

With shaking fingers, Nick buttoned his shirt and pants and put on his shoes and stockings. All the while he looked at the ground to keep from looking at Hugh's body. But he *wanted* to look and he knew it. Dressed, he turned away. "Hugh, I can't be your friend after today. I won't ever talk to you again." As he trudged away Hugh's voice continued behind him, taunting.

"Oh, yes you will. There's nobody else in the village who would fuck you and that's what you want. That's what you need, you just don't know it. You know what would happen if I told anybody what you just did with me? You'd have to stand up in front of your father and all those other hypocrites and confess, that's what! And they'd pray over you and tell you you'll go to hell and..." He went on and suddenly Nick realized that Hugh's voice sounded funny.

He half turned and was stunned to see that as Hugh ranted he was also crying. "Hugh...?" he asked uncertainly. He took a step toward him.

Hugh picked up a rock and threw it at him, catching him on the shoulder. "You think I'm nothing, don't you! Not good enough for you, don't you!" A second rock caught Nick on the chest and made him stagger. "My pa's a drunkard and I will be too. You think I'm not good enough for the likes of you even if I'm the only one."

"I don't think that at all. I'll go home and pray for both of us."

Hugh was crying harder, his face twisted. "Yes, you do that!" This time his seeking fingers found a large, hard clod of dirt and he hurled it with all his might. It caught Nick in the stomach.

"You don't understand, you stupid little bugger," Hugh cried. "I love you. I could've left this stupid village a long time ago but I was waiting for you to grow up. I've always known what you are, just like I've always known what I am and I was waiting for you. I wanted us to go away together like James and Angelica."

Nick retreated backward, more shaken than he had ever been by anything. What did Hugh mean — "always known what you are"? "I'll pray for you," he said again. "I'll pray for both of us." He couldn't stand either the sight or sound of Hugh a moment longer. The memory of their sin and the things Hugh was saying made him sick to his stomach. He turned and ran as fast as he could, toward the safety of home.

For days he lived in dread that Hugh would tell and he would find himself where Angelica and James had been. He knew that any punishment given him by the church or God Himself would be mild compared to his father's punishment.

But like Angelica and James, Hugh left the village in the night. Nick decided this was absolute proof that prayer worked. Before the congregation which had watched him grow up, Nick made an emotional dedication. He pledged his soul to purity, his body to chastity, and his industry to mankind.

Of the three, only the last was easy.

William Stuart stared at his youngest child, who now stood taller than he did. "What are you saying?"

Nick said it again. "I want to study medicine, Father, at university. I've been reading in the journals about such amazing – Father, there are so many new things – so many new discoveries and techniques! I want to learn how to transfuse blood, and how to use anesthetics. Don't you realize how much suffering, especially by women in labor, could be eased with the use of ether or chloroform?"

"If women were meant to have their children without pain God would have arranged it that way. And transfusing? Putting another man's blood into someone? That is as blasphemous as it is obscene! As for university, it ruins young men. That's all it's good for. I shan't have you exposed to that corruption." He smiled a crafty smile. "In any event, you don't have the educational background for it."

"I've been studying. With Father Spencer. He was a teacher before he became–"

At the name of the Anglican priest in the village, whose pretty, spired small church was all but empty on Sundays, Nick's father spat, "Studied! Behind my back? With that *Catholic?*"

Nick saw no point in arguing the difference between Anglican Catholicism and that of the Roman Church. To his father they were identical. "He's helped me more than anyone except you. He's a good man. I've taken my O levels with him and did very well."

"And when did this wonder occur, may I ask?"

Nick's face turned red. "Last year." His father looked shocked. "He says within the year I should be able to pass my A levels, if I continue to apply myself." He could not keep the excitement from his face and voice. "He is certain I will be accepted at university. I've been saving my money–"

"I can't believe you have deceived and lied to me. There is no need to study medicine elsewhere. You can learn all you need to know from me."

Nick went on stubbornly. "Father, I don't fault what you do here in the valley. But I don't want to treat cattle one hour and a man the next, a sick cat thirty minutes later and then deliver a baby. That's not wrong for you; it's what you want. I want to treat people, nothing else." He took a deep breath. "And I want to specialize."

"Specialize! In what? Upper right nostrils?"

"I want to care for childbearing women and their babies." The memory was sharp in his mind of his favorite sister, Mary, screaming in agony as she gave birth to an infant who died within moments. Mary followed her child a week later, dead from childbed fever. "I want to help prevent what happened to Mary from happening to other women."

"Mary died because it was God's will," snapped his father. "If you interfere with that—"

"But if it is God's will that someone die, doesn't it follow that she will die regardless of what a physician does? And haven't you interfered with God's will many times as a doctor?"

His father, who had grown more grim and more fanatical with the passing of six years, shot to his feet. "I have never interfered with the will of God! Never! And you — you are meant to stay here, to walk in my shoes. It is what we have planned your entire life."

"It's what you planned. I was never consulted," said Nick quietly. "I want to go to university, study obstetrics and gynecology and related surgeries. I've learned all I can from you and I thank you for it. Now I have to go my own way."

"You are eighteen and you will do as I say. You will end your association with that priest and—"

"No. I am going to continue my studies."

"If you continue against my wishes you will no longer be welcome in my house. I will not have rebellion among my children."

"You wouldn't do that, Father. Lock the door against me?"

"I will if you pursue the matter."

Nick lowered his head. It was a small village; if his father willed it, he would be an outcast, as much of one as his priestly friend. And when had he ever known his father not to carry through on a threat? "Is that your last word?" he asked.

"It is."

"Then I shall leave now."

"You headstrong fool. To think I favored you over your brother!"

"And made him hate me because you did."

They glared at each other over the chasm of their differences, the aging fanatic who was a good physician and the young man to whom "good" was not good enough.

He went, as he had said he would. Father Spencer took him in, gave him a pallet on the floor of the two-room cottage and access to the piles and mounds of books that heaped up and spilled over from bookshelves and tables. He became, as he had known he would, a pariah. Father Spencer eventually sent him to a good friend, a teacher at St. Thomas Aquinas, one of the finest schools. The friend, Laurence Northcliff, accepted Nick as a private student and when he was not at the school, crammed as much knowledge as possible into his brain. Nick scored exceptionally well in his A levels. He was ecstatic when he was accepted at Edinburgh. He wrote his father, never dreaming that his father would still be angry. There was no reply from the stony man in the rosy-stone house.

□

No one studied harder than the provincial boy with the frayed cuffs, too-short trousers, and empty pockets. And in his years there his vow of chastity was stained only twice when he was lonely and a fellow student smiled at him in a certain way.

He was disappointed when financial needs forced him to leave university equipped with only general medical knowledge. His dream of specialization would have to wait. He went to work for a year in a hospital in London and then opened his own practice which would serve the needy.

His vow to help mankind held firm in a little clinic he opened on the edge of the slums. The hours were long; he was frequently hungry.

One night some former classmates from Edinburgh came to the City, blew into his clinic in a brash, laughing crowd, and carried him off to a theatre.

He had never been in a theatre. Third only to blasphemy and fornication, playacting was the greatest of sins. Of course it was a twofold sin, since playacting always led to fornication. He had tried for a long time to throw off the restraints of the church, but they clung to him despite his best efforts.

The play his friends took him to see was *Hamlet* which, he knew from having read it, was not only about fornication but about incest and murder. He was angry that they had taken him to such a play.

He shifted uncomfortably in his seat through Act One, Scene One, wishing he were not sitting in the center of the row. He could not leave without creating a stir and stepping on toes.

And then Scene Two began. There came onto the stage an entourage, at its head a king and queen. Near them and yet apart was a golden-haired figure in plain dark medieval clothing which contrasted with the bright robes of the others. The king was talking about grief, but seemed hardly to be grieving. But the other ... the other...

Nick leaned forward, unaware that most other people in the audience did the same. The long-legged figure in black spoke. "...a little more than kin but less than kind..." It was an aside, spoken so that the king could not be sure what was said. Even so the voice that spoke it was resonant, and the words of bitter anger reached the farthest seats of the balcony.

Throughout the play Nick remained as he was, transfixed by that lean youth who prowled the stage, whose every motion was spare and fraught with violence about to be unleashed, violence that was only hinted at until the last act. The tension in the too-taut bowstring that was Hamlet was not released until the final moment when the golden head fell back against Horatio's arm.

Tears were running down Nick's face as Horatio said, "Good night, sweet prince. And flights of angels sing thee to thy rest..."

The curtain lowered.

The audience burst into thunderous applause. Nick could not applaud. His emotions had been sucked dry. He had not felt like this since that day of sin on the bank with Hugh. He fumbled his program open while behind, in front, and on either side of him people stood and applauded and called out, "Kit! Kit! Kit! Kit!"

He saw the name in print then, for the first time.

Kit St. Denys.

He was suddenly aware that the cast was taking bows and he had to stand to see. The entire cast took many bows, and then only the principal players were left, and finally only He alone, bowing to them over and over until He finally quit the stage and did not return.

Nick's friends laughed at him. "Look at old Stuart, will you? He's fairly dazzled!" "It's the red-haired girl who played the queen that's done it, I wager!" "No, no, Ophelia! It had to be Ophelia." "It's the queen, I tell you. Ophelia? That wasted, consumptive child?" "Come along, Stuart. What did you think of it?"

Nick, still a little dazed, said, "I think – it was wonderful–"

They clapped him on the back. "The saint has been corrupted at last! First the Theatre – and then loose women! Oh, how the mighty are fallen."

In the cheap seats on the last night of *Hamlet*, Nick Stuart sat alone, as mesmerized as he had been that first night. Every night that week he had returned to the theatre and had sat there thrilling to the same lines delivered by the same voice but always with some slight difference in inflection or emotion. He watched no one else on the stage. If Hamlet were offstage Nick was impatient until he returned. The money he used to purchase tickets was money that ought to have gone for meals in the pub near his surgery, but somehow it seemed more important to sit there in the dark and take into himself the beauty and subdued power of Kit St. Denys.

The theatre might well be an abomination as he had always heard. He no longer cared.

Each night he sat there in a fever, his shameful mind spinning fantasies more intense than any he had spun before in his darker moments. From habit, without even knowing he was doing it, he prayed for a miracle: that he might actually get to speak to St. Denys. And a miracle happened.

The last act this time was more lifelike than ever when something red splattered the stage each time Hamlet thrust or parried and his left hand was stained red. Then, when the last curtain call had been made, St. Denys held forth his left hand in supplication. What everyone had supposed to be fake blood still dripped.

"Ladies and gentlemen, I seem to have slightly injured myself. Is there a doctor present?"

Without thinking, Nick stood up. "I'm a doctor," he said and while everyone else was streaming toward the doors, talking in excited voices, Nick was pushing against the flow to find his way backstage.

He was guided to a dressing room where St. Denys sat white-faced, while a wizened little man held a red-soaked folded cloth against his wrist. Nick heard the little man say, "The doctor is here, Mr. Kit."

Nick concentrated on the injury itself, seeing it as a disembodied entity and not as a limb attached to his god. "I need to send for my medical bag," he said. "It wants stitches."

"There isn't time," said St. Denys. "I've a party to attend. I thought of stitches and had the wardrobe mistress bring needles and silk thread."

Nick was appalled. "Sewing needles? Ordinary thread? Unsterilized? With dye? Mr. St. Denys—"

"Sew it," St. Denys demanded.

Nick hesitated, and then stitched the wound. When he had finished, the actor's forearm boasted a neat royal purple welt. Throughout the procedure St. Denys had uttered not one sound other than one or two slight gasps, though his face was white.

When he had finished bandaging the wound, Nick looked into dark eyes that seemed to see into his heart and soul and mind.

Something stopped for Nick. Time? His heartbeat? He didn't know. He knew only that something stopped and something began.

St. Denys's eyes held Nick's. His lips parted as if to say something important, and then he asked, "How much money is owed you, Mr....?"

"Stuart. And — and nothing, Mr. St. Denys. It was a pleasure, I mean an honor, to do it."

"But a workman is worthy of his hire, so I've been told."

"Please. Not a penny."

"Then please accept my invitation to join our party."

"I couldn't." But he wanted to. Another hour or two in this man's presence ... wouldn't it be worth the loss of sleep?

"I wish you would. I must see the theatre manager before he leaves. Would you wait here and give some thought to the party? Otherwise I will insist upon paying you in money."

Nick nodded and St. Denys left the room. No, he would not go to any party. Neither would he accept money. He didn't even have to sit here waiting. He was not nailed to the chair; he could leave.

He glanced down and noticed a blond curl on his black sleeve. Slowly he pulled it off. It had a life of its own. He straightened it out. Released, it sprang back to its former shape. A thread of gold in the form of a question mark.

He was a man of integrity. He needn't act like a silly milkmaid at the first sight of a new hired hand. No. He need not go to that party.

But he knew he would.

6

In one corner was a bathtub which the old man, ignoring him, filled with hot water.

While he waited, uninfluenced by the St. Denys presence, Nick felt reality return. Here he was, in a theatre populated by women no better than painted harlots and men who did not know the meaning of the word "morals." Was he insane? He got up and started toward the door. Suddenly a young woman with stage makeup and red hair bounded into the room.

"Kit–," she said and stopped in surprise. "Who are you?"

"I – um – I'm the doctor."

"Oh. Then you took care of his arm? I thought I would faint when I saw real blood." She smiled and stuck out her hand like a man. "I'm Rama Weisberg. I played the queen." He was so taken aback by her gesture he did not take her hand and after a moment she withdrew it, an odd look on her face. "Didn't you like the production?" she asked. "Or was it just me you didn't like?"

"Oh – nothing of the kind. It's just – I've never met an actress before and..."

The way he said the word told her. "Actress? You say it as if it were the same as three-day-old mutton." She flounced from the room and disappeared into the hallway. Shortly thereafter, St. Denys returned, looking bemused.

"What did you say to Rama?" he asked.

Unhappily, Nick said, "I'm not really sure. She said I called her a mutton, but I didn't."

"Ah, well. She has a redhead's temper. Now then," he went on, letting the little old man help him remove his jerkin and the full-sleeved blood-stained white blouse.

"Your bath is ready, Mr. Kit," said the old man.

"Thank you, William. As I started to say, Stuart, have you decided about the party? You will go, won't you?" As he talked he sat down at the makeup table with its boxes and bottles, and started removing the sweat-streaked makeup.

The "No, I don't think so" died on Nick's lips. He gazed at the naked back and arms, wondering how it would feel to touch them. He was startled by the faint white crisscrossed lines that marred what was otherwise perfect. How in the world would someone like St. Denys acquire scars like that? The tips of the sweat-darkened fair mane lay in waves against the nape of his neck. Nick was near enough to notice a sparse sprinkling of freckles on his shoulders. His ears were hidden by his hair and the downward curve of his jaw was strong.

"If your wife is with you she is more than welcome to join us," St. Denys was saying.

"I don't have a wife," Nick said and did not realize that the way he said it told Kit St. Denys a great deal. "Mr. St. Denys—"

"Please, won't you call me Kit? Everyone does."

"Mr. St. Denys, I wouldn't fit in at your party. I'm just not the kind who enjoys that sort of thing."

Amused, Kit asked, "'That sort of thing'? I assure you, Mr. Stuart, it is only a late dinner, a bit of the grape, and laughter. It is not a bacchanalian orgy."

Nick's face grew hot. "I didn't mean that."

Kit turned toward him, his face free of the makeup. St. Denys was much younger and even more beautiful now. Nick was sorry for that. He had hoped that the glamour and sensuality were all an illusion and he could go home and forget he had ever spoken to the man. He still could. Couldn't he?

"Then you'll come," said St. Denys. "I won't take no for an answer." With complete unconcern, he stood up, and let the old man help him finish undressing. St. Denys had a body as beautiful as his face. Nude, he walked to the tub.

Well proportioned, long-legged, with ... Nick broke into a sweat; how would it feel to spread his hands upon the round warm flesh of his arse? Or see those gently swaying genitals tight, erect, and ready?

"I must leave here!" he told himself. There was a quagmire of sin in this room and he was teetering on the brink!

St. Denys stepped into the high-backed tub of hot water and, careful to keep his injured arm free of the water, he exhaled a gusty sigh of pleasure as the old man fussed over him with scented soap and a sea sponge. The servant kept darting resentful glances at Nick.

"Tell me, Stuart – what was your first name again? Or did you say?"

"Nicholas. My friends call me Nick."

St. Denys laughed. "I'm surprised. Given your sober demeanor, I assumed no one would call you anything less formal than 'Mr. Stuart.'"

That assumption irritated Nick though he did not know why.

"You said you had seen several performances, did you not? Are you particularly interested in Shakespeare?"

"Uh – yes. Oh, yes. Very interested. In Shakespeare. Yes, indeed."

"What is your favorite play?"

"Well – *Hamlet,* of course."

"Of course."

Nick knew he was being mocked. "Well, it is." Then it didn't matter because like Neptune rising from the sea St. Denys stood up in his tub and stepped out, grinning at him as if he knew the lustful thoughts darting in Nick's mind. Nick's face turned red.

"Only a few more minutes, Mr. Stuart. Then we can leave for the party." The old man helped him into his underclothes, trousers, and shoes. Then St. Denys said, "I can manage from here, William. Thank you. You go freshen up for the party."

"Very good, Mr. Kit." William favored Nick with one more disapproving glare and was gone.

"I'm ... surprised," said Nick. "You socialize with your servants?"

The answer was a cool rebuff. "William is not a servant. He is my dresser and has been for a long time. As such he is as much a part of any production as the rest of us. That I always have the right costume for any given scene is due to William."

Nick wondered how any man who had just been stark naked in front of a stranger could answer with such dignity. He was surprised at the actor's next words as he awkwardly pulled on his starched white shirt, easing his bandaged arm into the sleeve.

"You'll have to learn the ways of the theatre if you're to be around us," said St. Denys, matter-of-factly.

"I didn't know I was." A fine vertical line formed between Nick's eyebrows. The man took a great deal for granted! And yet ... it was immensely flattering.

St. Denys gave him a slow, deliberate look that seemed to pull secrets from him without his having to say a word. "But you are, aren't you." It was not a question.

Nick was dazed by the ferocity of the desire the quiet words aroused. "Yes," he said.

"I knew the moment I saw you that you were one of my kind. Something in your eyes."

A moment of paralyzing fear struck Nick. "One of my kind—" Hugh had said the same thing. If St. Denys and Hugh could recognize his daemon by looking in his eyes then so could others! Merciful Heaven— Then his fear was forgotten when St. Denys's sultry expression gave way to one of guileless charm.

"I'm terribly clumsy tonight. Devil of a time managing the shirt buttons. Ought to have kept William in here. It's a bloody inconsiderate thing to ask of a guest, but could you help me?"

Nick nodded. He fastened them, and his fingers trembled. His fingertips brushed the damp, hot skin of St. Denys's chest and abdomen as each button slid into its buttonhole. He was helpless against the sexual imagery that flashed into his mind. He wanted to feel that silky flesh against his own ... Then as he fastened the right sleeve button he saw the twisted little finger. Scars on the actor's back and a broken finger ... What mysteries did they represent? He glanced up once more into St. Denys's dark eyes.

"After the party," St. Denys said softly, "you will go with me to my hotel." That, too, was not a question.

"Yes..."

"You'll stay the night with me."

Nick hesitated the barest fraction of a moment. "Yes." He did not look away.

"Then let us be off, Nick."

It did not occur to Nick until much later that with those two "yeses" he had accepted everything and questioned nothing.

❐

He was relieved that St. Denys made no effort to force him to join in the festivities at Prince's. Instead, Nick stood about with an alcoholic drink of some kind in his hand, not tasting it, and watched St. Denys while trying not to be obvious about it. When he felt curious glances on him, his gaze immediately sought one of the dozens of paintings and photographs that lined the walls of the Upstairs Gallery.

As the band played into the early morning the dancing became more frenetic instead of less. Nick wondered how people who had worked until late had the energy to kick up their heels and whirl around the floor. St. Denys danced with this girl and that, laughing, tossing his forelock out of his eyes, and seemed to have forgotten Nick Stuart's existence.

Nick frowned with righteous disapproval at the dancers and drinkers and then smiled a self-mocking smile. Was this not irony? he asked himself, to condemn the sinfulness of drinking and dancing while all but drooling with the desire to fornicate with another man? Disgusted with his hypocrisy, he left the ballroom.

He discovered a side room filled with elaborate, massive dark furniture and enough potted plants for an arboretum. He poured his drink into the soil of a plant and sat down.

Should he stay or should he go? Suppose he stayed and St. Denys really had forgotten him. It would be humiliating to go out into that ballroom and find him gone. On the other hand, there was the bald fact that he wanted Kit St. Denys even if it damned his immortal soul. He decided to stay.

Just when his eyes were beginning to glaze from ennui, St. Denys breezed in. "Here you are," he said. "I was wondering where you had got to. You didn't have a very good time, did you? I shouldn't have insisted you come. I'm sorry."

"No," Nick lied, struggling against the quicksand of the soft couch. "I had a wonderful evening. Really."

St. Denys laughed. "*I* had a wonderful evening; you were bored. I daresay I would be bored out of my mind if I were at a gathering of doctors. At any rate, your wonderful evening is only about to begin." Nick's entire body went rigid with shock when St. Denys bent slightly and kissed him. Nick had kissed another male only once and that had been on a grassy hill in the Cotswolds.

"St. Denys–," he gasped. "With all of these people about!"

"It's all right. Many of them have gone. And they're my people. They know all about me."

"Well, they don't know about me!"

The answering smile was enigmatic. "They will." He added, "And the name, as I have said, is Kit."

Nick was an early waker and even the fact that he had not slept until nearly dawn did not change that. He sat up and looked with wonder at the man in bed beside him. The few hurried sexual experiences at university had not prepared him for the completeness of the night before.

He wanted to touch the jaw that was slack with sleep, and the curve of the ear. He wanted to run his hand the length of Kit's shoulder and arm. He wanted to again feel with his hands and mouth the fine skin, the places where pulses of life beat, the hard nipples, and the muscles and hollows of Kit's torso. He wanted to taste again for the first time another man's sex, an act so foreign to him he had refused more than once last night. But before the night was played out Kit had coaxed him into doing it and it had been both thrilling and repellant. He wanted to feel again the velvet heat of Kit's mouth around his sex. He wanted to again possess Kit as fully as any man or woman had ever been possessed, and in the act become, himself, the one possessed.

Kit stirred.

Nick started to say his name, started to caress him.

Suddenly a strangled cry of terror burst from Kit's throat. His eyes flew open but they seemed to look through Nick to something behind him. Gasping, crying out something Nick could not understand, he sobbed brokenly, an even greater shock than the scream had been. Only the word "Pa" was understandable.

"Kit—," Nick said, and shook him. "Kit, you're having a nightmare. Wake up." Kit flung his hands off and grappled with him. Nick broke free and cried, "Kit! Wake up!" The shake he gave him was violent this time.

The glassy look faded from Kit's eyes, though his breath still sounded like a choked gasp. "You—," he managed to say finally. "You – you're here. You're still here!"

Uncertainly Nick asked, "Do you want me to go?"

Kit reached out and painfully gripped Nick's wrist. "No—" His eyes never left Nick's face and with a sense of awe Nick saw the devils leave the dark, shadowed eyes, felt the hurtful grip on his wrist relax. Kit lay down again. "I don't want you to leave," he whispered. "Stay with me. No one else has ever made him go away so quickly."

"Who? What are you talking about?"

For a moment Kit's eyes were again hagridden. "I can't tell you. Don't leave me, Nick." He drew Nick down to lie beside him, their heads on the same pillow. Kit's hand slid across Nick's belly to curl around his side. "He's eating my soul, Nick," he whispered. "Sometimes I don't know which I am."

"I ... don't understand."

Kit's head moved beside his on the pillow. "I can't tell you. I can't tell anyone. You have to take me on trust."

They lay without moving, until eventually Kit went to sleep again, this time without the nightmares.

Nick was afraid to move even though sunlight soon flooded the room. Kit's arm remained across him; his breath was warm on Nick's neck. Nick lay wide awake, thinking about the mystery thrust upon him. "...made *him* go away..." Who? Kit was young and strong and rich. Who could possibly threaten him? Well, whoever "he" was, the great Kit St. Denys had become a terrified child for those few minutes.

Hesitantly he stroked Kit's hair. He had never felt this kind of tenderness for anyone and it was frightening. Then he relaxed. He knew it would end when Kit awakened and they resumed their separate and very different lives, but what harm could it do for a little while to pretend that the passion of the night before had been something more? They would meet some years in the future, both portly and balding ... He smiled and shook his head. Fat and balding? That was too much to imagine for either of them.

Nick dozed. He was awakened by Kit's tongue teasing his lips. He struggled to wakefulness.

"Come on," said Kit. "Everything's ready."

Nick sat up, disoriented, and raked his fingers through his rumpled hair. "What's ready?"

Kit just laughed and pulled him from the bed and led him into the bathroom. There was a narrow hip tub with fragrant steam wafting from it.

"Get in," Kit said. "I always start the day with a bath."

Nick sniffed. "What's that smell?"

"French scented oil," said Kit. "I borrowed it from my leading lady."

"Scented oil?" Nick said with ill-concealed disdain. "That isn't very manly, is it?"

Kit gave him a lewd smile, bringing a bright red blush to Nick's face. "I fail to recall that you complained about my manliness last night."

Nick got in the tub without any further protest. To his shock Kit got into the water also. "There isn't room," Nick protested.

"Depends upon what you need room for." Kit placed his soapy hands around Nick's neck then slowly slid them over his shoulders and downward.

The erotic, slithering touch had an instant effect. Nick had never been so close to fainting in his entire life.

❐

In the days and nights that followed, Nick sometimes found himself wondering if any of it had really happened.

He had left Kit's hotel that morning feeling every emotion known to man from elation to soul-sick guilt and back again. He prayed and tried to convince God that he was sorry for the sin and it would never happen again. But each time in the midst of his prayer, he would remember that night and an involuntary smile would cut short his prayer. Finally he stopped trying to convince God. He couldn't even convince himself.

Each day he found himself thinking Kit would contact him, ask to see him again, but he received no messages.

Gradually the hope faded. Well, what had he expected? He'd known there was nothing to it but a pair of bodies meeting in mutual heat. He had been an idiot to think for even a moment that it had been anything more.

He went about the routine of seeing patients in his surgery set up in an old brick building on the border of the East End. In the daylight hours it was not hard to put Kit from his mind, for there was no shortage of sick and injured people to tend to.

He wished more of them could pay him. And because he saw so many of the poor and lower class, the middle-class patients went elsewhere. There was something wrong, he thought when he was hungry, that a man was punished for wanting to do some good in the world.

Wistfully he remembered the nights he had gone to the theatre, so lost in the magic of Kit St. Denys he forgot he was hungry.

One night he shooed the last patient out the door and set about washing the instruments and putting away the medicines. He heard a knock at the door. "Oh, go away!" he muttered. "The sign says 'Closed,' doesn't it?" The knock came again. With a sigh he went to it.

Kit stood there, one arm leaning against the doorjamb. He almost glowed with good health and vitality, money and privilege. "Hello, physician. I've had a devil of a time finding you. You didn't tell me where your house of mercy was situated."

Nick was suddenly, acutely, aware of the shabbiness of his surgery and, for that matter, of himself – one had peeling paint and the other had threadbare clothes. He was both resentful that Kit should see him like this and elated that he had come.

"Are you not going to ask me in?" Kit asked.

"Oh – yes. Of course." Nick stepped aside and Kit entered, looking around.

"Don't your patients pay you?" he asked abruptly.

Nick bristled. "That is none of your concern."

"Of course it is. If you're starving you're no good to me or to yourself. Do they?"

"When they can."

Kit's gaze was level and questioning. "Leave this. I need a Company doctor. My people are forever getting ill or getting hurt. The physician I had has retired. I'll pay you well." He made a vague gesture. "You don't need these people."

"They need me. There is no other doctor in this area."

Kit's lip curled. "Do you think they appreciate your sacrifice? You could lay down your life for them and most of them would step over your corpse without a backward glance."

Nick's temper flared. "You don't know anything about these people! You have money, a good life ... you know nothing."

Kit shrugged. "I know more than you think." He moved no closer, nor did he touch Nick, but Nick felt as if he had been caressed when Kit said, "I could find any number of doctors. I want you. I want you for my people. And I want you for myself. Please." And softer still, "You helped me in a way no one else has done. I need you."

"I can't."

For a long moment there was silence. Then Kit smiled and gave his head a little shake. "Well. If I can't hire you away from your pauper patients, then at least let me buy you dinner. You don't look as if you've had a decent meal for a year."

"I do quite well, thank you."

"Dinner. I insist."

Nick hesitated. There had been little conversation the other time. What would there be for them to talk about? It was on his tongue to decline, then he heard himself say, "I must finish here first."

"Go ahead. I'll observe. Perhaps I'll find myself playing a physician someday."

Nick felt clumsy with Kit's eyes upon him as he performed the routine tasks and locked the bottles of liquids and pills away. As he worked he answered Kit's questions about the method and reason for sterilization, the reason for the white coat instead of the black wool which other doctors of his acquaintance favored.

Nick's answers were clumsy; talking about what he did was not something that came easily to him.

When he had put everything away and locked the door to the surgery, he left with Kit in a hired gig. He could not have said what restaurant they went to, but he knew it was a fancy one. He imagined what his thrifty mother and father would say if they could see him in this place with its silky-voiced waiters and glittering crystal, its wine list and potted palms.

He felt again that Kit was taking him to a world where he did not belong. He let Kit order, and sat in silence whenever gentlemen, sometimes accompanying a lady, would pause beside Kit's chair and address him as an old friend or admirer.

Kit glanced at him after one obnoxious and obviously half-inebriated gentleman had gone his way. "Shall I have the food sent to a private room? Would you be more comfortable?"

Nick said, "Of course not," but the relieved expression on his face made Kit summon the waiter, speak a few words, slip some money into the waiter's pocket, and stand up.

"Come along," said Kit and led him toward the back, up a short flight of stairs to a small, dimly lit room just large enough for a table and two chairs, with a grill through which, if one wished, one could watch the diners below. Nick relaxed as he sat down.

Kit stood a moment at the grill, then joined him at the table. "I'm sorry you were uncomfortable belowstairs. We need never dine in public, you know. Most fine restaurants have private rooms like this."

Nick's heart beat a little faster. There it was again: that assumption they would be together often. When he said nothing, Kit gazed at him for several moments, unsmiling.

"I think you do not like me, Mr. Stuart."

"Not like you? How could anyone not like you?"

"There are those who find it quite easy. They say I'm arrogant. Which, of course, I am."

"I don't think so."

"You don't know me yet. But then, no one does."

The dinner arrived just then. Nick kept a cautious eye on Kit's expert use of the extra cutlery. In his parents' home things were plain and functional. There were a spoon, a knife, and a fork laid at the table, accompanied by a teacup and a solid, thick plate. The food was plain as well – boiled beef or mutton; thick-crusted bread and butter churned from milk given by one of their own cows. There was never anything like the alarming dish that was served with flames leaping up from it, and he had socialized so little at university that such bizarre things had never been encountered.

As the evening went on, Nick's apprehension of a silent, awkward dinner disappeared. Kit was charming and entertaining, telling him stories of the theatre through the courses and after the clutter had been cleared away.

"...and there I was," Kit said, "flailing about with the sword that wasn't there, going through all of the motions and feeling like a fool – especially when it came time to deliver the death blow."

Nick laughed. "But why didn't you just stop the play and get a sword?"

"Theatre is the realm of the imagination. Had I stopped, it would have destroyed the illusion even further. As it was, people realized I had no sword while they were watching, but the image they remembered afterward was complete with sword."

"I've never met anyone so different from everything I ever knew," said Nick. "I envy you. You have imagination. I've always wished I did."

"I'm sure you do."

"No. I see what is. I'm not capable of pretending. I used to see fellows at university – poets and the like, and wish I could think like that."

Kit smiled. "We each have our place, my friend. People with imagination tend to soar around in their own little world. You realists bring us back to earth – sometimes with a thump. And yet you and I are in the same business."

"I don't quite follow."

"We're healers. You heal the body with potions and pills. A jester heals the heart with laughter and a tragedian, with tears."

Nick gazed in wonder at him. There was nothing about this man that was ordinary – not his person, not his language, not his thoughts.

Kit moved slightly and with the movement seemed to throw off the serious mood. "We've talked enough about me this evening. Though wonderful and fascinating creature that I am, I could keep you enthralled all night. Where do you come from, Nick?"

"A little village in the Cotswolds, not far from Gloucester."

"A country lad, eh?"

"In every way. Plain people. My father is a doctor and an elder in the church. I helped my father with lambs and calves and babies. I helped him pull teeth and lance boils and stitch wounds."

"So that's where you learned your fancy needlework! And you will go back there to live and practice someday?"

Nick shook his head. "No. My father and I don't get on. I'm not sure the entire Cotswold country would be large enough for us both. I miss the countryside, and there is much about the City that I detest, but I think it is where I can do the most good. I'm thinking..."

"What?"

"Oh – nothing. Just a thought I have about – I told my father and he all but frothed at the mouth."

"You strike me as any father's ideal son. What could you possibly have said?"

"That I want to specialize."

"In what?"

"Obstetrics and gynecology."

"It sounds dreadful. What is it?"

"Delivering infants and treating the ailments of women."

"Hm. Haven't women been giving birth for several thousand years? And why women? Is not a man's health just as important?"

"You sound like my father!" Nick's brows lowered and his voice was a little sullen. "I don't have to explain to you or to him or to anyone."

"The boy is bristly!" Kit put his hand on Nick's. "I may have sounded like your father, but I assure you I don't harbor fatherly feeling toward you. Or brotherly. Or even cousinly." His smile was mischievous. Then he touched his napkin to his lips. "My friend, the hour is late. Shall we go?"

With every step he took from the room, through the restaurant, from the restaurant to the vehicle, Nick tried to think of a way to justify going to bed again with Kit St. Denys even though it was a terrible sin. To his disappointed relief he was spared the decision. Kit delivered him to the surgery and drove away.

Sunday next, Kit appeared again, unannounced, and again insisted upon Nick's dining with him. They went to the same place. This time Nick ordered food familiar to him, and thoroughly enjoyed the boiled beef. This time when dinner was finished, Kit said, "Tell me what it's like in your little Cotswold village."

"It's truly beautiful there," Nick answered, and in a wave of nostalgia painted verbal pictures about the rolling green hills and clear water, the rosy-stone cottage, his mother's gardens, one that produced vegetables and one which put forth a blaze of colored blossoms.

"And everything revolves around the church," he said. "Prayer every day. Sundays and midweek we went to church — twice."

"So you are religious?"

Nick's forehead puckered. "I — yes, I suppose I am. I believe in God. I believe in sin."

"And in the goodness of mankind?"

"I don't believe there is any except what is given by the grace of God to those who repent." Nick was amazed that he was saying these things. He had not thought them for many years and he had seldom gone to church while at university. Why were they suddenly coming from his lips as though he were a missionary?

Kit put his elbow on the table and leaned his chin on his hand. "Repent of what?"

Nick was taken aback. "Well — of whatever Satan has led them into."

"I don't believe in Satan."

"You — you don't — you don't believe in Evil?" Nick was horrified; the clamorous memory of thousands of sermons rushed to the forefront.

Kit's smile slipped. "Oh, my blue-eyed Puritan. I believe in evil. I've seen evil. I lived with evil. But I also believe that a man or woman can achieve goodness through their own efforts. It's not a gift from your Jehovah, a pat on the head for saying what-a-bad-boy-am-I."

Nick said nothing; he did not know how to counter such an argument.

Kit went on, not noticing his distress. "My stepfa— my father was a good man. My friend Lizbet is a good woman. I have friends who are good people though they would not be made welcome in your Baptist Heaven." His smile was disarming. "I, on the other hand, am a perfect pagan; I live for life. I have no hope of ever achieving Christian perfection nor do I wish to."

As before, he signaled the end of the evening by touching his lips with his napkin. "Shall we go?"

Nick did not move for a moment. What had he gotten himself into? He had met many sinners but they knew they were sinners and some cared and some didn't. But to not believe in sin and redemption—! He should shake the dust of this place from off his feet. He should run and never look back. He should—

His hand lay tensely curled in on itself on the tabletop. Kit's hand descended upon it.

"Will you—" Kit paused as a waiter entered, bowed, and removed the dessert dishes. "Will you spend the night with me again?" His voice was quiet, gentle.

The hair on Nick's arms stood up. He wished Kit would try to force the issue, for then he could say no.

Instead, Kit said quietly, "I fear I feel a kind of fatal attraction to you and I don't know why. You're not my sort at all." He shrugged. *"Je ne sais quoi?"*

Nick swallowed. "Someone like you must have many lovers."

"But none like you." Kit smiled an ingenuous smile. "I've never before shared a lover with God."

Nick blanched at the blasphemy.

But he did not return to the surgery that night.

Or the next.

Nor for many nights to come.

Days he spent with his patients and their endless problems. In between he argued with himself that he should stop his madness while he still could, and set about finding the proper wife for a young physician. But when the surgery was locked and Kit appeared at the door the proper wife was forgotten. As was any notion of sin.

7

They gradually slipped into being "we." Bit by bit each deepened the roots he had sent into the other's life. The one unresolvable conflict was Nick's refusal to exchange his surgery and its privation for the easier, more profitable work of being doctor to the Company. Kit finally surrendered that point.

Nick attended rehearsals whenever he could; it gave him much pleasure to see Kit in his dual roles as director and star. He attended every performance possible. Sometimes he wondered how he had tolerated his dull life before Kit. They were together every night through the rain-drenched summer and autumn through the frigid winter.

One Sunday when ice covered everything and hung in thick daggers from the rooftops, Nick coaxed an unwilling Kit out into the country, determined to teach him to ice-skate. Kit fell several times, dragging Nick down to lie sprawled on the ice with him. When the day was over, Kit said, "Look what a good teacher you are!" and proceeded to do spins and backward skating Nick could not do.

"You liar!" Nick bellowed. "You knew how all along!"

Red-nosed, red-cheeked, howling with laughter, Kit sailed around the pond, calling, "But it was such fun having you teach me."

"I'll get even," said Nick. "See if I don't."

Kit tried without success to teach him how to play a guitar.

"I can't," he finally protested. "It hurts my fingers and I need them to be sensitive."

"That's just an excuse," retorted Kit.

"Of course. But it's a good one. And true."

And though there were many nights that they went to plays or dinners or parties, many winter evenings were spent alone in Kit's suite with the fire crackling while Nick read medical journals and Kit read scripts or theatre publications. On nights when Nick felt as lazy as an overfed cat he asked Kit to read to him and, always glad of an audience, Kit obliged. Sometimes Nick would say, "Play something for me, won't you?" And as he got out the guitar and tuned it, Kit would grumble, "Other people pay me to entertain them." But he was pleased nonetheless and was soon singing love songs or bawdy backstreet ballads. Other times Nick had to say nothing and Kit would know he wanted to hear some of Shakespeare's sonnets.

Then Kit would stretch out on the couch with his head in Nick's lap and recite the ones Nick loved the most. It was still difficult for Nick to show affection, but at these times he would wind locks of blond hair around his fingers and marvel at the fullness of the emotion to which he could not fix a name.

A grand party was planned by the Company for Kit's twenty-sixth birthday. But that night Nick forgot about him, forgot about time, forgot about everything except the exhausted sixteen-year-old girl in a sordid tenement room, struggling to deliver a second twin. The first had uttered a weak cry and died. With every fiber of his being he wanted to save the second.

At last he held in his hands the unmoving, wet fruition of twenty hours of weariness for him, and agony for the young mother.

"I won't lose you too," he vowed. Quickly he cleaned the baby's mouth and nose and breathed a light puff of air into its lungs. A second light puff and a third. The tiny creature sucked in its first air and a moment later gave a healthy howl of protest.

The closemouthed, slovenly midwife started to cut the cord with a pair of scissors she picked up from the table, which was still covered with the leavings of the family's last meal.

"Good God, woman!" snapped Nick. "Not those. Use my instruments."

She shot him a poisonous glare. "Been doin' me job for longer'n you been born. I reckon I know how." Nonetheless, she put the scissors aside and picked up the shiny, clean scissors that Nick had laid out.

The cord cut, Nick handed the baby to his grandmother, who was hovering in the background, and turned his attention to the girl.

"It's almost over, Mary," he said. "You have a son. A healthy, living son." She tried to smile through her pain.

Hours afterward, he lay down on his bed without bothering to turn back the covers. Drifting into a tired sleep he mused over the midwife's snarled words: *"Been doin' me job for longer'n you been born."* Yes, he thought. And that was why so many women died of fevers and so many babies died without ever opening their eyes. Dirty instruments, use of superstitions instead of knowledge – he remembered seeing the woman put a sharp knife under the bed to cut the pain as he entered the room. The midwife had looked apoplectic when he gave the girl a brief whiff of chloroform.

With every infant he delivered, with every mother he saw suffering or dying from puerperal fever, he was more sure that his calling and his mission lay in obstetrics and gynecology. Kit's opinion to the contrary, he knew he could make a difference.

His drooping eyes flew open. Kit! The birthday party. He was to have been there nearly eleven hours ago. His first thought was to dress and go to the hotel. Then he lay back down. Kit was not a child. He would understand; he knew Nick's time was not always his own. He went to sleep.

❏

Across the City, Kit sat the night in terror, the suite lit, a bottle of whiskey in his shaking hand, listening to the scratching on the window and the tapping at the door as the thick-bearded, hulking figure in the dark blue coat tried to get in.

"'Arry! I know you're in there, 'Arry. Let me in, boy. Let me in. 'Arry! Do it now!"

"Go away!" Kit screamed when he could stand it no longer. The whiskey bottle went crashing against the door. "Go away," he screamed again and swung his arm, knocking over an unlit lamp, spilling kerosene upon the carpet. "You're dead. You're dead. I killed you. Oh–," he cried with a raw sob, "Nickie, God damn your bloody soul, where are you?"

The door swung open and he felt the breath stop in his throat. Rourke was going to kill him with his rotting corpse's hands. Kit sank to his knees, unable to stand.

"Kit?" said Francis Mulholland, coming in. "I heard something break as I went by. Are you ... God, my God." He knelt beside him. "Kit, what is it?"

Kit stared at him as if he had never seen him before.

When Francis gripped Kit's arms to pull him to his feet Kit's face lost its color and he fainted.

❏

Nick arrived late the next morning, having given himself the day off. He was tired but pleased. He had gone to the cluttered room that

•95•

was the home of the new mother and infant, her mother and father, and three brothers, and had found mother and child both doing well. It would, of course, be a few days before he would know for certain whether any of the thousand and one ills of postpartum women and newborns would set in, but for now everything looked rosy. He was smiling as he unlocked the door with the key Kit had given him – and stepped into something out of a bad dream. A flower vase lay broken in front of the mantel. A tall clock lay stunned on its side. Draperies hung by one end of a rod. A lamp had been knocked over. It looked as if there had been a violent struggle. The place stank of stale whiskey and vomit.

Nick's mind played the scene – an intruder, an attempted murder, assault– Fear washed over him as he remembered the nightmare and Kit's terror of "him." The bedroom door was closed; he flung it open. And sagged in relief. Kit lay asleep. Whatever had happened, he was all right.

He started to reach out toward Kit when a man came out of the water closet, a man wearing Kit's dressing gown. Nick recognized the good-natured face and gangly frame: Francis Mulholland. At the same instant he realized the bed had hosted more than one person. The actor stopped and appeared flustered.

"What are you doing here?" snapped Nick.

His voice roused Kit, who raised halfway up on one elbow, a rumpled, absurd caricature of himself. "It's all right, Francis," he said in a hoarse, unsteady voice. "I'm fine now. You needn't stay."

Francis cast a resentful glare at Nick, who strode out into the sitting room while Francis dressed. Baffled and angry, he waited.

In the bedroom Francis finished putting on his clothes and then went to Kit. Kit leaned his cheek against Francis's chest. "You're a good friend," he said.

"But you want him." Francis's words were bitter and accompanied by a jerk of his head toward the sitting room.

Kit looked up, his eyes red, his face stubbled. "I wish I could say you're wrong, Francis. But you're not and we both know it. Oh, God, I feel sick." He sat without moving until his head stopped spinning. "Help me into my dressing gown, will you? I must maintain some shred of dignity."

Francis pulled the dressing gown up Kit's fumbling arms and tied the sash. "You look bloody awful," he said. Then he dropped a light kiss on Kit's drooping head and walked from the bedroom. He favored Nick with a resentful glance but did not speak to him as he left the suite.

Nick could not bring himself to go into the bedroom. The door opened and Kit came out, groping and dizzy. "Nickie," he said, and made it to the couch before collapsing.

"You slept with Mulholland, didn't you," Nick accused. "I am gone one night in nearly a year and you go to bed with someone else."

Kit leaned his head back and put one hand over his burning eyes. "I needed someone. You weren't here. You promised you would be."

"I was delivering twins. One of them died. The woman could have died. I thought that was a little more important." He heard the angry defensiveness in his voice.

Kit lowered his hand and looked at him. "Twins?" he asked, with an odd expression on his face. "Yes. I suppose it was. I'm sorry about the baby."

"I want to know what Mulholland was doing here."

Kit covered his eyes again. "It wasn't what you think."

"You went to *bed* with him. What else could it be?"

"I don't see that it's any of your bloody business."

"I think it is." Nick looked around at the destruction in the room. "What happened in here? Did you and Mulholland get carried away?"

A humorless grimace touched Kit's lips. "Yes," he said. "That's what happened. Francis and I fucked on every piece of furniture in here and finished up in there."

"You have the morals of an alley cat!" Nick's disgust was scathing.

Again the humorless grimace quirked Kit's mouth. "Alley cat? Are you calling me a pussy? Ah, Nickie. I'd send your teeth down your throat for that if I had the strength."

"You were drunk last night."

"As a lord. Francis and I, we sat here and downed a fifth of whiskey before we commenced our wild activities."

"Damn you," Nick choked. "I hope I never set eyes on you again. You are rotten to the core." He slammed the door as he left. He was heartsick. As his cab neared his surgery, he noticed a small church he had never seen before. "Stop here," he told the driver, who pulled his aged horse to a stop. Nick got out and paid his fare.

The church was Anglican, and though small and in a working-class neighborhood, tried its best to be High Church. Nick averted his eyes from the statues of the saints and the votive candles. He had never expected to pray in a place that skirted the forbidden edges of idolatry. He closed his eyes and tried to find God.

He tried the prayers he had learned when young, and he prayed for God to forgive him for the vile sins he had committed with Kit. He could not feel the warmth of forgiveness as he once had. He knew why. He tried to whisper the words "God, I am most heartily sorry for what I've done." The words stuck in his throat. He wasn't sorry. He'd never tried to put a name to what he felt for Kit, but here in the chill of this place, with the blank plaster eyes of the Anglican idols watching him, he knew. He loved Kit in the way God meant him to love a woman. It was as simple and as soul-damning as that.

He rose from his knees. As he neared the door a priest came in. "I didn't know anyone was here," the priest apologized. "May I help you, my son?"

Nick's answer was an involuntary bark of laughter. "Nobody can help me, Reverend. Nobody."

He found another cab and returned to the hotel. Kit was sitting where he had left him. Kit looked up at Nick. He looked so vulnerable that Nick was wrenched inside.

"I ... suppose I ... jumped to a ... a wrong conclusion."

"You suppose," Kit said as if mulling over a new idea.

Nick ran his fingers through his hair. "Kit – you just don't know how difficult all this is for me."

"All what?"

"You and I. It's wrong, you know. What we're doing."

"You're unhappy with me?"

"You know I'm not. That makes it worse. I *should* be."

Kit shook his head. "Poor little Puritan. Torn between Jehovah and a pagan. How do you ever manage to forget that burden of guilt long enough to enjoy yourself?"

"I don't know. It's just ... you make me forget it. Everything about you tells me I have no reason to feel guilty. But sometimes in the middle of the night when it's quiet and you're asleep I feel–" He stopped, reluctant to go on.

"Feel what, Nickie? You may as well spit it out."

"I feel as if God is watching me."

"And He's upset that you are enjoying life."

"No! He's angry because I am sinning! Kit, you didn't grow up as I did, knowing God is watching everything you do."

"Well, then? Do you want to end it, Nickie? Do you want to leave me and go back to your prayers?"

Nick's eyes were dark with desperation. "No! But I know that's what I *should* do. I – I don't know how I would live anymore, without you. That's why I can't bear the thought that I'm not the only one."

"Ah. So that's it. If you're going to jeopardize your eternal soul for my favors, then that gives you proprietary rights." He said it with such a flippant edge Nick was at a loss how to answer. Then Kit took him unawares by saying, "Nickie, close your surgery for a fortnight."

"A fortnight! I can't leave my patients that long."

"Just once? Can't you just once? *The Tempest* has two more performances and I desperately need a holiday. So do you. Come with me to St. Denys Hill."

"But I have women due to deliver."

"There are other doctors, you know. You look as tired as I do."

"Well ... I am." Nick smiled. "I'm bloody tired." He looked at the puffy face, which had never looked less handsome. "I don't know ... perhaps you're right. Maybe we do need a holiday. Both of us."

Kit's bloodshot eyes brightened. "Think of it, Nickie. For fourteen days we'll have not a care in the world. And I assure you, God is too busy with this wicked city to pay any attention to St. Denys Hill. We'll ride horses, eat pheasant if we like, sleep in a different room every night if we wish. There's a pond in the woods; we'll bathe without a stitch on and then make love in the grass with no one to know but the birds. We'll picnic on Jester's Knoll. 'A Jug of Wine, a Loaf of Bread – and Thou Beside me singing in the Wilderness...'"

He seemed lighthearted and Nick suddenly realized he had not seen Kit this playful for weeks. And he could see in the dark eyes that this was something Kit wanted a great deal. He smiled. "Very well. But you must promise I don't have to sing in the wilderness. I can't carry a tune. When are we to leave?"

"Sunday next."

"But I can't go that soon! I must arrange for another doctor to see to my patients."

"You have four days. Surely you can find someone."

"I – don't know."

"Find someone. Offer him whatever he wants. I'll pay it."

"I'll pay my own expenses, thank you very much."

"Such stiff-necked pride, little Puritan. Such stiff-necked pride."

❑

In the end, Nick had to accept Kit's offer. No physician of his acquaintance would do it for the amount of money he could offer. So much for altruistic physicians, he thought sourly.

Then they were off in a carriage, bound for St. Denys Hill.

"I'd rather take a motorcar," Kit said. "But there are no roads fit to drive upon out there."

"My prayers were answered. I don't want to ever ride in one of the things."

"People like you hold back progress," Kit observed.

"I can't see that a noisy machine that scares one out of one's wits could by any stretch of the imagination be called progress. Now a new inoculation for puerperal fever would be progress."

"But a motorcar could get you to your patient with puerperal fever, whatever that may be, much sooner."

"If it didn't stop functioning."

They laughed. It was amazing. Only a few hours from London and already Nick felt as if a load had fallen from his shoulders. Then Nick thought of something new to worry about as he eyed the back of the driver's head. "Uh ... I presume there are servants at the Hill?"

"Of course. It's a large place."

"Won't there be talk, my staying with you and all?"

"Ah, my Nickie, master of the euphemism. By 'staying with' I presume you mean 'sleeping with.'" He grinned. "Like my father, I hire people who are honest, trustworthy, and who understand my proclivities. And I pay them well to maintain their discretion. Some of them have been there since before I – since before I left. Some of them worked for my father."

Nick leaned back. "I've told you everything about my life before we met. Do you realize you have told me nothing? I know that you are a great actor and the most complicated human being I've ever met and you are very rich. Nothing else."

"Very." When he looked at Nick, his eyes were shuttered from within. "There is much more to me than you know, Nickie-mine."

"And when will I know the dreadful secrets?" Nick asked, and laughed.

"Perhaps soon. Perhaps never. Look about you. I believe this must be the most splendid place on earth."

They had passed through a village that reminded Nick a little of his own. The land here was rich and green with spring. On a low hill he could see the spire of a church. To the west, on a steep hill that seemed to have been upthrust violently from the earth, were the remains of a castle. At frequent intervals the river Derwent could be glimpsed shining like a young girl's ribbon. A little farther on was a stretch of wild moorland.

"You are on my land now," said Kit. "I will never let the moor be tamed. In a few minutes you will see the house."

Nick glanced at his lover's profile. Kit was leaning forward, smiling. "You love it here, don't you."

"Yes. Oh, God, yes. Whenever I come back I think I shall never leave. But then the stage calls me and I must. There it is."

They passed beneath a canopy of ancient, sheltering trees, then between two massive stone pillars and up a long driveway. The great house was silhouetted against the brilliant blue of the sky. Nick's mouth fell open. He had known Kit was rich but this place was far more than he had imagined.

He had expected a massive kind of Norman castle. Instead he saw gray stone and an amazing number of windows.

Kit seemed to know what he was thinking. "When you see it with the sun shining full on the windows it looks like a glass house. Hardwick Hall is the only grand home that has more."

Nick was too awed to say very much. They were met by a gathering of servants who seemed glad to see their employer. And then Kit took Nick on the Grand Tour. They walked from the Great Hall with its wainscoting and tapestries and pillars through the dining room to the drawing room and the Lesser Hall. Kit pointed to the gallery above.

"I used to hide there and watch parties to which I was not invited." He then took Nick upstairs to the gallery and then to the library. "This was the first room I ever saw in this house," he said, and watched Nick's reaction.

Nick looked puzzled. "I thought you were born here. What—"

Kit put his fingers to his lips. "No questions yet." Most of the nude statues were gone now, given to his father's friends and servants as mementoes of him. Kit had kept his favorites: the four-foot-tall replica of Michelangelo's David, which he and his father had acquired on an Italian holiday, and the Antinous. One was smooth, the other pitted with time and the tip of the perfect nose was missing.

Nick had never seen a nude statue and he stared, first at the unabashed genitals carved with such care and then at the expertly executed muscles and veins and facial features. "If this is what the ancient gods looked like no wonder the Greeks and Romans worshipped idols."

Kit laughed. "Oh, dear Puritan. You do have such a strange way of looking at things. They weren't gods. They were just men. Glorious men," he added, "but men."

"I don't understand how the artists did it," Nick said, overcoming his ingrained revulsion to graven images. He gingerly touched the Antinous's raised arm, which was broken off at the wrist. "It's a surprise to find it cold."

"Michelangelo said the figure was always in the stone. It was the sculptor's work to free it. Not too different from an actor. We're given words on paper and we have to make it live."

"Who was he? Was he a real person?"

"As real as you and I. He was Emperor Hadrian's *amoroso*. He drowned himself when he was eighteen. No one knows why. There were thousands of statues of him and it's believed this is pretty much what he looked like. This statue is believed to have been done from life. It's more than seventeen hundred years old and priceless."

Nick could not stop looking at the face of the boy who had been adored by an emperor. He glanced at Kit and then back at the statue. "You look like him."

Kit laughed. "I don't think so."

"But you do."

"You flatter me. He was declared a god by Hadrian, you know. Are you going to declare me a god when I'm dead? Well, even we future gods have to eat. I'm starving."

The tour ended there. They dined at opposite ends of a large table until Kit groaned and said, "For godsake, bring your dinner down here. It's like shouting across a lawn tennis court."

They slept that night in Kit's boyhood room, surrounded by things given him by St. Denys.

The next morning Kit had two horses saddled. "I'm out of practice," said Nick. "And the horses I rode were plow horses. No kin to these sleek beasties."

He found the skill returning, though, and his thoroughbred moved so effortlessly it was like flying. "Where are we going?" Nick asked.

"I want you to see the Dower House."

There, in the charming house half-surrounded by woods, they spent the afternoon in each other's arms. When they left Nick said with a teasing laugh, "What a perfect place for a tryst."

Kit's smile was enigmatic. He saw no reason to tell Nick about the hours he'd spent there with Rawdon McPherson years ago.

The third day was a continued tour of the Hill. "Some of these rooms I've seen only once," Kit said. "Some I've never seen at all. There is one ... but I shall save that one for the appropriate time."

"This is so enormous. Why would one family build such a huge place?"

"It took a century and a half to build. It had to be grand, you see, because the St. Denys family used to be quite important. Politics, the Church, everything of importance had a St. Denys finger in it. That meant entertaining on a royal scale. And, of course, when one is entertaining His Majesty, or Her Majesty, as the case might be, one has to have a great deal of space." He made an encompassing gesture that took in the mass of stone that was St. Denys Hill. "From these rooms the St. Denys women were launched into society and here the St. Denys men hatched plots, at least one involving gunpowder and Parliament."

"Your ancestors were involved with Guy Fawkes?"

"To their eyeteeth. When the plot failed, I think there was a temporary exodus of St. Denys men."

Nick shook his head. "It's like being in a book." He looked around the room they were in, a large one with the typical wainscoting. One corner was filled by a curious bed with thick bunches of colored plumes. Every inch of wall space was taken up with tapestries, framed and unframed.

"It's called the Cut Velvet Room," said Kit. "Don't ask me why. I had the best of the tapestries brought here for display." He showed Nick one of a white deer pierced by an arrow. "This is my favorite. It was done by Mary, Queen of Scots. Duncan St. Denys almost lost his head because of his support for that unfortunate lady, but like every St. Denys he landed on his feet."

He pointed to a smaller one of flowers. "Anne Boleyn did that one."

"This is like a museum."

Kit laughed and kissed him. "Precisely. The bed, so I was told, was that of Bonnie Prince Charlie. How will it be to sleep in the bed of a prince?"

The bed was uncomfortable and Nick remarked the next morning, "Now I know why princes and dukes and so forth were always plotting mischief. They had backaches and headaches and were just in very rotten moods."

"Why, Nick! You've made a joke. See? I am a good influence on you after all." Kit dressed and said, "I'm going to let you entertain yourself for a while. I have some things that need doing. You know where the library is. Or if you wish, take a horse and enjoy the countryside. My home is your home."

Nick decided to accept the offer of the horse and spent the day exploring the estate. Passing the Dower House, he wondered if they would return there. He hoped they would. It was so much smaller, so much more intimate, he was more at ease there.

❐

Kit's time spent going over the household accounts with the butler and housekeeper was a matter of form. They were professionals and he trusted them.

He then went to the secret room he was saving for the "appropriate time." Only he knew of its existence. A small room accessible only through a trick panel, it had been a "priest hole" in the days of Cromwell when men and women caught celebrating Mass had their noses slit as a permanent and horrible warning to others. Kit thought it a fitting place to face his own dark secrets.

An easel was upon the stone altar and upon the easel was a painting of Jonathan as he would look had he lived. Kit had taken the first photograph St. Denys had had made of him and had directed an artist how to paint from it. The face in the painting was more fragile than his, the eyes a trifle closer together and sad, the mouth weaker and filled with pain. He peered intently into the painted eyes.

"Shall I tell him the truth?" he asked the image on the altar. "I've told no one else, not even Francis and I've known him for many years. I know I could trust Francis; he would lay down his life for me. But Nick ... I have known him a year. Can I trust him? Dare I? I love him, Jonathan. Far more than he does me. If he does at all."

The image on the altar sometimes seemed to speak to him; today it was silent. He sighed. "If I tell him what I was and what I did, if I tell him the truth about Pa and the daemons inside me I would be giving him a loaded gun pointed directly at my heart. He could destroy me. And perhaps he would. He's a Puritan at heart and they are experts at judging others. And yet ... and yet ... how can I even pretend to myself that I love him if I don't trust him with the truth?" He smiled crookedly at the almost-mirror image in the painting. "Jonathan, at times you are not much help."

That evening Nick was mystified by Kit's sudden switch in mood. He was quiet, almost withdrawn. Several times Nick found Kit looking at him in an odd, questioning manner. More than once Kit seemed on the verge of saying something but each time he did not. Even in bed he seemed distant.

Kit lay awake, pondering the question he had asked Jonathan's picture. By morning he decided to risk it. As soon as an "appropriate time" came he would lay his past bare for Nick and let the Devil take the hindmost.

But the next day was warm and perfect, no fit day for exposing violence and sorrow. They picnicked and took the promised dip in the pond in the woods, in water that was icy and sent Nick leaping from it almost as soon as the water touched his skin. Kit scrambled from the water and with laughter wrestled him to the ground. Nick's yelping complaints about the damp leaves and the roughness of the ground soon dissolved into groans of pleasure.

The week passed and no "appropriate time" for revelation presented itself.

❑

The second week they were there Kit hosted a gathering of his father's old friends – "I promised him I would do this whenever I was in residence," he explained. "And I don't mind. Most of them were my friends too. And Lizbet will be here. You must meet her if you never meet anyone else. You'll love her."

Except for Lizbet Porter the guests were well-dressed and well-off men from all over England. To Nick's disgust some of them were excessively effeminate. He wondered how Kit could tolerate their butterfly hands brushing at his lapels, touching his face and hair, pressing his hands while looking soulfully at him with eyes like those of moonstruck calves. They made Nick shudder. Fairies! he thought with loathing.

One man annoyed him more because he was *not* effeminate. He was a handsome gray-haired man who seemed to talk to Kit far more than he needed to. Kit introduced them, with the slurring words that showed he had had too much wine.

"Nickie, meet Rawdon McPherson. An old, old, old friend. Rawdon, Nick Stuart. My latest conquest." He laughed and leaned on McPherson. McPherson gave Nick a curious glance and put one arm around Kit's shoulders.

"Old man, you're smashed and the evening is young." He inclined his head toward Nick. "A pleasure to make your acquaintance, Mr. Stuart. Come along, Kit." As if he owned Kit, he guided him back to a gathering of their friends.

"Conquest!?" Nick muttered to himself. He wished he had never come to this place. He left to wander the halls with their portraits of Kit's long-dead ancestors and ancestresses.

It was not much consolation, but there was one guest he liked very much. Kit had been right about that. Lizbet Porter was now plump and gray-haired but still pretty. Kit had hugged her when she arrived, and he kept one arm around her when he introduced her to Nick.

"This is my Lizbet," he had said. "My first friend. The only real mother I ever had."

Nick found Lizbet alone in a flower-filled alcove and sat down beside her. "Hello." He gave her an understanding smile. "You couldn't bear them either, eh?"

"Them?" she asked, looking puzzled.

"The fairies. I don't know how—"

"They don't bother me. Why do they bother you? I think some of them are quite nice." She softened her words with a smile. "I've known some of the men here for many years."

Nick tried again. "Why are you out here? Didn't you come to visit Kit?"

"He's busy with his other friends just now. We keep in touch by letter. I'll let them enjoy his company. I am to dine here tomorrow evening, you know."

"I didn't know, but I'm glad. May I ask you something?"

"If you wish."

"Why did he say you were the only real mother he ever had?"

Lizbet's face grew still. "What has he told you of himself?"

"Almost nothing. He's more closemouthed than a clam when it comes to himself. Were you his nanny?"

"In a manner of speaking. Mr. Stuart, I'm not free to tell you anything he has not. It isn't my place. But whatever I did for him he has more than repaid me. He has made certain I will never want for anything. He's bought me a house not far from here." Her eyes took in the ancient splendor around them. "He has asked me many times to live here, but it's too opulent for me. I would feel as if I were on stage all the time." She looked back at him and Nick had the feeling she was assessing him. "He is very vulnerable, Mr. Stuart. I pray you are worthy of his confidence."

Suddenly he stiffened and scowled. He heard Kit's voice and that of someone else. The acres of marble gave parts of the house the qualities of an amphitheater.

Directly across from the alcove was a stairway that led to the gallery. Footsteps were descending the wide marble stairs. McPherson and Kit came into sight, laughing, and McPherson's hand was on Kit's shoulder. Kit abruptly sat down on one of the steps. McPherson stopped and sat down beside him.

"Feet are wobbly," Kit said. "Need to rest." He leaned back against the step above, sprawling in loose-limbed invitation.

McPherson kissed him. Nick heard McPherson say, "Meet me at the Dower House. Midnight."

Nick heard Kit laugh, a drunken giggle. "Do you think I'm mad?"

Nick heard McPherson laugh too. "I know you are. You were totally mad as a child. A mad, beautiful child." He kissed Kit again. Nick's boiling blood buzzed in his ears. Then Kit's arms were around McPherson's neck, and he made no sound of protest when McPherson's hand slid beneath his shirt and down inside his trousers. "You do want to meet don't you!" McPherson said. "It's been a long time, Kit. Meet me."

Kit hiccoughed and gave a lewd laugh. "If you don't let go, I won't *need* to meet you."

Nick leaped up, ready to kill one or both of them. Lizbet seized his sleeve and said in a low voice, "Don't." He glared down at her and tried to pull free.

Just then one of the effeminate guests came fluttering down the broad marble corridor. "Oh – my goodness – look at this." He recited in a high-pitched sing-song voice, "Kit and Rawdon up in a tree, k-i-s-s-i-n-g – not to mention a little naughty grab-and-tickle, naughty, naughty, naughty!"

"Harold," said McPherson, withdrawing his hand and getting to his feet, "your timing is impeccable."

Laughing, Kit scrambled to his feet and lurched the final few steps to seize Harold and whirl him around in an impromptu, inebriated waltz until they both tumbled down, laughing.

Nick's eyes left the exhibition of Kit and the fairy and settled again on Rawdon McPherson, who stood watching them, bemused and not at all drunk. For the first time in his life he hated someone. McPherson walked over to Kit. "You're drunk as a bricklayer, my dear. Drunk as a bricklayer. Don't forget. The Dower House at midnight." He disappeared down a hallway and soon rejoined the other guests in the Lesser Hall.

Kit stood up unsteadily and tried to bring order to his rumpled clothes. Harold was even drunker than Kit. "What y'going t'do at the Dower House, Kit? Who's invited?"

"Nobody is invited. Jus' me. Harold, have you seen Nickie? I can't find him anywhere."

"Oh, he's prob'ly with th'others. C'mon." He tugged at Kit's sleeve and as they disappeared Nick could hear Kit satirically declaiming Juliet's lines in a falsetto.

"Roooo-me-o, Rooooo-me-o, wherefore art thou, Roooo-meeee-ooooo?"

Nick was trembling with rage. His own words about the Dower House came back to him – "a perfect place for a tryst."

Lizbet Porter said in a quiet voice, "Kit is as he is, Mr. Stuart. He is unique and those who love him must love him without condition or reservation. If you can't do that you have no place in his life."

Nick stared at her in disbelief. "I am to excuse his behavior? Accept unfaithfulness?"

"If that is what it takes. Now I believe I will join the others. Are you coming?" Reluctantly Nick walked with her back to the Lesser Hall.

The evening had degenerated into a game of charades at which Kit, even drunk, was the acknowledged master. Nick did not take part; he was not asked to. He watched the faces of the men, all old enough to be Kit's father. But obviously that made no difference to Kit! How many of them, he wondered, how many of them had Kit slept with? McPherson, surely. Was he the only one? Had Kit slept with all of them? Was that the tie that bound them all together – they'd all had Kit at one time or another? And there was McPherson again, going through pantomime gestures, almost as accomplished at charades as Kit.

Damn him, thought Nick. Damn that smug, handsome face. Damn them all.

He looked at Kit's laughing, flushed face. *Kit, I love you. Why don't you realize it and stop making a fool of me?* he asked silently.

8

By eleven o'clock the guests were gone. McPherson was the last to leave and Nick was certain he saw a significant look pass between him and Kit. And then he and Kit were alone. Kit had stopped drinking when the charades had started and seemed more sober than he had earlier.

He looked at the buffet which was a shambles of melted ices and crumbled bread. "Thank God for servants," he said. He yawned. "I'm very tired. It was fun, wasn't it, Nickie?"

"For you, I suppose," said Nick, his voice sharp. "*I* didn't enjoy it."

Kit said crossly, "You are harder to please than anyone I've ever seen. You don't like this and you don't like that and you don't approve of this and you don't approve of that and — quite frankly, you're as fussy as an old maiden aunt."

"At least I don't act like a whore," snapped Nick.

Kit started to retort, then he turned away. "I'm not even going to dignify that by asking what you mean. You're being tiresome. Come to bed." He started to walk away. Nick caught his arm; Kit stared at him a moment and jerked his arm free.

"Don't turn your back on me!" Nick ordered. "I was there in the south hallway. I saw you and McPherson on the stairs."

"You were spying on me?"

"I'd gone there to get away from your mincing nancy friends. The last thing I expected was to see you and McPherson pawing at each other."

"Whatever are you talking about? He kissed me. I kissed him back. What of it?"

"He had his hands all over you."

"Again — what of it? I didn't plan it."

"Didn't you?"

"No, I did not. We made a nostalgic trip to the balcony, that's all. Talked about my father. He and Rawdon were good friends."

"You were acting like a bitch in heat on the stairs. Perhaps you didn't plan it but you seemed to enjoy it."

Kit's brows drew together and a muscle jumped in his jaw. With supreme effort he kept his temper. "I will not stand here and defend myself against your stupidity. Are you coming to bed or not?"

"Why? Isn't it almost midnight?"

"Nickie, I am too sleepy for conundrums and I am getting a headache. Stay down here and argue with yourself. I'm going to bed." He walked away and Nick followed him.

"And as soon as I am asleep you will be off to the Dower House to meet McPherson, won't you."

Kit stopped again. "Is that what this is all about?" He sighed. "Nickie, I have no intention of meeting Rawdon at the Dower House or anywhere else. He just wishes I would."

"*He* believes you will. *I* believe you will."

Kit started up the stairs, refusing to respond to Nick's accusations with anything other than an exasperated shake of his head. They reached Kit's old bedroom suite. Kit turned to him and said, "There are twenty other bedrooms if you wish to sleep alone. God forbid you sleep with a sinner."

"Do you want me to?"

"I want you to do whatever makes you happy – if there is such a thing."

Nick followed him into the bedroom. "Just tell the truth about you and McPherson."

Kit started to undress and was standing there barefoot and shirtless before he answered. "Rawdon was the one who taught me how it could be between two men, but he did it because I wanted him to. I was sixteen. He said I seduced him and perhaps I did. We've been together off and on, though not often."

"And others, besides him?"

As if explaining something simple to a simpleton, Kit said with infinite patience, "Nickie, there were many men. I don't know how many. I remember very few names and fewer faces."

Nick found it hard to breathe. "And of those there tonight? How many of them?"

"Only Rawdon."

"*'Only Rawdon,'*" said Nick with sarcasm. And then, "'Many men.'"

"I admitted it, did I not? Would you rather I had lied? It wasn't just sexual. You know that. I needed them to keep–" He couldn't tell Nick about Rourke. Not now. Later, when they were both calmer and this little quarrel was over and Nick could laugh at his jealousy, he would tell him everything. "I needed them to keep away the nightmares."

"'*Many men,*'" shouted Nick. "You don't even know how many!" He dealt Kit a backhanded blow to the jaw that sent him staggering. "You are a bloody whore!"

Kit was as stunned by the twisted expression of torture on Nick's face as he was by the words and the blow. He held his hand to his face, which flamed with the mark of Nick's hand. "I would let no other man on earth strike me," he said through clenched teeth. "I would let no other man speak to me as you have. Don't ever do it again."

"The truth, Kit! The truth, or don't you know what that is?" Nick's eyes were blind with tears of rage and betrayal.

"Since we have been together there has been no one else. I give you my word."

"Your word! I've watched you with your theatre friends. Touching, always touching each other. And what of Mulholland? He spent the night in your bed quite recently. But I am supposed to believe that the Great Male Whore of London changed his ways."

Kit lowered his head like a bull about to charge. "No. I wouldn't expect you to believe that. You're perfect. You don't have flaws. So how could you understand anyone who does?" There was a moment of quivering silence. In an effort to give peace one last try, Kit said, "Nickie, I need you. We need each other. Don't do this to us."

"I am doing nothing. You are the one who has done the harm. You don't even know what I have gone through, do you. I have put my immortal soul in danger for you. I defied God for you. And you repay me by playing the whore with half the men in England."

A bubble of hysterical laughter rose in Kit's chest. "Half, Nickie? Only half? My God, how did that happen?"

Nick's fury would not let him see the absurdity of it. "You bypassed the ugly, the insane, and the dead."

It was then that Kit swung from the heels and knocked his lover flat on his back. He stood over him, fists clenched. "I need you more than I've ever needed anyone. But by God I will not tolerate this. I've been faithful to you. I can't make you believe me so to hell with you. Sleep elsewhere. We'll talk in the morning when your hot head has cooled off and you can see what a fool you've been tonight."

Nick got up. There was blood on his chin. He said nothing, but walked out without a backward glance. Kit slammed the door behind Nick and locked it.

Nick slept in his clothes, and at the first light of day he set out on foot. He was to the village before Kit awakened, and was in a coach on his way to London before Kit knew he was gone.

❒

Lizbet arrived for the dinner and went to the small dining room that had once been a lady's boudoir. She stepped into the room and was surprised to see the table unset, and Kit sitting alone in the dimness.

"Kit?" she asked, "why are the candles not lit?"

He seemed to rouse himself from a stupor, and got up to light the two nearest candles. "Lizbet. Forgive me. I meant to send my man to tell you there would be no dinner this evening. It seems you have come for naught."

She sat down in the chair at his right hand. There was a glass and a nearly empty whisky bottle. He reached for it and she moved it out of arm's length. "What has happened? Where is your friend?"

"Gone. He's gone. He walked out sometime during the night." Kit picked up his glass and tossed down the whiskey in it. "The bloody fool is *gone!*" He hurled the glass at the wall. Lizbet jumped when it struck and shattered.

"I don't understand."

"Do you think I do?" Kit raked his hands through his hair. "What will I do without him, Lizbet? He was so important to me. As long as I had Nick and the theatre I didn't need anything else."

"But what happened?"

"He saw Rawdon kiss me—"

"I ... know. So did I."

He was taken aback. "Oh. Well, like a fool he put more importance to it than it had. He said unforgivable things and I let him get away with it. I should have stopped him with the first word."

"Forget him. He was never worthy of you. I knew that from the first moment I saw him. Put him out of your mind."

The eyes that burned into hers had an almost maniacal gleam. "Forget him? Oh, no, Lizbet. Forget him? I'll make him sorry he

•113•

insulted me. I'll make him sorry he walked out on me. I'll make him sorry he was ever born."

She put her hand on his arm. "Don't think like that. No good can come of it. Please, Kit. Forget him. You have a good friend in Francis Mulholland and I know he almost worships you."

Kit looked into her eyes. She loved him. She thought of him as her son. She wanted nothing but his happiness and she automatically hated anyone who wronged him. She knew him as well as anyone could and yet she did not understand how deeply hurt he was by Nick's defection. He mumbled something in agreement with her wishes, all the while promising Nick Stuart that he would rue the day he had called Kit St. Denys a whore.

❐

Exhausted and emotionally drained, already regretting his hateful words, Nick arrived at his surgery. He would write to Kit at once. Explain. Make Kit see his side of it. At least try.

As he unlocked his door he saw an envelope on the floor, slid in under the door. He knelt and picked it up. It was a letter dated ten days earlier, in the spidery hand of his sister Agnes.

> Father is ill and has made his peace with Our Heavenly Father. He asks for you. No one else can comfort him no matter how we try. He wants you. He has the mistaken notion that you care about him. Mother wants you to come home at once before it is too late.

❐

As he rode on a railroad train hurtling across the countryside Nick tried to strike a silent, desperate bargain with God.

Let my father live. I am most heartily sorry for what I've done. I didn't honor my father. I went against his wishes. Worse of all I let Satan tempt me into terrible sin— But just let my father live and I'll forget Kit. No — I've already forgotten him. There will never be another man. Never. I will marry, have a dozen children if that's what You want. I know my father and I don't get on but he is my father and I don't want him to die. Please, I am so sorry. Let my father live...

It was like going back in time. From the splendor of the Hill to the country village in the rich earth and lush uplands of his boyhood. His stomach clenched as the train approached the depot, from which he would have to hire a cart or some other conveyance to take him to the village.

Then he was at the depot, stepping down in the early afternoon. There was an old-time coach of the kind that once held England together on the network of roads. He felt lucky that the coachman was no one who recognized him, thus saving him from questions and comments.

◻

It was after dark when he arrived at the stone cottage that had sheltered generations of Stuarts. Light shone through the many-paned windows. He paused to smell the heady scent of his mother's flower garden. In the light from the window he could see the silhouette of the water pump that stood near the door.

This had once been his home, his window, his pump. Why had he ever left the simple goodness of this life? Kit had called him a fool. Oh, yes, that was what he was. A fool. He was now a stranger in his own land. He lifted his hand to knock, then lowered it, opened the door, and went in. Agnes stiffened when she saw him, and did not smile. She gave a curt nod of her head toward their parents' bedroom and returned to reading her Bible. Nick felt the silence, no different now than it had ever been, come down on him like an oppressive memory. With Kit he had gotten used to talk and laughter and ... He gave his head a savage shake. Dear God, even in the midst of family tragedy he could not forget!

As he went into the bedroom he could smell the sickly sweet odor of flesh being eaten away by cancer. His mother was beside the bed. He said softly, "Mother."

Red-eyed, she looked up, accusation in her face. "Why didn't you come sooner?" she asked without even a greeting. Then she got up and leaned over her husband. "Mr. Stuart," she said. "Nicholas has come at last." She turned and with a heavy step left the room.

Nick looked down at his father. Could this wasted, ancient man really be the father whose disapproval had caused him so much distress? His father's body made a slight ridge beneath the thin, often-patched blanket, the flatness relieved only by the small humps which were his hands, his genitals, and his feet.

"Father," he said in a low voice. His father's eyes slowly opened.

"Nicholas." It was a dry, barely audible whisper. There was a faint attempt at a smile. "Mrs. Stuart believed you could cure me."

The smile disappeared and he closed his eyes in exhaustion. "I wish we could have..." His voice trailed off.

A lump rose in Nick's throat. "Father, I wish I had taken time to tell you how much I owe you. I learned so much from you. I wonder how many hundreds of hours we rode together and walked together and worked together."

His father's eyeballs moved beneath the thin flesh of his lids. "Both ... should have said ... things. You didn't know how ... proud I have always ... been of you." He drew a shallow, painful breath. "Nicholas ... stories about you ... we heard them ... not true I know..."

"Stories, Father?" he asked in fear.

"Lies. Dreadful lies. Jealous people. Lies. You consorting with ... actors ... and loose women..." The eyes suddenly flew open. "Tell me ... not true."

Nick tried to swallow the boulder-sized lump. "It's not true, Father." And with a bitter wryness, he acknowledged that now, at least, he was telling the truth. "I – I – now that I have my education and can make my way in the world, I'm going to find a wife. Yes. A wife. I'll have a huge family, Father, and–"

"The Church. You will ... return to the Church...?"

"Yes, Father."

Slowly, slowly, his father's right hand crawled out from beneath the blanket. "Take my hand in ... promise."

"Yes, Father," Nick whispered and took the hot, dry hand.

His father died within the hour.

Miserably, Nick told himself he could have arrived early enough to ease his father's final days if he had not preferred to waste his time mired in sin with another man. He would carry the guilt with him always.

❐

The funeral service at the church the following day increased the weight of his guilt. There were so many sins of which he was guilty! he thought as he listened to the minister and when the people prayed, he prayed with them, in humble contrition.

❐

Nick stayed at the family home for three months, in part to help his mother settle his father's estate and, he admitted to himself, also to avoid any chance of seeing Kit.

He walked by the hour out among the green hills of his home, but he saw little of the beauty. The only emotion he felt was anger, equally toward Kit and toward himself. Kit had seduced him; he had been willing.

He saw some of his father's patients and almost agreed to his mother's request to live there with her and Agnes. There was something tempting about it: he could practice medicine there among the humble people from which he came and with whom he belonged.

He sold off his practice in London.

For a month he was assiduous about following in his father's footsteps. He, too, delivered babies and calves with equal dedication. He treated gout and grippe in people, hairballs in cats, and ulcerated udders on dairy cows. And then the desire to specialize began to burn in him once again. He wrote to doctors in Edinburgh, and even to two well-known obstetricians in America. As if arranged by God, two things happened within a week.

He learned that in the settlement of his father's estate he received a much larger inheritance than he had expected. And he received a letter from America. New York City. It was from Dr. Ferris Sanborn and it was a cautiously worded letter of encouragement. Dr. Sanborn wanted to know more about him, about his education and experience, and he wanted to see letters of recommendation.

For the letters, Nick had to return to London. He dreaded it, certain he would see Kit there. But without the letters he had no chance. He made the journey and as the cab took him to the office of a colleague, he asked the driver to go by the Xavier. Like picking at a scab, he thought sourly. He was startled to see no playbills.

"What's playing at the Xavier, do you know?" he asked the driver, as he descended from the cab a little later.

"I ain't the thee-ater sort, gov'nor," the man said. He slapped the reins against his horse's rump and moved off through the traffic.

Nick asked the same question of his colleague, Mr. Fitsch.

Fitsch said, "Oh, nothing at all. I understand that young firebrand, St. Denys, has taken his company off on a tour."

"Oh." Nick could not believe he had forgotten. Kit had been full of enthusiasm about the European tour. Belgium, Germany, Italy, France, Denmark, Russia, Hungary. It was scheduled to last the better part of a year. Nick felt a sharp twinge of sorrow. He was off for America; Kit was off for Europe. The separation was as final as death.

He shook off the thought. He had a new life to prepare for. The visits with Fitsch and the three other colleagues were pleasant and each one gave him glowing letters of recommendation. He sent the letters on their way across the sea and returned to his mother's home to wait.

By the time the answer came from Sanborn Nick, his mother, and his sister were getting on one another's nerves. And he knew if he had to midwife one more sheep he was going to jump off a cliff. His brother cursed him because he should have received much more inheritance than Nick; he had six children to feed and Nick had none. But worst of all every night was troubled by dreams of Kit. Nothing but time and distance would cure him of those.

Mr. Sanborn – Nick caught himself; they called surgeons "doctor" in America; he would have to remember that – Dr. Sanborn offered him a residency at Our Lady of Blessings Hospital with the possibility of a chance to work with him in his private practice should everything be mutually satisfactory. The amount of money Sanborn named was princely compared to what Nick was accustomed to getting.

He spent no time debating the issue. Within the week he was on the deck of the steamship *Prince Charlie,* watching his homeland fade from sight in the early morning fog. He stood with his back straight, his hands folded on the rail, his eyes dry and smarting.

He expected never to return.

There was a new land, a new life ahead of him. He had his medical books and diplomas in his trunks. Of Kit there was nothing tangible: the pictures, tickets, theatre programmes, small gifts Kit had given him had all been either destroyed or given away. In a tenement not far from his former surgery a pale, consumptive girl was combing her lank locks with a gold-handled comb and looking at her gaunt face in a gold-handled mirror. He hoped the mirror made her feel pretty.

In his right hand was the only memento he had kept of Kit. A photograph. He dropped his gaze to it. So beautiful, he thought. So wicked and deceitful.

Slowly he tore the photograph into a dozen tiny pieces and cast them upon the water. Kit St. Denys was now but a bad memory that would soon be erased.

There was the sound of a soft footstep. He glanced to his left and saw a young lady also leaning against the rail. He had noticed her in passing when they had left England. Her eyes were dark, and her dark hair was drawn back in a thick bun at her neck. Her hat was plain, with jet beads and a single black feather. Her frock was black.

He studied her surreptitiously. She was a handsome woman, and likely a widow. Respectable. She looked intelligent. This was the kind of wife he needed. A lady but one who was down-to-earth. With a wife like this lady he would have peace of mind. A wife and family would exorcise the devil inside him that had drawn him to Kit.

He tried to think of something to say. It was so easy to talk to ladies when they were patients! What did one say to them socially?

Then the opportunity was gone, for the lady, perhaps realizing he was thinking of approaching her, turned away from him and joined a gray-haired man and a little girl.

Nick was disappointed; she was married, not widowed, and had a child. Then he ridiculed himself: had he really expected it to be that easy?

At dinner he found himself at the same table as she, and he wondered at the propriety of her being there rather than at a separate ladies' table. Nor did her husband, who looked like a sour old stick, seem very pleased. Nick made a determined effort to concentrate on his dinner.

There was laughter when one of the men there said, "But of course this New Woman nonsense is just that, is it not, Mrs. Jameson? You are clearly not a subscriber to it!"

She spoke coolly. "But I am, sir. I intend to give my daughter as good an education as you intend to give your son, if you have one."

"Well, of course I do. Five. A man can't have too many sons! And four of them are at Harvard and the other at Yale. Fine boys." He added testily, "And I have four daughters and let me assure you, they are good, decent, normal young ladies who wouldn't dream of defying me or their husbands."

"Nor did I, sir. But my husband, God rest his soul, treated me as an equal. He and I were of one mind when it came to our daughter."

The man said with the hint of a sneer, "And where will this educated daughter of yours attend school? At Harvard?"

There was general laughter and he saw her cheeks stain red. "No, sir, not at Harvard."

"I thought not!"

"She will go to Vassar. Harvard has not the sense to admit women. Yet."

Nick's ear sharpened with interest. "Woman" was considered a demeaning phrase by most ladies. None but the despised suffragettes used the word "woman." He looked at her, really looked at her for the first time. Was she a suffragette? She didn't look very militant. And she had said, "God rest his soul"; she was, then, a widow. And she already had a child. Better and better. He was annoyed when the man turned to him for help.

"Well, what do you think of this silliness, eh? Females wanting to go to Harvard! What won't they think of next?"

Nick smiled at the young lady. "I'm not quite sure what or where Harvard is or whether it's a good school, but why should a female be denied opportunity if she has as good a mind as a man?"

The man and the other men at the table looked at him as though he were a traitor in their midst. The lady put down her napkin and Nick leaped to his feet to pull out her chair. "May I escort you back to your room, Mrs. Jameson?"

The man he had mistaken for her husband got up and threw down his napkin. "Indeed, sir, you may not escort my daughter to her room. And we will thank you to keep your unwanted advances to yourself. Daughter, come along." He took her elbow and propelled her away from the table.

At least he now knew her name. Mrs. Jameson.

In the following days he watched for her and one day came upon her again at the rail, staring out at the endless sea. She smiled at him.

"I apologize for my father's rudeness the other evening, Mr....

"Stuart. Nicholas Stuart, at your service."

"Mr. Stuart. He means well. It's just that he has an old-fashioned concern for my welfare."

"As well he should. There are a great many scoundrels in this world, Mrs. Jameson. They prey upon helpless females."

She touched her gloved fingers to her lips and looked down, but not before he had seen the sparkle of laughter in her eyes. "I am not helpless, Mr. Stuart. I have my wits. And I have a little gun which my dear husband taught me to shoot. And I can run very, very fast."

For a moment he was take aback, then he laughed. "As you say, madam. You have your wits. And your charm is not a negligible weapon." He listened to himself with amazement. He – Nick Stuart – was actually playing the gallant with a pretty female. The age of miracles was not over!

He became Mrs. Jameson's constant companion on the voyage, though he saw her under the watchful eye of her father, the Reverend Daniel Carlisle. The little girl was named Alyce and she celebrated her fifth birthday aboard ship.

Nick liked Mrs. Jameson. He liked her a great deal. She was levelheaded, charming, and – as he had already learned – independent-minded. She had lost her husband of six years to undulant fever a year earlier and her father had taken her and Alyce on a cruise to facilitate the healing of her grief.

One night she managed to elude her father's eagle eye and met Nick almost at the place where he had first seen her. She looked melancholy.

"What is it?" he asked.

"I was wondering ... Stephen has been gone only a year. I thought I would never stop grieving and yet here I am, enjoying your company and ... I haven't stopped grieving, actually. It's just taken a different turn and ... and where I saw only darkness now see flashes of prismatic color–" She broke off. "I sound foolish."

"Oh, no. It's a lovely thought," he said, and added without thinking, "I wish everyone who grieves could find healing."

Sympathy warmed her face. "You, too, have lost a beloved mate, haven't you."

He had not thought of it that way and yet that's what had happened. She had lost her husband to sickness of the body. He had lost Kit to the sickness of his promiscuous soul. It was a loss as complete as hers and just as final.

"Yes," he said after a moment. "But it's nothing I can talk about."

"I understand."

"Mrs. Jameson, you are quite the finest lady I have ever met. I will be living in New York City. Since we are both free, would you do me the honor of letting me call upon you?"

She smiled. "I live with my daughter on Long Island. It is only a short ferryboat ride from the city. It would be a great pleasure to me if you would call, sir." Her eyes never left his. "My father will disapprove, but then, you are not asking to call on him, are you."

He laughed. "Only if you say I must." Still smiling, he lifted her gloved hand to his lips. "Mrs. Jameson, I am looking forward to getting better acquainted."

"Please," she said softly, "I know it is highly improper, but won't you call me Bronwyn?"

"Mrs. Jameson ... Bronwyn ... I believe this will turn out to be the most momentous journey I have ever taken."

He was happy. He had found the lady he would make his wife. It had been easy, after all.

❐

In the small white church with the tall thin spire, the Reverend Daniel Carlisle with reluctance said the words that joined his daughter and the Englishman in holy matrimony. Bronwyn stood before him in flowers and veils, and beside her stood the man she had with unbecoming haste decided to marry.

Carlisle was all too aware of the meaningful glances the ladies of his congregation darted toward his daughter's midsection. His next sermon, he decided grimly, would be a strong lesson on the evils of gossip.

He had been beside himself when Bronwyn had announced she was marrying that Englishman only one month after they had met on board ship. Poor Stephen – dead less than a year! To the shame of an improperly short mourning period was added the shame of a hasty marriage.

Reverend Carlisle had pleaded with her to reconsider. What did she know about the man? At least wait a year, properly mourn the father of her child. At least give him time to have Stuart investigated. She had been adamant.

It was his own doing. He should have been stricter with her after her mother died. He should have allowed the schoolmasters to use the birch when she was headstrong. But maybe it wasn't her fault. Maybe that Englishman had bewitched her with his handsome face and intense blue eyes. And yet he said he came from sturdy Puritan stock. Suppose he had been a Jew? Or, God forbid, Catholic. Or Anglican, which was nothing more nor less than backdoor Catholicism.

He looked down into Bronwyn's face, turned upward toward her new husband, and he softened. Her love for the man, hard to accept though it was, shone in her eyes. And maybe, just maybe, Stuart would grow on him.

•122•

□

As Nick said his vows, promising to honor and cherish her in sickness and in health, keeping himself only to her until death should come between them, a part of himself stood aside and watched incredulously. He was actually taking a wife. An attractive, independent-minded woman with a child. He was going to be responsible for two other people from this day forward. He would be sharing his life with this woman he did not even know.

He would be sharing his bed with her. The thought panicked him. He had never shared a bed with anyone but Kit. His few sexual adventures at university had taken only minutes from his life and had been soon forgotten. He had never wakened with his arms around anyone but Kit.

He shut down the memory. He did not want to even think of that name ever again.

He had a new life. He had a stepdaughter. He had a fine wife. He had respectability. Soon he would find the perfect house. His whole future was before him, with the promise of a partnership in a thriving practice if everything went well. He heard himself say, "I will."

He lifted the flower-bedecked veil and gave his bride a chaste kiss on the cheek. Her cheek was soft beneath his lips. He had never yet kissed her mouth.

And unbidden the thought came: Kit would find this all very amusing.

□

"He's not in England, Mr. St. Denys," said the nondescript little man who was one of the most reputable detectives in the country. "Nor is he in Edinburgh. His colleagues will say naught except that he asked for letters of recommendation which they freely gave. His family claims not to know where he is. If anyone knows his whereabouts they are not disclosing them."

Kit, his eyes ringed with dark smudges of weariness, stared at the man. He had hired this man the very week he had left for the Continent on tour. The fool had had eight months to find Nick and here he was, saying he could not find him.

"Royster, it is your business — for which you have charged me a great deal — to find him."

The man cleared his throat. "It may be a long undertaking, sir."

"I don't care how long it takes."

"I may have to travel extensively."

"I don't care where you have to go."

"I can't do it alone. I will have to hire additional detectives."

"Hire them."

"It will be very expensive."

"I don't care what it costs."

"We will find him."

"Yes," said Kit. "You will."

Royster hesitated, then said, "If I may be so bold, sir ... might I ask what it is the gentleman is guilty of?"

"No."

"Ah. Well, sir, we will find him," he said again.

And Kit repeated, "Yes. You will."

The door closed behind the detective.

Had Nick seen Kit's eyes he would have been chilled to the marrow of his bones.

"I have set the hounds on you, Stuart," Kit said. "I will run you to earth if it takes the rest of my life!"

Without Sanction

America, 1896–1900

9

"P alpitations, Doctor," said pretty Mrs. McWorth, and panted to prove it. "I get so light-headed sometimes."

Nick touched the bell of the stethoscope to her chest and listened to the pumping of her heart. With a little sigh she straightened her spine, thus thrusting her ample bosom at him.

Nick was of the opinion that a large part of Mrs. McWorth's trouble was the man to whom she was married, a millionaire with a tight hand on the dollar. And that part he could do nothing about. There was, however, advice he could give.

He folded his stethoscope and said, "Mrs. McWorth, I find nothing wrong physically. However..."

"It is unusual, Dr. Stuart," she said, interrupting him, "for someone with hair as dark as yours to have such blue, blue eyes — no, violet, actually. Your eyes are violet, did you know that?" She giggled. "Why, a man with eyes like yours could just about have his way with any girl. Even if she were married."

"You are avoiding the issue, Mrs. McWorth. The color of my eyes has nothing to do with your health."

"My health? You just said there is nothing wrong."

"Physically."

Alarm made her shrink away from him. "Dr. Stuart! Surely you are not suggesting that I am — am not competent mentally!"

"Of course not. Mrs. McWorth, I have no medicine to give you, but I have two suggestions I would like you to follow."

"Anything, Dr. Stuart. Why, after the way you cured Mrs. Knopf and Mrs. Lippencott, I trust you with all my heart."

"There is no comparison, Mrs. McWorth. They had surgery."

She rebuttoned her bodice. "Anyway, I trust you."

"Very well. First, I want you to loosen your corset lacing. You ladies may as well tie those strings around your pretty necks and hang yourselves with them. If you must wear them at least be sensible."

Horror crossed her face. "Undo my corset, Dr. Stuart! And look like a — a huge cow? As to 'sensible' — one cannot be both sensible and fashionable."

"You are a handsome woman, Mrs. McWorth. You will be a handsome woman even if your waist measures twenty-four instead of twenty-two. Loosen your corset by two inches. If you do, your light-headedness will vanish. What good is being in a fashionable frock if you are blue from lack of oxygen?"

"Oh, Dr. Stuart, you are so silly!" Her forehead puckered. "But my husband will divorce me if I look fat. He has said so. He will cut me off without a penny."

"Then, forgive me, madam, but you are married to a fool. My second suggestion is this: leave the house more often. Involve yourself with the Altar Guild or the Ladies Aid Society. Anything to keep your mind occupied with something other than your own troubles."

"But my husband would never allow it."

"Tell him it is your doctor's orders."

"But he doesn't like you."

Nick laughed. "So you are able to defy his edicts when it pleases you!"

She blushed, and smiled. "I daresay you are right. Well ... what charity would you suggest?"

He shrugged. "There are so many. I may be prejudiced, but I would say St. Cecilia's Orphanage. My wife is one of the directresses; I shall be glad to speak to her about you."

"An orphanage! But my dear Dr. Stuart, no one in my family has ever had anything to do with an orphanage! You do mean ... go there, in person, don't you. I — I am too tenderhearted. I could not bear to see those unfortunate children."

"Force yourself," he said without pity. "Now, Mrs. McWorth, if you don't mind, I have other patients who are waiting."

She walked to the door, accompanied by the soft swish of her skirt hem against the floor. "I will consider it, Dr. Stuart."

Nick had been in his own practice less than a year. The ten months he had spent with Dr. Ferris Sanborn had ended by mutual consent. They, like Nick and his father, did not get on. Sanborn thought Nick was too radical, too quick to try new, unproven techniques and Nick thought Sanborn was a stubborn fool knee-deep in tradition. The final disagreement had been over the use of chloroform.

"If God had meant women to bear their children without pain," Dr. Sanborn had said coldly, "He would have created them that way."

This was like listening to his father's pet arguments all over again and it had been the last straw. "If God had meant women to bear their children without pain He would not have led Morton to pioneer anesthetics," Nick had retorted. "And I expected something better from you, Dr. Sanborn. That is the reasoning of a medieval monk!"

So Nick and Dr. Sanborn had parted company and Nick had set out on his own. He had searched for the right kind of place, a place where he could combine living and working.

He and Bronwyn and Alyce had been living in a flat near the hospital, but living in the city made him edgy. It was noisy, it was crowded, it stank worse than London. Everything went too fast, from the boys zipping along on their bicycles to the electric trolley that whizzed along faster than anyone needed to go. Skyscrapers fifteen stories high threatened to blot out the sun and many-armed poles containing cat's cradles of telephone, electrical, and telegraph wires were everywhere. It was like living in a confounded spider-web. He wanted out of the city and Bronwyn, who had never been comfortable there, agreed.

He found a house in a pleasant area not far from Long Island City, a comfortable distance from New York City but a ferryboat ride to the hospital, the shops, the restaurants there.

The house was a three-story yellow structure described by the estate agent as "Italianate with a piquant touch of Second Empire as evidenced by a splendid mansard roof and happy dormer windows." Nick had been suspicious of any windows described as "happy," but Bronwyn had fallen in love with the place, declaring it perfect for rearing the ten children she wanted.

A deep porch ran the width of the front, and Bronwyn had filled up both ends with plants on pedestals and wicker rocking chairs for her many lady friends. Rising above the center of the porch and overtopping the rest of the house by a half story was a square tower complete with a widow's walk. Nick was enamored of the view from the widow's walk – the five acres of gardens and woods that surrounded his home and the glimmer of the river in the distance. No matter where one looked there was a flower garden.

A side entrance led into the three rooms Nick took over for his surgery. He appropriated the library with its existing floor-to-ceiling bookshelves for his office and gave the rest to Bronwyn to decorate as she pleased, cautioning her to keep in mind their financial situation.

Bronwyn was rather overwhelmed by the responsibility. The rectory where she had lived had not changed in furnishings or manner her entire life. She and her first husband had never had a permanent home. And now she was entrusted with decorating a fine old house that had seen better days. Nicholas, she thought with exasperation, was not much help. He refurbished his surgery, painting everything white except the floor, put chairs in the waiting room, a table in the examining room, a locked glass-fronted cabinet for his medicines and instruments and a relic of a desk with a locking rolltop in his office.

At first Bronwyn consulted him with questions such as, "But Nicholas, what do you think about this color for the sitting room? Or is this better?"

He always gave her a blank look and then answered with a shrug, "Dearest, I don't care. Whatever you think."

At last she quit asking and tried to make sense of the different colors, fabrics, and furnishings. He sometimes flinched when he was given the figures of what it all was costing, but he never once harped on it. He was a good man, an excellent husband in almost every way, and she loved him. She wished he would let himself be included in her part of their life.

Holding two samples of carpeting, she sighed and her mind drifted. Just like the intimacy of their bed, she thought wistfully. She did not know if other married couples were intimate more often than they were, and she would never dream of asking, but she sometimes lay in her bedroom burning for him to come in there and touch her and kiss her the way— She cut off the memory of her first husband. Nicholas was just shy. They had been married only two years. Time would make him more at ease. Wouldn't it?

They had moved there in March, and so as summer came on Bronwyn discovered that she had a natural affinity for green growing things and became an avid gardener.

With amusement, Nick would wander out into her gardens and find her wearing a bonnet, gloves, and an old frock, furiously digging more holes in the ground in order to plant another slip of something or another. He teased her by calling her "gopher." Her pride and joy was the gazebo she had designed for the back garden.

Stone urns and fountains that had sat long neglected were cleaned out and either planted with greenery or kept filled with water for the birds.

In a few days a man was to come and tell them what their next project would cost – a bathroom and water closet. That was one thing they agreed upon wholeheartedly.

On this lovely summer day Bronwyn placed a new rosebush into the ground, and was patting the earth around it when a shadow fell over her. She looked up to see Nicholas smiling down at her.

"I've been watching you out here, my little gopher," he said. "You look adorable."

"Oh, I'm not!" she said, laughing. "I'm dirty and–"

He pulled her to her feet and kissed her. "Nicholas," she said, red-faced. "What on earth – out here where everyone can see – and besides, I'm filthy."

"You have a smudge of dirt on your cheek. I think it's very sweet. And who is here to watch? The servants have the day away and Alyce is spending the day with your father."

There was something about the perfume of the fresh air and flowers, her voice, the healthy pink glow of her face. Something. He kissed her again. "Bronwyn..." His voice trailed off. He kissed her again and felt more desire for her than he had felt on their wedding night.

In token protest Bronwyn whispered, "Oh ... Nicholas ... now...?"

He removed her dirty gloves and dropped them to the ground. Then he scooped her up in his arms and carried her into the house.

❏

The unexpected intimacy in midmorning was soon forgotten by Nick. Bronwyn could not forget it. She longed for it to happen again.

As for Nick, he was happy these days. Or maybe content was closer to the truth. He kept busy with his private practice, busy working with future obstetricians at St. Jerome's Hospital, and on the vestry of the church.

When home he spent time with Alyce and with Bronwyn. Alyce was, in his mind, his own child.

Then, a few weeks after the midday love that he had already forgotten, he examined her and looked into her eyes. He was pleased and she was ecstatic.

"Well," he said. "It would seem we're going to have a baby."

"Oh, Nicholas!" She threw her arms around his neck. "It's the answer to my prayers." She knew that the baby would be the answer to everything. Nicholas would love her with every atom of his being now. How could he not? She was going to bear him a child. And it must have happened on that sunny morning.

◻

Kit's eyes were hard as he stared at the detective. "It took you long enough."

"I told you it would take a long while. You said you did not care."

Kit got up and walked to the window of his hotel room, gazing down into the street without seeing any of the dozens of cabs or people walking or the many kinds of carts and wagons.

"You're certain of what you've just told me?"

"Yes, Mr. St. Denys. I even have the name of the man who sold him the house."

"A house," Kit mumbled. "A *wife,* of all things! My God. Nick Stuart building a nest." It was a sneer of contempt.

"Sir?"

"Nothing."

"Do you want me to wire my man to do anything further?"

"No." Kit went to the secretary writing desk and returned in a few minutes. He held out a bank draught. "I believe this covers everything, does it not?"

The man took it. "More than sufficient, sir. Very generous of you. I hope I can be of service to you another time, sir."

"I'm sure you do."

The man left and Kit was alone with the knowledge for which he had waited two years. And now that he had it, what was he going to do with it? In his imagination he had rehearsed many scenes of confrontation with Nick. Now he realized that not one of the scenes had been crafted in the belief he would actually see him.

After a few minutes, he roused himself from his musings and left the hotel. He went to the office of his booking agent and was shown right in by the young man who served as secretary.

•132•

Flannery held out his hand to one of his most profitable clients. "Kit. I've been wondering when we could plan the next tour."

"I've got it planned."

Flannery looked puzzled. "Oh? I know you talked about going back to Copenhagen and—"

"America. I want it to begin and end in New York City."

"But I thought we agreed to wait a year or so to go to America. I thought—"

"I've changed my mind. I want to go to as many cities as you can get us into, ending with an extended run in New York."

"Of course. But there are certain ... problems with playing in America. You see, there is—"

"I don't want excuses, I want bookings. See that I get them. Get us in anywhere you can within three months."

"Three months! Kit, I can't do it that quickly. The best theatres are already booked, as I started to say, and there are diffi—"

"Three months, Flannery. I don't care if it's a horse barn in Toronto. I want to be there in three months. If you can't do it I'll find someone who can."

"I'll do it, I'll do it." He looked curiously at Kit. "You are the most unpredictable man I've ever worked with."

Kit's smile was tight. "Oh, no, Mr. Flannery. I'm in all likelihood the most predictable. I have a goal in mind for everything I do. Nothing is random."

That was a lie and he knew it. He should have said, "Nothing I do in the theatre is random." God knew his personal life was a rocket out of control. Since Nick's defection Kit had frantically searched for a replacement. He had hunted in pubs and nightclubs, theatres and opera houses, backstage and on stage, among performers and watchers. There had for a month been a blue-eyed Spanish bullfighter. Most of them he could not abide.

He needed Nick. His nightmares had worsened and he had twice been frightened by waking hallucinations of Tom Rourke following him in the streets of London. He slept little and when exhaustion threatened he took laudanum in order to sleep; other times he drank cognac to forget the loneliness and the dreams. The mirror told him it was all taking its toll. He was thinner, with shadows beneath his eyes and cheekbones. His work was not suffering, but he knew it was only a matter of time before it, too, showed the strain.

He left Flannery's office and went to the theatre for a consultation with his stage manager. He knew Maurice would balk. But now that he had made up his mind to go to America nothing was going to stand in his way. He was a sick man who had been told the cure for his illness was in another country. His cure was to find Nick and tell him to go to hell; then he would be cured of his need. He would move heaven and earth to get where Nick Stuart was.

❏

Other than medical journals, Nick did not read. He brought a newspaper home from the city every night for his wife and trusted her to keep him informed. He was far more interested in the discovery of the malaria bacillus than he was in the doings of President McKinley; far more interested in a new technique for doing a cesarian section delivery than he was in another of the endless wars, this time between Spain and the United States. The only bit of news that caught his attention was that of Queen Victoria's Diamond Jubilee.

Bronwyn had put the paper down in front of him at breakfast, folded with the photograph of the Queen on the front. "She must be as old as the hills," she remarked with a yawn.

He glared at her. "She is the Queen of England. She has been Queen for three-quarters of a century and she is a great lady."

His tone had been accusing, as if she had committed some gross error. Taken by surprise, she apologized, though not sure what it was she was apologizing for. Then she said, "Nicholas, are you homesick for England?"

He stared at her. Then with a sigh he said, "I suppose I am. It is so different here."

"Then why don't you go home for a visit?" She had her fingers crossed beneath the table. She didn't want him to go and leave her alone with the house, the servants, Alyce, and her baby which was due in five months.

"Go home...?" he said. Unbidden images moved across his mind. Kit, his mother, lush green hills— It lasted but an instant and was brushed aside. "No," he said. "Perhaps I will return someday to visit my family. But not for a while. And maybe never." He smiled at her. "I have everything I want right here, with you and Alyce."

Her eyes misted. "I am glad. So glad."

"And speaking of Alyce, I am considering riding lessons for her. Would her lovely mother approve?"

"This summer? I don't know. She's very young."

"Your father told me when you were Alyce's age you were riding everywhere. Winning prizes, he said."

"My father sometimes exaggerates my accomplishments. As to the riding lessons..."

"I bought her a pony."

"Nicholas! Without my knowing?"

"It's a very gentle old pony that belonged to the children of a colleague and they have outgrown her. He said Meg – that's the pony's name – hardly ever goes faster than a trot and that she's as even-tempered as an animal can be. In fifteen years he says he's never seen her kick or bite."

"Well..."

"I bought her for almost nothing."

"But–"

"I was afraid if I didn't she would end up at the knackers."

Bronwyn melted. Who could not love a man who kept a pony from the knackers? "Nicholas, you are so softhearted. Did you think about the lessons before or after you bought the animal?"

He grinned. "After, actually. Wait till you see her. She will be brought over this morning. But don't tell Alyce. I want to be there when she first sees the creature."

"What about tack?"

"That is part of the price."

"You are a dear." Bronwyn got up, kissed his cheek, and went to look in on Alyce.

Nick drank another cup of tea and then he, too, left the table. The newspaper lay where it had been put. If he had picked it up and turned to the theatre section he would have seen a column headed:

Famous St. Denys Repertory Company
To Arrive in August for First American Performances.
Americans Eagerly Await This British Invasion

The column was by one of the best-known theatre critics in the United States; he was not even cautious in his praise. He, who had sniffily withheld complete approval of either Ellen Terry or Sarah Bernhardt, was ready to embrace Kit St. Denys.

□

When the column was forwarded to Kit in London, he laughed.

"What an ass the man is," he remarked to Francis and Rama. "He has never seen us perform. Now he has no choice but to review our performances well. We could mount a production of 'Three Blind Mice' or 'Little Bo Peep' and he'd have to equate it with Shakespeare."

His friends laughed with him. They, like the rest of the Company, did not realize that the American tour had been put together in haste, nor did they realize the driving reason behind it, nor did they know that a discussed European tour was delayed for another two years. All they knew was that they were going to America and they would be playing in American theatres and that they would begin and end in New York City, which was becoming the theatre capital of the world. They had no doubt it would be a triumphant tour.

There was a hesitant knock at the door. Rama opened it. A roughly dressed young man stood there, cap in hand, his dark hair rumpled and his blue eyes showing boldness overlaid with uncertainty.

"Beggin' your pardon, mum," he said to Rama. "I was told to come here and ask for a Mr. St. Denys."

Rama glanced at Kit and saw him appraising the young man. A spasm of distaste crossed her face. She turned toward Francis. "Francis, I think we'd better leave. I don't think we're needed here any longer."

Francis cast a wistful glance at Kit, picked up his coat and hat, and followed Rama.

□

The boy continued to stand just inside the doorway. Kit looked at him and said nothing for a moment. Then he said, "You'll do." He made a slight gesture. "There is the bathroom, and toilet articles. I want you bathed and shaved. While you're doing that I shall order you up a meal." As an afterthought he asked the boy's name and at once forgot it.

He never remembered their names.

10

Kit was not bothered by the stares of the other passengers on the railroad train that chugged its way through the woodlands of Ohio. He heard his name whispered by a girl across the aisle. He smiled at her. Her eyes widened and she blushed, then whispered to the girl beside her. He returned to watching out the window. Let them stare, let them whisper. Wilde had said something about that sort of thing: "The only thing worse than being talked about is not being talked about." Talk meant ticket sales.

The thought of Wilde distracted him a moment. He and Wilde had crossed paths many times when Kit was younger; Wilde often came to Papa St. Denys's gentlemen-only parties, and they saw one another around the theatres as Kit grew older. Once he had found Kit alone at the Xavier Theatre and had kept him fascinated for several minutes with his droll stories and cutting wit. Then he had whispered, "There is no one like you anywhere else in this hideous world, my Kit. You are summer lightning and cool shadows scented with jasmine..." As he spoke his clear gray eyes looked deep into Kit's, and Kit had been mesmerized. And then Wilde's large hand had travelled downward to fondle him. The spell was broken by Wilde's attempt at a passionate, tongue-thrusting kiss. Kit's reaction had been instant; he bloodied the Irishman's nose.

Thereafter, Wilde had avoided Kit as if he were plague-ridden. Wilde had then proceeded to get involved with the very handsome and quite mad Douglas boy who had pushed him to disaster. It occurred to Kit that Wilde would be coming out of prison sometime soon. He wondered what the playwright would do then? Rumor had it that he was forbidden to have contact with his two sons or any of his old friends. His name was soiled beyond hope.

With a slight shrug he dismissed Wilde and his troubles. It was nothing to him. He had his own problems to deal with.

The Company had just finished the grueling eight-month tour that began in New York City. The cities where they had appeared rolled through his mind with the precision and monotony of the railroad wheels: New York, Montreal, Buffalo, Boston, Philadelphia, Boston again, then Washington; small towns throughout the South, towns that still showed the aftermath of the war; New Orleans, where the air was heady with the scent of magnolias and reeking with the stench of open sewer ditches. Northward through Missouri and Kentucky, to Cincinnati and Chicago, where winter forced a long, unscheduled stay and the thaw found them ankle-deep in mud. "There isn't as much mud in all of England," Rama had complained, "as there is in Chicago!" Chicago to Cleveland, and then they were in New England again, in the spring, and saw hillsides golden with daffodils and jonquils. And now they were on their way once more to New York and their final six-week engagement of *Cyrano de Bergerac*.

Bleakly Kit wondered how he would find the strength. He was exhausted. They all were. And raspy voices, sore throats, aches and pains were plaguing them all. One performance had been delayed a week when both he and Rama lost their voices.

His mouth twisted. If they'd had a good *doctor* traveling with them it might not have happened. Stuart. On their first visit to New York there had not been time to deal with Nick Stuart. But this time he would have the leisure to say what he had crossed an ocean to say— His thoughts were interrupted by Rama's voice. "Kit?"

He smiled up at her. Her copper-colored hair burst out in an uncontrolled, unfashionable mass from beneath an astonishing hat.

"Rama. I was just thinking of you. Sit down."

"And I know what you were thinking," she said, making herself as comfortable as she could on the stiff seat. "About *Cyrano.*"

"More about my aches and pains."

"Poor baby," she said without sympathy. "I wish we were doing something else. Cyrano is a wonderful part for you. But Roxanne is such a muttonhead."

"Just like you."

She kicked his shin. "You just want to do it because it has such a wonderful death scene at the end."

"Of course. I love death scenes. I do them bloody well, if I say so myself."

"You don't need to. You die with such heartrending grace you always have the theatre knee-deep in tears. But Roxanne, really! ... poor dotty old lady spending her life creeping about in a convent because of some simpleminded fellow with a pretty face — just the way I do for you."

"Ah. Well, would you like to play Cyrano and let me play Roxanne?"

"Your feet are too big for Roxanne."

"And I would look bally awful in a dress."

They laughed together, drawing more curious stares from the other passengers in the train.

"I wonder who they think we are," mused Rama.

"Not who. What." He leaned forward and leered at her. "They think I am a white slaver and you are one of me gi'ls."

She giggled. "They do not. They think I am your mistress. God knows," she said with a sigh, "I wish I were."

He leaned back, smiling. "Believe me, if I ever decide to take a mistress it will be you."

"Well, make it soon. I'm not getting any younger. Where are we staying?"

"At the Marlborough."

"That's rather posh, isn't it?"

"Compared to what, pet? St. Denys Hill?"

She laughed. "I keep forgetting you come from such a rarified upbringing."

"To be sure."

"I suppose we have separate rooms, you and I."

"Separate. But very, very close."

◻

The staff of the Marlborough bowed and scraped to a quite satisfactory degree when the famous young actor appeared in their lobby, on his arm a red-haired woman who "must be one of those actresses." The whispers followed their progress across the electrically lit lobby and up the ornate curved stairway.

Rama held her head high in her most haughty fashion, and Kit bestowed regal smiles upon the gaping employees. Behind them toiled three liveried boys with their trunks.

Then Rama's room was reached and the play ended. He left her there, her hauteur forgotten as she sighed, removed her hat, laid it on the bed, and sat down, her elbows on her knees and her chin on her hands.

She wouldn't see him until morning. Unless he got drunk.

In his suite, Kit tossed coins to the servants and then inspected his quarters. Sitting room and bedroom, bathroom and private water closet. The most luxurious place he had been in since the tour began.

He went to the window and peered down at the busy street, colorful with the hats and parasols and dresses of the women, many of whom were followed by servants. The streets were thick with every kind of vehicle, with horses and without. While he watched, a motorcar made a series of loud popping noises, frightening horses and bringing shaking fists and curses from the drivers of the horse-drawn conveyances. Noisy, smoky, nasty things, he thought. Powerful things. He intended to buy one as soon as he was home again.

He whistled as he put on a fresh collar. He liked to prowl about cities new to him, explore their murky corners. But first he had to take care of business, and that meant going to the Barclay Theatre. Opening night was only three days away because of the delays caused by the weather. They would have to rush the rehearsals and stage setup.

He paused outside Rama's door, thinking he should take her with him. But she was tired from the journey, and at any rate, if he met someone interesting it would be awkward having her there. He once more crossed the lobby of the hotel, smiling and tipping his hat to the ladies he passed.

A hansom bearing the hotel's crest was waiting just outside the door. Kit climbed in. "Barclay Theatre, please."

He had not expected to get the Barclay on such short notice. But, as his booking agent was pleased to tell him, the scheduled performance by Mrs. Fiske had been cancelled unexpectedly because of her health. That had concerned Kit somewhat, as Minnie Maddern Fiske was someone whose work he admired though they had not met. But one actor's distress was usually another actor's blessing, and so it had turned out.

The hansom pulled to a stop in front of the Barclay. Kit stepped out and then stared in disbelief.

The playbills which should have advertised the coming performance of the St. Denys Company blazed forth the name of the performances for the present day and the following five weeks: Miss

Maude Adams in *Midnight Belle*. His gaze swung to the playbills on the other side of the theatre. After Miss Maude Adams vacated the premises there was to be a revival of *Rip Van Winkle* with Joseph Jefferson.

"There had better be some sensible explanation," he said grimly.

In the theatre he found the manager's office tucked away in a side hallway, well away from the columned foyer and wide, carpeted steps. He charged into the office without knocking. A cherubic man sat at a desk piled high with papers of every kind. The cherubic man smiled and then froze.

"You know who I am?" Kit said coldly.

"I, um, yes indeed, Mr. St. Denys. I've been trying for weeks, simply weeks, to reach you. You see, there has been a mistake made—"

Kit leaned toward the man, his fingers spread upon the only clear spot on the desk. "Say that again."

"I ... said there has been a mistake. I tried to reach you for weeks! Months!"

Kit's eyes impaled the sweating manager. "Yes, there was a mistake. You made it and you'd better have an explanation. And you are a liar. If you had tried to reach me you would have succeeded."

"I– I–"

"I want an explanation, Mr. Grant. Now."

"You ... are not associated with the Theatre Trust. I can't book any but actors who are approved by the Trust."

"What the bloody hell are you talking about? Who, and what is this Trust?"

Grant scrambled for a piece of paper and grabbed a pen. "Here. Talk to one of these gentlemen. They can explain it to you. Or – or talk to Mrs. Fiske. She knows."

"Knows what?"

Grant mopped his gleaming face. "I – really don't want to – discuss it, Mr. St. Denys. Please. Talk to one of those gentlemen. They'll explain everything."

Kit snatched the paper from Grant's hands. "Mr. Grant, as soon as I can retain an attorney you will have your balls sued off for breach of contract." Kit turned on his heel and stalked from the office, through the foyer and out onto the street. Not until then did he realize that his teeth were clenched so tightly his jaw ached.

A hansom with a jaded, bony horse delivered him to the address on the paper. Kit strode into the building, past several desks, and stopped at the desk of a young man whose good looks gave him a moment's pause. Then he demanded, "I want to see Erlanger. Now."

The young man said primly, "Whom shall I say is calling? Do you have an appointment?"

"No, I don't. The name is St. Denys. I'm not leaving here until I see him."

The young man got up, walked to a set of speaking tubes on the wall, and said something. A moment later he came back and sat down. "I'm sorry, Mr. Erlanger is not in."

"You little—"

The young man ignored him and smiled at someone behind him. "Go right up, Mr. Frohman. Mr. Erlanger is expecting you."

Kit's head jerked around. Frohman. The other name on Grant's list. The man was courtly looking, a head shorter than Kit, and delicate in appearance. He reminded Kit a little of Papa St. Denys. "Charles Frohman?"

"Why ... yes." The gentleman smiled. "I'd know your face anywhere, Mr. St. Denys. Welcome to our city, sir."

"Oh, yes. I've been given a fine welcome. At the Barclay."

The smile did not waver. "I see."

"I was told Erlanger was not in."

"He's not in to *you*," said the young secretary.

Frohman raised a manicured hand. "Gently, Freddy. Mr. St. Denys is a guest in our country. He's also an exceptional actor. I saw you in London, Mr. St. Denys. I wrote you about representing you in America."

"Did you? I don't remember. My booking agent sees to all of that for me. I'm not here to chitchat. I want some answers and I was told you and Mr. Erlanger could give them to me."

Frohman put a friendly hand on Kit's shoulder. "Come with me, Mr. St. Denys. We'll have a glass of wine and an illuminating conversation. I'm certain we can come to an accommodation."

"We'd better," said Kit darkly. His fury was cooling under the calm, pleasant demeanor of the other man. He felt a moment's trepidation as Frohman led him into a cubicle only a few feet square and clanged a wrought-iron door shut. Within seconds Kit gasped as the floor beneath his feet moved and he clutched at Frohman. The gentleman laughed. "It's only an elevator, Mr. St. Denys. Quite safe, I assure you."

Kit's resentment returned at the patronizing tone. He had been on a lift once before but had forgotten about it. The groaning thing stopped and the door opened. Mr. Frohman led him down a hall to a door with a name etched upon it:

A.L. ERLANGER

He pushed the door open into a room as cluttered with gewgaws as any lady's parlor and called, "Abe, are you here? It's Charles. And a friend."

The figure who emerged from a closed door on the right took Kit by surprise. His first impulse was to laugh. Erlanger was short, almost as wide as he was tall, plain almost to ugliness, and hairy. As if determined to make himself even more unattractive than Nature had already done, he had a fat black cigar stuck in his mouth.

He grinned. "The famous Kit St. Denys, I presume. I thought you'd find your way up here. I would've been disappointed in you if you hadn't."

The elegant Mr. Frohman sat down and indicated to Kit to do the same. "Abe, Mr. St. Denys was not prepared for the cancellation at the Barclay. He was not notified."

Erlanger took out his cigar and widened his eyes in mock innocence. "Oh, my Great-Aunt Nellie's corset cover! I am so sorry about that, Mr. St. Denys."

Mr. Frohman said with a touch of annoyance in his voice, "Abe...," and to Kit, "Mr. St. Denys, won't you please sit down? Tall men who are standing when I'm sitting make me feel inadequate."

Kit ignored him. Instinct told him the power and the authority in this matter rested in the repulsive little toad with the cigar.

"I want to know what is going on," he demanded.

Erlanger replaced his cigar, took a drag on it, and exhaled choking smoke. "Mr. St. Denys, I could pretty this up, I suppose. But they tell me you're a real shrewd cookie. The thing is, you see, that solely for the protection of the artist," – again the unpleasant grin that made a mockery of his words – "*solely* for the protection of the artist the Trust was formed. This way the actor and playwright are protected. The actor will always be assured of a quality house in which to perform. He will always be assured of receiving the monies due–"

"That is horse shit, Mr. Erlanger. I want to know one thing: Why is my contract with the Barclay not being honored? Why are Maude Adams and Joe Jefferson playing my dates?"

Erlanger tapped the end from his cigar. "They cooperate."

"I was told that Mrs. Fiske lost the theatre because of her health. That wasn't true, was it," said Kit, and it was not a question.

Erlanger's face became the color of old brick. "That woman!" he spat. "That redheaded hellcat and her bastard husband! Before I'm through she won't be allowed to perform in barnyards!"

"Abe, Abe," said Frohman softly. "You are getting overwrought."

Kit's voice was icy as he said, "Mr. Erlanger, Mr. Frohman, I don't know what the game is. But I do know you have not seen the last of me. And I give you my word: I and my Company will perform in this city. And I give you my further promise that when we do we will outdraw any production you are backing."

❏

The Company came into Kit's suite one by one or in couples and threes until they were all there, from Rama to the wardrobe mistress. They were cheery, expecting him to announce the beginning of rehearsals for *Cyrano*.

An uneasy silence fell when Kit did not join in the banter and, indeed, looked very serious. He did not mince words and there was no way to soften the blow.

"My friends, I do not know when or where we will perform." He went on to tell them of the stranglehold the Trust had on the theatre.

"There must be somewhere!" Francis protested.

"I have inquiries out and have interviewed several theatre managers. No one is willing to take us. Apparently the Trust has blacklisted us."

"Then let's go home," someone said with anger. "We don't need this bloody city. Let's all go home."

"I can't," said Kit. "I told Erlanger I would perform here and I will. I will not let them make me run."

He let their dismayed outbursts go on for a little while and then quieted them again.

"Each of you will have to make up your mind. Stay or go. If you go I will pay your fare back to England, give you all the money due you, and add a little to help until you get settled once more. If you stay ... I can promise you nothing. I don't know how long it will take to find a place. I don't know if we can even mount a successful production in the face of their opposition."

The impact of his words left them stunned.

Rama was the first to put it into words. "Oh ... Kit. No. Break up the Company?"

"I would rather rip my heart out but I don't know what else to do. You have all worked so long and so hard. We have triumphed everywhere we have played. And it's *not* over for the Company. Let us say it's a respite. When I have done what I vowed to do, I'll come home. And when I do, the St. Denys Repertory Company will triumph again."

He believed it. He made them believe it.

"Within the week I must know which of you need immediate funds to return home."

"We'd feel like we were abandoning you," said Tom.

"No. You must do what is best for yourselves, your careers, your families. I know some of you have families waiting at home who have not seen you for a long time. Go to them."

He wished they would all leave. These few minutes had been harder on him than a full evening's performance of *Hamlet*.

Francis asked, "What if we stay, Kit?"

"You will have to find work. You can work in the theatre if you are willing to swallow your pride and work for the Trust. In fact you would probably work steadily." He drew a deep breath. "Now please. If you don't mind, I think I need to do some serious thinking alone. Consider your decisions with great care. Friday next we will meet in the dining room for a grand dinner and say farewell to those who are going home."

They left more subdued than they had come. Kit saw accusation in the eyes of some; anger in the eyes of others. Disbelief in most of them. He turned away to the window so he did not have to watch them go. He stared out into the darkness of what had become a hostile and foreign city, and leaned his forehead against the cool glass.

He was thirty different kinds of fool, he thought. Bringing the Company halfway around the world in pursuit of a man who wanted nothing to do with him. He was surrounded by friends and people who wished him well and yet he was lonely. He shut his eyes. If only Jonathan had lived he would never be lonely. "Christ...," he whispered. If Jonathan had lived he would never have killed his father and Kit St. Denys would never have existed. The sneering black-whiskered face of Tom Rourke suddenly leered through the window at him, his red lips spread, wetness like blood gleaming on his beard.

Kit's head jerked back, his heart gave a violent leap. He pulled the curtains shut. When he turned he realized he was not alone. Francis Mulholland leaned against the door, watching him with compassion.

"It will be all right. I shan't leave you," said Francis.

"How did you know?" Kit asked in a barely audible voice.

"I always know."

❐

That night the nightmares came as both Kit and Francis had known they would. Francis held him while Kit sobbed in terror of whatever mysterious phantom it was that tormented him so.

11

Before he went down to breakfast, Nick went into the master bedroom where Bronwyn now slept alone. It had been her decision because of her discomfort, which was proportionate to her increasing size. They had not shared a bed for several months, and though he wanted to regret that fact he knew to his shame that he did not.

Going in, he saw she was just stirring to wakefulness. She smiled up at him. "I dreamed about you," she said.

"I hope it was a good dream." He lifted her hand to his lips. "What shall I have Cook bring up for you today?"

"Mm. I don't know. I think I'll breakfast with Alyce this morning." She stretched and yawned. "Of course, if Cook just happened to have some of those sinful English scones you have addicted me to..."

He laughed. "I'm sure she does. With currant jelly."

"Oh, I shall be as big as a barge."

"Then you don't want a scone and currant jelly?"

"Did I say that? I think I'll take two. And a cup of tea." She reached up and put her arms around his neck. "I love you," she said.

He kissed her cheek. "I love you. Now if you will unhand me, madam, I will look in on the other woman in my life."

Bronwyn grunted and shifted position. "This child must be wearing boots with spurs."

"Obviously a boy, judging from all the trouble he has caused you."

"What shall we call him, Nicholas? You have never said what name you prefer for a boy."

"Well, I suppose Daniel after your father is inevitable."

She patted his knee. "As a middle name, Nicholas. I promised. Isn't there any name you like? Of course, I would like to name him Nicholas Daniel."

"Oh, no," he laughed. "That will not do. I guess I have no affinity for any name except—" He caught himself. "—except James."

"James Daniel?" She made a face. "It's not very rhythmic."

"Oh, name him what you will. Name him Fauntleroy if you want! Anyway, it's probably a girl and we've already settled on Amelia." He gave her a perfunctory kiss on the forehead and went into the nursery to check on Alyce and found her still asleep. Her blanket had slipped to the floor; he picked it up and covered her again, tucking it in around her.

Downstairs there was waiting for him his tea and buttered scones fixed to perfection by the English cook he had been lucky enough to find. One more thing to make Reverend Daniel Carlisle unhappy with his son-in-law: English nanny for Alyce and now an English cook. "Nothing American is good enough for you, eh?" Carlisle had once said. "Your daughter," Nick had retorted and that had ended that particular argument.

◻

At that same hour Kit was glaring with murder in his eyes at the cowering manager of the Barclay Theatre.

"I told you," Grant sniveled, "the Trust controls all the theatres of quality in the city. I can tell you nothing else!"

"There is a theatre somewhere. You will tell me. Because if you don't, we will picket your theatre at every performance from now until Hell freezes over."

The man gulped. "Well — well — there might be one — but it's—"

"But me no buts. Write down the particulars."

Grant snatched a pen and paper and wrote down the name of the theatre. "It's closed now. But it's owned by a Judge Philip Wescott—"

Kit nodded decisively. "I met him."

"For godsake don't tell him I told you about it."

Kit folded the paper and put it into his money wallet. When he did he saw the other paper he carried with him everywhere in preparation for the day when he could put it to use: the directions to Nick Stuart's house. But he had no time to bother with that traitorous weasel now. He returned to the Marlborough House and sent a note around to Judge Wescott.

At two o'clock he was picking at his portion of a fine luncheon, eating almost nothing, while across from him sat a distinguished gray-haired gentleman. Wescott was influential, wealthy, a member of the American aristocracy, and he had friends even wealthier than he was. And he was, Kit suspected, "a member of the club." Though they had met during the Company's first run in the city, he had forgotten Wescott's existence until the cowed manager at the Barclay mentioned him.

Over the pheasant, Judge Wescott said, "I can't believe you'd even remember an old fellow like me. After all, we only met twice..."

"Three times." Kit smiled. "As for being old! The word hardly applies to you. What are you – forty perhaps?"

"Forty-five. Soon I'll be known as Old Judge Wescott."

"Age is subjective, is it not? Michelangelo's David is four hundred years old and it's still breathtaking." He smiled a smile that added: "And so are you."

He saw the familiar look of desire in the judge's eyes and knew he had not been mistaken. He was not in the least attracted to the man but if sleeping with him would get him a theatre and save the Company he would do it. Nick would tell him he was a whore. Who the bloody hell cared what he would say or think?

"I need help, Judge Wescott."

"Call me Philip. Please." The look, the smile, were caresses given in the presence of dozens of other diners.

"I need a theatre, Philip. I have, it seems, run afoul of some cretins who call themselves the Theatre Trust, and one A.L. Erlanger in particular."

"I heard."

Kit was not surprised. "Then you know the situation in which I find myself. Can you help? I was told you own a theatre."

"Who told you that?" Displeasure crossed the judge's face.

"I can't tell you. Do you, Philip?"

"I ... um ... yes." He dropped his voice. "But it's rather questionable that I do, since I acquired it as a result of a bankruptcy. Not very ethical."

"I don't care about the ethics of it. I need a place to perform. Will you lease it to me?"

"Oh, no, Kit. It won't do at all."

"Why?"

"It's in deplorable condition. The previous owner let it sit unused for a long time and it hasn't been in use since I've owned it."

"Then why did you take it?"

"The lot is someday going to be worth a great deal of money if I read my city development right."

Kit slumped a little. Calculatedly. He gave Wescott a mournful, dejected look. "You were my last hope, Philip. My last hope. Some of the Company wanted to cut our losses here and just go back to England. I see now that they were right." No kitten abandoned in a howling, icy, windblown rain had ever looked more vulnerable. "I've never given in to anything before," he said in a low voice.

The judge's struggle was obvious. Kit looked away from him as if to hide his pain.

"All right. I'll take you to see it. If you can make use of the place, then I suppose ... if the place can be made suitable for you I'll be glad to let you use it."

"Thank you! I don't know how I can repay you."

Wescott's eyes brightened and he laughed. "I'm sure we can think of a way."

"When may I see it?"

"I've no engagements the rest of the day. If you please, we can go there now."

❐

The theatre, once called the Flambeau, was off Broadway. And though separated from Broadway by only a short distance, it seemed a million miles away from the splendid theatres on what was being called the Great White Way.

Boards covered the windows. The brick exterior had been painted white and the paint had peeled off in leprous patches. Fragments of obscenities showed against what remained of the white paint. There was a heavy padlock on the door, but the door was chipped and gouged and the padlock bore the marks of a saw blade.

"It once was a nice little theatre," Wescott remarked as he undid the padlock. The door opened with a creak.

It was like entering a cave. Slivers of light came through cracks and breaks in the wood covering of the windows. Kit lit the lantern he had brought.

"Vandals have gotten in more than once," Wescott said, though it was obvious.

Seats were ripped from the floor. The air was heavy with dust and fallen plaster. The curtains had been torn from the stage. More obscenities were scrawled over the interior walls. A stench wafted from an overflowing toilet in the water closet.

"It would take a fortune to make it usable," Kit said, heartsick.

•150•

"Now you know why the Trust wasn't interested in it."

"Damn," said Kit. "Damn." He sighed. "I don't believe I need to see anything else."

They left; the padlock was replaced.

"I'm sorry," said Wescott. "I'll ask around, see what I can find, but they control every theatre of quality. Not just in this city but across the country. I'm surprised you did not find yourself locked out on your tour." He paused. "I don't suppose you'd ... ah ... want to visit an elderly but spry judge this evening? Have dinner, spend the night?"

Kit shook his head. "I'm sorry, Philip. I'd be rather dreadful company at this point in my life. I'm uncertain what to do now, or where to go. I won't give in to them. Another time. I give you my word."

The corners of Wescott's mouth drooped in disappointment but he said he understood.

Kit returned to the Marlborough, and as he passed the desk the clerk called his name. There was a note for him left by a lady. He tipped the clerk and took the letter to his room. His name was on the envelope in a dainty, feminine hand and he assumed it was another I-love-you-madly-let-us-fly-away-together letter, but instead he found an intriguing message:

Mr. St. Denys, first let me express my admiration for your work, though I have been privileged to see you but once. I was overwhelmed with the power of your portrayal of Henry the V. The theatrical grapevine has it that Erlanger & Co. have painted you into a corner. They did it to me, as well, and other of my colleagues. The others yielded to them. I shall not. Perhaps we could find a way together to defy these evil creatures who would stifle us and prevent us from working where we wish. I would be honored if you would call upon me tomorrow at seven o'clock in the evening.

> Yours in adversity,
> Minnie Maddern Fiske

He felt a resurgence of hope. Mrs. Fiske was a great actress. She was the "redheaded hellcat" referred to by Erlanger. Anyone capable of irritating Erlanger had to be worth knowing.

But first, while he was unable to get a theatre, while he was still in as foul a mood as he had ever been in his life, he would take care of the unfinished business that had inspired the American tour.

❐

The ferryboat ride to Long Island passed almost unnoticed, for Kit's mind was on the coming confrontation with Nick. Telling him what kind of rotter he was and then telling him to go to Hell would be more satisfying than anything he had done in years. And while he was at it, if the opportunity arose to tell the truth about Nick to the bitch who was Mrs. Stuart, so much the better. It would be no more than Nick deserved.

At the dock he rented a riding horse and set out, following the directions given him by the detective. He rounded a curve in the road and came upon the house which had been hidden by the woods. He stared at the yellow monstrosity with its lavender shutters and hideous scrollwork on every horizontal piece of wood in sight. He snorted in derision. No one had ever accused Nick Stuart of having any taste!

He dismounted and hitched his horse to the iron hitching post just outside the gray stone wall that separated the house from the woods and the rest of the world.

A sign suspended from a wooden arm proclaimed that this place was where one could find:

Nicholas M. Stuart
Physician
Surgeon
Specializing in
Obstetrics & Gynecology

So, thought Kit, Nick had proceeded with his plans to specialize. Respectable, successful physician-surgeon, was he? How much respectability would he have left when the truth was known? None, if Kit St. Denys had anything to do with it! He closed the gate behind him and walked toward the house.

Glancing at the array of plants and furniture on the porch, he thought, *How very domestic!* There was no answer to his knock. He knocked again, louder. He could imagine Nick cringing inside, having seen him approach, afraid to answer the summons.

The door opened. He found himself looking down into the face of a blonde-haired little girl who gazed solemnly up at him. "Good afternoon," she said in a prim voice, "Dr. Stuart, my father, is awfully busy today in his surgery but my mother is in the garden. She will speak with you. Please come with me."

He was so taken off guard by her adult demeanor that when she emerged from the house, left the porch, and started around the house on the flagstone path he followed her as if on a lead. From the back at least, she was reassuringly just a little girl with a blue hairbow and high-buttoned shoes. There was another gate between the front gardens and the back gardens.

The little girl said, "My father put the new fence in so that my baby brother will not be wandering out."

"You – have a baby brother?"

"Not yet. But I will have. My father has promised me a brother. I would rather have a sister, but I didn't want to hurt his feelings."

"I ... see."

In the center of the flower-lush garden was a gazebo and in the gazebo was a dark-haired lady fanning herself with her wide-brimmed hat. The little girl approached the lady and gestured toward the man behind her. Kit was excruciatingly uncomfortable and wished he were a million miles away. The lady smiled at him and motioned him closer.

She held out her hand and he bowed over it. "I am Mrs. Stuart, sir. My husband is occupied with his patients. May I be of assistance to you?" Her smile was artless; her voice musical.

Kit was trapped, unsure what to say. He had expected to find Nick's family consisting of a screaming brat and a haggish banshee. "I – am an old friend of your husband, madam. I came to pay my respects and ... see how he is faring."

She smiled, her dark eyes bright. In spite of the girth she thought was camouflaged by her lap robe, she was a handsome woman, with splendid dark eyes. And Nick was a fool for dark eyes.

"Why, he is doing very well. What is your name, sir? Perhaps he has mentioned you."

"Yes," said Kit. "Perhaps. My name is St. Denys. Kit St. Denys. I am–"

"The actor!" she exclaimed, her eyes wide.

"Then he has mentioned me?"

"Oh, no. I didn't even know he knew you. But I've seen you perform, sir! My first husband, God rest his soul, and I went to the Xavier Theatre to see you in *Hamlet*. It was wonderful, Mr. St. Denys.

I will never forget it. And to think my husband knows someone as famous as you and he never mentioned it. How surprising."

Bitterly Kit thought, *Not surprising at all, given the nature of the beast.* "To be expected, madam," he said, smiling his best, most dimpled smile. "You see, Nick was not quite the sophisticated sort the rest of us were. Simple country lad, you know."

She sighed. "He's told me very little of his life in England. He doesn't talk a great deal, you know."

"I know."

"Would you do us the great honor of taking dinner with us? Nicholas should be free from his patients in half an hour and Cook always has dinner ready on the button."

Kit felt panic. "I – don't believe so, Mrs. Stuart, though it is kind of you to ask. You see, he and I had quite a falling-out over a difference of ... opinion and I am not certain he would welcome me. Let me return another day. When will he be free?"

"He has no patients on Friday."

"If you have no objection, I shall return then."

"I would be honored."

"And Mrs. Stuart ... would you be so kind as to not tell him I was here? When I see him I want it to be a surprise."

"I understand. And I shall enjoin secrecy on my little minx here." She held out her hand and once more he bowed over it. "I am looking forward to seeing you on Friday, Mr. St. Denys. And this time I will insist upon your joining us at our table."

"As you wish, Mrs. Stuart."

He felt a light tug at his coat and looked down into the little girl's blue eyes. "My name is Alyce," she said. "I think you look like a prince."

He was nonplussed but managed to thank her, even though the real princes he had seen had been rather ugly. Her mother reproved her. "Alyce, one does not make personal remarks to strangers. It is impolite."

The little girl sighed. "Yes, Mama."

Kit thawed toward her. She was a child who was trying her level best to learn the difficult rules of adult society. He remembered another child who had struggled to adjust to adult, polite society. It was not easy.

He took his leave of them and, swinging into the saddle, sat there for a moment looking at the house, wondering just where the surgery was. He pictured a scene wherein he would walk into the surgery, filled no doubt with pregnant ladies, and tell them exactly what their precious Physician and Surgeon was.

Giving a short, sharp bark of self-mocking laughter he turned the horse's head and rode back to the ferry landing for the return to the city.

□

Nick pinched the bridge of his nose and rubbed his tired eyes. The last patient had just left. There had been a steady stream of ladies and children. Yes, he specialized in women's ailments, but he could not turn away a sick child, could he? Today he had even patched up a couple of injured male laborers. He knew Alyce and Bronwyn would have eaten dinner two hours before. He thought again about interviewing associates. There was a young fellow at the hospital who had expressed an interest. Perhaps he would talk to the boy.

He put away the last of the bottles of medicines and removed his instruments from the porcelain tub where he sterilized them. Beside the sterilizer were a half dozen pairs of rubber gloves, another of the newfangled methods he employed to the amusement of some of the older doctors in the city. He washed the gloves in strong soap and water and put them aside to dry. Last, he removed the stained but clean white coat. To old surgeons who still maintained an "operating coat" of black wool, never cleaned and seldom replaced, Nick's white coat was on the same level as the rubber gloves and his lack of whiskers. Nick was not the only young doctor using the new methods, but because he was British and resented, he was the most visible.

He didn't care. He lost fewer mothers and babies than any of the old fogies and his surgical patients didn't have chin whiskers dropping into their incisions. That had been a retort that had not endeared him to some of his colleagues while it had made a hero of him to others.

He yawned, and left the surgery. He was so tired he knew he would be sound asleep within seconds of touching the pillow. Bronwyn had gone to bed early and she smiled drowsily up at him when he bent to kiss her cheek and wish her a good night. The second part of the nightly ritual was to look in on Alyce and, if she were still awake, read her another chapter of the book *Alice's Adventures Underground.*

She was still awake, sitting up with a book on her lap. She could read very well, but she loved having him or Bronwyn read to her. He sat down on the bed.

"Are you ready for more adventures, my Alyce?"

She hugged his neck. "Papa, I want you to read this one tonight."

"What – no *Alice*?"

"Not tonight." She put into his hands her favorite fairy tale, *Rapunzel*.

"Ah. The beautiful princess with the long golden hair."

She pointed to the artful drawing of the prince, who gazed up with rapture at the captive princess.

"The prince was here today, Papa."

He rumpled her hair and laughed. "Of course. Did he ask to climb your plaits?" he asked as he took hold of one braid and shook it playfully.

"Of course not," she sniffed. "Don't make fun of me, Papa. I'm not a child. He was here and he talked to Mama and me."

"And how did he get here? In a golden coach?"

She frowned. "That would be quite silly. He rode a horse. It was one of Mr. Murphy's horses."

"Hm. Well, pet, few princes ride rental ponies." The idea struck him as very funny. "I'm sure it set everyone on the island laughing like loons to see some chap riding along in tights and jerkin–"

"Papa!" Alyce thumped her hand down on the bed. "He really did come but he didn't wear clothes like that! He was dressed almost like you and he talked the same way you do. He was from England and he used to be your friend. You didn't tell me you had a friend who was a prince, Papa."

As if his eyes were yanked back to the cover of the book, Nick stared at it. The prince was tall, lean, with beautiful features that were both strong and sensitive; the prince had flowing fair hair that hung in waves to his collar.

Nick's mouth went dry.

What he was thinking was insane. It was impossible. Abruptly he put the book down.

"I'm sorry. I don't want to read that book."

"But, Papa–"

He stood up. "I said I don't *want* to, Alyce! Must you always have your way?"

She looked down and mumbled, "No."

Guilt struck him like a blow. He had scolded her on more than one occasion when she was being wayward or headstrong, but in this instance... "See here, Alyce. I'm sorry. I acted like an old bear." Then, wheedling, "Why don't we read some more of *Alice* instead. I'd like to know what happens when she—"

Still not looking at him, she slid down beneath her counterpane and shook her head. "You may read it alone, if you wish. Good night, Papa. I don't want a story tonight after all."

He cursed himself and got up. He took two steps toward the door and returned to the bed. Without saying anything to her he reached for the *Rapunzel* book. He again studied the picture of the prince and thought with self-contempt, *What a fool you are, to be sure. There is no resemblance at all.*

With that he laid the book back where it had been and went to bed.

12

"Damn him," Kit muttered to himself over and over as the ferryboat crawled through the gray water. "Damn him. Damn him."

He wondered if he would ever stop hearing the words of that woman *("My husband...")* and the little girl *("My father...")* – as if they owned him! As if they really belonged in Nick Stuart's life! And not only they but the nameless little creature being carried in the woman's body as well. *("My father promised me a brother...")*

He had known that Nick had a wife because the detective had told him so. But Kit had known without being told that she was a harridan, a harpy, a bitch, a she-devil, a seducer, the embodiment of all the evil women who had ever lived.

His hands tightened to white knuckles on the railing. Why couldn't she be what he had pictured? What right had she to be sweet and gentle and kind? What right did Nick have to throw this innocent woman into his path? Through that dark-haired Madonna Nick had more power to hurt him than he had ever possessed before. Kit's hands hurt on the railing. Nick could not be allowed to have that kind of power over him. He didn't want to hurt the lady but what choice did he have? Nick had betrayed his trust and had to be punished. If the woman and child were hurt too, was that not Nick's fault?

His mind ran around and around the questions until he was almost too numb to think. Reaching the hotel, he pretended not to see Rama in the lobby and hurried upstairs where he locked the door. There he paced and argued the same argument without end.

He had to do what he had come to do. It was not his fault that Nick had dragged a woman and child into it... When he could bear his own agitation no longer he left the hotel and hurried into the streets to find distraction. Nervously he noticed it was almost night-fall. He walked quickly, with no direction, and was caught up in a crowd and carried along on its current. When he tried to extricate himself he stepped back on someone's foot.

He turned to apologize. "I'm sor—" His words were cut off by horror. He was looking into the face of Tom Rourke.

"That's quite all right," the man was saying, but Kit did not hear. He was pushing his way through the crowd, not hearing the protests of people he shoved aside.

He ran back into the hotel, sweating and disheveled. Rama was not in her room. Francis was not in his room.

Alone! he thought. Alone – and it was night – and his father was out there, nearby.

But he couldn't be. He was dead.

But he wouldn't stay dead!

In an effort to get control of himself, he sat down and seized a pen.

Think, he told himself. Think of things to write. Write to Lizbet. Yes, that will help. That will be like a medicine. Write to Lizbet.

And the writing did calm him somewhat. He had to plan and think what to say because he deliberately wrote lies. He painted a bright picture of success, of standing-room-only crowds at the Barclay. Time enough when he got home to tell her what really happened.

He bent over the sheet of paper, his neck and shoulders cramping with the terrible tension, his handwriting jerky. The letter was finished when he could think of no more lies; he glanced at the letter and saw that he mentioned a dainty handkerchief he had bought for her. He did not remember writing that but it was a nice touch. Tomorrow he would find a handkerchief for Lizbet, some ridiculously elaborate thing.

He opened a bottle of whiskey and swallowed two drinks. Though the suite was chilly, from time to time he brushed clammy sweat from his forehead and glanced uneasily at the windows, hidden behind the heavy drapes.

Distract yourself! he ordered. Get angry. Yes. That will help, too. You've plenty to be angry about.

He wrote to his booking agent, a bitter letter telling him what had happened, demanding to know how it had happened without his knowledge, and severing their connection.

There was no one else to write to. He had scripts to read but knew he could not concentrate on them. He began to make nervous drawings, at first of nothing in particular, and then as the lines darkened he realized they had form and substance. He had sketched the wrecked stage of the Flambeau. Hesitantly at first and then as though his hand were possessed he added more lines, changed others.

He stared at it. It was the same stage but the curtains were whole, there was the hint of a set, it was a stage waiting for a performance. An omen? He bit his lip, then seized more paper and wrote again.

He wrote to his banker and his solicitor, giving them instructions for the forwarding of a very large amount of money, and authorizing a mortgage of the Xavier Theatre, if necessary.

He put those letters aside and scribbled one more, one addressed to the Trust, which in the morning he would take to the newspapers.

"I accuse," said the first sentence. "I, Christopher St. Denys, accuse you, Messrs. Erlanger and Frohman and other cohorts of the Theatre Trust, of strangling the theatre..."

For a page he went on, read it over, tore it up, and rewrote it. He wrote it several times before he was satisfied, and then he put it aside.

This time the letters were at an end. There was no more distraction to be had. He sat shivering in the suite that seemed as large as St. Denys Hill and twice as empty, a cavern of malignant shadows where the spirit of an evil long-dead man might lurk. The silence was oppressive. He got up and with shaking hands made sure the drapes were drawn as tight as possible and all the lights were on. He hated the way his hands trembled when he poured another glass of whiskey; he hated the weakness inside him that governed him at times like this.

Several more whiskeys followed. He wobbled to bed and fell fully clothed upon it, on his side, eyes staring at nothing, his knees drawn up, lights still burning in every room.

He thought again of the yellow house across the river and of the man inside that house. He thought of the good days he and Nick had had together, of the laughter and the caring, of the fun it had been to take that naive country boy and show him the world of theatre and teach him about love between men. He thought of the few happy days at St. Denys Hill and how he had intended to tell Nick about Jonathan and Rourke and ... Why hadn't he? If Nick had known, perhaps he would have understood and they would still be together.

He heard a voice and only half realized it was his own. His words spilled over like the tears that streaked his face. "I trusted you, Nickie – No one but Jonathan and Lizbet and Papa St. Denys – I trusted them – you made me feel safe – but *they* didn't abandon me – Nickie, I need you tonight and you're so close– McPherson didn't mean anything to me – I tried to tell you–" A sob shook him. "I saw the Devil tonight – why aren't you here with me, God damn you – you self-righteous tin saint! – I hate you – God, but I hate you– you're so close, Nickie – just across the bloody river – I need you so much – why aren't you here– you should know I'm here–"

The whiskey gradually won out and he slept, a restless sleep that suddenly broke into splintering terror as Tom Rourke burst into his dreams, his bearded face contorted, his entire being covered with blood that pulsated with a life of its own and he had Jonathan by the throat and was choking him, choking him, choking–

Kit jerked upright, heart pounding. He knew he had screamed; it still hung silently in the air. Something – someone moved behind the drape–

He leaped to his feet, staggering a little from sudden dizziness, and jerked the drape back.

There was nothing there except the weak tea-colored sun just rising in the foggy morning.

He fell back on the bed, drained, and slept until noon.

He was pale that afternoon when he set out with his letter to the Trust rolled like a scroll in his hand. Bruiselike marks lay beneath his eyes. As he walked toward the cabstand he tried not to look into the shadows for Tom Rourke. The sun gradually warmed away the chill inside him and he was able to laugh at his night terror. What a fool he was. Tom Rourke was dead.

He went first to the offices of the *Sun*. The editor glanced at the letter, shook his head, and laughed.

He went to the *American,* where he was dismissed out-of-hand, and then to the *Evening Post.*

The editor at the *Post* read it, then handed it back. "Mr. St. Denys, I have much admiration for your work and can empathize with your feelings. But even if I agreed with your position, I could not print that."

"Why not?" Kit demanded.

"My dear sir, it is a fallacy that newspapers exist to print news. Newspapers exist to sell products. In order to do that we must have advertisers. In order to keep advertisers we must pander to them. We carry a lot of theatre advertisements. If I printed that, the Trust would pull the ads of every theatre they control – and we would lose thousands and thousands of dollars."

"And the moral justice of it? That means nothing?"

"Mr. St. Denys, moral justice is keeping food on the table and clothes on the backs of my family and my employees and their families. Good day, sir."

The editor of the *World* at first would not speak to him, but relented when Kit refused to leave. He asked Kit in with every show of respect and read the letter. He read it twice before handing it back.

"You are right about them, Mr. St. Denys. I myself accused the Trust of fraud for sending second-rate road companies and advertising them as the original. I know full well what they are and what their methods are."

Kit leaned forward eagerly. "Then you will print this?"

"No. I'm sorry."

"But ... why?" Kit asked, bewildered. "If you know, then ... why?"

Mr. Norris looked away from Kit's eyes. "Call it cowardice if you like. But when I wrote my editorial there was an organization of well-known actors who promised to hold out against the Trust. Richard Mansfield was its president ... until the Trust bought him. When he defected to the Trust the others melted away; you'll find them all now acting in Trust-controlled theaters. I could not defy the Trust alone. It would not have been fair to the stockholders and the others who depend—"

"I've heard that speech before. And you cannot say they are all acting under the Trust. Mrs. Fiske is not."

"She is the exception."

"And I."

"And you."

Kit got up. "Good day, Mr. Norris. I see I can look for no help among the newspapers of this city."

Norris hesitated. "Try the *Dramatic Mirror*. It's just a theatre weekly, but the editor there is enough of a fool to print it. And you're quite right; no one else will."

Kit emerged onto the street and was lucky enough to find a hansom waiting at the curb. "Do you know where the *Dramatic Mirror* offices are?" he asked the driver.

The driver did and in due time deposited Kit where he had been not long before. Puzzled, he studied the building and realized that the Empire Theatre, where Erlanger had his offices, had been built around another building, and it was in this smaller, surrounded building that the *Mirror* was located. Doubtless it was a Trust tool also; Norris had sent him on a wild-goose chase. He almost got back into the cab. Then he said, "Wait for me. I shan't be long."

Inside he found a busy room. Actually, he thought, it wasn't so much busy as chaotic. A young lady with eyeglasses was working at a furious pace at a typewriting machine. There were stacks of magazines, books, and newspapers everywhere. Theatrical posters adorned the walls. He grinned at the sight of a large cartoon of the elegant Frohman and the toadish Erlanger, both with pig trotters instead of hands, trampling small figures of actors and actresses beneath their hind hooves. The caption read:

Beauty and the Beast
both engaged in beastly business

He must have been wrong about the *Mirror*'s being a Trust paper. He'd been wrong about a great many things lately. He approached a young man at the nearest desk. "I beg your pardon, my name is St. Denys. I must speak to the editor."

"Harry?"

"Well ... if Harry is the editor."

"Editor. Manager. Owner. Right this way." The young man beckoned to him to follow and talked over his shoulder. "Say, you aren't *the* St. Denys, are you? The actor? Sure you are. I've seen your pictures. Never saw you on stage but I heard you're dynamite." He talked so fast, Kit was a little lost. The boy knocked on a door and opened it. "Man to see you, Harry." With a flourish he ushered Kit in and closed the door behind him.

Kit saw a tall, slim man of indeterminate age, with thinning hair and a thick mustache. The gentleman rose.

"And I know who you are!" the man said, extending his hand. "It is a pleasure, Mr. St. Denys! My wife has spoken often of you, wishing she could work with you."

"Your wife, sir? Are we acquainted?"

He chuckled and motioned toward a large portrait of a delicate, plain-faced woman with luxurious red hair. "Mrs. Fiske, sir. Minnie Maddern Fiske. I'm Harrison Fiske." He laughed. "Erlanger called me Mr. Minnie Maddern in public, thinking it was an insult. Not a bit of it! My wife's a genius."

"As they say, it is a small world, Mr. Fiske." Kit smiled. "I received an invitation from your wife to call upon her this very evening."

"I'm not surprised. My Minnie is always a few steps ahead of the rest of the world. Now, then, I assume you came here for a purpose."

Kit handed him the letter. When Fiske had read it he looked up, smiling.

"It would be an honor to print this, Mr. St. Denys. There is a *caveat,* however. We are a weekly with a small circulation. Actors, managers, playwrights who are with the Trust are forbidden to read the *Mirror.* Hotel newsstands that sell Trust theatre tickets – and there are many of them – are not allowed to sell the *Mirror.* In short, your letter will be read by a small but select minority."

"But it will be read."

"It will indeed be read."

They shook hands. "Until this evening, then."

"I look forward to it."

Kit's cab was still waiting. He felt good about events for the first time in several days. The Trust could be brought down. It had to be. He had never run from a fight in his life. And he had won most of them. He was whistling a cheerful pub tune he'd learned as a boy when he left the building. He hoped Erlanger was looking out the window.

His next stop was the Fifth Avenue home of Judge Wescott. The place reminded Kit of a certain kind of dowager, the kind who has inherited millions, whose family has been around since Adam and Eve and therefore does not need to put on airs to impress anyone. The mansions around it seemed garish and overblown in comparison.

The butler conducted him to the library and left. Kit looked around, remembering with nostalgia the St. Denys library as he had first known it, and his new father's unabashed collection of male nude statues. He shook his head. Poor Philip Wescott. Poor Philip living in such neutered and strangulating respectability! No matter how much he might like to, he would never dare have even one male nude statue let alone dozens. And that thought led to the beautiful statue of Antinous and Nick's remark that Kit looked like Antinous.

Nick. Kit frowned. He had managed to put that traitor out of his mind for a few hours and here he was back again. Would he never be rid of him? And he answered his own question: not until he saw him again and the final act was played out.

His thoughts were interrupted by the arrival of Philip Wescott, who clasped Kit's hand in greeting.

"What a pleasant surprise. I was sitting down to a late luncheon. Will you join me?"

"Another time, Philip. I'm sorry to have disturbed you at your mealtime."

"'Another time.' Is that all I shall ever hear from you, Kit? If not the pleasure of my company, what does bring you here?"

"I want the theatre. The Flambeau. I want you to do whatever legal things are necessary for me to take possession of it at once."

Wescott was amazed. "I can't believe you are serious. Kit, you saw the place. And you didn't even see all of it. You must reconsider. I would not be able to sleep at night if I allowed a friend to—"

"Philip, I want it. Have an engineer go over it for structural damage and if the walls will hold the roof and the floors will hold the audience, then I want it as soon as possible. I have already written to my people in London to send the money."

"I think you are a little mad."

Kit's smile was tight and without humor. "More than a little, I suspect. How soon can I have the place?"

"Within the month."

"I want it this week. I have enough for earnest money."

"Kit, I think you have done this on impulse and will change your mind."

"You haven't known me very long, Philip. If you had you'd know I never change my mind."

Philip Wescott gazed at him in wonder. "How I wish I had that kind of courage. What is it like to be so sure? There are so many things I'd do if I did not have to consider whether a certain thing is wise or acceptable..." He sighed.

"Consider this, my friend: one of us is far more likely than the other to end his days in poverty or get his head broken. I leave it to you to guess which is which."

"You may be right. I shall start the process tomorrow, then. You should have the engineer's recommendation within a day or so."

They shook hands on it. The judge held Kit's hand longer than was necessary. Kit returned to the cab and ordered the driver to take him to the shopping district. He had an important purchase to make.

He stopped the cab and got out in the middle of the dazzling shopping district known as Lady's Mile. Building after building displayed every kind of dress, coat, hat, bonnet, glove, shoe, boot, scarf, fur, and jewelry. Every kind of adornment or gewgaw a lady with money to spend could ever want.

Women passed him in chattering twos and threes, many accompanied by serving-girls carrying the purchases. He saw several gentlemen pass in the company of two or more females and the gentlemen each wore a pained expression, as though he would much rather be suffering the attentions of a dentist.

Kit glanced at the name over the door of the store he chose: Lord & Taylor. A fine name, at least. Inside he was assailed with the scents of perfume and the rustle of long skirts and the light voices of women. A lady who was examining a corset looked up, saw him, turned bright red, and hastily put the corset down.

He tipped his hat to her. A salesgirl flirted with him, her expression saying she would run away with him right then and there even though she didn't know his name. When he left a few minutes later he had what he had wanted. It was called a handkerchief, but it consisted of about four square inches of cambric and a six-inch-wide border of lace. Lizbet would declare it the most impractical thing she had ever seen and she would love it.

That evening he could not have said what he ate or what kind of wine he drank. When he arrived at the restaurant in the Brevoort and Harry Fiske introduced him to his wife, Minnie Fiske held out her hand and Kit lifted it to his lips. She was a very feminine lady, not beautiful, but striking, with hair even redder than Rama's.

"Mrs. Fiske," he said, "the portrait in your husband's office does not do you justice."

She laughed. "Harry, you did not tell me he would be such a flatterer. And please, let us be friends. Call me Minnie. I shall call you Kit, if you've no objection."

"I would be pleased."

During dinner the conversation was pleasant, mostly about theatre, without bringing in the Trust to spoil appetites. When the dessert had been cleared away, Minnie said, "Kit, I have a proposition but it would be better discussed in private. Have you time to join us in our suite? You men may have cigars and brandy, if you like, and I shall tell you what is in my mind."

And so a little later Kit found himself in the modest suite, a glass of brandy in one hand and in the other the script for *Tess of the d'Urbervilles*.

"I knew when you walked in tonight that I had found my Angel Clare," said Minnie Fiske. "The actor who was to play the part decided he would rather work for the Trust. And then I discovered you were in the city and I knew it was an omen. Be my Angel Clare, Kit. Angel Clare is beautiful and high-minded until he is faced with the need to forgive the woman he loves. He has just confessed to her that in the high spirits of youth he sinned with a woman. Tess accepts that with love. Then she feels safe enough to confess her own story of seduction at the hands of a cad, the child that resulted, and its death. He, of course, cannot accept it . He married a pure virgin only to find out that she is in reality soiled goods."

And Kit knew exactly the expression that would be on Angel Clare's face. The same expression of revulsion he had seen on Nick's face as he said the words: "You are a whore."

"Take the script," Minnie was saying. "Read it. I want you to do it but I shall not make you feel obligated. I realize it is a supporting role to that of Tess, but—"

"I want very much to do it."

"But you haven't read the script yet."

"I trust your judgment. And my instincts. As to being in a supporting role to the great Minnie Fiske, I will accept that gladly."

She smiled. "Even if we must play in a livery stable?"

"We will have a theatre. I'll see to it. He held out his hand as she had earlier. "Done?"

"Done!" she said and gripped his hand.

❐

Nick was annoyed with Bronwyn. In his office on a small inlaid table was the silver-framed family photograph taken of himself, Bronwyn, and Alyce not long after the wedding. In front of the photograph lay a newspaper she had put there, telling him — no, *ordering* him — to read the article she had circled. Stubbornly he had refused. Now, two days later, he gave in. If he didn't the thing would lie there forever. He considered throwing it away, but if he did she would ask him about the column and he would feel like a fool.

The house was quiet, everyone but himself was in bed, the surgery was cleaned up, and he had no more excuses. He took the paper and sat down at his desk, unfolded the paper, and found the column.

"My God," he gasped. There was a small drawing of Kit by the newspaper sketch artist. It was not a true representation but it was recognizable. Why was his picture in the newspaper? He dreaded to find out, but something in him made him read on.

NEW SALVOS FIRED IN THEATRE WAR

Theatre war? What nonsense was this? Then he realized the column was by the theatre critic for the newspaper.

Kit St. Denys, the brilliant British actor who has recently taken up residence in our fair city, has fired his first guns in the theatre war. In a letter printed in the *Dramatic Mirror,* he accused Messrs. Erlanger, Frohman and others of nefarious schemes to destroy not only careers but the theatre itself. That the charges are wild and unfounded is fact, but one wonders why one of Mr. St. Denys's stature should feel the need to attack these gentlemen. One wonders if he is

Nick put it down, reading no further. He could feel his pulse pounding in his temples. "...recently taken up residence..." *Recently taken up residence—!*

Alyce had been right all along. The prince had been there. The prince of seduction and deceit. He hurled the newspaper into the fire. Kit! In New York. What did it mean? Dear God, what was he planning to do? Why had he come there? What had he told Bronwyn? What was he *going* to tell Bronwyn?

Nick shuddered.

He did not know which was stronger in him: the fear that Kit would ruin him or the longing to see him again.

Needing to do something, anything, he went to Bronwyn's room and shook her shoulder. "Are you awake?" he asked.

She blinked owlishly at him. "What is it? Is Alyce all right?"

"Alyce is quite all right. Bronwyn, I read the column. Why did you give it to me?"

"He was here. He said he wanted to surprise you, but when he didn't come back I thought you should know. He said you were friends in England and had a falling-out."

Nick gave a short, angry laugh. "Did he indeed! He is a wicked man, Bronwyn. You are not to entertain him in this house ever again."

She twitched her shoulder away from his hand. "Men! Alyce and her little friends have disputes all the time but they always make up. Why can't grown men be as adult as little girls? He was your friend and you should make up. Now go away and let me sleep."

He straightened. Was she demanding that he reconcile with the one man who could ruin their lives?

There was no foolishness as destructive, he thought, as the foolishness of the innocent.

13

An ocean away from New York, Lizbet Porter, known to the local people as Miss Elizabeth, walked down the lane from her small house not far from St. Denys Hill, to the village where twice each week she went for the post.

She was a mysterious personage to the people in the village. Her walk and her talk were so fine it was whispered she was a vicar's daughter who had been ruined many years ago. When the postmaster made it known that she frequently received letters and parcels from Young Mr. St. Denys, the solution to the puzzle seemed obvious: she had been betrothed to Xavier St. Denys, who had gotten her with child, and she had given birth and then had been callously cast aside to make her own way while he raised her child. That this did not much match the known kindness of Xavier St. Denys did not matter in the least. It was a romantic story and allowed them to feel morally superior to the upper class.

Lizbet was ignorant of these stories and continued to call for her post, and talk cheerfully to anyone in the tavern.

The tavern owner also served as the postmaster. After squeezing and bending it first, he handed her a thick letter. "Another letter from Young Mr. St. Denys I see, Miss Elizabeth. Almost like a parcel, I'd say."

She smiled in delight. "Yes, it is."

"What do ye suppose be in it, t'make it so fat."

"I don't know."

"He's in America now, is he?"

She nodded. "Of course." She almost added, "And you know that as well as I do, you old fake." With a wicked urge to foil his avid interest, she tucked the letter into the pocket of her coat instead of opening it there. "Cheerio, Mr. Sand."

"Cheerio, Miss Elizabeth." He was clearly disappointed.

She went back out into the fog. She liked walking in the fog. There was an eerie mystery to it and the droplets of moisture were like damp velvet on her face. Sounds were different in the fog, something she had not realized until Kit had once pointed it out to her. Smiling, she slipped her hand in her pocket.

Kit. Her boy. She had thought of him like that for years. No son could be better to his mother. He provided the house she lived in, everything she needed or wanted. If anything, he was too generous. She had a Dresden china teapot he had given her and in it was money she had not spent and he kept sending more. He sent her books and scripts, and linen shirtwaists, and kid gloves and boots, and fur muffs. There were shelves of splendid hats in her bedroom. The sweet dear. Where did he think she spent her time that she could use such splendid things? She preferred her stout walking shoes and wool skirt and in winter nothing could keep her warmer than her heavy coachman's coat and scarf, bought from Mrs. Darby when her coachman husband died. Still, she treasured the luxuries because he had chosen and sent them. And as soon as he came back she would trot them out and wear them to dinner at the Hill.

There had been a time, when she first moved to the country, that she had returned to the City two or three times a year to appear in whatever plays she could get parts in. Gradually she had tired of that and had since become more and more a country woman. Miss Elizabeth.

She gave a start, thinking someone was behind a tree beside the lane. Then with a breathy laugh she discovered it was just the old apple tree with the stunted, twisted trunk. It looked rather like a gnome in the fog.

Her little house welcomed her with warmth to remove the damp chill of the fog. She saved the letter for teatime when she could revel in it. It was almost like having tea with Kit. She brought water in from the well, heated it, and took a bath and not until she was wrapped from head to toe in a soft, warm flannel nightdress and robe, did she fix her tea, sit down beside the fireplace, and open the letter.

"Oh...," she said in soft pleasure when the handkerchief, carefully folded and wrapped, came into view. "What a lovely thing." She put it aside and unfolded the letter.

Dearest Lizbet, I hope you find pleasure in the handkerchief. I was assured by the young lady salesclerk in this very posh shop that *the* Mrs. Astor (who speaks to no one but God, I gather), always buys this style. I hope it makes you feel frightfully rich and snooty.

I wish you were here to see the Company in our latest triumph...

He went on for three pages telling about the city and exulting over the adulation they were receiving at the Barclay:

queues every night ... I like it so much in this wonderful city I am seriously considering buying my own theatre and remaining for a few years. Of course I'll send for you. I need my Lizbet here to take the wind out of my sails once in a while...

She frowned slightly and folded the letter. Something was askew with the letter but she did not know what it was. It almost sounded a little *too* cheerful. No mention as there usually was of illness or houses less than capacity or an isolated poor review or the miserable traveling conditions. Well, she had the address of his hotel. She would simply write him and ask. He should know better than to try to pull the wool over her eyes.

Then she blew out the lamp and went to bed.

❐

Out in the deepening fog a man, barely visible, watched the cottage. When the lights had been out for several minutes the shadowy figure detached itself from the trees and swiftly, quietly, approached the house. He tried the door and grinned. No one in the country locked their door and this one was no exception. On silent feet he walked through the parlor to the bedroom where Lizbet lay asleep.

He leaned over her.

❐

Lizbet's eyes flew open as a hand clamped over her mouth and nose. She tried to struggle but she was crushed against a man's chest. Buttons cut into her breasts.

"Now, ye slut, I'm goin' t'take me hand off your mouth. Ain't nobody goin' to hear ye anyway but I can't stand a screamin' woman. Scream and I cut your throat. Understand?"

She nodded and gave a stifled cry of pain as he grabbed a handful of her hair and twisted her head back so that she was looking with uncomprehending fright into his swarthy, bearded face.

"Where's me boy?" he demanded.

"I – don't know what–" And then she did know. She gasped, suddenly recognizing a face from more than fifteen years in the past. "Rourke!"

He laughed and threw her flat on the bed. "The same. A deserted pa just lookin' for his long-lost boy. I longs t'clasp 'im to me bosom. Now where is he?"

"I don't know." She squealed as he struck her.

"Don't give me that shit, whore. I been watchin' and I been askin' in the village. I know he's tourin'. But where?"

"Please," she begged, "don't bother him, Mr. Rourke. He's happy. He's got a good life. Don't–"

The laughter was loud and cruel. "A good life? I reckon he does! He was always a smart 'un. Get hisself adopted by that rich old fairy St. Denys. Inherited a lot o' brass, so I hear. And is makin' more. Well, I figure 'e owes 'is old pa a living."

"He – he thinks you're dead."

"Of course 'e does! 'E tried to kill me, th' little bastard! That son of a whore! But I ain't dead. And I ain't of a mind to work no more, neither. 'E could keep me in th' lap o' luxury. And 'e will, too, or 'e'll be sorry."

"He has no reason to help you." She tried to sound defiant and sounded like a scared child.

"Oh, I think 'e does, lady. I think 'e'll pay plenty to keep 'is fancy theatre friends from knowin' who and what 'e really is. The bee-yoo-ti-ful Kit St. Denys – 'Arry Rourke, a river rat, a little thief who could steal a man's back teeth afore he knew it. And, I 'ave me a suspicion, 'e's a fairy too, just like old St. Denys. See, I talked to th' servants at that fancy pile o' rocks." He laughed, an evil cackle.

Lizbet suddenly lunged for the heavy porcelain pitcher on the washstand beside the bed. She swung it with all her strength. He caught her hands in midair. The pitcher flew from her fingers and smashed to pieces on the floor. His teeth were bared in hatred as he flung her back on the bed and struck her repeatedly across the face. She fought as well and as long as she could, scratching his face, biting, thrashing about but she was no match for him. To her horror she felt against her thigh the evidence that the struggle was exciting him. She fought harder and when she could fight no more and had strength enough only to breathe, he took her, holding her pillow over her face as he tore into her body.

When he was satisfied he stood up, righted his clothes, and took the pillow from her face. Her head was thrown back, her eyes stared at nothing, her mouth was open in a scream that would never be heard.

He cursed his stupidity. He had throttled the best source of information without learning a thing! Within a few minutes he had ransacked the little house and had found a small treasure of things to pawn and the Dresden teapot yielded at least two hundred quid in paper and coin. Every drawer was emptied and he found the thick packet of letters, tied with a ribbon, but the damned things had no address on them. He dragged her to the floor and tore apart the mattress. There was nothing there. On the shelf in the wardrobe he found a scrapbook.

Curious, he looked through it. It was of nothing but 'Arry. Oh, no, he thought with a sneer. Not 'Arry. 'Arry wasn't good enough for the likes of him. Kit. The book was of nothing but Kit. Newspaper stories, pictures, programmes from the theatre, old tickets. Had he cared to, he would have seen that each programme was autographed "With all my love to Lizbet. Kit."

As he was ready to leave he noticed a letter that had fallen to the floor unnoticed and he picked it up.

He read it laboriously. Then he grinned. Now he knew where his boy 'Arry was. With the letter was a fancy handkerchief. He put the letter in his pocket and dangled the handkerchief in the air before his eyes. Might as well take it too. It was a mighty fancy piece of work. It would likely get him the favors of a whore and he wouldn't have to pay money. He crammed it in his pocket as well. As he strode to the door he paused and stared down at Lizbet, lying facedown on the pieces of the broken pitcher, half-naked, her gown twisted around her torso.

He spat at her.

"Bitch," he said and walked out into the mist.

He had his plans made before he was past the village. He had enough money now for several weeks of high living and then a ticket to New York City. There he would find his "long-lost son" and he would never have another care in the world. But first the high living!

◻

Rourke lived a little higher and a little faster than he had planned. Food, drink, whores, they all took money. And soon the money he had stolen from Lizbet was gone, as was the money he'd gotten from pawning her belongings. And he still did not have a ticket to America.

He considered the alternatives: he could work, ship out again; or he could steal. Shipping out was not attractive; he wasn't a kid anymore and it was too much work for too little money. He planned a small burglary but a chance meeting with a friendly stranger in a pub changed his mind. The stranger, Liam Finney, had a better idea – one burglary which would get them a bargeful of money.

They schemed to rob Sir Brackney's house while he was taking a Parisian holiday. Finney had worked as butler there and knew the house like the back of his hand and so drew a map. Rourke would take the top floor and Finney the ground floor. Everything would be split fifty-fifty.

The burglary went without a hitch and Rourke was mentally spending his money until, as he noiselessly crept along a hallway with a sack of swag in his hand he blundered against a tall clock. The noise woke the servants. The butler and the chauffeur both came charging out of the servants' quarters, one with a gun and the other with a fireplace poker. Rourke surrendered meekly. Finney was never seen again.

Rourke laughed to himself to think that the Court believed they were sentencing a petty thief to six months. If the rum-heads had known the truth they would have sentenced him to the gallows.

While he served his sentence he resigned himself to the fact that he would have to work his way to America after all. He saw no reason to change his plans; since the brat was buying a theatre he would obviously still be there when his fond papa got off the boat.

In the meantime, he scrubbed his cell, walked in the exercise circle, dutifully went to chapel, and was a model prisoner.

◻

The Company had made their decisions and Kit had to regretfully accept them. The only ones who elected to stay in New York were Rama and Francis, both of whom had found work tutoring, and neither of whom could leave Kit while there was a chance he would need them.

Most of the actors booked passage on the *Princess Lucille* and so could end the tour as they had begun, in one another's company. Kit hired the private dining room of the hotel, brought in a chef trained in Paris, and threw a grand farewell dinner the night before the *Lucille* was to leave port.

Beside each plate was an envelope with a name, and in each envelope was the amount of wages owed and a generous bonus as well to see them over the arrival home.

Everyone tried valiantly to keep spirits up. Jokes were told and they laughed. Reminiscences cropped up and they cried. Everyone had a story about a play or about Kit or about his or her own embarrassment on stage.

And when the food was gone and the drink was running low and time was running out they called for Kit to recite to them. They called out plays, scenes, characters, and lines and he knew them, sometimes to laughter, sometimes to tears – Bottom, Lady Macbeth, Juliet, Romeo, Hamlet, Calaban, Shylock. And then it was over.

He lifted his glass in one final toast.

"To the Company. Severed from one another for but a little while. When I have accomplished here what I have set out to do I will come home and we will be together again – triumphant, unstoppable, the acting company to whom all others will be compared. To the Company."

"To the Company," they echoed.

Within the hour they were gone. Kit returned to his suite, despondent and lonely even though his people would be there for one more night. He did not want to see them. He would not be at the dock in the morning. He could not bear to say good-bye a second time.

He was sitting alone, staring into the fire in the grate, when his head suddenly jerked up. He sat erect, looking intently into space. Someone had called him. It had been a call – no, a wail, of such anguish that it was unbearable. It had been a woman, a woman in pain. It had sounded so much like Lizbet that the hair stood on his arms and the back of his neck. It did not come again. He relaxed a little; he must have fallen asleep sitting there and had a dream.

All the same the air in the suite seemed changed. Eerie, somehow. He shivered, even though he knew that once again he had drunk too much and was merely being visited by daemons of the grape. He went down to Francis's room, where he was welcomed with open and protecting arms and there he spent the night.

"What would I do if you'd decided to go back too?" he asked Francis as they lay in peaceful companionship.

"You would find someone else," said Francis, ever truthful. He nuzzled Kit's hair. "You'd forget me."

"I might find someone else," Kit admitted. "But I'd never forget you. I never forget anything." He sat up, hugging his knees. "Francis, did I tell you that Nick Stuart is here?"

Francis felt as if a curtain had fallen between them. "No," he said tersely. "And if he is I don't want to know about it." He turned away.

Kit looked down at him, at the bare shoulders and the curve of the arm on the outside of the cover, at the back of the neck and the brown hair. This was a man who would lay down his life for him and yet he wanted the unattainable man across the river. He lay down and put his arm over Francis.

"I'm sorry," he said. "I'd forget him if I could."

Francis's voice was muffled. "I don't own you."

Kit lay awake long after Francis was asleep. He did not feel safe from the nightmare tonight.

The next morning, while shaving, Kit had an inspiration. "Francis!" he called.

Francis came into the bathroom, buttoning his shirt as he asked, "What?"

"Resign the tutoring position. You don't like it anyway. Come back on my payroll."

"As what?" sniffed Francis, still smarting from the mention of Stuart's name. "Your gigolo?"

"Don't be an ass. I need someone at the theatre to supervise everything. There are carpenters and electrical workers and so on and so forth, and they all have their own supervisor but I want someone of mine there for them to answer to."

"I don't know anything about that sort of thing," Francis protested. "I'm an actor, not a builder."

"You know honesty, don't you? I can't be there to watch over it all. Please? You know you'd rather work for me than tutor those empty-headed girls. Besides, I pay better wages."

"Well, that's true enough. But if I resign my tutoring position and find out I can't do what you want me to do, then where will I be?"

Kit turned, grabbed him by the collar, and kissed him, deliberately smearing shaving lather on his face. "Then I'll hire you as my gigolo."

Francis swore good-naturedly as he shoved Kit away and wiped the lather from his face. The confidence Kit had in him, the teasing kiss, these almost served to wipe away the memory of the name of Nick Stuart.

"I'm going to the theatre after I breakfast with Judge Wescott. Join us, why don't you, and then come to the theatre with me."

Francis made a face. "Wescott. I don't like him."

"Why? Because he wants me to go to bed with him?"

Francis snorted. "If I were jealous of every man and woman who wants to go to bed with you I'd be green as grass. No, I just don't like him. I shall breakfast alone, thank you, and join you at the theatre."

"As you wish. Francis ... if it's any comfort, the judge holds no attraction for me."

The answer was quiet. "He would if the night was dark enough and you were frightened enough."

Kit looked away, not wanting to admit the wrenching in his belly at the thought of the night terrors that held such power over him.

He ignored what Francis had said. "The theatre. In two hours."

Kit decided to walk to the restaurant since the day was clear and beautiful and promised to be warmer than March usually was. He strode along, dodging ladies' parasols, rowdy children, the traffic of wagons and carriages and gigs and the occasional motorcar. He noticed them without noticing them, for his thoughts were on the first readings with Mrs. Fiske. The more he dug into the character of Angel Clare the more the character intrigued him. There were times when he felt an uncomfortable similarity between his inner flaws and those of Angel Clare, but that was a notion that he did not examine too closely.

Without warning he was staggered by a sharp blow across his ear and a voice bellowed, "You liar! You goddamned liar!"

He put up his hand to ward off a second blow, grabbed the walking stick that had delivered it, and found Abraham Lincoln Erlanger at the other end.

"Are you mad?" Kit demanded, glaring down at the short, stocky man who was dancing around in a fury. His ear throbbed with pain.

"No, but you are, you lying bastard!" Erlanger hauled back on the walking stick. Kit let it go and Erlanger fell ignominiously on his back on the sidewalk, his buttocks landing in a small pile of dog manure, his legs in the air. Kit did not even try to stop his burst of laughter.

Erlanger scrambled to his feet, his face scarlet. "I'll show you! You can't accuse the Trust and me personally of criminal acts and then assault me in broad daylight and get away with it!"

Kit started to walk away.

"Oh, no you don't!" Erlanger grabbed Kit's arm, spun him half around, and punched him on the jaw.

Kit St. Denys vanished in the blink of an eye and it was 'Arry Rourke who reacted, sending a hard fist straight toward Erlanger's nose. A geyser of blood spurted forth and Erlanger staggered backward, his hand over his nose, blood streaming between his fingers.

A young policeman seemed to appear from nowhere. "You're under arrest," he said to Kit.

"Fuck yourself, Officer. He attacked me."

"Seein' as how you're bigger than him and he's bloody and you ain't, I'd say the evidence says otherwise."

Kit started to retort, then realized he had been set up. "You came with this disgusting little toad, didn't you! Very well. How much did he pay you? I'll double it."

The policeman started to splutter an indignant protest then gave Kit a conspiratorial grin. "A twenty-dollar gold piece."

"Would two of them do anything to soften your position?"

"If you take it I'll have your badge, Kelton," Erlanger snarled.

"Come work for me, Kelton," said Kit. "I need a watchman for security."

"How much?"

"Name it."

"Twenty-five a week."

"Done."

"Where?"

"The old Flambeau. Do you know where that is?"

"I'll find it. When do you want me?"

"Start tonight."

They shook hands. Erlanger stood watching them, his hand still on his streaming nose, his eyes darting from one man to the other. "St. Denys, you and that redheaded witch Minnie Fiske think you're going to undercut us, don't you. You think that old relic can be fixed up into a decent theatre, don't you. Wrong, St. Denys, on all counts. I promise you: You will never perform with her there. You may never perform anywhere in this city!"

"Oh, I believe we will, Mr. Erlanger. I believe we will." With exaggerated politeness he lifted his hat. "Good day, Mr. Erlanger."

Behind him the little man's voice rose to a shrill scream. "I'm warning you, St. Denys! I'm warning you!"

By the time Kit arrived at the restaurant his anger had grown. He should have taken the little monster by the throat and shaken his teeth out! The obsequious headwaiter showed him to the private room where Judge Wescott was waiting. The waiter withdrew and closed the door.

Philip Wescott's smile was instant and warm. "Kit. I was beginning to think you were not going to make it." Then the smile disappeared. "Good Lord, man, what happened? Your ear is bleeding."

"Is it?" Kit drew out his handkerchief and gingerly touched his ear. The handkerchief came away red.

"Here," said Philip. "Let me do that. I can see it." He dipped his own handkerchief into the water goblet and gently dabbed at Kit's painful ear. "It's swollen as well. I think you need a doctor."

A self-mocking little smile touched Kit's lips. "Yes. I do indeed need a doctor but the one I need is not available."

"Any one would do."

"Oh, no. I need a certain specialist."

"Are you going to tell me what happened?"

"I was attacked by a toad." Philip looked at him as if he had lost his mind. Kit laughed. "The honorable A.L. Erlanger attacked me with a walking stick."

Philip looked shocked. "Attacked you! What did you do?"

"I bloodied his nose and sent him flying into dog shit." Kit's eyes narrowed. "He also threatened me. He said Mrs. Fiske and I will never perform in this city."

Philip shook his head. "Don't underestimate him, Kit, or the others. They're very powerful and they have a great deal of money behind them. And scruples were something they left behind in grammar school."

"They," said Kit, "should not underestimate me. Enough of that. Any more talk of that vile little man and I shall lose my appetite."

"I took the liberty of ordering the crab for you."

"Thank you. Now then ... do you have the deed?"

Philip drew from his pocket the folded deed to the theatre. He placed it in Kit's palm and closed his fingers over it, keeping his hand on Kit's for several seconds. Their eyes held. Philip said nothing more personal than, "The theatre is now yours — lock, stock, and barrel, for better or worse." His eyes pleaded for something he could not put into words.

Kit chose to ignore the pleading. Someday, maybe, he thought. And at the same time he knew Francis was right. If it were dark enough and he was frightened enough the judge would find his wish coming true. Kit raised his glass.

"To the St. Denys Theatre," he said.

"To the St. Denys Theatre," Philip echoed.

14

Alyce gasped in delight. "Papa, look! It looks so real!" She lowered the stereopticon which Nick had bought for her the day before and held it out to him.

He already knew, of course, that Niagara Falls seemed to thunder downward before one's very eyes when viewed through the stereopticon, but he took it and made suitably impressed noises as if seeing it for the first time. He passed it to Bronwyn, who took it and was almost as excited as Alyce.

It was a quiet Sunday afternoon at the Stuart house. Smells of cooking ham and sweet potatoes curled throughout the house from the massive black range in the kitchen where Cook reigned supreme.

Alyce took the stereopticon, removed the Niagara Falls with care, and put on a card showing a charging locomotive.

Nick glanced at the clock. Sunday afternoons such as this seemed to last forever. Any minute now his father-in-law would be coming to spend a few hours as would Bronwyn's Aunt Grace and Aunt Grace's daughter Lorelei; and if this Sunday proceeded like every other Sunday spent with Bronwyn's relatives, Nick would have a disagreement with her father, hear all about Aunt Grace's female trouble while she diagnosed herself and asked for free medical advice, and Lorelei would play the violin – badly – and Bronwyn's father would read from the Bible – not forgetting to denounce stereopticons, phonographs, and motorcars as works of the Devil – and finally Alyce and Lorelei would get into a quarrel that would end with Alyce giving Lorelei a pop on her pug nose or the other way around. He suppressed a sigh.

After the baby was born perhaps they could once more go horseback riding or walking for miles or even go to the amusement park. Until then they were stuck with scripture and Lorelei's violin. He glanced surreptitiously at Bronwyn.

She looked pretty with her thick dark hair drawn up into a pompadour and a knot, though the child within her had made her look, as she put it, "like an East River barge." Her frock was loose and of a dark material that looked hot. She looked pale and tired. As well she should be, he thought. The final two months of pregnancy were difficult for most women and no man, however sympathetic he might be, could know what they felt like, physically or mentally.

Alyce tired of the stereopticon and put it away. "Mama, do I have to play with Lorelei?"

"Yes, dear."

Alyce sighed heavily. "I don't like her very much."

"She's your cousin."

"Well, I know that." She brightened and touched the enormous bow at the back of her head. "Why don't you play with her, Mama. She likes you."

"And what would you be doing, pray tell?"

"I could ride Meg."

Bronwyn fixed her with a severe look. "Young lady, you know you do not ride Meg unless your father can go with you. Meg may be old and gentle but if she became frightened she could run away with you."

It was on the tip of Nick's tongue to say, "That's easily solved! I'll go with her." But he daren't. The Sunday afternoons were a tradition and Bronwyn, for all her progressive social ideas, liked certain traditions. Change them at your peril!

"Papa?" Alyce appealed to the Court of Last Resort.

"Your mother is right, Alyce. Besides, you needn't put up with Lorelei very often."

Bronwyn gave him a withering look.

She had given him many withering looks of late. It had been almost a fortnight since he had wakened her, angry about the newspaper column regarding Kit's challenge to the Trust. He had stayed angry for a day or so and the atmosphere had been cool. She still dropped hints that two grown men should be able to resolve their differences.

He glanced at the clock again but he did not see it. He saw Kit. So near — just across the river — and he knew where Nick lived — the by-now-familiar feeling of desire and fear tore through him again.

He was almost glad to have his thoughts interrupted by the day girl announcing, "Your father is here, ma'am."

The afternoon had an added torture. Nine-year-old Lorelei not only played the violin but she also recited *Horatio at the Bridge* in its entirety. The recitation, however, was more natural and less histrionic than Lorelei's recitations usually were.

Aunt Grace beamed. "I know it is immodest of me, but wasn't that splendid?" she asked.

"It was indeed," Daniel Carlisle agreed. "Though I could wish the poem were something more devotional – *Thanatopsis,* for instance."

"Lorelei, why don't you and Alyce go play for a while?" Aunt Grace said. Lorelei dropped a perfect curtsey and Alyce reluctantly left the room with her. "Lorelei has a new elocution teacher at Miss Squires's Academy. She isn't socially acceptable, you know, but she is accomplished." Her voice dropped as if sharing a scandalous secret. "The new teacher was an *actress.*"

"Found the error of her ways, did she?" asked Bronwyn's father. "I presume she has put her feet on the road to salvation."

"I would like to think so, but I believe there was some kind of financial failure or something of the sort with the company she was with. But the acting profession's loss is the Squires Academy's gain. And maybe through the example of the girls and the other teachers at the academy Miss Weisberg will, indeed, find salvation."

The name sent an unwelcome presence flashing across Nick's memory. Rama Weisberg – red hair – petite – hated him – adored Kit – Kit! Kit! Kit! Was the whole world in a conspiracy to make him think of his seducer?

"If the ladies will excuse me," he said, "I feel a sudden need for fresh air." He bowed to them and went out into the garden, out to the gazebo. Another conspiracy! He could not even sit in his own house without Kit's complicating things! And the gazebo was little help; there was the place where Kit had stood and talked to Bronwyn. Alyce had pointed out to Nick the exact spot.

He left the gazebo and went out to the stable. The new stableboy, hired when his predecessor was discovered drunk and smoking cigars in the stable, was busy grooming Nick's gelding. Nick had spoken to him for a few minutes when he was hired, taking him on the basis of a recommendation from a fellow doctor at the hospital, and had given him no further thought.

"How goes it, James?" he asked.

The boy looked up with eyes that were a disconcerting dark blue. "John, sir. My name is John."

"Oh – I beg your pardon." Now he did feel awkward. He wasn't at ease with domestics and hired help and in all likelihood never would be. "Um – is everything all right out here in your, uh, little kingdom?"

"Sir?" The boy's expression was puzzled.

"Nothing. Are there any problems?"

The boy nodded. "Mrs. Stuart's filly, sir. When I was exercisin' her this mornin' I noticed her limpin' a little on her right foreleg. I looked at it and think maybe the vet'narian ought t'be called. I think she's got a tendon flarin' up, sir."

Nick's eyes took on a light of interest. He smiled. "I'm a doctor, remember? When I was a boy I helped my father take care of many a horse. Bring her out into the sunlight."

He stripped off his coat and rolled up his sleeves. He had completely forgotten the company in the house. He walked out into the sunlight and as John came out leading the dainty filly, Nick found himself staring at the boy. He didn't remember his hair as being so blond, and only the fact that it was lank and wanted washing kept it from being almost the color of Kit's. Angry with himself for noticing, he turned his attention to the filly. She was, indeed, limping.

He knelt and gently felt. She nervously shifted her feet and started back with a whinny when he touched her right foreleg. "Easy, girl. Easy, girl," he soothed her, while John stood at her head and murmured to her. Nick got up after a few minutes.

"It's definitely inflamed. Do you know how to apply liniment and wrap?"

"Of course, sir." Then with quiet dignity he added, "I learned from my pa, too. He's head of the Astor stables."

Nick looked at him, surprised. "Why are you not working for them? You would make a great deal more money."

"I did work for them." An expression of distaste crossed his young, plain face. "I didn't like them, sir. I won't be talked to like that by anyone, man or woman, like I was a dog to be kicked."

"I see." He reached up to take control of the filly from the boy and his hand accidently brushed John's. Nick was stunned by the shock that rocketed through his body and struck him deep inside. It had been such a long time since his flesh had come in contact with that of another man! Oh God, he thought in dismay, knowing he wanted to stroke the golden-haired forearm, wanted to put his arms around the compact body and crush it to him, wanted to look at John's nakedness and touch him everywhere...

"Sir? Is something wrong? You look awful funny."

Nick dropped his hand and managed a laugh. "And so I should. I completely forgot about the Sunday company. My wife will likely hand me my head on a platter." He pulled out his watch. "They should be gone in an hour. Put plenty of liniment on that leg and wrap it well. Tie her in the closed stall and give her plenty of water and rest. I'll look in on her tomorrow."

"Yes, sir."

"Please saddle the gelding and the pony in an hour or so."

"Yes, sir."

The boy started toward the stable, leading the filly. Then he paused and said, "Sir, hope I'm not oversteppin' my bounds, but you're the first employer I've had that didn't act like I was some kind of simpleton."

Nick smiled. "That's called condescension. I came from a small village, John, and when I first went to university they treated me that way the moment I opened my mouth and they heard my accent." He took his coat from the hook where he had hung it and left the stable.

Still shaken by the unexpected lust, he knew it was not John he wanted. He knew what he had to do. One could not rid oneself of a daemon by prayer; he had prayed to no avail. One could not exorcise a daemon by running away from it; the daemon was in one's heart and would go wherever its host went. One could exorcise it only by facing it and tearing it from one's heart as if it were a cancer. His mouth thinned. As if it were a cancer? That's exactly what his feelings for Kit were.

"I have to see him," he muttered. "And I would rather be eaten by sharks."

The rest of the afternoon crept in its snaillike way to a conclusion. Long before Aunt Grace and Lorelei and Reverend Carlisle left, Bronwyn looked exhausted.

At last they were gone, but not before Lorelei pinched Alyce's arm and Alyce pinched hers in retaliation.

Bronwyn leaned against Nick. "I am so tired, Nicholas. I think I will lie down." He walked with her to her bedroom.

"This will be the last company Sunday until after the baby is born," said Nick. "Doctor's orders." He helped her lie down and covered her with a light blanket.

Her smile was wan. "You just want an excuse not to see Aunt Grace and Lorelei and Papa. But I agree."

"I've had the groom saddle the gelding and Alyce's pony. I'm going to take her for a ride. Oh, and Cleopatra has developed tendinitis, so I'm having the groom doctor it with a poultice."

"Poor Cleopatra. I can hardly wait until I can ride again." She sighed. "Remember the rides we took at dawn when we first married? So romantic, with the mist from the river, and the silence..."

He lifted her hand to his lips. "Just get my son here and we'll take many dawn rides if you wish. And we'll bicycle again and go to the amusement parks again. Whatever you want to do. I have to change clothes. We shan't be gone long."

While Nanny helped Alyce change from her lace blue-sashed frock to her little divided riding skirt, Nick put on his comfortable clothes and riding boots. A little later he looked with pride at his stepdaughter as she sat astride the fat little pony, looking for all the world like an equestrienne. The lessons at the riding academy were worth the money, he thought.

She rode well and the little pony was gentle and slow. Nick's gelding sometimes trotted sideways with impatience, wanting to run.

"Papa," Alyce said as they trotted, "why must I be nice to Lorelei? She isn't nice to me."

"That's the way civilization is run, sweetheart. You are the hostess and she is the guest. At least, that's the reason your mother gives me."

"It isn't fair. If someone's mean to you shouldn't you be allowed to be mean back without getting in trouble? If they do it to you first?"

"Not if you're civilized."

"Well then, I don't like being civilized. I'd – I'd rather be a red savage Indian." The frown suddenly left her pretty face. "Papa!"

"What? You sound as if you've made a great discovery."

"Papa, you said I have to be nice to her because I'm the hostess and she's my guest. Well then, when I visit her she's the hostess and I'm her guest and she has to be nice to me and I can pinch her till she screams."

His eyebrows quirked. "Alyce Rachel Stuart, that is a perfectly uncivilized idea."

She burst into peals of giggles.

As they rode back the twilight shadows were lengthening and the temperature beginning to chill. When Nick tossed his reins to the stableboy he gave him a curious glance. How had he ever seen in this plain and unkempt boy any resemblance to Kit? There was none at all. And he was at a loss to explain the explosion in his gut that afternoon.

The maidservant curtseyed as he came in the back door.

"There's a ... gentleman to see you, sir."

"I'm not attired to meet a gentleman," he mumbled. "And I smell like horse. Oh, well. How long has he been here?"

"About a quarter of an hour, sir. He arrived by foot." She said it disapprovingly, with an air of disdain.

"A quarter of an hour? Then I'd better see him at once." In the parlor Nick found a thin man with a striped suit and vest, and an old-fashioned collar so high his chin looked imprisoned. Though young, his head was bald except for a curl of brown hair on his forehead, a fringe around his ears, and a luxurious handlebar mustache.

Nick held out his hand. "Nicholas Stuart, at your service. You are here to see me, sir?"

The man had bounded to his feet when Nick entered the room. "Glad to meet you at last, sir!" he cried.

"How may I help you? Please sit down."

They both sat. "Well, I've come with a proposition." The accent was Irish. Now that Nick was closer he could see that the suit of clothes was threadbare, the collar had seen better days, the shoes were worn, and he had no chain and fob stretching across his belly. Technically, then, he was obviously not a gentleman.

"What kind of proposition?"

"Me name's Kelly, Dr. Stuart. Well, sir, it's a proposition that'd mean a lot o' hard work for little pay."

Puzzled, Nick asked, "Why would you make such a proposal? And why to me, Mr. Kelly?"

"I asked another gen'leman of medicine and he gave me your name. Sir, I come on b'half o' other folks in the Bowery. We're packed like sardines in a hold, sir, families of eight-nine-ten all livin' in one room with new babies and gran'parents all livin' there too."

"I've heard conditions are appalling, but I don't know what I could do."

"Nothin' about conditions, sir. That's just the way o' the world. I was in a worse place when I lived in Lon'on. But we don't have a doctor to our name, sir, not one. A bunch of us got to thinkin' maybe there wouldn't be folks droppin' dead like summer flies if we had a doctor."

"But I specialize in pregnancy and female illnesses."

The Irishman grinned. "We got plenty o' females, sir, and they tend t'be lusty breeders. Un'erstand, ye'd be there to treat us Irish. We'll take up collections to pay you, though it wouldn't be much. You wouldn' have to touch no kikes or niggers or Chinamen or wops."

"Mr. Kelly, I'm sorry. But my practice here occupies me most of the time and then I also spend time at St. Jerome's hospital. I wouldn't have the time."

The vivid sparkle went out of the man's eyes and his face became bitter. "Coulda saved the two bits it cost to come here. An' I got me suit out o' hock, too. *And* I had to borrow a collar from me brother."

"I'm sorry. I wish I could help. I would be glad to pay your ferry fare home."

"Never mind. I ain't one for charity."

Looking at him, Nick saw his long-ago surgery in London, on the edge of squalor. He remembered the long, long hours and the hunger. No, he could not possibly do that again. And then he remembered the women, the fleshless, pale women worn out from bearing child after child and trying to survive with little food. He, too, had struggled to survive there but he had been able to leave it behind him. They were still there.

"Mr. Kelly ... see here, don't accept my no as a flat refusal. Let me consider it for a few days. There are many things involved. I might see a way to be there in a surgery for only a few hours a week and that would have to suffice."

The brightness came back to the freckled face. "Sir, it would be God's own blessin' on us if you could. Just a few hours, sir, would save some lives, give some ease." He leaped again to his feet. "I'll be goin' now, sir. Me friends will be happy—"

"Mr. Kelly, I haven't committed myself."

"I know, sir. But I c'n tell by lookin' at ye that ye're a compassionate man and I know ye will do it because o' that."

Nick gazed at him. "Mr. Kelly, you had a long walk here. You must be hungry. Would you like something to eat before you leave?"

"Why, that'd be most welcome, sir. As long as you let me pay what I can." He dug into his pocket and produced a penny. "It ain't much, but it's what I got except for me ferry money."

Gravely, Nick took it. "Come to the kitchen, Mr. Kelly. I'll tell Cook to fix you a plate."

Nick knew, just as sure as he knew the sun came up in the east, that he would do as this man requested. Bronwyn would not like it, for it would mean another day when his attention would be elsewhere. But neither could he call himself a physician if he turned his back on people in need.

"We have a place all picked out for our clinic," Kelly prattled on as they went to the kitchen. "It used t'be a kike business but–"

"Mr. Kelly, one thing must be understood at the start. I will turn no one away. I will treat whoever comes to my door, whether it be a Jew, a Negro, a Pole, or an Italian. Everyone. If that is not acceptable then you will have to look elsewhere."

For an instant Kelly's jaw became pugnacious. "But, sir, who wants the same hands touchin' him what touched a kike or a nigger?"

Nick frowned. "I have no doubt there are Jews who would feel the same way about being touched by hands that had touched a mick."

Kelly's nostrils flared. "Sir, that is a fightin' word."

"I have given you my terms, Mr. Kelly. Take it or leave it. As far as my hands and my instruments are concerned, they are immaculate before touching anyone."

The hard jaw softened. "Well, sir, if that's the way the candle burns, then that's the way it burns. We'll do whatever you say, sir."

"Good." Nick gave brief instructions to Cook to feed Kelly and then he went to his study. He was already beginning to regret his impetuous decision. He smiled wryly. Kit always told him he was too hidebound and not reckless enough. Committing himself to work in the worst part of the city for very little money ought to be reckless enough to satisfy even Kit.

15

Nick met Kelly at the hospital and hired a cab to take them to the Lower East Side. The cabdriver balked at penetrating clear to Oliver Street. "I ain't takin' nobody there. I'll take ya as far as is safe and ya can walk from there."

Kelly looked at Nick and shrugged. "He's afraid we'll eat the horse," he said.

"Would you?"

"On a bad day."

They had to walk several blocks through neighborhoods that became denser with people, increasingly drained of beauty. Nick had never been down into the very worst of the London slums and in his eyes the New York slums that he saw now were a thousand times worse than any in his homeland. He was self-conscious of his fine clothes, sharply aware of the suspicion in the faces of the people they passed.

"I see no Negroes," said Nick. "Nor Chinese nor Italians. I thought you were concerned that I might treat some of them."

"Just a bare chance, Doc. You don't think us Irish are going to live with 'em, do you? In fact, us Irish will be out o' these dumps someday soon and then they can have 'em because they aren't ever goin' t'get out." He grinned. "Big advantage, bein' white."

"Mr. Kelly, what I said I meant. No one will be refused treatment."

"Hey, Kelly, who's the swell?" someone called.

"The new doctor I brought back," Kelly hollered, his hands around his mouth. Nick felt like a prize of some kind.

A tail of noisy children attached themselves to their wake and followed along hooting and tugging at Nick's coattail until Kelly chased them away. Two of Kelly's friends joined them, and a few minutes later they were at the place Kelly called the "old kike store," which was to be the clinic.

It would make a pretty poor one, thought Nick, but it would be better than nothing. Kelly and two of his friends stood expectantly beside the door as Nick finished his brief tour of the small building. It was filthy and infested with spiders, but it would have to do.

"Well?" Kelly asked impatiently. "What is the verdict, Doctor?"

"Sure, Doc," said one of the friends, beaming, "it'll do fine, won't it? Get some brawny lasses down here wi' mop buckets and we got a clinic!"

"It will take more than that, Mr...."

"Daley, Doc. Sean Daley."

"Mr. Daley. You men have to take responsibility for getting it cleaned up and painted."

"Painted?" he squawked.

"Painted. Every inch. I won't have people coming into a sty. Get me a cabinet and an examining table and some chairs. Get me someone to help out, boy or girl, man or woman, doesn't matter, someone pretty strong in case I need help with a patient. Put a door on that open doorway. Paint everything as light a color as you can find, preferably white."

"That's — a lot of work," said the third man.

"Ye sure a good scrubbin'..." The second man's voice trailed off under Nick's stare.

"Doc wants it painted, we'll paint it," said Kelly in a no-nonsense tone of voice.

"Thank you, Kelly." Nick looked hard at the other two. "If I am to come here for almost nothing in the way of money, gentlemen, the least you can do is cooperate with me. I want the work done within a week. Then I will come back and inspect it. If it doesn't meet my standards you will have to do it again. Is that understood?"

"Yes," said Kelly firmly, ignoring his friends.

"Good." Nick left the dirty former cobbler's shop and stepped out once more into the noisy teeming street. Peddlers' pushcarts lined both sides of the narrow brick street, with an occasional cart pulled by a horse who looked too decrepit to interest even a knacker. Voices — of both sexes and all ages — filled the air with a continuous shrill cacophony. Women haggled with fishmongers and grocers over unhealthy-looking fish and shriveled vegetables, or picked out live chickens at the poultry shop. There was not a doorway without chattering women or sullen men, not a foot of broken sidewalk without its running, screaming, or fighting children.

Nick paused in surprise and watched two young women who sat on little stools in a doorway under an awning and nursed their infants while two other young women sat near them occupied with some kind of sewing. One of the nursing mothers glanced up and saw Nick. Immediately her face darkened with confusion and anger; she removed the protesting baby from her breast and hastily covered herself. The other woman looked up at him as if daring him to disapprove.

Nick and Kelly walked on. "It doesn't seem like a very healthy place to nurse a baby," Nick said. "The dirt in the street, the flies..."

"Considerin' the rooms they live in, Doc, the street is better."

Nick had read somewhere that there were more than a thousand people per acre in this part of the city, at least one hundred thousand of them living in tenements with complete families in one or two squalid rooms. The death rate was horrendous, largely from tuberculosis, influenza, malnutrition, and childbearing diseases. He could do nothing about tuberculosis, influenza, or malnutrition. But by God he could try to do something about the other.

"Ready to go, Doc?" Kelly asked. "I'll see ye safe to the polite side o' town. Ye don't want to be down here alone for a while." He grinned. "And check your pockets every once in a while. Some of these kids are slick."

It was amazing, thought Nick, how little actual distance separated the slums from Millionaires' Row. Shacks and incredible mansions within minutes of each other. He wondered if the Astors and the Vanderbilts and their kind even knew places such as Oliver Street existed. And if they did know, did they care?

By the time Nick got to the hospital he was an hour late to do his rounds and teach his residents. He looked into the birthing ward, though none of the women were his private patients. His patients preferred to deliver at home and Nick encouraged them in that. He suspected there was less likelihood of contracting sickness there than in the hospital. But in the short time he had lived and practiced in the city, he had gained a reputation for being one of the best obstetricians and was frequently consulted by other doctors, much to the chagrin and irritation of some of his older colleagues.

The young doctor who had expressed an interest in practicing with him, Chad Galvin by name, was beside the bed of a pale-faced, anxious girl. The doctor looked relieved when Nick stepped up beside him and spoke to him.

"Dr. Stuart, I wonder if you would look at Mrs. Tucker? I see no cause for concern but she is in a great deal of discomfort."

"First baby?" Nick asked.

The girl nodded.

He asked a few other questions, pulled the screen around the bed, and examined her. "You're doing well," he said with a smile. Then he indicated with a slight nod of his head that he wished to speak to Dr. Galvin. He took him down the room and said, "She's presenting breech."

Dr. Galvin, young and untried, in his first six months of practice, gulped. "I've never done a breech. I've never even seen one done."

"I've done several. Send for me if she starts labor. If the baby doesn't right itself, and it may, it will have to be done manually."

"What about caesarian section?"

"Only if there is no other way. I've done three and lost one of the mothers."

The younger man nodded.

"Dr. Galvin, we spoke once in rather general terms about your working with me in my surgery on Long Island. No specifics were mentioned, but are you still interested?"

"Yes, sir!" The smooth face lit up. "It would be a great privilege, Dr. Stuart! I've watched you work for months now and I have great respect for you. I'd learn more working with you than I would with anyone else."

"Well, I don't know about that," said Nick dryly. The boy's enthusiasm made him feel like an elderly crock. "But sometime soon you must dine with me and my family and we can discuss particulars."

"Yes, sir! Sir, must we wait for that? Could we have dinner this evening and talk? I don't want to wait a day longer than necessary!"

Nick smiled. "Of course. Have you a suggestion?"

"It's a special occasion, isn't it? Why don't we go to the Brevoort. It's a hotel, but their dining room is said to be very good."

"That will be fine."

"Would you also look at Mrs. Swanson? She's fifty and is pregnant with her sixteenth child."

"Good heavens. She should be giving us lessons."

"But there's something wrong."

Nick examined Mrs. Swanson, a huge woman whose belly was an enormous mound. As with Mrs. Tucker he asked questions, many questions and examined her again. She looked sharply at him. She was no young girl who was intimidated by doctors.

"Is something wrong with the baby?" she asked. "There is, isn't there. I should know. I haven't felt any movement at all."

Nick took off his rubber gloves and laid them aside to be scrubbed. "Mrs. Swanson, I'm sorry. There is no baby."

She looked stunned. Young Galvin nodded and said softly, "As I thought."

"No baby! Of course there is."

"There is a mass, Mrs. Swanson. A large tumor. It is impossible to tell exactly the size or extent of it. I would guess it has engulfed the left ovary and has spread into the abdomen."

Her large face was colorless. "Am I going to die?"

"Not all tumors are cancerous. But even benign ones can grow to such size they inhibit normal functions of the organs."

"Can you ... can you cut it out?"

"I can try. And I may fail. It may be too involved with other organs and tissues to remove. It would more than likely involve surgical removal of the uterus and fallopian tubes. I can't tell you now. And it's not a decision I can make for you."

Though her smile was a tremulous one she said, "Kind of a drastic way not t'have more babies." She looked from one doctor to the other. "What should I do?"

"I can't tell you that. You have a family to consider. Fifteen children, I believe?"

She nodded.

"And all living?"

"Every one. The youngest is five. Two sets of twins. The oldest of my children is fifteen. I don't know what to do." Tears came to her eyes. "I'm scared."

"Yes," he said softly. "I know. Why don't you rest here, tell your husband what the situation is. Or do you wish Dr. Galvin or myself to tell him?"

"I will. We been married a long time, Doctor. I reckon we can say about anything. Doctor, before I talk to him, tell me what choices I got."

Nick peered into the frightened face. Her eyes were steady. She was tough. "Mrs. Swanson, if the tumor is benign you might live with it for many years. If so, you might therefore be risking your life in surgery for something that is not, at this time, life-threatening. On the other hand, if the tumor is malignant, you will most certainly die without surgery."

She smiled a tiny smile. "Can't tell me which horse to back, huh, Dr. Stuart?"

"I wish I could, Mrs. Swanson, but in all honesty I must tell you there is a great deal medical science does not know. Dr. Galvin and I will look in on you tomorrow after you have talked to your husband."

Leaving the ward, Nick went to the lecture room, where he spoke as he did twice a week to new doctors considering specializing in obstetrics and gynecology. He did not do as well this day; he was distracted by his own words to Mrs. Swanson: "There is a great deal we don't know."

Where did tumors come from? How did they start? Why hadn't medical science found a way to ascertain the extent and nature of a tumor without cutting the flesh open? Why wasn't there more they could do for a patient like Mrs. Swanson? Medical science was thousands of years old. Why didn't they know more? Would they ever know more? Would the work of the German, Roentgen, someday allow them to see into the body? He had read several articles about it, some acclaiming X-rays to be the discovery that would lead to the cure of almost everything, other articles that ridiculed the work of the physicist as anything but useful. There had also been articles by religious leaders, including his father-in-law, denouncing the discovery as the work of Satan. He held back an angry frown. He had returned to the Church as he had promised his father, he'd even put in his time on the vestry and was grateful that his term was over. He did not and never would believe that the Church had the right to meddle in affairs of science.

When the day was over, he asked a colleague whose home was not far from his to tell Mrs. Stuart he would be home late.

He was tired as he met Chad Galvin at the Brevoort for dinner. They talked for a few minutes about Mrs. Swanson, and about Nick's practice. Chad, in midsentence, stopped and looked up with an eager smile. "Look, Dr. Stuart. It's Mrs. Fiske. My mother knows her and says she is one of the bravest women in the country. My mother admires her a great deal, says she is a really great actress. I think she's handsome for an older lady."

Without much interest Nick glanced where Chad indicated. He saw a petite, red-haired woman he guessed to be in her middle thirties – "older lady" indeed! As the lady made her way behind a waiter to a table, she was followed by a thin man with a luxurious mustache, who was in turn followed by a tall man with blond hair, a man who bore a striking resemblance to Kit.

God in Heaven. It *was* Kit. Nick could not move.

Chad chuckled. "What do you think? She's something, isn't she?"

Nick did not hear him. He was devouring Kit with his eyes. He looked much thinner ... was he ill? He didn't take proper care of himself ... Every passionate and tender and laughing moment they had shared rushed through Nick's brain in a tangled skein of riotous emotion. He prayed Kit would not see him.

His prayers were answered. Kit did not look in that direction and when he was seated, his back was to Nick. Nick dragged his gaze back to Chad.

"I must be going," he said.

"But we haven't had dessert."

"You may stay, if you like. I feel – indisposed toward dessert just now. Please, Chad. Stay. I need to catch the next ferry home."

And he escaped into the cool early-spring air.

Ever since he had learned Kit was in the city, he had told himself it was such a big city they would never see each other unless Kit returned to Nick's house or unless Nick sought him out.

And now, having seen him only a few feet away, how could he forget him again? His daemon had returned to haunt him.

□

Kit picked up the stack of letters that had accumulated for the past three days. Every minute of those days had been spent consulting with the contractors to be certain his wishes were being followed, or at the theatre itself, or reading the script with Mrs. Fiske. When he had time to think, he missed seeing Rama around the hotel every day; her job at Miss Squires's Academy required her to live on the premises.

He sorted through the letters, thinking he ought to hire a secretary. He was disappointed that there was not one from Lizbet. Usually she wrote at once when she received a gift, telling him he should not have spent the money, scolding him for not delivering it in person, wishing him love. There was a letter from his solicitor, protesting the orders to mortgage the Xavier but enclosing the papers that accomplished it.

Kit held them in his hand. He did not really expect to lose the Xavier and yet ... it was possible. This document could be the instrument that would take away his adopted father's most cherished legacy to him. It would be like losing part of himself. Then with firm resolve he put the document into the small metal box with other important papers. He would not lose the Xavier.

There were a half dozen letters from female admirers; one contained an address and a key. They made advances in varying degrees of explicitness. There was even one written in a heavy, masculine hand and the erotic suggestions were not at all veiled. Too bad, thought Kit, *that* one hadn't included a key.

And last there was the envelope from the housekeeper at the Hill, with her regular report of expenditures. She was required only to send it to the solicitor in London, but since she did not trust solicitors she always sent Kit a copy as well. He tore it open. Odd. Instead of the usual columns of figures and notations it was a letter written in the housekeeper's crisp hand.

> Dear Young Sir,
>   Tis with grief I have to write to inform you of terible loss to us and to yourself. Miss Elizabeth has been most foully murdered and the monster what done it has not been caught.

For a moment he puzzled over the identity of the unfortunate Miss Elizabeth. When realization struck him it was like a fist in the belly, driving the wind from him. Lizbet! Dead – murdered? It could not be! He read frantically on, looking for confirmation that he was mistaken.

> She were discovered by the dairy lad. Poor thing, she had been beaten and smothered and the sheriff said she had been violated. The monster had stole money and likely other things too and vanished into air. There was no clues. We arranged for her to be buried here at the Hill with Mr. St. Denys and his family and we hope you approve of going ahead. There was a nice funeral service in the village church and the rector said she was a good woman. There is only a simple marker at her grave now as we thought you would want to see to that on your return. All the staff here wants you to know we simpathize with your grief, Young Sir, because we know you and Miss Elizabeth was the best of friends.

Best of friends? he thought, too stunned by grief to cry. Best of friends? So much more than that! More his mother than his mother had ever been.

Who could have killed her? And why? Why would anyone think a woman living in a cottage in the country would have anything worth stealing?

Lizbet – who had given him his love of theatre, who had coached his first lines, who had taken him in more than once, who had washed blood from his face, who had taken him to Papa St. Denys and started him on his new life, who had stood by him through the years, who would have fought the world, the flesh, the Devil, and man-eating lions to protect him – Lizbet was dead.

He was jarred by a sudden memory. He had heard a woman cry out in his mind. The woman had sounded like Lizbet.

Tears spilled over and slid down his frozen, emotionless face. He dashed off a letter to his solicitor:

> I want you to immediately take whatever steps must be taken to officially issue a £5,000 reward for the apprehension of the fiend. Nothing must hinder bringing the monster to justice.

As he posted the letter he felt more helpless than he had when Jonathan died. He wanted to seize the killer, beat him with his own hands, choke the life out of him. And all he could do was offer money.

He told the dreadful news to Francis, and then went to Miss Squires's Academy for Young Ladies to tell Rama. They had known Lizbet slightly, and knew how important she was to him without knowing the reason.

In the chill formal parlor at the Academy, Rama's eyes filled with tears. "Oh, Kit, I'm so terribly sorry. It must be like losing your mother."

Kit kept his face free of the turmoil inside him. "She was my mother as far as I was concerned." He picked up his hat. "I must be going. I thought you would want to know."

"Yes. Oh, yes. Kit ... how are you about ... this?" She said it awkwardly, not knowing exactly what to ask.

He pretended not to hear the question.

How did he feel about it? Grief-stricken – and also frightened. He had four great pillars upon which he had constructed the framework of his security: his mind; his acting; Lizbet's support; Nick Stuart's love.

But Nick Stuart's love had proved shallow and worthless.

His acting career was threatened by the Trust.

And now the oldest and firmest of the pillars had been violently ripped from his life.

He was terrified that without the other three he would lose the only one he had left.

And Rourke's dead ghoulish presence was out there, waiting.

16

Minnie Fiske was puzzled but pleased. Something
had happened to Kit in the past few days but she did not
know what. Whatever it was had improved his already
uncanny concept of Angel Clare. He brought to it now
a vulnerable quality that had not been there before. In
fact, it had not been there even in her interpretation of
the character when she first read the script. Angel Clare
had been so easy to condemn before; but now, when he
brokenly begged Tess to forgive him, there was some
uncertainty. Should not Angel Clare be pitied at least a
little for the foolishness that had cost him the woman he
loved as well as putting her feet on the path that led her
to murder and the gallows?

One afternoon he knocked at her door and when she opened it
she saw him standing there with a little-boy-at-Christmas grin.

"Kit," she said with suspicion, "you are up to no good."

"On the contrary, dearest Minnie. I'm up to a great deal of
good." He spoke to someone behind him. "Bring it in, Mr. Morris."
He entered the parlor and behind him was a small man staggering
under the weight of a square wooden cabinet with a handle on top.
"May we put it here, Minnie?" he asked and without waiting for an
answer moved a vase of flowers, a lamp, and two books from a table.

Minnie watched him with open-mouthed curiosity. When the
small man, with a grunt of effort, put the cabinet on the table, she
saw what it was.

"A Graphophone Talking Machine? Kit, what in the world...?"

"Minnie, I give you the twentieth century, right here in your
parlor."

Morris bustled about. He removed the machine from the case,
set it up, put on a wax cylinder, positioned the reading horn, and
then stood at attention. "Ready when you are, folks," he said with
the smile of a proud parent. "Yessir, we're going to make a bundle
from this."

"Kit, what is going on?" she asked again.

"We're going to make a record, Minnie. Some key scenes with just Tess and Angel. We'll reproduce them and sell them to stores that sell Graphophones and records. What we make from the records will likely not amount to much, but the publicity the play will get will be priceless. The Trust can stop our newspaper advertising. They can't stop our records."

She looked skeptical. "I don't know. I've never heard myself on one of these ... contraptions."

"Ma'am!" cried Morris, insulted. "This is not a contraption. It is a delicate, superb machine, the machine which has reached the pinnacle of perfection. No talking machine will ever surpass it. Why, one cranking alone will allow you to reproduce or record as many as five—"

She coughed delicately. "My apologies, Mr. Morris. Well, then. Mr. St. Denys, your humble handmaid awaits."

When they had finished, they both sat and waited tensely for Morris to reproduce what they had done. He removed the smaller horn into which they had spoken and replaced it with a longer horn with a much larger bell. He repositioned the cylinder and cranked the machine. Minnie found herself clutching Kit's hand and not breathing. There was a moment when there was no sound but a slight scratching and then it came, Angel's first light and flirtatious words to dairymaid Tess and her confused, blushing reply. Minnie looked with delight at Kit. Two other scenes had been recorded: the words of Tess confessing her seduction by Alec D'Urberville and the angry and bitter words with which Angel abandons her.

Minnie was so excited she could scarcely sit still. "It's wonderful. But will it not give too much of the plot away?"

"Trust me. It gives just enough away. The ladies will know enough to come with a half dozen handkerchiefs. So what is your verdict? Shall we do it?"

"Oh, yes!"

"And I've made an appointment with Mr. Virgil Wendelin for photographs of Tess and Angel, and whoever is doing Alec. We will have posters everywhere, and while we're at it we may as well have folders and souvenir programmes made up. All you need do is provide the names of the remainder of the cast. And he has agreed to take group photos in costume for the programmes."

"My word. You've arranged for everything."

"I hope you don't mind my plunging in with both feet. I will pay for it all and consider it an investment."

"Then I suggest we start reading with the rest of the cast at once. I've reserved the small ballroom here for our rehearsals until your theatre is ready. When do you think that will be?"

"Within six weeks. The electricity is being installed this week and as soon as there is light I shall pay double the wages and have them work around the clock."

"Good. Have you the dimensions of the finished stage? We can work within an imaginary framework in the ballroom and start blocking."

He nodded. "And what about the scenic artist?"

"Hired. And the electrical lighting artist?"

"I have him." He laughed. "He was fired from a Trust theatre for saying they were a 'bunch of crooks no better than Boss Tweed,' whoever Boss Tweed might be."

She filled him in on the local history of a few years past, adding, "In my opinion, at least, he's right. And now, something I've been meaning to ask for several days. What of Miss Weisberg? Would she consider playing Izz?"

He did not even want to predict how Rama would feel about playing a minor role. "I will be glad to ask her."

❒

Miss Felicity Squires, proprietress of the Young Ladies' Academy, was flustered to have this handsome man unaccompanied by a wife arrive in her office for the second time. She was dashed with disappointment when he asked again to speak with Miss Weisberg, teacher of Elocution and Deportment. With the pull cord that rang in the upstairs dormitory for the spinster teachers, she summoned Miss Weisberg. Rama arrived, looking unlike herself in the black dress with the high collar, a gold watch on a gold chain hanging upon her bosom. As she had done the other time, Miss Squires sat at the desk, hands folded.

Kit smiled his most potent spinster-charming smile. "Miss Squires, I must speak with Miss Weisberg alone."

"I can't allow that, Mr. St. Denys. Our school's reputation is synonymous with our teachers' reputations and our teachers' reputations must be guarded at all times. No spinster may be allowed to entertain a male person unchaperoned."

Her back to her supervisor, Rama rolled her eyes in mock desperation.

"But it is a matter of grave urgency." He looked soulfully at her. "We are cousins, you see, and it is of a serious and delicate family matter I must speak. I know a lady of refinement such as yourself will understand."

She hesitated and then yielded. "Very well. But it is against the rules. And I shall guard the door to be sure no one knows you are alone."

"Thank you."

She left the room. Rama fell into his arms. "Oh, Kit, I'm dying here! It's deadly, deadly, deadly! And these dreadful clothes — and I have to wear a binder because I am too 'well endowed'! Are we ready to perform again? Is the theatre finished? Oh, say it is! I'm going mad!"

"I have a part for you."

"Wonderful! I don't even care what it is. Lady Macbeth? Titania?"

"Izz."

"What?"

"The part of Izz in *Tess of the d'Urbervilles*. Mrs. Fiske thinks you're perfect and so do I."

"Mrs. Fiske!?"

He realized he had made a tactical error. "Rama—"

"Then it's a small part?"

"It's small but important."

She turned abruptly away from him and looked out the window. "I am a leading lady, Kit. I am *your* leading lady. Something you have forgotten while I've been cooped up in this genteel dungeon."

"It's just one play. Then you'll be my leading lady again. The theatre will be a success and we'll build another Company, maybe bring back the ones who went home. Please, Rama. I want you to do it."

She chewed her lower lip. "Only if I also understudy Mrs. Fiske. Will she agree to that?"

"She will," he said fervently, not knowing whether she would or not. If she objected he'd talk her into it. He stood behind Rama and nuzzled her hair. "If it's any consolation, for about two minutes Izz thinks she's going to be Angel Clare's mistress."

Rama snorted, then gave a provoked little laugh. "Then she had about as much chance as I." She sighed. "But what of money, Kit? Here I have a secure job and a regular income."

"But it's a dungeon."

"But once *Tess* is over ... what then?"

"I told you. We'll build another Company. Why not? We can divide our time between New York and London. I'll own a theatre both places."

"And what about the Trust?"

"Everyone working for us will have no association with them. Not that they would have much choice." He put his arms around her from behind and she put her hands over his, leaning back against him. "Then you'll do it?"

"As if you doubt it. I can't resist you. Who can? When do you want me?"

He reached into his inside coat pocket. "Next week. It so happens I have a script with me."

She took it and whacked him with it. "Bloody sure of yourself, Mr. St. Denys! Bloody sure of yourself!"

He felt more cheerful than he had since learning of Lizbet's death.

He was not prepared to arrive at the theatre and walk into a quiet auditorium. There should have been hammers thudding and saws rasping and feet thumping and men's voices engaged in talking and cursing and joking. Instead there was silence. There was no one but Francis, standing alone in gloom on the half-finished stage.

"What's wrong?" Kit asked, going up the side steps and joining Francis. "What has happened?"

"They're gone. The entire lot of them. Carpenters, painters, all of them."

"Gone where, for godsake!"

A voice spoke behind Kit. Kelton, the bogus policeman Kit had hired away from Erlanger, joined them. "The Trust hired them away," he said, shaking his head. "I was afraid o' that."

"I was paying them more than anyone in the city. I made sure of that!" Kit said, his eyes darkening with fury.

"But the Trust found out what you were paying," said Francis. "And doubled it."

Kelton spoke up. "And it's bein' said around town, Mr. St. Denys, that your theatre is dead."

"They do not know me, Kelton. I'll get the workmen if I have to bring them from England."

Kelton fidgeted. "Well, sir, I suppose I'll need t'be findin' myself a new job, eh?"

"It would appear so, Mr. Kelton."

Kelton looked hopefully at him. "But maybe I could just hang around, sir? I could sweep and things like that, or anythin' else you need done. I — why, sir, I got me a wife and five children t'feed."

Kit said, "All right, stay." Then he said to Francis, "I'm going back to the hotel. Coming with me?"

They left Kelton standing there. "Why didn't you sack him?" Francis asked. "If you want my opinion, he's the cause of this. I don't trust him. I think he's been telling the Trust everything you're doing."

"Don't you think I know an honest man when I see one?"

"I doubt it."

Francis's doubts about his judgment annoyed Kit more than he would have admitted and they made the cab ride to the hotel in silence. As they walked past the desk, the clerk called discreetly to Kit, "Mr. St. Denys, a word, sir."

Kit went toward the desk. Francis went on through to the restaurant. It seemed that these days, whenever Kit was around, Francis found himself eating. He was distressed that he was too heavy to fit into any of his old costumes.

"Mr. St. Denys, there is a gentleman waiting to see you," the soft-voiced hotel clerk said. "In the Gentlemen's Sitting Room."

The Gentlemen's Sitting Room was a fashionable cave of dark carpet, dark paisley drapes, dark-toned floral wallpaper, several brass spittoons, and large, threatening potted palms. One of the ugliest rooms I've ever seen, he thought. Depressing. He avoided it whenever possible.

A solitary figure stood beside the fireplace, one hand on the mantel, the other in his pocket, his head slightly lowered. "Sir?" Kit asked. "Are you the gentleman—" His breath stopped for an instant. "Nick?"

Nick looked up and into Kit's eyes.

"What are you doing here?" Kit asked, his voice icy.

"I have been fighting myself for weeks, Kit. I had to see you."

"You mistake me for someone who gives a damn."

"Talk to me, Kit."

"I gave you a chance to talk to me two years ago. You weren't interested then; I'm not interested now. Go home to your wife and kiddy."

"Please talk to me."

Kit shrugged. "I have no desire for this interview. Or for you, for that matter." He kept his voice cool, his face expressionless. Finest acting of my career, he thought. "Would you like to talk here or would you trust me enough to come to my suite?"

"I'd like privacy."

Kit led the way upstairs. In the suite Nick looked around. Luxury. Of course. Kit liked things to be luxurious. He sat in the chair Kit indicated and took the wineglass Kit offered. Kit did not sit, but leaned against the desk, one ankle crossed over the other in a show of unconcern.

"You came to my home," said Nick, searching Kit's face, trying to find a clue there of what went on in that mind he could never fathom.

"I did."

"Why?"

Kit's smile was humorless. "I intended to wreck your cozy life. Your cozy ... *respectable* ... little life. I'm certain you don't have to ask why."

"What stopped you?"

"Conscience. Didn't know I had one, did you?"

"Kit – don't. What stopped you?"

"Your wife."

"My wife? What is that supposed to mean?"

"I mean, if she had been the viperish shrew I expected I would have told her without turning a hair." He frowned and his voice dropped. "She's lovely. You don't deserve her."

"For once we agree."

There was a silence so complete they both jumped when the mantelpiece clock struck the hour.

"Nick, why are you here?"

"I can't stop thinking about you. You're like a – a damned disease. I don't *want* to think about you. And sometimes I believe I'm cured of you and then, without warning, you're back in my mind. I promised my father on his deathbed – I promised God, too, for that matter, that I would never be with another man, that I would never even want another man, especially you." He looked so woebegone Kit almost felt sorry for him. "And here I am. Promises broken."

"Only one? Or both?"

For a moment Nick looked puzzled. Then he mumbled, "Only one."

"I am sorry about your father. When was it?"

"Just after I left the Hill. I was called home."

"So our lives parallel yet again." He told him about Lizbet, and saw compassion in the blue eyes.

"I'm sorry, Kit. Truly sorry. It was a horrible thing to happen. I know what she meant to you." He stood up. "I must leave here. Seeing you is bringing back too many memories."

Kit's voice was a gentle caress as he asked, "All bad, Nickie?" He saw what he wanted to see in Nick's eyes.

"Don't call me that." Nick tried to say it as a warning, but it came out as a helpless plea and he hated himself for his weakness.

Kit said, "I am going to ask you two questions. Will you answer them truthfully?"

"I suppose I owe you that much."

"Did you ever love me?"

The look of astonishment on Nick's face was all the answer he needed. "How can you even ask?"

"And the other question ... Nickie, are you happy?"

"I have every good thing a man could want."

"That is not what I asked. Are you happy?"

"I'm ... content."

Kit made a face. "'Content' is for cows chewing their cud or old lazy cats asleep by a fire! I am proud to say you were never content with me."

Nick pictured his carefully hoarded guilt as black sheep trying to escape through a half-open gate. He slammed the gate shut; he had to keep those black sheep safe or he was lost once again to wickedness. His voice was sharp when he said, "I was a great many things with you. Angry, crazy, jealous, sinful—"

At the last word Kit's eyes sparked. "You were *happy*. Admit it! For one year in your life you were happy. I taught you how to be young and enjoy life. I taught you to stop acting as if your body were a piece of badly made baggage fit for nothing. I taught you to make love, damn it! Until you met me you hadn't a clue!"

"And you learned nothing from me?"

"Oh, yes. I learned how to tolerate a fool."

They glared at each other in mutual hurt and anger.

"Fool?" Nick demanded. "You are calling me a fool?"

"You called me worse than that."

Nick reached for the door. Kit grabbed his arm and turned him half-around. "You are not going to leave here until you admit you were happy with me!"

"You're right," said Nick, throwing Kit's hand off his arm. "I was happy. But *you* are the one who changed all that. *You* are the one who changed everything. *You* are the one who made me see how wicked our ways are."

"You lie. It was you and your damned Puritan condemna–" Suddenly there flashed through Kit's mind a scene he had never allowed himself to see: he and Rawdon on the stairs at the Hill as they must have looked through Nick's eyes. He had been aroused by the liquor and by Rawdon's expert caresses; he could not deny it. "My God," he said.

Nick turned again toward the door. "There is no point in pursuing this. It's just pouring salt in a wound."

"Nickie – wait. That night at the Hill, with Rawdon–"

"I don't want to hear about it."

"I was wrong. I should have shown at least a little common sense and decency."

"A *little* decency is all you ever showed."

Kit bit back his furious retort and said instead, "You damned me without giving me a chance to defend myself. Well, that's the way of your kind; I accept that. But you have to accept me as I am, too."

"I don't have to accept anything."

"You do." He touched his fingertips lightly to Nick's cheek. "Nickie, like it or not we're bound together with a threefold cord that cannot be broken no matter how we try."

"What are you talking about?" Nick asked, recognizing the words as being from the Old Testament. The question was a feeble attempt to fend off the surge of longing that was building in him.

"You know the words, Nickie. 'A threefold cord is not quickly broken...'"

"That – doesn't even – make sense," he protested. He looked at his hand, gripping the door handle so tightly his fingers hurt. He closed his eyes as Kit's warm lips and tongue touched his neck, just below his ear.

"Threefold, Nickie," he whispered. "Our bodies, our minds, and our souls."

"I thought you didn't believe in souls..."

"I do now."

"Oh, God..." Nick did not know if he uttered a prayer or a curse as Kit's body pressed against his back and Kit's hands made him burn with an intensity of need he had not known for two years.

"Give us an hour together, Nickie. For old times' sake. Just an hour. Just to make up for all the pain we've caused each other. An hour, Nickie. In memory of happiness."

Nick turned to face him. "If I do," he cried, "I am damned."

Kit framed Nick's face with his hands. "Then we'll be damned together," he said and kissed him.

❏

It was much more than an hour before they disentangled their naked limbs on the bed. Kit raised up on one elbow and looked down at Nick.

"Welcome home," he said, smiling.

Nick smiled and brushed Kit's forelock out of his eyes. Then the smile faded and he started to speak. Kit put one finger on Nick's lips.

"Don't say anything. If you say anything you'll say too much. Let me say it for you: it can't be as it was before." He removed the silencing finger. "I know that. But—" He lowered his head and gave Nick a lingering kiss. "—but let me have whatever part of your time is unspoken for."

"Yes. Oh, yes."

"I warn you — I won't share you with God again."

In answer Nick pulled Kit's head back down for another kiss and when they drew apart he said, "Kit, your nightmares ... do they still come if you're alone? Do you still need ... someone?"

Kit drew back. "I need you. But if you can't be with me then I have to find whatever sanctuary I can find. You have to accept it. Take me as I am or let us end it here and now."

"Then I suppose I have no choice, do I," said Nick, "but to take you as you are."

"You can't know how thankful I am that you're here," Kit said, and added quietly, "but if you ever leave me that way again I will hunt you down and kill you and then myself."

He was deadly serious as he spoke. His words were not just theatrics; Nick knew he meant it.

◻

Escapes were neither easy nor common from Dartmoor. But Tom Rourke, model prisoner, had stood prison life as long as he could. He hatched several elaborate schemes for escape but discarded them. He worked out a plan with two others to flee from a work detail in the moors by jumping a stone wall, but the day of the planned escape he was assigned to other work inside the prison. A damned lucky day for him. Of the two would-be escapees, one had been killed outright and the other brought back and beaten nearly to death by the warders.

Rourke decided it couldn't be anything that involved someone else. Every time he tried working in tandem with some other bloke it ended bad. So he bided his time. Warder Peabody was about his size and build. He lured Peabody into his cell one night by pretending to be sick. With one well-placed and expert blow he broke the warder's neck, switched clothes, and walked out of the prison a free man.

The search for the escaped convict in the warder's uniform was pursued vigorously. A reward of fifty pounds was offered. His body was found a few days later, floating in a river.

Or so they thought.

A country bumpkin had captured him and intended to collect the reward. All he collected was his death and a warder's uniform.

A steamer called the *Dazzling Lady* set out from Liverpool on a beautiful April day, its destination New York City. One of the stokers was a brawny man with a gray-streaked black beard and mean eyes that kept everyone at a distance.

Thinking it was a fine bit of humor, Tom Rourke shipped out under the name of St. Denys.

With every load of coal he shoveled into the red maw of the boiler he told himself aloud, "Soon. I ain't goin' t'have t'work no more. Live like a bloody gen'leman. Th' brat'll pay through the nose t'keep his secrets."

The other stokers, sweat-streaked and black with coal dust, were happy to give him all the room he wanted. That old man had the muscles of a youngster and underneath the grime was the kind of pallor a man got only in prison. He was crazy, talking to himself while he shoveled and laughing to himself in his bunk.

An American stoker named Jones claimed to know what made the crazy old man tick. "I used t'live in Loosiana," he whispered to his bunk mates. "Lived with a Creole gal for a while. She taught me a lot about voodoo. I tell ya, that ol' man's got th'evil eye. I'm keepin' away from him. Don't want him puttin' no spell on me!"

One of the others laughed. "I reckon you think he c'n change into a bat or somethin'."

"It wouldn't surprise me none," said Jones.

17

When Nick lied to Bronwyn the morning after his reunion with Kit, he waited with detached expectancy for the shame that would follow.

"I'm sorry, dearest," he said. "There was a patient at the hospital who needed me and by the time I had her taken care of I was too tired to come home. I'm sure you understand." He braced himself for her disbelief and suspicion, prepared to lie and lie again if necessary.

She looked at him with the same trust as always. "Of course I do. I knew that would happen when I married a doctor."

Nick was puzzled at first that the sense of sin which had hounded him all his life seemed no longer to be in evidence at a time when it should be breathing down his neck. In place of the guilt there was the sporadic fear that God and the Holy Spirit had given up on him. He'd heard many times that if one persisted in spitting on God's offer of Salvation, then the divine hands would be washed of him and he would be left to his descent into the fire that burneth forever. And in the case of men such as he who gave himself over to the unspeakable abomination of lying with another man as with a woman, special torments had been devised in Hell.

But if he had already committed an unforgivable sin his soul was damned and there was nothing he could do about it. He loved Kit and needed to be with him. He had denied that love, had cursed it, and fought it as long as he could. Yet to his surprise none of it affected the love he had for Bronwyn, Alyce, and the unborn child. He was amazed how easy it was to divide his loyalties.

He spent one night a week with Kit, using patients or lectures as an excuse for staying in the city. On the nights he was not with Kit, he blanked from his mind any speculation about him and the nightmares and other men.

One evening Kit, in a glum mood, took him to his theatre. Nick did not know what to say. When, at Kit's repeated urging to tell the truth, he said it looked like half-finished chaos, Kit sighed.

"I know. I thought to have it finished in a few weeks. Now I don't see how it is possible. The Trust managed to hire my entire work crew away except for that fellow." He made a vague gesture toward a strapping young man. "He's loyal, anyway. But there's not much he can do alone. I have to find workmen. And I have advertised to no avail. I won't admit defeat if it takes every penny I possess."

"What kind of workmen?"

"Well, I wanted skilled craftsmen, but at this point I'll take what I can get."

"Come with me to my clinic. There are a lot of men there who either can't find work or can find nothing but menial work for starvation wages. Some of them, I'm sure, don't even want to work, but if they do..."

"An inspired idea, Nicholas! Sheer genius. I'll come look them over. When do you go again?"

"Wednesday. All day." He chuckled. "I can just imagine your reaction when you see how the poor live."

Kit's smile was ironic. "Oh, Nick. One of these days I will have to tell you a story about a poor little rich boy."

❐

The rehearsals in the hotel ballroom were going very well. Kit was pleased with the actors Minnie Fiske had assembled, and after a tense beginning Rama was fitting into the troupe as if she had always been there. Mrs. Fiske had no difficulty in letting Rama understudy the role of Tess, and told Kit in private that she very much liked the young lady.

She looked archly at him and added, "Might there be a romance in your future? The girl is obviously in love with you."

"We are such wonderful friends, she and I," he said with a smile, "that I wouldn't want to ruin it by mixing in romance."

On Wednesday he went to the clinic with Nick, who by now was recognized and accepted by the people of the neighborhood. Kit, however, was a different story. As Nick had been at first, he was an object of curiosity and resentment. He had rejected Nick's suggestion that he dress a little less grand for his trip to the slums. Instead he put on a linen shirt and stiff collar with a black tie, an elegant rust-colored suit and vest with a watch-and-chain, and finished it off with a jaunty black homburg.

Nick had shaken his head. "You'll be lucky if you don't lose the watch and the hat."

"I want to hire workmen. I'd have a better chance getting them if I look like I can pay them. I can always get another hat and watch."

The neighborhood people often stopped talking or smoking or arguing to stare after the handsome rich man who was with their doctor. A young woman with a bold, saucy face fell into step beside Kit and said in a bantering low voice, "Ye're a pretty fellow, to be sure. I'd give ye a bit o' snug for a bit o' stiff, if you're willin' when ye get away from yon." She jerked her head toward Nick.

"Ah, me dear, me stiff would be willin' but yon taskmaster won't let me out of his sight. Some other time."

"Do I have your word? Molly's me name. Molly O'Shaunessy."

Kit stopped walking and tipped his hat to her. "And a lovely lass you are, too, Molly O'Shaunessy." She gazed after him, dazzled.

The men for the most part either glared or stared. By the time Nick and his companion had reached the clinic, they had collected a sizable following.

Joking with the woman had not come easy, for each step further into the slums had brought Kit closer to his past. The voices, the sounds, the smells, the sights of poverty – different and yet terribly the same. How many Harry Rourkes were here? He caught a glimpse of a blond-haired, sullen boy with a soiled, delicate face who might have been himself or Jonathan. Was there a Tom Rourke in that boy's life? Cold sweat trickled down his sides. It was a mistake to have come here. A mistake. He half expected Pa to step out from the crowd—

"We're here." Nick's voice cut into his morbid thoughts. Nick got up on the stoop and raised his arms. "News," he called, "I have some news for you." They quieted down. "The gentleman with me is in need of workmen. Will you hear him out?"

There was a chorus of agreement. Kit made himself look into their faces. Tom Rourke was not among them. The grimy blond boy was in the forefront, scowling, and no doubt calculating his chances of making off with the watch, chain, and the wallet that was in Kit's coat pocket.

"Gentlemen," he said, his voice carrying to the farthest man. "My name is St. Denys. I own a theatre. Just now the work on the theatre is at a standstill because of some underhanded shenanigans by my rivals. I want thirty workmen who can follow directions, who can do carpentry, cleaning, painting, men who are not afraid of heights. There will be about six weeks' work and I plan to work in two twelve-hour shifts. I will pay fifty dollars a week, seventy-five dollars a week to a foreman for each shift. Because of the problems I have had with desertions, you will sign a contract with me if you are hired. There will be no payment until the work is completed. Anyone not fulfilling his commitment will be paid nothing."

"Ye mean we could work for five weeks and not git paid at all?" asked one incredulous man.

"Exactly. The only exceptions would be someone provably ill or affected by other situations he cannot control. I will tolerate no drunkenness on my time. I will tolerate no lateness and no shirkers. If the work is done well and done in less than six weeks there will be an additional fifty dollars bonus per man." He gazed around, taking the measure of the faces made hard by poverty. He looked at Kelly, with his pugnacious face and curl of hair on his otherwise bald head. "You there. Are you capable of being a foreman?"

Kelly grinned. "For sure I am, Mr. St. Denys."

"Good. Then, gentlemen, if there is a tavern nearby we can begin interviewing. Mr. Kelly, you will assist me." He smiled and saw the hostility thaw. "And I'll buy a drink for every man hired, to celebrate." His gaze rested again on the sullen blond boy. "You there," he said, "do you want to work?"

The boy started, looked around, and asked, "Who, me?"

"Yes, you. What's your name?"

"Mickey."

"Well, Mickey, if you can do what you're told, you can work for me too. These men will need a lot of water carried to them. They're going to work hard and work up big thirsts. Can you do it?"

"Sure!"

"Then come to the tavern with us and sign up."

Kit walked at the head of an increasing group, Kelly at his side. Kelly took him to a tavern called Killarny, and the sign had been painted over more than once. Again Kit was assailed by an almost nauseating sense of familiarity. The smell of cheap liquor, dirty corners, and chewing tobacco and cigars. He called for the man behind the bar to give him a table, a place to write.

In less than two hours he had his thirty men hired, as well as an additional foreman and the boy. He left them drinking their cele-bratory beers and returned to the clinic to sit silently in an unobtrusive corner, observing the people, watching Nick whenever he emerged from the examination room.

Kit had never seen this side of him. The arm around the elderly woman's shoulders, the gentle way he took the howling baby from its mother ... Was this how he was with the little girl, Alyce? And with his wife? And how he would be with the soon-to-be-born infant? The idea was troubling. Nick as family man had never been quite real. Until now.

❐

The workers from the East Side proved to be a blessing. Kelly, it turned out, had done carpentry in Ireland. One of the other men had been a stagehand in London and Francis was delighted not to have to explain to an amateur about the grid, pin rails, the rope system that was to be used to raise and lower scenery, the difference between the hanging of the working curtain, the drape, and the asbestos curtain. The man knew what teasers and tormenters were. He was, in short, a godsend and Francis hired him for permanent work. The men for the most part were hardworking or at least adequate for the work.

Each day when Kit came in to see what had been done, Francis could proudly point out visible progress. The one fly in Francis's ointment of pleasure was that all too often that damned Stuart was with Kit. Once, for an instant, it had occurred to Francis that he could rid Kit of Stuart forever if he just told the man's wife what was going on. He was more ashamed of that momentary thought than of anything he'd ever done in his life.

After a fortnight, Kit stood between Nick and Francis at the back of the auditorium. "It looks wonderful," he said. Several of the men stopped working and grinned at him and each other with pride. "You're doing very well."

"I wouldn't have believed it possible in such a short time," said Nick. The comment mollified Francis a little.

Repairs to the stage floor had been finished and the floor varnished, sanded, and varnished again until it gleamed. Overhead all was ready for delivery and hanging of the sandbags, lines, curtains, and scenery. Broken glass had been replaced. The electrical workers had finished and were gone and light would flood the stage. The auditorium floor, like the stage, had been refinished and needed only the seats, which were to be delivered within the week. From the smallest to the largest, the holes in the plaster had been replastered and the whole painted a cream color.

The next major phase, to be started while waiting for the seats, was the renovation of the dressing rooms and water closets, one for the gentlemen and one for the ladies. New makeup mirrors and wardrobes were being built, and in the largest dressing room – "Mine, of course," Kit said with a laugh – there was a private water closet and bathroom and a locked cabinet which would hold the daggers and jewelry he used in the roles of royalty. Some were paste, costume things, he told Nick, but others were antiques from St. Denys Hill and had precious and semiprecious stones. Nothing of enormous value, but they added such an air of authenticity he had to use them. Besides, the things had lain around unused for generations.

"And now I can show you the upstairs," said Kit. "They are making quick work of it as well."

"Upstairs?"

"There was a loft full of trash, everything from old flats to pigeon droppings when I looked at it." He led the way to the outside stairway that led to a landing and a door. "Take a look." He threw open the door. The loft was now a flat in the making. The floor was being painted by a man in bibbed pants. The walls were papered with something subtly floral. The tiles in the fireplace were darkened by the stain of past fires but other than that they were clean. "This has all been done by Bill," said Kit. "You're doing a fine job, Bill."

The man looked up uncomfortably, grunted something, and went back to painting.

"Through the other door is the–"

Nick laughed. "I know. The bathroom. It's a wonder you're not waterlogged."

"Hold out your hand," Kit ordered.

Nick obediently held out his hand and Kit put two keys on Nick's palm.

"One is to the front door of the theatre and the other is to this room. I can make no greater commitment than that, Nick. The theatre is my life; I'm giving you unrestricted access to it. And if you need to stay the night, even if I should not be here, I want you to use this room. As they say in Spain, *mi casa, su casa.*"

The images he had tried so hard to kill flashed across Nick's mind and something inside him cried, *But what if I found you with somebody else?*

With that uncanny sense that had always mystified Nick, Kit seemed to read his mind. "There hasn't been anyone in the past month, not since the night you came to me." His smile was radiant. "There hasn't been one single nightmare since that night. They're gone. You cured them."

"That's the best news I've ever heard!" said Nick with such warmth that Bill sat back on his knees and looked at them. Nick was acutely conscious of the man's curious gaze.

Kit laughed. "Never mind Bill. He understands."

❐

Two weeks later the cast of *Tess* were allowed for the first time into the St. Denys Theatre. They inspected every corner of the stage and dressing rooms and were delighted.

Minnie Fiske, whose opinion was the one Kit wanted most to hear, stood alone on the stage as Kit stood at the farthest place from her.

"It is splendid," she said without raising her voice. "Can you hear me?"

"Yes," Kit replied. "Damn the Trust. Our show will go on. Can you hear me?"

She threw back her head and laughed. "Dear boy, I heard you loud and clear and soon all of New York is going to hear you!" He ran to join her on the stage. "My husband has the advertising copy all ready," she said, gripping his hands. "All we have to do is insert the date and to the printer it goes!"

"Yes. I have one more thing to show you."

"I don't know if I can bear any more excitement!"

It was raining, so Kit held an umbrella over her and took her to a large brick building behind the theatre. He turned on the electric lights. The organized mess of creation was everywhere.

She clapped her hands. "Oh, Kit! Is this your building as well?"

"It is. As you can see, *Tess*'s flats are coming along and on that side I've got people making other properties that we'll need."

The pieces of what would be the box set for the Durbeyfield cottage were painted and drying. She walked toward a huge flat that was finished and standing up, a painting of mammoth upright stones with other mammoth stones horizontally atop them.

"Stonehenge," she whispered. "Kit, it's breathtaking."

"And will be even more so from the audience's viewpoint. Tomorrow the lighting artist is to consult with me. And here..." He took her into an adjoining room where costumes hung on racks. "...every costume and property we have used, properly labelled."

"It must have cost a fortune," she breathed.

He said only, "Enough," not adding that the Xavier in London was no longer his. That still hurt.

One by one and in pairs the rest of the cast was finding their way to the warehouse and were impressed. In a body they returned to the theatre, where Kit made the announcement they had all been waiting for.

"Four weeks from tonight," he said as they gathered around on the stage, "we will open. We will begin rehearsal tomorrow morning at eight o'clock. There are posters to distribute, so each of you take a handful. Has anyone heard the record?"

Several had. Three had bought the record and then had had to buy a Graphophone on which to play it.

Kit went on. "Ladies and gentlemen, be prepared to be here no fewer than twelve hours a day, maybe more. The wardrobe mistress and costume designer tell me the costumes are almost finished and require only final fitting. The ladies will be here every day and the times you are not required on stage they will take care of the last-minute adjustments. We'll have the dress parade in one week, at which time we will make any final changes in lighting and curtain cues."

"What curtains?" someone asked.

Kit laughed. "I assure you, they will be here. My greatest regret is that we will not have time to open *Tess* out of town and work out any kinks, but time is of the essence. I learned this afternoon that the Trust is also preparing a production of *Tess*. We must open before they do. We still have an enormous amount of work, an enormous number of hours before us. But we will open and we will be so good I *dare* them to open a production and compare it to ours. You may invite two guests to the dress rehearsal if you wish. Are there any questions?"

No one had any. In their faces he saw nothing but determination to beat the Trust at their own game. He wished them a good night. Rama was the last to leave.

"It's a fine theatre, Kit," she said. "I wish—"

He put his arms around her. "What do you wish, little Rama?"

She sighed. "I guess my nose is askew because Mrs. Fiske saw it before I did. And saw it before you fixed it up. I always assumed I would be part of whatever you did." She sighed again. "Francis told me Stuart is back." There was such distaste in her voice that Kit dropped his hands.

"Rama, you are one of my most trusted and beloved friends, but I will never again hear anything against him. Do you understand?"

Defeated, she searched his face. "He is that important to you?"

He gently rubbed the knuckles of his right hand against her jaw. "He is to me what you want to be. I don't know how else to say it."

She nodded and stood on tiptoe to kiss his cheek. "Then all that is left for me is to say, be happy."

❒

Nick wrote a note a few days later and sent it to the theatre by messenger.

> I will not be there tonight or for several days, perhaps weeks. My wife is nearing her time and I don't wish to leave her alone. I feel so torn. I want to be with you but I want to be with her – indeed, I must be with her at this time. You know how I feel. I hope I can attend opening night but I cannot promise. What is it you theatre people say before a show – "break a leg"? (Pray don't! Your favorite doctor will be otherwise occupied!)
> Yours, N

Kit was disappointed, but he had not tried to fool himself by pretending things would be as before.

And then he had no time to think about Nick. The seats were late arriving, the curtains were late arriving, the stage manager quit without notice to work for the Trust. Francis stepped in as stage manager, untried in that capacity, but he proved to be good at it. The rehearsals stretched to eighteen hours and sometimes twenty hours a day. Exhaustion showed in the faces and tempers.

Each night Kit dragged himself upstairs to his newly finished flat, and often fell asleep without even undressing.

"Doesn't matter," he mumbled as he drifted into numb-minded sleep. "Doesn't matter if we all drop dead soon as it's finished. Only thing matters is beating them. Beating the Toad."

❒

A glittering crowd attended the opening night of *Tess of the d'Urbervilles* in the new St. Denys Theatre. There were hushed comments about the soft beauty of the interior with its cream and gold colors and the painted medallion in the center of the proscenium arch which bore the St. Denys coat of arms. In the balcony was a block of seats reserved for the workmen and their wives, dressed in the best clothes they owned or could borrow, some of the styles out-of-date but with shoes shined, collars high, and hair piled into pompadours. Kit had insisted on it, over the protests of his financial manager.

"Free seats don't make money, Mr. St. Denys, and you are in need of money at this point."

Kit had looked at him and said, "The men who want to come, will come and be seated without charge. They may never see another play."

"So what?" the man had retorted. "People like that could not possibly care or benefit from it."

Kit had become livid. "I said they will be seated without charge, Mr. Fletcher. I did not say it was open for debate. And as of tomorrow morning you are no longer in my employ."

In the cast, in a nonspeaking walk-on as a young villager was the fair-haired boy, Mickey, whom Kit had hired to carry water to the workers. Kit had been touched to discover that after rehearsals started, the boy was sneaking in and hiding in the balcony to watch, mesmerized by the world of make-believe. When Kit found out and asked him if he would like to be in the play the blue eyes had lit as if with a thousand candles.

People like that—! Kit thought, infuriated all over again every time he remembered.

The night was a triumph. Kit felt it even as he, as Angel Clare, knelt in agony of soul at Tess's feet to beg her forgiveness of his desertion. He felt it as Tess lay a gentle hand on his hair and said, "There is nothing to forgive." He felt it as the lawmen laid hands on him while Tess slept. He felt it as Tess awoke, saw them, and looked at him with full knowledge that it was all over and that the gallows would be her destiny.

The curtain fell. The audience as one leaped to their feet, and for ten minutes of crying and applause and bravos would not let the curtain calls end. At the back and in the aisles, were other actors and actresses who had come to the theatre, some directly from their own performances, to see the end of the play. Tall, handsome Maurice Barrymore stood in the back of the orchestra, tears in his eyes.

Kit withdrew and let Mrs. Fiske take the last curtain calls alone.

When the lights came up, he saw that Nick's reserved front-row seat was empty and his absence marred the otherwise perfect evening.

An exquisitely beautiful woman came backstage and said in a musical voice to the cast, "Splendid. Splendid." She took Minnie Fiske's hand and said, "Dear Minnie, you were heartrending tonight. And you, sir..." She held out her hand to Kit. "You were wonderful."

"Thank you," he said. "Thank you." He knew he should resent her because she was acting under the auspices of the Trust, in the theatre he should have had. But he could not be angry at the gifted Maude Adams.

The newspapers the next day could not praise *Tess* enough. Words and phrases such as "glorious," "Wagnerian," "breathless," "ecstasy," "victory," "intelligence and restraint," "a miracle of emotional expression, humanity, and genius," "perfect casting" were thrown about with abandon by critics who were commonly pitiless.

❏

The men who comprised the Trust were unhappy. A.L. Erlanger was infuriated that some of the reviews were in newspapers that were forbidden to advertise non-Trust performances. It smacked of betrayal to have that hell-cat's play praised! The Trust withdrew plans to mount a competing production of *Tess*.

❏

On the night *Tess* and the St. Denys Theatre opened, there was across the river an event of such magnitude that Nick Stuart completely forgot about Kit's big night.

At nine o'clock in the evening, after sixteen hours of labor, Bronwyn gave birth to James Daniel Stuart, in the lying-in room Nick had prepared. Young Dr. Galvin had come to assist, but he did more watching than assisting.

Nick held his infant son in his arms and looked with adoration at the ruddy little face, squashed nose, puffy eyes, and rosebud mouth. With one finger he stroked the inky black hair.

Bronwyn smiled a tired but happy smile. "What do you think, Papa?"

"I think he is the most beautiful creature I have ever seen in my life." He laid Jamie in Bronwyn's arms. "And I think he just said his first word – 'Da-da.'"

She gave a faint little laugh, then looked down at the baby. "He is a handsome boy, isn't he? He'll look just like you."

Nick smiled. "Far handsomer than this old dog." He took Jamie from her and handed him to Nanny. "I want you to rest now. Time enough to see Master Jamie."

She nodded, still drowsy from the small amount of chloroform Nick had administered. Within seconds she was asleep.

He thanked Chad for coming and then retired. Before he went to sleep, however, he went into the nursery where Nanny slept in a cot between Alyce's bed and the cradle. Alyce was standing there looking down at her new brother.

"He's funny-looking," she said. "He looks like a monkey. A hairless monkey."

"A little," said Nick, smiling. "But he'll look much better in a few days." He picked her up.

She looked at him sadly. "Now he's here, will you still be my father?"

"Now and forever. And you know I keep my promises."

She hugged him. "I know. You promised me a baby brother and here he is."

18

The desk clerk glanced up and then stiffened. This large, uncouth man did not belong in his hotel. Then the man surprised him by putting a five-dollar gold piece on the desk. The clerk reconsidered. A lot of people with money were eccentric. "May I help you?" he asked, pocketing the coin after a discreet look around.

"St. Denys," said the man, his teeth showing in the gray-streaked beard. "What's 'is room number?"

"He's no longer here. He has other rooms now."

"Where?"

The desk clerk considered suggesting that another gold piece would get that information, but the man looked kind of ... off-putting. "He has rooms over the theatre he owns. The St. Denys Theatre."

"I ain't from 'ere. Write down how t'get there."

The desk clerk wrote it down and slid it across the counter. "Are you ... a friend of his?" It didn't seem likely, but then he knew St. Denys had at one time or another taken most of the men in the city upstairs. Except himself, in spite of hints! Surely this untidy specimen was not thinking *he* would appeal to Kit St. Denys! That was too absurd for words.

The man took the paper in grimy hands, folded it, and put it in his coat pocket.

❐

Tom Rourke left the hotel and set out for the theatre. It was a long walk, but he had just come from stoking coal on a steamer for a month and did not even feel the exertion. He found the theatre and watched from across the street. From another pocket he drew a photograph he had stolen from the bitch friend of his son. He studied it. While he watched, no one looking like that had gone in. Just then two men came toward the street from behind the theatre. They were arguing, their voices belligerent. Rourke crossed the street in order to hear better.

The taller and better-dressed of the men shouted with an English accent, "I said you are dismissed! Don't argue and don't set foot here again!"

The other man made an angry gesture. "You can't fire me. He's the only one what can and he ain't here."

"Get out. I told him you were not to be trusted! I told him there had to be some way the Trust knew everything we were doing. Now get out of here, Kelton. Don't come back. Ever."

"You'll regret this, Mulholland! I'll get even!"

Two gentlemen in bowler hats passed by just then and stared at the two angry men.

Kelton stalked away, pausing just long enough to lift his middle finger to Francis. Francis Mulholland stood there a moment, rubbing the back of his neck. He gave a start when a tall, bearded man approached him.

"Beggin' your pardon, sir, but I couldn't help overhearin'. That chap lost his position, did he?"

"Yes, what of it?"

"Well, sir, I'm lookin' for work. Kind o' down on me luck, you see. These Americans, some of 'em don't take kindly t'hirin' somebody like me, big and rough-lookin'."

"Well, I do need an extra set of hands, and I ought to help out a fellow Britisher." Francis looked him over. "You seem strong enough."

"Like th' bishop's ox," said Rourke with a grin.

"If you're not afraid of hard work..."

Rourke held up his big hands. "I been stokin' on a steamer, mister. I got coal dust in every pore. That ain't work for a sissy."

"When can you start?"

"Now."

"I need a stagehand to carry large, heavy pieces of props and scenery. They sometimes have to be moved fast. You have to follow directions to the letter."

"I ain't a dummy," Rourke said, offended.

"You're hired." He glanced again at the big hands. "There is soap and water in the bathroom. Please get off all the grime possible as some of our pieces are white or light-colored. Somehow thumb-prints all over Stonehenge might destroy the mood." The man just looked blankly at him.

"Come inside with me and I'll get your name for the payroll. I'm Mr. Mulholland and you will answer to me."

As he led Rourke around to the back of the theatre, Rourke noticed the stairway that must lead to the "rooms over the theatre." Excitement shot through him. The brat lived up there. The brat with the answer to everything in his life! He had to get a glimpse of him.

"Mr. Mulholland, Mr. St. Denys is so famous and all, when do I see him? I ain't never seen anyone real famous except I saw the Queen once."

"Oh, he's in and out." They were behind the theatre and Francis motioned to the building behind the theatre. "There is the warehouse where we keep the flats – the painted scenery – and the props. Everything has its proper place there and you must become acquainted with it." He unlocked the theatre's back door and took his new stagehand in, down the hall with doors on either side.

"These are the dressing rooms," Francis explained. "But you will have no need to enter them." He pointed out the bathroom and water closet. "Mr. St. Denys does insist on cleanliness as much as possible. Avail yourself of the facilities there." A balding man came toward them, carrying a chair.

"Mr. Mulholland," he said, "I'm takin' this over to the warehouse to be fixed. If Mrs. Fiske sat in it tonight, she'd land on her backside for certain."

"Thank you, Kelly. Kelly, I just sacked Kelton and this is our new stagehand ... what did you say your name was?"

"Ah – Smith," said Tom Rourke, in case either one of these knew 'Arry's real name. "John Smith."

"Kelly, why don't you take Smith with you to the warehouse and then finish showing him about the theatre. I need to speak with Mr. St. Denys. Smith, Kelly here is just below me in authority."

Rourke said, "Why don't I carry the chair, Mr. Kelly. Firm believer in gettin' in good with me bosses."

Kelly grinned. "You and me is goin' to get along fine, Smith."

Rourke walked beside Kelly, the chair under one arm. "What kind of chap is this St. Denys, anyway?"

Kelly shrugged. "He pays good money. Damn good money. And I like 'im. He's got balls; don't think he's afraid of nothin'. There's talk he's a–" He cut off his own comment. "He's a good man to work for. We work hard but so does he. And he let us and our families come for free to the first time they did *Tess.*"

"Pays good, does 'e? 'E's rich, then?"

"Can't say for certain, but I'd reckon he is. Some say he's got castles and the like back home. And he bought this rundown theatre and put in electricity and everything, fixed everything that was broke, bought new curtains and all, so he must be rich as they say." If he had looked at "Smith" he would have seen a smile of immense satisfaction. They had reached the warehouse and Kelly said, "He might be here. The door's open."

They walked in and Rourke's gaze swept the room which was filled with flats and other pieces of scenery, some in the process of being repaired. Footsteps came toward them and Rourke tensed.

"Mr. St. Denys," called Kelly.

Kit paused and glanced at the two men. His eyes froze on Rourke's face and he paled.

"Mr. St. Denys, this is your new stagehand. Name of Smith."

◻

Kit licked his lips and after a moment of hesitation he came toward them. He was trembling inside, nauseated. This man, this Smith, looked so much like – but it couldn't be – how many times had he thought he saw – He held out his hand, aware it was clammy but hoping Smith would not notice.

"Mr. Smith. Good to have you with us." Had Smith noticed the sweat on his upper lip? The cold hands? Had his voice quivered at all?

"Thank 'e for the job, Mr. St. Denys."

Dear God – the voice – the voice was the same – but Pa was dead – he could see his own hand plunging down twice, see the blood pooling out into the black fur– Insanity. This was insanity. He dropped Smith's hand and took a step backward, his terrified eyes still on Smith's bearded face.

"Mr. St. Denys, Mr. Mulholland is lookin' for ye. He needs to talk with ye he said."

"Th-thank you, Kelly." Kit walked away from them and not until he was outside the warehouse in the sunshine could he breathe. He'd have to find some reason for Francis to fire Smith. He could not have him around. It would drive him mad. He broke into a run and did not stop until he was halfway up the stairs to his apartment. He heard Francis call to him.

"Kit, wait. I need to see you."

He plunged into his apartment and seized a whiskey bottle and put it to his lips, not bothering with a glass. He gulped the liquor, choking. Francis came in and jerked it away from him.

"Kit, what the bloody hell is wrong?"

Kit stared at him with wide, staring eyes. "I'm sick, Francis. I am quite mad. Oh, God. Oh, God. I am mad."

"What's happened, love? You were whistling not an hour ago."

"I can't tell you," Kit whispered. "Hold me, Francis. Tell me I'm not going to end my days chained to a wall in some lunatic asylum..."

"Now, now. Why would you say a thing like that? You're tired, that's all. And what with Lizbet's death and everything else ... But you're not mad. Not even close to it."

Kit managed a shaky laugh. "I – I'm – you're right. I don't know what got into me."

Francis smiled. "You need old St. Francis, that's what. Do you want me to stay with you tonight?"

Almost Kit said yes. But Nick had sent a note saying:

If all is well with my wife and son I will be there for the performance tonight and afterward if you are of a mind to have me stay.

After all, there was the phrase "if all is well" ... Suppose all were not well? Suppose Nick did not come? He would be alone and he knew the nightmare would torment him tonight. He knew it.

He squeezed Francis's shoulder. "My dear friend, I think not tonight. I'm all right now. It was just – a fit of some kind, I think. Too many hours rehearsing."

Francis sighed. "Will you send for me if you change your mind?"

"You may be sure of that."

❏

Tess was having its fourteenth performance that night and it was the first performance Nick saw. And like most of the rest of the audience, many of whom had already seen it once, he had tears in his eyes. The acting was restrained yet so powerful that he forgot he was watching Kit.

The ovation, as it had been every night, was prolonged and thunderous.

Nick waited until the crowd thinned before going back to Kit's dressing room. On stage the stagehands and property master were returning everything back to Act One, Scene One for the next night. A brawny, bearded man came out carrying one of the "stone" altars from Stonehenge, the one upon which Tess had slept. Kit had shown them to Nick and told him that they would be made of a combination of wood, *papier-mâché,* and thin pieces of stone. Nick assumed they would be very heavy. It surprised him to see the man carrying one beneath his arm as if it weighed nothing.

As he went toward the room at the end of the hall, he congratulated each cast member he saw, having learned in his years with Kit before that it didn't matter whether the actor knew who you were or not. He paused as Mrs. Fiske came hurrying down the hall, laughing, her face shiny with makeup and perspiration.

"Mrs. Fiske," he said and she stopped. "Mrs. Fiske, I'm not saying anything new, I know, but you were magnificent."

She curtseyed. "Thank you, sir. I have a magnificent cast. That is the secret." Then she opened the door to her dressing room and disappeared.

Nick knocked lightly on Kit's door. While waiting for it to be opened, he glanced around and saw the big bearded man who had been carrying the altar. The man studied him with a look that seemed to be curious, and then went on his way, presumably to get something else that would be put in the property room until needed for the next performance. Then the man was forgotten because Kit was at the door.

The old dresser, William, filled the bathtub while Kit took off Angel Clare's sweat-soaked shirt and laid it aside. Kit smiled at Nick in the mirror.

"I'm glad you're here. I was getting worried. I presume mother and baby are doing well?"

"Perfect. I still can't believe I have a son." Nick caught sight of his foolish grin in the mirror. "He's probably unique in the annals of infancy." He drew up a chair and sat close to Kit as he removed his makeup. "I've read the reviews every day. They're going to run out of adjectives before long."

"I know," said Kit with a laugh. "I hear Erlanger and Company are having collective fits. I received a lovely note from your wife the other day thanking me for the gift."

"It was — is — a beautiful christening gown. I can't imagine your buying it."

"I must confess. I had Mrs. Fiske buy it for me. My inclination was toy soldiers or something wind-up."

"Well, in another two weeks, Jamie will undoubtedly be walking. You can get him toy soldiers then."

"Of course."

"You look tired."

"I can't imagine why." He uttered a little groan of pleasure as Nick got up, stood behind him, and kneaded the tension-knotted shoulders and neck.

"I used to do this after every performance, remember?" said Nick.

Kit turned his head slightly so that his cheek rested for a moment against Nick's arm. "How could I forget? Are you staying here tonight?"

Nick tilted Kit's head back, leaned over, and kissed him. "Oh, yes. It seems much longer than it has been."

Kit's left eyebrow quirked. "How much longer is it?"

"You are such a nasty, vulgar child."

Kit chuckled, then said, "Sometimes I wonder how I, at least, survived these past few two and a half years."

"I know. I—" He stopped. William, as disapproving of Nick as he had always been, had emerged from the bathroom.

"Your bath is ready, Mr. Kit." He directed a poisonous look at Nick and Nick thought the more things changed, the more they stayed the same. "Am I to go now, Mr. Kit?"

"Please. And be sure to lock the door when you leave."

Nick knew what was in Kit's mind and he blushed deep crimson. The memory of the morning after their first night together and the shock he felt when Kit got into the bathtub with him—

"Kit, don't even think it. The theatre is full of people!"

"So was the hotel, *mon cher*. Hundreds of people."

"Well, I'm not getting in there with you. This time. I'll just watch." He followed Kit into the bathroom, where an ornate, claw-footed tub stood in its pristine glory, with lions carved onto its side and at one end the inglorious and dangerous but vital water heater. As Kit climbed into the steaming water, Nick asked, "I've always wondered but never had the courage to inquire ... how do you come by those scars on your back?"

Kit did not answer, but slid down into the water.

"Kit? Is it something you don't want to talk about?" He was startled by the sudden haunted expression in Kit's eyes.

"It's nothing I *can* talk about. Suffice it to say that I received the scars from the same man who gave me this." He held up his right hand and Nick saw again the bent little finger. "I'm not ready to talk about it. Perhaps I never will be." Then with an obvious changing of subject he said, "Grab the sponge and douse me, will you?"

Nick took off his coat and rolled up his sleeves. Kit looked up at him, his left eyebrow again lifted in suggestive mischief. Nick leaned over and squeezed out the heavy sea sponge over Kit's head, and Kit spluttered. When Nick straightened his eyes turned toward the bathroom door.

"What was that?"

"What?"

"I thought I heard the outer door open." He stepped to the door and, annoyed with William for forgetting to lock the outer door, he shut it, locked it, and returned to Kit. "I think someone must have come looking for you."

"Impossible. William locked the door."

"He's getting old. Getting forgetful."

"His memory is better than mine." As he had the first time Nick sat in a dressing room, Kit rose from the water like a young sea god. "Dry me," he said.

Nick picked up the thick towel that was folded over the brass stand. "Don't think you're going to cozen me into—"

"Into what?" Kit asked, all innocence. "I just want to be dried. And you're so much better at it than I am. I promise I won't make one single voluntary advance to you."

The water dripped from Kit's hair, leaving silvery trails down his face and neck. Dozens of shiny trails slid over his shoulders, chest and belly and his slowly lifting cock. Kit looked down at it and back at Nick with that same innocent expression and said in wonder, as if he'd never seen such a phenomenon before, "Now where did that come from, do you suppose?"

"Kit, you promised—!"

"I said no *voluntary* advances. I can't help it if John Thomas has a mind of his own."

"Well, John Thomas can go to Halifax. I can ignore him."

"To be sure," Kit murmured.

Nick tried. He toweled Kit's hair and face and got as far as his lips before, with a sheepish grin of surrender, he dropped the towel and tasted Kit's mouth and his damp, slightly soapy-flavored skin as he proceeded downward. Kit shivered.

"Ah, Nickie, Nickie, you do learn your lessons well!"

□

The lock on the dressing room door yielded again to the thin wire in Tom Rourke's hand and he noiselessly stepped in and crossed to the bathroom door. He opened it far enough to spy, grinning in lecherous enjoyment at what he saw. Just like he thought. His son was one o' them. And since he'd had to pick the lock open again, he'd almost missed seein' the brat with his fancy-man on the floor at his feet. The little bugger would pay plenty to keep this quiet! He licked his lips, aware that he was getting hard as 'Arry twisted his fingers in the other nelly's hair, threw his head back, and gave a low cry of ecstasy.

Rourke scurried from the theatre and into the first tavern he could find. It took only two whiskeys to find a whore willing to go into the tavern's storeroom with him. She was old and broken-down but cheap and willing to do anything. He threw the money in her face when he was through.

□

The nightmare came as Kit had known it would. It was far more terrible than any he had ever had before...

Rourke was flaying Jonathan's dead body and his brother's rotting flesh was striking him, his face, his hands, his arms, his nude body and he could not get away from it – and then Rourke was stabbing him over and over in every part of his body—

With a hoarse snarl Kit fell upon Rourke, his strong hands about Rourke's throat tightening, tightening—

"Leave me alone," cried Kit. "You're dead, you're dead– Die, damn you!"

Nick, brought to shocked wakefulness, choked and struggled but Kit was strong. Lights danced behind his eyes when suddenly he broke Kit's hold. He shoved him back and pinned him to the bed. Kit's teeth were clenched, the muscles in his neck stood out in cords, his head thrashed like a thing alive by itself.

"Kit!" Nick shouted. "Kit! Kit! Wake up! Kit!"

The glazed look went out of Kit's eyes. "Nickie ... what did I do?" he whispered, trembling as if with palsy.

"You tried to strangle me." He released Kit's arms and slowly moved away from him. "You said the nightmares were over."

Kit did not answer at once, then he said, "Xavier St. Denys was not my father. My real father was a monster; the scars on my back are from his whippings, and he broke my finger for no reason at all. My mother was no better than a whore. I had a brother. A twin. Pa killed him and tried to kill me. He nearly succeeded. I killed him instead." He put one hand over his eyes. "Sometimes when I am half-awake at night I wonder whether I am Jonathan or Harry ... sometimes I truly don't know where he ended and I began. I loved him. He was innocent and gentle..."

In a voice that sometimes broke, sometimes halted, sometimes fell quiet for minutes at a time, he told Nick everything. When he had finished the clock ticking in the bedroom was very loud.

Kit realized his face was wet; he had not been aware of crying. Nick's face was wet, too. He pulled Kit into his arms so that Kit's head was nestled between his chin and shoulder. "Why didn't you tell me this in England? If I'd known, perhaps things would have been different."

"I couldn't tell anyone. If I could have, it would have been you."

"Dear Lord, it's all like a play, isn't it? A tragic play."

"Not all tragic. There was Papa St. Denys, and Lizbet, and the theatre and my friends. And you."

"But what triggered this dream tonight? Do you know?"

"This morning Francis hired a man named Smith. He's the image of Pa. He even sounds like him. Absurd? Of course it is. I know it. But absurd or not I'm going to tell Francis to have Kelly dismiss him. I can't have him around here."

"No. Don't do that."

"I can't look at him every day! I can't."

"When I was a boy I was deathly afraid of heights. My father took me out into the country and forced me to climb the tallest tree he could find. I climbed it, bawling like a calf all the way up. And then he went away and left me to get down alone. Went home. I stayed there for hours, until after nightfall, terrified I'd fall out. Then I got so angry at him I forgot I was afraid. I inched my way down, hating him more with every minute that passed. But I should be grateful, I suppose. At least I've never again been afraid of heights."

"You think I should keep this man on?" Kit doubted the wisdom, and was afraid of the idea.

"I do. The only way you'll ever get over these nightmares is to convince yourself the monster is really dead and couldn't possibly be Smith. Face him. Face your fear. I'll be here; you won't be doing it alone."

"Good," said Kit. He laughed shakily. "I don't think I could do it on my own."

◻

In a tawdry room little different from the thousands of other tawdry rooms he had stayed in all over the world, Tom Rourke stripped off his shirt. He stared into the cracked mirror on the wall, concentrating upon the two hairless ridges of scar tissue near his left nipple.

He would've died if that knife had been in the hands of a grown man instead of his sissy son. He had come out of his faint and had found himself covered with his own blood. The boy was gone. He had staggered out into the street, crying for help. Luckily Blackie Stonebed had been passing by, drunk but not too drunk to help a friend. Blackie had brought a doctor and the two of them had taken Tom Rourke back into his house and laid him down on the bloody sheets. The doctor later thanked his own skill and the fact that Tom Rourke was too mean to die young.

When he recovered he had begun to search for the kid. He wanted to smash his pretty face to pulp and then fuck him like he had his brother and if it killed him too, so what? The world wouldn't miss 'im. But 'Arry had vanished. He might never have found him, but a long time afterward he'd heard an actor in a pub telling how a certain famous actor was nothin' more than a mud-lark who'd somehow wormed his way into money, a lot of money. The actor mentioned the name "Lizbet Porter." Rourke's ears sharpened. Wasn't "Lizbet" the name he'd beat out of Jonathan that last day? Some instinct in his gut told him the "famous actor" was 'Arry.

He bought the man a drink and asked him questions. The description of the famous actor, Kit St. Denys, convinced Rourke. "And he's rich, you say?" he asked, to which the man replied, "Like bloody King Midas."

That day Tom Rourke's ambition changed from smashing the pretty face to bleeding his son dry of money.

As he looked in the mirror, his fingers rubbed the ugly scars and his face tightened with hatred. But there was no rule that said he couldn't get even for the stabbing first. No rule that said he couldn't scare the bloody shit out of the brat first.

He wondered if 'Arry had known who he was, there in the warehouse. He'd looked like he did. Rourke chuckled. He looked like he'd seen a ghost. Then he sobered. But if 'Arry did recognize him, then he would have to move fast, before 'Arry found some excuse to sack him or call the police.

There had been too many delays already. Enough was enough.

19

The dedication of James Daniel Stuart was an Occasion, and little Jamie was dressed in the white, lavishly laced christening gown Kit had sent. Although the church did not christen in the same way other denominations did, Jamie's grandfather held him before the congregation and dedicated him to a life of Christian service. Nick stood beside Bronwyn remembering the intense excitement that such ceremonies had once held for him. He felt like the worst hypocrite in the world when he, along with Bronwyn and the congregation, agreed to see that the child's feet were set upon the Christian path.

After the ceremony, family and friends adjourned to the yellow house for an afternoon of visiting with one another and enjoying the beauty of the flower gardens, abloom with their early-summer blossoms. There were many gifts brought for Jamie, but Jamie was interested in nothing except drooling all over the strings of his bonnet and crying in the rusty voice of an infant for his dinner. Bronwyn took him from the gazebo to the upstairs bedroom and nursed him.

Nick came in not long after and stood watching her. "That is the loveliest scene," he said softly. "Madonna and child."

Her cheeks blushed a little. "I didn't know you were there. And I'm afraid I'm far from being the Madonna."

"Not in my eyes."

A little later, with Jamie asleep in his basket in the gazebo, Bronwyn seated nearby chatting with friends, and Nick also nearby discussing with Chad Galvin the particulars of setting up a practice together, someone said, "What in the world is someone like that doing here?"

Nick heard and glanced up and his heart skipped. Kit was making an entrance through the gate, dressed for riding but looking as elegant as if he were in formal evening wear, his guitar slung on his back. Nick looked at Bronwyn and she laughed at him. "Bronwyn, what is he doing here?"

"I was determined that you and your friend should make up," she said. "And today was the very best day to do it. He, at least, wants to make amends or he wouldn't have sent that beautiful christening gown. Now go on. Speak to him."

For an eternity they looked at each other across the chasm of a few feet. Nick felt as if the entire world were watching him, drooling with avidity to see the look on his face and hear the tone of his voice. His lover, his wife, himself. Together. His heart pounded in his ears. He was angry with both Kit and Bronwyn. What right had she to invite him? Should Kit not have had better sense than to come? Feeling that his movements were wooden, he walked toward Kit and held out his hand.

"It's good to see you after such — such a long time." He could feel Bronwyn's approving smile behind him. Their handshake was perfunctory and brief.

"Your good lady was most insistent in her letter this morning," said Kit. "I am never able to resist a charming lady." He looked beyond Nick and smiled at Bronwyn. "I wonder if I might see the object of all this celebration?"

She laughed. "But of course! Why else do you think you were invited? You are to worship him like everyone else."

Nick did not go with Kit to the gazebo, fearing it would look suspicious. Instead he busied himself getting two glasses of punch, one for Bronwyn and one for Kit. The few seconds' delay would alleviate any speculation. He was startled to see Kit seated at ease beside Bronwyn, holding Jamie — awkwardly, to be sure, but Jamie was not protesting. Words passed between them; Bronwyn and Kit both smiled. Kit returned Jamie to his mother, took his guitar, and tuned it.

As Nick stepped up into the gazebo, he heard Kit say, "I have a confession, Mrs. Stuart. I did not even see the christening gown until today. But I do have a gift for the young gentleman that is of my own choosing."

Soft notes were plucked from the strings and Nick was stopped in his tracks by the sound of Kit's singing, something he had not heard for a long time. How could he have forgotten how sweet and clear Kit's voice was? Tears came to his eyes as he listened to the words of some soothing, loving old English or Irish lullaby, sung by this man who as a child had never known a parent's love. For the first time Nick knew he could no longer keep his two lives separate.

He had been living in a dream world to think he could. The two parts had touched; the edges had blurred.

His gaze moved from Bronwyn and Jamie to Kit and back again. God help me, he thought in agony, if I ever have to choose between them.

The song ended. The other guests applauded, and several ladies dabbed at their eyes with dainty handkerchiefs. Reverend Carlisle scowled his disapproval at the secular music which undoubtedly had tavern origins. Kit looked up at Nick. His smile was rueful, helpless, and devastating.

He stood up, bowed to Bronwyn, and once more slung his guitar on his back, looking for all the world like a traveling troubadour. "Mrs. Stuart, I regret that I must be going."

"So soon! But you just arrived."

"I have a business appointment in the city and it cannot be delayed."

"Do come again when you can visit," she said, looking squarely at Nick and stressing the last word. "You will dine with us soon, won't you?"

"It would be a pleasure."

Nick put in, "If you must leave already, at least I will be a good host and walk you to your horse."

They fell into step beside one another and did not speak until out of earshot of the others.

"Are you angry that I came?" Kit asked.

"I was. Angry at you both. Not now."

"Her letter was delivered by messenger this morning. I wondered how you would feel about it."

"It's ... difficult for me, seeing you together."

"I don't wonder." He glanced sideways at Nick. "I saw it in your face. You know you can hide nothing from me. Don't worry, Nickie. I will never put you in a position of having to decide between us. With her you can have a home, and you are such a domestic puppy you need a home. With me, what can you have? Passion. Which is rather a flimsy reed to lean upon."

Nick's voice dropped as if the trees around them could hear. "It's more than just passion and you know it."

"Yes. I know. But you can't leave them."

"No."

"I rest my case." He reached into his inside pocket and removed a small book, handing it to Nick. "I bought this for you long ago, in England, at a rare book shop. I took it to the Hill, to give it to you there, but ... well, things fell out as they did. I've carried it with me all this time, thinking that when I found you I would throw it in your face to make you feel guilty. Now I give it to you as I meant to do so long ago and far away."

It was a small volume bound in soft brown leather. In faded gilt letters it said: *The Sonnets by William Shakespeare*. The printing date inside was 1766. On the flyleaf were words written in Kit's fine hand:

> Without the sanction of Society
> without the sanction of the Church
> without the sanction of God,
> I love you

Nick could not swallow the lump in his throat. "Thank you. The sonnets. I loved to hear you recite them."

The gentle breeze fanned their faces. A cardinal called his mate somewhere in the trees.

"'Why, fearing of Time's tyranny, might I not then say I love you best?'" Kit quoted softly. "I remember that was your favorite."

"I remember so many things." In the sunlight he could see fine lines radiating from the outer corners of Kit's eyes and other fine lines leaving faint trails across his forehead. He knew such lines were on his face as well. They were no longer boys. "Time's tyranny." Why was the word "love" so much easier for Kit to say than for him? "I don't think I could live without you, Kit."

"Of course you could. You have." Kit looked up at the almost painfully blue sky, accented with a few lazy clouds that seemed painted on. "I feel like kissing you here and now." He burst into laughter at Nick's consternation. "Oh, Nickie! You always take me so literally. I must be going. Your guests will be talking." He swung up into the saddle and gazed down at Nick. "When will I see you again?"

"Tonight."

Kit nodded. "Until tonight."

Nick watched him ride away, then put the book into his pocket and returned to his wife, his children, and his guests.

At the theatre Kelly was furious. "I told that bastard to be here at four o'clock and he isn't here yet." There were some heavy pieces that needed moving from the warehouse to the stage in preparation for the performance that night, and Smith was the strongest man in the crew. Kelly pulled two workers from another job and sent them to the warehouse for the pillars.

Rourke, at that moment, was sleeping off a bout with whiskey from the night before. After this night he planned never to work again.

Before going to his room for a brief lie-down before getting ready for the performance, Kit went to the office of the recently hired business manager.

"How are ticket sales, Mr. Shepard?" he asked.

Shepard, a gnarled man who looked older than his years, had been hired on the basis of Judge Wescott's recommendation and so far was proving his worth. He had already discovered some over-payments, and there were things missing that Kit suspected had been taken by the Trust's spy, Kelton. The business manager grinned.

"Couldn't be better, Mr. St. Denys. Sold out every night this week, as we have been since we opened. There are perhaps a half dozen tickets left for Saturday's matinee." His grin became wider. *"And* one block of tickets for tonight's performance was bought by an agent for Ava Astor."

"Well, well. So La Divine Astor is going to desert her Trust friends and come see us. We'll give her a performance she will never forget."

"Indeed you shall, Mr. St. Denys. And you'll be glad to know that if sales keep up as they have been, you may see a profit by the time the run is finished. A *small* one, understand, but a profit nonetheless."

"That is good news!" Kit was relieved. He had lost the Xavier Theatre and had mortgaged some of the land St. Denys Hill stood upon. He didn't want to lose that too.

From there he went to his rooms over the theatre. Performance before La Astor – and afterward he would be sure to meet her and charm her beyond all endurance. If she chose to invest in the theatre it would be a godsend. And then afterward, there would be Nick and a night of love in all its manifestations.

He took a bath, read the script of Ibsen's *A Doll's House,* which Minnie wanted him to direct and produce, and then went to sleep, his mental clock set to wake him in an hour. He hated taking time to rest, but the nightly performances and worry about money were taking their toll. He woke refreshed and joined Francis for dinner.

❏

There was an hour every day when no one was in the theatre, Rourke had learned by observation. Between the placing of the last prop and the time set for the cast and crew to return, the building was deserted. He chose this time, at twilight, to come to the theatre and go up the stairs to his son's rooms. He knocked on the door, but there was no answer. He tried the door; locked. The ever-present thin wire appeared in his hand and within moments he was inside.

Looked like a bloody female's place! he thought in contempt. Pictures, fancy tables, la-de-da china gewgaws, Oriental rugs on the walls. He saw a statue of a naked man and spat on the floor. He tiptoed to the bedroom.

Empty.

"Damn," he muttered. Stay or try again later? Just then he heard footsteps coming up, then heard a key in the lock. He hid in the wardrobe in the bedroom. He heard someone – it had to be 'Arry – walking around the parlor and then there was a slight squeak as if they had sat down. Rourke cautiously left the wardrobe and peered out into the parlor.

The brat was at a small desk, writing something. Rourke took a step forward, when someone knocked on the door; he ducked back into the bedroom and peered through the crack between the door and the frame. The brat got up and went to the door. A man came in with something wrapped in a cloth. 'Arry took it out. It looked like a dagger with a jewelled hilt. Rourke licked his lips. Real jewels? Of course. 'Ad to be: 'e was rich, wasn't 'e?

The brat inspected it. "It looks fine," he said. "You do good work." He counted out some money into the man's hand. The man bobbed his head and left. But 'Arry, instead of returning to the desk, left the apartment. Rourke cursed. A few minutes later he followed. The brat was not in the dressing room, but he soon would be.

Rourke looked in the dressing room's tall wooden cabinet. Gor! Jewels everyplace. Rings and knives and swords and crowns – looked like th' bloody Tower. He tucked a jewelled dagger with intricate carving into his coat, sure it was the one the man had just brought back. Then he hid behind a folding screen in the corner. If he had to wait all night it would be worth it.

❐

Kit was whistling as he let himself into his dressing room, puzzled that the door was unlocked. He was certain he had locked it. He decided to go ahead and get dressed without William's help tonight.

As he pulled on the loose, soft-collared shirt, coat, and trousers of Angel Clare as a student on holiday, he thought it would be a joy to do Shakespeare again and put on the crown of Richard or Lear, or the bright colors of Romeo. Or maybe the intense black of Hamlet. He especially enjoyed the role of Hamlet and Nick had been urging him to do it again. Perhaps he would forget directing Minnie in *Doll's House* and get back to what he loved best to do.

He stood back to inspect his image and was satisfied. He sat down to apply the makeup.

"'Arry. Me boy."

His heart stopped beating. His breath stopped in his throat.

"'Arry. Don't ye want to give yer old pa a kiss?"

Kit leaped to his feet, sending the chair clattering over backward. There was a bare instant between seeing Rourke and the moment when Rourke was on him, the huge hands on his throat, the big body toppling him backward onto the makeup dresser. The little pots and powder containers flew off the dresser and smashed against the floor.

Kit was paralyzed by terror. All he could do was gape at the grinning, evil face over him.

"Can't ye even fight, ye little bugger?" Rourke sneered. His thumbs pressed against Kit's Adam's apple and he choked. "Yeah, I know you're a fairy-queen, me boy. And if ye don't want everyone else t'know it, ye'll pay me and pay me good and keep on payin' me as long as I want it. An' what would your fancy friends say t'know you ain't no St. Denys at all but me own long-lost boy who tried t'kill me!" His eyes glittered with hatred. He eased the pressure on Kit's throat. "Reckon I better be careful. Don't want t'kill the goose with th' golden egg, now do I!"

•242•

"You're dead," Kit gasped. "You're dead. You're not real."

"Oh, I'm real all right. Ye bastard! Ye whoreson! Tryin' t'kill your own pa!"

Kit's numb mind told him – This isn't real, it isn't real, it's just another nightmare, Nick will save you from it–

Rourke shook him savagely. "Well? Will ye pay or not?" He removed one hand from Kit's throat and slapped him with the full force of his arm.

Kit's head snapped back. The pain was real. As real as it had been on that last day in the shack the day they buried Jonathan. The big hand cracked his face again. He tasted blood.

"You ain't nothin' but a coward, a pussy. You make me ashamed to be your pa," growled Rourke. "Won't even fight t'save your skin."

"You killed my brother," Kit choked.

Rourke laughed. "Yeah, and that ain't all I done to him. He was a little fairy just like you. But he died happy, gettin' his brains buggered out. Didn't lose much when he croaked."

Blind rage devoured his fear. Kit jerked his knee up, hard, to smash into Rourke's crotch. Rourke gasped and staggered back; the dagger fell from his coat and clattered to the floor.

With no thought except to kill this beast once and for all, Kit launched himself toward Rourke and drove him backward into the cabinet and then to the floor.

Rourke's fist smashed Kit face once – twice – Something crunched; pain exploded in Kit's face and blood streamed from his nose. They grappled, bucking and rolling. Kit was blinded by blood from a gash on his browbone; he gagged on the blood in his throat. Suddenly Rourke overpowered him, and was holding him pinned flat against the floor. He lay on top of Kit, hard and aching to punish the brat as he'd punished his brother, as he'd punished that Porter slut and many others. He forgot the millions he would get from blackmail. All he could think of now was the hated face, the spittin' image of his bitch wife. "I'll teach you," he snarled. "I'll teach you. Ye worthless man's cunt, I'll split ye in two–"

Kit flung out his hand and his fingers closed upon the dagger – repaired, polished. And sharpened.

With all the strength he possessed he slashed the knife deep across the soft throat just under the dark beard. Rourke stiffened. Gurgled. Blood rained down upon Kit's hands, his face, his clothes.

Rourke fell on him. Kit shoved the heavy body aside and got to his knees. Sobbing, he raised the knife in his slippery hand and plunged it downward.

Again.

And again.

And again.

And again.

And again.

There was no thought. There was only the mechanical lifting of his arm and its downward plunge and the sobs.

Again.

And again.

And again.

❒

William's feelings were hurt that Mr. Kit would lock him out of the dressing room. He'd known for a long time that Mr. Kit would like for him to retire and didn't know how to suggest it, but this was an unkind way to do it. Sadly he turned away and left the theatre. He had never gotten drunk in all his seventy years. It was time.

❒

It was Kit's custom to go to each room before a performance and greet each performer, make a joke, ease some of the high-strung nerves. They wondered why he didn't come this night. Rama and Francis, meeting in the hallway, spoke of it. Rama had an instant answer.

"I suppose," she said in a tart, low voice that no one but Francis could hear, "that he's been cavorting with Stuart upstairs!"

Francis did not want to admit she was right, but she probably was. He went on his way, to make a last-minute check backstage.

❒

Minnie Fiske was mystified, for she, Kit, and her husband always had a small glass of sherry together before the opening curtain. Well, Kit was a man, after all, and they were a mysterious species. She drank her little glass of sherry with just her husband for company.

◻

Members of the audience craned their necks and whispered excited-
ly as a grandly dressed party of twenty took the box seats to the right
of the stage.

"It's one of the Astors, Ava I think," was the whisper that snaked
through the audience.

"It's all the Astors," whispered somebody else. "Look at the
diamonds! Think they own the world."

"Don't they?"

◻

Nick had been delayed at the hospital and arrived just in time for the
opening curtain, still wearing his workday suit of clothes. Impatient,
he sat through ne'er-do-well Jack Durbeyfield's discovery that he
was in reality Sir John d'Urberville. He fidgeted through the arrival
of the young farm lasses and their dancing among the flowers, with
each other for partners as there were no men present at the moment.
He sat up in eager anticipation as the moment came for the three
Clare brothers to appear, at which time Angel Clare would first set
eyes on Tess.

The action on stage faltered. Minnie Fiske began throwing in
lines that Nick knew were not in the script. He tensed. Kit never
missed a cue or an entrance. Never. The actresses carried on,
valiantly improvising. There was the sound of hushed, distressed
voices backstage. Two of the Clare brothers came on and they, too,
Nick knew, improvised, waiting for Kit's arrival.

Then the speeches and the acting floundered. Francis Mulholland, stage manager, stepped forward. "Ladies and gentlemen, there
is a slight delay in the continuation of the play. We beg your
indulgence for but a few minutes and then we shall continue."

The curtains slid closed. Nick was out of his seat before the
curtains met in the center, almost running backstage. He seized
Mulholland's arm as he left the wings.

"What's wrong? He's never missed." He saw worry on Mulholland's face.

"Wait—" Francis turned to the cast, who were crowding around
him. "Get back to your places. Every one of you. Kit will be here
any moment. He's been delayed and your heads will roll if you're

not in your places when he gets here." Reluctantly, they did as he said, shepherded along by Minnie Fiske, whose forehead was wrinkled with concern. "Come with me," Francis said to Nick. "I tried to get into the dressing room but there's something blocking the door. I'm afraid he might have fallen."

They ran to the dressing room and, putting their shoulders to it, managed to shove the door open against Rourke's legs. The door of the cabinet had sprung open when Rourke struck it and the floor was littered with fallen paste jewels, crowns, rings, knives. Two figures were in the center of the room. None of the rubies were as red as the red that pooled out around the man on the floor. None of the rubies were as red as the red on Kit's face and hands and clothes as he mechanically lifted the knife and drove it into the chopped flesh of the man's chest.

Nick and Francis looked in horror at Kit and then at each other.

"My God – what – it's Smith! Why–?" choked Francis.

Nick knelt beside Kit, ignoring the puddle of blood. There was no point in checking the bearded man's pulse, for his eyes and mouth were both eternally stretched wide in disbelief. Nick knew instinctively who he must be. It did not matter where he came from or how he got there.

"Kit," Nick said softly, "Kit, it's over. Give me the dagger."

Kit did not look at him. He kept his eyes fastened upon the corpse. He lifted the dagger and plunged it in again.

"Kit ... give it to me."

The terrible movement of Kit's arm was sluggish, as if he had barely enough strength left to raise it. Nick reached for the knife.

"Be careful, man!" cried Francis. "He may turn on you! My God, oh my God, this is – oh, God–"

Nick caught Kit's wrist in midplunge. For the first time Kit seemed to realize he was not alone. He looked at Nick, his face a crimson mask. When he spoke it was in a blood-freezing, conversational manner.

"'Yet who would have thought the old man to have had so much blood in him? ... What's done cannot be undone...'"

"That's from *Macbeth,*" said Francis. "Kit, don't you realize what you've–"

Nick put up a silencing hand. "Kit. I'm going to take the knife." He had to pry it from Kit's grasp. Kit seemed not to notice. Nick was stunned when Kit looked away from him and began to once again plunge a knife visible only to him, into the chest of his father.

"'Yet who would have thought the old man to have had so much blood in him?'" he said again. "'What's done cannot be undone...'"

"Kit," cried Nick, seizing the crimson hand. "Don't you know I'm here? For godsake, look at me!"

"'Yet who would have thought the old man to have had so much blood in him? What's done cannot be undone...'" Then Kit fixed his glazed eyes on Nick. "Where is my brother?" he whispered. "What have you done with him?" He clutched Nick's arms and cried, "Where is my brother? What have you done with him?" Before Nick could react, Kit folded forward and fell unconscious into Nick's arms.

20

The story exploded into the public consciousness in bold sensational headlines:

FAMED ACTOR GOES BERSERK
WORKMAN MURDERED BY ACTOR
MURDER ON BROADWAY
ST. DENYS INSANE?

Words such as "frenzy" and "bloodbath" were everyday fare for several days.

Tess shut down. The theatre was temporarily closed.

Against the protests of Nick, and Kit's other friends including Judge Wescott, Kit was taken into custody and sent to the New York City Lunatic Asylum on Blackwell's Island to await indictment.

Nick tried to see him, but was not granted admittance. Enemies became allies as Francis and Rama and Nick racked their brains for a solution. Harrison Fiske contacted a friend who was a clever muckraking newspaper reporter. The reporter gained access to the asylum and a series of articles appeared blasting the inhumane conditions there.

"Thirteen hundred men and women in a place built for three hundred," the newspaper trumpeted. "Foul food. Beastly conditions unworthy of Nineteenth Century enlightenment. Epidemics of cholera, dysentery, influenza sweep through regularly. Patients die of starvation or mistreatment. Some are shackled to walls in filthy cells. That anyone, let alone a gentleman such as St. Denys, should find himself in such a snake pit is deplorable."

Kit was removed from there to Petrie Mental Asylum, a private institution. "Asylum as in sanctuary," the director told Nick in an unctuous, soothing voice. "A place where the patients can be safe and sheltered."

"When may I see him?"

"Are you his brother or other blood kin?"

"No."

•248•

"Then, I'm sorry. Until the Court decrees otherwise he can have no visitors other than family members. You understand. He is accused, poor creature, of a heinous crime."

Through the spring and early summer Nick waited, sleeping little, dreaming often. Kit was indicted and brought to trial five months later. At the trial Nick saw him for the first time since that dreadful night and almost cried out in protest. This gray-faced, gaunt man with the vacant eyes and irons on his wrists and ankles – was this his beautiful Kit? What were they doing to him there?

Throughout the trial Kit sat silent and unmoving, his face blank, his eyes empty, and Nick knew that though Kit's body was alive and present, Kit St. Denys was no longer there.

The State called the medical examiner, who testified that the deceased had been stabbed in the chest forty-four times at least, quite possibly many more. Nick and Francis Mulholland were called as adverse witnesses to describe what they had found in the dressing room at the St. Denys Theatre. The dagger, still showing Rourke's blood, was introduced as evidence as were drawings by police artists and photographs of the deceased, and photographs of the accused covered with blood at the time of his arrest.

The defense attorney called a physician who testified to Kit's battered condition, which was obvious – the broken nose, the scar on his browbone. He showed photographs of Kit before the tragedy. Francis Mulholland testified he had hired Rourke who had given a false name; he broke down on the witness stand. "If I hadn't hired him," he wept, "this never would have happened." The hotel clerk testified that a man identical to the deceased had gotten Kit's address from him. Kelly testified that the deceased had used the name Smith and had asked many questions about Mr. St. Denys.

Nick was the last witness. To save Kit's life he had to tell Kit's story, and the journalists were all there scribbling as fast as their pencils could go. He told the Court everything Kit had told him about the hell of his childhood and the abuse at his father's hands. His words fell into a hushed room as he told them about the nightmares.

The prosecution, on cross-examination, asked the one question Nick had been dreading: "How do you come by the knowledge of these nightmares, Dr. Stuart? They sound like the sort of thing only an ... intimate ... would know of. A wife, perhaps, or a–"

"Your Honor," said the defense attorney, "I object to this question as irrelevant."

To Nick's relief, the judge agreed.

The newspapers sold record numbers of papers with headlines such as:

ST. DENYS VICTIM KILLER'S OWN FATHER
GUILTY VERDICT WILL BRING DEATH PENALTY
WILL ST. DENYS HANG?

The judge ruled Thomas Rourke's death at the hands of Christopher St. Denys, born Harry Rourke, to be justifiable homicide. Though the defendant had killed to save his own life, the judge added, and was therefore exonerated of criminal manslaughter, there remained the question of public safety. The defendant was deranged, and though the Court might be disposed to pity the Court must also take into consideration whether public safety would be served by releasing him. It was the Court's decision that Christopher St. Denys be declared a menace to society and returned to protective custody until such time as a competency hearing could be arranged.

Nick leaped to his feet shouting, "No! You can't do that! You can't!" He tried to shake off the restraining hands of the bailiffs, but was forced back into his seat, sick at heart.

❐

Nick stood at the barred window of the asylum and looked out over the grounds. Summer had come and gone; the leaves of the trees had turned. On the other side of the bars the world looked colorful and happy.

The Petrie Asylum was a private one, and Kit's money was legally untouchable. Grieving and outraged by his fellow judge's decision, Philip Wescott was paying for Kit's care. The plainness of Kit's room was depressing, with its walls of muddy green. A narrow cot. A commode. A small dresser bolted to the floor. No curtains ("He might hang himself"), no pictures ("He might shatter the glass and commit suicide"), no books (they looked at Nick as though he were simpleminded when he asked), nothing of the things Kit had loved, the things that made life civilized. Around the grounds, though aesthetically disguised by shrubbery and trees, was a brick wall with iron spikes atop it.

Nick leaned his forehead against the inside bars. Then he straightened and turned toward Kit.

Kit lay curled up on the cot, his eyes open but blank. Whatever he saw was happening only in his mute inner world.

"Kit, I wish I knew if you even heard me," said Nick softly. He put his hand on Kit's shoulder. Kit neither shrank away nor looked at him.

Nick sat down on the bed beside him. "Your friend Wescott is pulling strings to get the hearing before him as soon as possible. Then he will grant my petition to be your guardian. As soon as I can, I will take you home. You'll recover there. How could you not? With the laughter of the children, and Bronwyn's kindness, and my love – how could you not?" His voice cracked on the last word.

❒

"Mrs. Fiske is keeping the theatre going for you," Nick told him on another visit. If anything could penetrate the fog that enwrapped Kit's mind, it would be news of the theatre. "She's paying rent to your account, and she's in rehearsal with *Doll's House*. She sends her best wishes and hopes for your recovery. Miss Weisberg has returned to her tutoring job but as soon as you are performing again, she's leaving it for good to perform with you."

When speaking to Kit he never looked away, afraid that if he did he would miss a flicker of response.

Kit's hair had been allowed to grow long and shaggy and hung to his shoulders; he had not been shaved for several days and a rough beard darkened his jaw. He smelled sour as if he had not been bathed for a long time. To Nick that one detail was heartbreaking. How often had he teased Kit about growing gills or becoming waterlogged? For all the money they charged, they could not even see that he was properly groomed!

As the weeks passed Kit became very thin and Nick noticed ulcerations forming at the corners of his mouth. Kit would not open his mouth for Nick's concerned inspection. When asked about the ulcerations, the physician in charge said, "He won't eat. We have to force-feed him."

"Force-feed him? And how is that done?"

The doctor fidgeted under Nick's questioning stare. "There is a steel gag we use to pry the mouth open and keep it open. And then we pour down what we can through a tube. When the patient starts vomiting we know it's time to stop." At Nick's angry expression he said, "Well, we *can't* let them starve, can we?"

"Give me some food. Now. Let me try."

He was given a small bowl of broth and he returned to Kit's room.

"Kit, please hear me. You must eat. You must keep your strength up until you can leave here. Please, love, eat. For me. For your Nickie." He held a spoon close to the sore lips. After what seemed an eternity, just as he was ready to give up in defeat, Kit's mouth opened. Nick spooned in the broth. Kit swallowed, and Nick could tell it was painful. But with coaxing Kit took another spoonful and another.

"Let me see your mouth. Please. Please hear me and listen."

Again there was a long pause before Kit opened his mouth. His tongue, gums, and the visible part of his throat were raw and inflamed. Nick shook with fury.

"They won't do that to you again if I have to go to court!"

Before he left he stormed into the administrator's office and demanded an end to the forced feeding. He lay before him his own credentials as a doctor and said, "I will hire a private nurse if necessary to come here every day and see to this matter if you are unable to do so. But be assured, if that is the case it is going to become public record."

The forced feedings stopped.

❏

Every day he went to the asylum. Every day he held Kit's unresponsive hand and vowed, "We will win out over this, Kit. You'll get well. You'll act again. You'll be the greatest actor in the world again, very soon."

Kit, as always, did not seem to realize anyone had spoken to him.

"It's hard to believe the world can go on without you in it," said Nick. "I read the *Dramatic Mirror* now, just so I will know what's happening in the theatre. Someday you'll ask me and I'll be able to tell you. Mrs. Fiske said to tell you that the Trust has competition from a couple of brothers named Shubert, and the Shuberts have bought several theatres and have offered them to her as soon as she wishes to use them. Isn't that good news? Maybe before long the Trust will disappear like snow in April."

❏

It was a winter day with thick snowflakes turning the air to living lace when Nick came to Petrie Asylum to take Kit home. He was now the legal guardian, thanks to Judge Wescott's string-pulling and quick judicial ruling. Nick was excited as he helped the nurse dress Kit for the journey across the river. Kit's clothes hung on his bony frame and he neither assisted nor fought them as they put on boots and coat, hat and gloves. His hair had been cut at last and his beard removed.

Unannounced, the psychiatrist who had been treating Kit strode into the room. Nick had asked many times to consult with him and had always been refused. "Stuart, what do you think you're doing?" he demanded.

"Taking him home."

"You're a fool. You don't know what you're letting yourself in for. You're not trained—"

"But you are and you've done nothing for him."

"Are you prepared if he becomes violent again? Are you?"

Nick ignored him. He hoped the trip out into the cold snowy air would arouse Kit's interest, but Kit moved through it like a tall, handsome puppet.

❐

Bronwyn met them at the door of the house, her face warm with pity. "Mr. St. Denys, welcome to our home. It is your home for as long as you wish it to be." Nick had warned her, and she did not expect Kit to respond. She was shocked by his appearance.

Nick said, not expecting an answer, "You remember my wife, don't you?"

He led Kit upstairs to a room on the second floor, a room with two windows that looked out toward the gardens now white with snow. The walls had been painted a soft blue and Bronwyn had put up white curtains and framed prints. There was a soft, comfortable bed. The room was across the hallway from the newest bathroom in the house and there was a washstand in the room, with a bowl and pitcher of water.

"It's your new home, Kit. Until you are well again."

Kit, under Nick's guidance, walked into the room and sat down on the bed at Nick's suggestion. So he did hear and accept things into his mind. Nick's optimism grew. If he talked enough, every day, Kit would come out of his numbed world. There was no longer any doubt about it.

Kit lay down and curled up in his customary fetal position. Within seconds he was asleep.

Nick watched him for several minutes, then left. He paused outside the door, biting his lip. Then, unable to forget the psychiatrist's warning and all too aware of his responsibility toward his family's safety, he reluctantly locked the door.

❐

Days passed into a week, then two. Nick took a leave of absence from the clinic, turning it over to young Chad Galvin. This left him his hospital duties and his private patients. He figured and refigured his financial situation, knowing he would have to hire a nurse to look after Kit. In desperation he bit the end of his pen as he did the figures once more. Feeling like a beggar, he called upon Judge Wescott the next day. He had, after all, told Nick he would help in any way, to any extent. But it hurt Nick's pride to ask.

The judge welcomed him, and gave him a glass of wine which he gulped. The judge's eyebrows lifted and then he asked, "And how is our friend, Stuart?"

"The same, I'm afraid."

"I understand you took him home two weeks ago. The asylum called me."

Nick smiled. "I'm not certain the ink was even dry on the decree before I was there. You're welcome to my home, Judge, any time you wish to see him."

A shadow passed over the lined face. "I ... probably will not. I saw him at the trial, and once in the asylum and I don't have the inner strength you have. I can't bear to see him less than he was. I care about him very much. But I can't see him like that."

"It's hard for me, too," said Nick, with a tinge of resentment. "I have a purpose in coming here, Judge Wescott. I need your help again. For Kit."

"Anything I can do, I will do. What is it?"

"I have cut my patient work as much as I can, but he needs someone with him during the time I'm away. He needs to be fed and dressed. I don't have time to do it."

"And you need a nurse." The judge went to his desk, opened a drawer, and withdrew a leather-covered book of bank draughts. He had one written before Nick even answered, "Yes."

Nick took it. "I can't thank you enough."

Wescott waved his hand in casual dismissal. "Money is all I can give him, Stuart. It's little enough, after all."

The nurse Nick hired was one with whom he was familiar from the hospital, a tall, broad-shouldered Englishwoman called Mrs. Drew. Since Nick did not know when or if Kit might react physically, he made certain to hire someone strong enough to handle him. When Nick closed the surgery for the day or came home from the hospital, Mrs. Drew reported what kind of day she and her patient had had, and then left.

Nick would bolt down his supper and listen with half an ear to the chatter of his wife and daughter. He was never aware of the silent reproach in Bronwyn's eyes when he touched his napkin to his lips and excused himself from table. A few minutes later he would carry a supper tray upstairs, where he would coax Kit to take food from the spoon in his hand.

Each time he went into the bedroom he found Kit sitting on the bed, his knees drawn up, his back wedged into a corner. He never looked directly at Nick. And yet he did as he was told, volunteering no motion of his own. Like a featherless, nest-bound bird he opened his mouth for food.

Nick talked to him while feeding him. He spoke of their time together, the good times. He talked of the plays. He often mentioned Rama, and Francis, and Mrs. Fiske and *Tess*. None of it passed beyond the lightless dark eyes.

Bronwyn, whose affection and gentle heart had more than enough room in it for Kit, found herself finishing dinner night after night across from an empty chair, while Nick was upstairs.

Even Alyce noticed the changes.

"Papa doesn't read to me anymore," she said one night as Bronwyn tucked her into bed. "He doesn't play with me anymore. Doesn't he love me?"

Bronwyn kissed her forehead. "Of course he does. But you know he is a good doctor and wants his patients to get well. That's why he spends so much time with Uncle Kit. He has to in order to make him well."

The little girl sighed. "I wish he'd get well and go away."

Bronwyn straightened and stared at the shadow of herself on the wall. *So do I,* she thought. *So do I. I want my husband back.* At once she felt mean-spirited and small. *Heavenly Father, I did not mean it in that way. I want him to get well for his own sake. Truly I do.*

And she did. For a while she had gone upstairs for a few minutes each day to speak to Kit. But it became too distressing. She stopped going.

Nick was upstairs one morning when Bronwyn knocked lightly at the door. "Nicholas, there is a lady here to see Mr. St. Denys. A Miss Weisberg."

"Tell her to come in." Would seeing his old friend bring a reaction? Nick wondered.

Rama entered slowly, her stricken gaze fixed upon Kit. "I – I had to see him," she said to Nick. "I couldn't bear not knowing how he was."

Nick said nothing, but withdrew across the room so that Rama could sit down on the bed. She put her hand on Kit's.

"Kit, do you know me? It's Rama. Don't you think you've played this role long enough? You're very good at it, but it's time to change the bill. Francis misses you, too. Why don't we do *Taming of the Shrew* again? You're wonderful as Petruchio and you know I'm a marvelous Kate. Remember the line at the end? 'Why there's a wench! Come on and kiss me, Kate.'" Her voice quivered. "And then you kiss me and laugh and fling me over your shoulder and stride away ... everyone loved that part – Kit, say you remember. Say the line, won't you? 'Kiss me, Kate...'"

Nick's voice was soft. "It's no use, Miss Weisberg. I've tried everything."

She got up, dabbing at her eyes, and joined him at the door. Suddenly they were both stunned to hear Kit's voice.

"'Arry."

The one word, spoken in a dead tone, made Nick gasp and go toward Kit, Rama on his heels. "You spoke, didn't you!"

"'Arry."

"Kit, talk to me. Talk to Miss Weisberg. Tell us what you are thinking just now. Please, Kit. Talk to me."

"'Arry."

Nick and Rama exchanged puzzled, distraught glances. "Talk to me, Kit, do," Rama pleaded. "I don't know what you're saying. What do you mean?"

For the smallest fraction of a moment he looked puzzled but alert, as if he were seeking an answer to her question. Then he seemed to call back the enigmatic small step he had taken and withdrew again into his silent world.

Nick pleaded with him for several more minutes to speak again, but Kit sat in the corner with his arms locked around his drawn-up legs, his forehead on his knees, his face hidden. At last Nick gave up and with a sigh of defeat he left the room with Rama, locking the door behind him. Nothing was said until they were downstairs in his office.

Then Rama cried in distress, "You keep him locked up like a criminal?"

Nick could not answer her to justify it. He shook his head.

She seized his sleeve. "What was it he said?"

"I'm not sure."

"Was it even a word? Please tell me it was a word and not just a — a sound."

"I don't know. I think it was a word. No. I'm certain of it."

"But what?"

"I don't know, Miss Weisberg." His voice was sharp. "I didn't know ten seconds ago, how could I know now?"

"You're supposed to be able to heal people, aren't you? Do it!"

A muscle worked in his jaw, and he burst out, "Don't you think I want to? Don't you think I would give anything I own to see him be himself again?"

"Would you? At least this way you have him under your thumb. You can control him. You never could before!"

Nick went white. "Miss Weisberg, I want you to leave before I forget you are a woman and strike you for what you have just said."

With a final scathing glare, Rama left and Nick was alone. In a house filled with people, he had never been so lonely.

Nick had begun keeping a journal when he brought Kit home, hoping Kit's progress would yield some scientific and medical insight. Instead of a record of healing the journal had become a disheartening story of an odyssey to nowhere. Most entries read simply, "No change today."

He opened the journal, dipped his pen in the ink, and wrote the date at the top of the page.

> Kit spoke today. But was it intelligible speech? Or was it just a guttural protest against my constant badgering? Might it not even have been wishful thinking on my part? I wish I knew. I wish I could see into his mind. If the mind is even there.

He closed the journal and put it away. As he did so, his eye fell on the book of sonnets Kit had given him and he picked it up. The verses Kit had written in the front cried out to him. He said them aloud.

"'Without the sanction of Society, Without the sanction of the Church, Without the sanction of God...'" He picked up a pen and interlined his own wistful words to make it a poem to Kit. "'Without the sanction even of yourself, I love you.'"

He closed his eyes and bowed his head. "Heavenly Father, I haven't prayed for a long time and I have no right to do it now and I hope what has happened to him was not Divine punishment for what we did together—" His voice broke. "If that is so, then I beg You to punish me instead. He is not the one who betrayed a trust; I am. Make him well. I will promise anything, do anything, give up anything, just heal his mind. Do with me what You will; the sin was mine."

As a boy he had often believed he felt God speak to him. He waited now in the silence of the room, a silence broken only by his heartbeat. God was as silent as the room.

❐

The winter passed, with its freezing temperatures and snow and ice. Little buds appeared on the trees and jonquils pushed their way upward and soon thrust their cheery little faces toward the sun.

Through the winter Rama and Francis had made regular visits, but it became more and more difficult for them to face the living dead that had been their beloved friend. The visits became fewer and finally stopped.

Mrs. Drew proved to be a jewel. Professional, compassionate, and honest. She gave Nick a complete report every evening. She documented what Kit ate and drank and reported every sound he made, though they were not many.

She was waiting in his office one night when Nick came in carrying a thick book he had bought just that day. He noticed Mrs. Drew's curious glance and showed it to her.

She made a face. *"Principles of Psychology?* Are you studying mumbo jumbo now, sir?" Then she looked half-afraid he would be angry with her for her familiarity.

Nick sighed. "I don't know if it's mumbo jumbo or not, Mrs. Drew. Some of what I have read about it makes common sense and some of it is beyond my ken. But I can't do anything for him with what I already know."

"Yes, sir. Sometimes I think I am taking money under false pretenses, I do so little for him. I talk to him, Dr. Stuart, that's almost all I do."

"You more than earn your wage, Mrs. Drew. Would you like a glass of sherry before you leave?"

"Indeed I would, sir."

When she had gone, he dined with his family and as soon as he could, he went upstairs with the tray. Kit lay on his side, his left arm curled under his cheek, and refused to take any food.

Nick put down the tray and looked at him. "I've got a book, Kit. I hope it will tell me what to do. It's a new science, psychology, that may be able to unlock minds. That's all I need, isn't it – the proper key. Talk to me, Kit. If you remember what we were to each other, say my name."

Kit's lips moved. "'Arry," he said. And again, "'Arry."

□

One spring day not long afterward Nick glanced out the window of the surgery and saw his little family in the garden. Bronwyn was sitting on a blanket on the grass while Alyce swung in a swing that dangled from the oak tree. As he watched, Jamie pushed himself to his feet and walked toward his mother in the unsteady, staggering lurch of a toddler. With a grin of delight Nick excused himself from the waiting patients and ran outside.

He scooped Jamie up and held him giggling up in the air. "I got to see him take his first step! You little scapegrace! You thought you'd fool me, didn't you." He lowered the little boy and gave the chubby neck a tickling kiss. He was still grinning when he put Jamie down. "Go on, now. See if you can do it again."

Bronwyn looked at him oddly and without a word picked Jamie up and went in the house. He looked after her, puzzled. "What's wrong with Mama, Alyce? Did I do something to anger her?"

"Jamie walked two weeks ago, Papa. I heard Mama tell you." She turned away from him and followed her mother into the house.

Nick stood there in shock. His son had walked – she had told him – and he hadn't even heard her.

He went to Bronwyn. She was crying. He put his arms around her. "I'm sorry, dearest. I know I'm ... distracted these days. But–"

She would not look at him. "Yes. You are. Oh, Nicholas–" She turned then, pleading with her eyes and voice. "Nicholas, your friend is not getting any better. He can't do anything, he can't even talk to you and yet you spend every spare minute waiting hand and foot on him and ... Yes, Nicholas. Your son can walk. I told you and you didn't care."

"That's not true. I love you and the children. You know I do."

She took a handkerchief from her dress pocket and blotted her tears. "I know you do. That's why I don't understand what's happening to us. All I know is that if Mr. St. Denys were not here, we would be happy." Drawing a quivering breath she blurted, "I want him to leave here, Nicholas."

"He's ill, Bronwyn. I can't send him away. You've got to understand ... it's for only a little while longer. He is getting better," he lied. "I can see improvement every day." He put his arms around her and felt her resistance.

"And if he does not get well?" she asked in a hollow voice.

"He will. I told you. He's better already."

Bronwyn stepped back and stared at him. "Prove it," she said bitterly. "Let him take his meals with us. With the family. If I must share you with him at least I will be able to see you."

Nick flinched. That silent, numb figure at the dinner table... "He's not ready. When he is, he will join us."

"And then he will be well and he can go home?"

"I hope so. Oh, I hope so," he said fervently.

21

April passed and then May.

June.

Kit looked intently at him and the intensity was disturbing.

Nick urged, "Talk to me, Kit. Just say my name. Say anything. Who are you?"

Kit drew up his knees and hid his face against them.

July.

"Who are you? Do you know who you are? Can you say your name?"

A flicker.

"'Arry."

That word again – if it were a word. "Say your name. You're Kit. Kit St. Denys."

"'Arry."

Nick wrote in his journal that night:

Kit spoke again, that same guttural sound of several months past. If only I knew what he is trying to tell me. It sounds like "airy," but what can that possibly signify? Airy. Airy. I refuse to believe it is only meaningless babble. I am so tired, so drained. Sometimes I fear I will join him in his madness. Bronwyn's eyes reproach me. I know I neglect her, but I don't mean to. I will make it up to her and the children as soon as Kit is well.

He stared bleakly at the page. And what if Kit were never well? He could neither answer nor acknowledge the question.

When he woke the next morning he was conscious of having awakened with the answer to something important and then had fallen asleep again. What was the answer and what was the question?

He was writing out a prescription for a tonic for Mrs. Allen and only half listening to her as she chattered on about her cat.

"He just hasn't been himself, poor thing, since Mrs. Thomas's dog chased him under the porch. Why, he just shakes all the time. I wish you were a veterinarian, Dr. Stuart. I'd bring in my Harry for you to examine."

He chuckled and handed her the prescription. "My days of treating cats are over, Mrs. Allen, but–" His eyes widened and he almost put his hands on her plump shoulders. "Mrs. Allen, what did you say your cat's name is?"

"Why ... Harry. Short for Harrison McTavish. He's a pure-bred– Why, Dr. Stuart!" she exclaimed when he planted a kiss on her cheek.

"Harry, of course! Thank you, Mrs. Allen. Thank you. And if you want to bring dear Harry in to see me after hours, you're more than welcome."

Harry, of course. 'Arry. Kit had said he was raised a river rat in London. Of course he'd drop his *h*'s. Nick's patients were surprised at the sparkle in his eye.

"You don't seen as tired today, Dr. Stuart," ventured young Mrs. Zorns.

He laughed as he placed his stethoscope against her abdomen to listen for the baby's heartbeat. "I'm not, Mrs. Zorns. I found a piece to a puzzle I've been trying to put together." He listened then straightened, smiling. "And I believe, my dear lady, that you are going to have twins."

The last of the patients left and for the first time without even bothering to sterilize instruments and put medicines away, Nick hurried upstairs, taking the steps two at a time. He burst into Kit's room.

"I know what you've been trying to tell me," he said. "Harry. You're trying to tell me you're Harry." He crossed the room and sat down on the chair beside the bed. "But you're not. You're Kit. You had a bit of a nasty shock, that's all, and you've temporarily forgotten your name. But now–"

Kit pulled away from him and huddled into himself like a timid, frightened rabbit. "'Arry," he said again, but this time it was in a pleading tone which left Nick more puzzled than ever.

"I don't understand!" Nick cried. "I don't understand. Why are you so afraid of me? Kit St. Denys is afraid of nothing."

Jonathan stared at the man who sat there, a strange man. He did not know where he was. He did not know who this man was or who the woman was who dressed him and fed him. And he did not know where his brother Harry was. Harry would know everything. Harry would take him away from here.

❒

Two days later there appeared on Nick's doorstep a heavyset man who introduced himself as Dr. Hesse, currently practicing in Philadelphia but originally from Berlin. He had read of the St. Denys case, as indeed who had not, and he asked to examine him. When Nick asked for his credentials he was told that Dr. Hesse had studied psychiatry with the great Wilhelm Griesinger.

Nick's hope soared. He had read of Griesinger. He leaped at the chance and in his mind Kit was as good as cured.

Hesse took rooms in New York City and came every day to work with Kit. He declined to discuss his methods of treatment, informing Nick that it was too complicated for anyone not in the profession and ordered that during the hour he was there no one else should approach the room: it was too distracting for both patient and doctor.

He was an obnoxious boor, but Nick gritted his teeth, followed orders, and tolerated him for Kit's sake. He noticed that after each session with Hesse Kit had an odd expression in his eyes; the only way Nick could describe it was "wary," as if uneasy or afraid.

One evening as Nurse Drew prepared to leave for the day, she fidgeted and asked to see him in private. He groaned inwardly; she must be giving notice and he needed her. He took her into the library and closed the door. She stood there twisting the strings of her purse, her gaze on the floor. Strange, he thought. Mrs. Drew was one of the most straightforward women he had ever known and now...

"Mrs. Drew, what is it? Has something happened?"

She bobbed her big head. "Aye, Doctor. But it's—" Her face reddened.

"What is it?"

"Well, sir, it's that witch doctor you hired."

"Witch doc— Oh. Dr. Hesse. Mrs. Drew, forgive me but you have no grounds to criticize psychiatry. You know nothing about it."

"Sir, I don't know about psychiatry, you're right, but I know there's something wrong about that witch doctor."

"What are you talking about?"

"Well, sir, whenever he's here I find something else to do since I can't take care of my patient. Yesterday I went upstairs just to see if Mr. Kit was all right. I just don't trust that man. The door was locked. I wondered what he was up to. I went up this morning and I suppose he'd forgotten to lock it and I started to go in..." Her face burned brighter. "Sir, I can't say what I saw, I just can't. But it was something very, very bad. And if that man is to be in this house, then I can't be. And sir, he is a bad man and you oughtn't trust Mr. Kit with him." Her shoulders moved in shrug. "I guess that's all, sir."

Nick's mind supplied a dozen scenarios of what must be happening in that room and if even one of them was true he wanted to kill Hesse. "Did he see you, Mrs. Drew?"

"No, sir. I closed the door quiet. I was close to being sick. If I'd confronted him he'd have said it was my word against his and him being a doctor and all. I didn't know what to do except tell you."

"Yes," said Nick. "You did the right thing, Mrs. Drew. And Mrs. Drew, please don't quit on me. I need you. He needs you."

She smiled, bobbed her head again, and left.

Nick did not go to the hospital the next day. He feigned sickness. Hesse showed up at the regular time, not knowing Nick was home. Nick paced his office for several minutes, perhaps a quarter hour, before going upstairs. He tried the latch. The door was locked. He could hear Hesse's voice murmuring in a low tone. Noiselessly Nick put his key in the keyhole and silently opened the door.

Kit lay on the bed, his face unchanged; he might as well have been carved from wood. His shirt was open to the waist and his trousers were half-unbuttoned. Dr. Hesse was kissing the unresponsive mouth while his right hand was working with dexterity at the rest of Kit's trouser buttons. Had there been any doubt of his intentions the bulging front of his own trousers would have dispelled it.

Nick moved with a cry of outrage. Hesse lifted his head and scrambled to his feet.

In two strides Nick crossed the floor and hauled the psychiatrist from the room, out into the hall, and slammed him against the wall. "What the bloody hell do you think you were doing?" he demanded. "What kind of animal are you? He's a child. How dare you take advantage of a child?"

"I told you not to interrupt!" the man blustered. "I was nearing a breakthrough!"

Nick shook him like a dog shakes a rat. "You unspeakable—"

Hesse tried to keep his dignity while squeaking, "It is clear you have a closed — ouch! — mind. I have developed a theory that the sexual organs have a direct nerve link to the mind. After all, the sexual instinct — ow! you're hurting me! — is the most basic of instincts second only to the need for food. Surely you don't think I took pleasure in what I was doing! Why — I find it disgusting! But I had to do it because if I could trigger that instinct it would prove my theory—"

Nick shoved Hesse toward the stairs. "Damn your theory," he snarled. "My attorney will be contacting you for return of every cent I've paid you. And believe me, if any man is—" He cut off the rest of his furious thought: *if any man is meant to awaken that instinct in him, you are not the one.*

He all but threw Hesse down the stairs and then returned to Kit, who lay unmoving. Except for his eyes. For the first time he looked at Nick and there was something there ... shame? Nick wondered. A tear slid down Kit's temple.

"It's all right," said Nick as he righted Kit's clothes. "I don't know how many times this happened but it will never happen again. There will be no more like him. We'll get through this together, you and I."

Kit turned his head away and once more withdrew into himself.

❏

Not long afterward Nick received a letter from a Dr. Fanton of Baltimore, another psychiatrist who offered to treat Kit free of charge. His credentials were impressive. Nick tore it up and threw it away.

❏

August.

Images, fuzzy and faint, battered weakly at the wall behind his eyes. Pa — big, dark coat with brass buttons, black beard — Ma was gone — Something lay on the bed. It was a small, frail boy who lay unmoving.

He whimpered and fell on his knees beside the bed. It was Jonathan. It was Jonathan who was lying there hurt. And he — he was not Jonathan; he was Harry. Pa had hurt Jonathan.

He pulled his brother into his arms and rocked him, stroking the blond hair so like his own, and promised to care for him. But Jonathan did not answer him. Pa had killed him.

From the doorway Nick watched, stunned, as Kit cradled his wadded-up blanket and crooned to it.

"Harry?" he said.

Kit's head snapped up and he leaped to his feet with the quickness of a tiger. Before Nick knew what was happening Kit was on him, his hands around his throat.

"Bastard!" he screamed. "Bastard! You killed my brother!"

He had the strength of madness as he shoved Nick against the door, his eyes blazing with hatred, his teeth bared. "Damn you! Damn you!"

Nick felt oddly calm as Kit's hands closed around his throat as they had once before. He clawed at Kit's wrists. "Wait," he managed to gasp. "I'm not – Pa. Jon's – away somewhere – kill me – and you'll – never find – him–"

Kit froze. "What?" He loosened his hold on Nick just enough so that Nick was able to bring his arms up and break away, almost falling into the hallway. He quickly shut and locked the door and leaned against it, breathing raggedly.

"Is there no end to it?" he cried. "God – God – he finally speaks and it is to threaten my life! I don't know how much longer I can bear it."

But he had to bear it. The alternative was the madhouse.

❐

Not Pa ... of course he wasn't ... but who was he? And that on the bed ... that wasn't Jonathan it was a blanket ... Jonathan, help me! I'm alone and scared...

Kit's rage was over as quickly as it had come. He was exhausted. Falling onto the bed, he was soon asleep.

❐

The heat of August bore down upon the yellow house. Flowers turned brown in the garden. Everyone and everything was listless.

Only Kit was consumed with the energy that had replaced his lethargy. He paced the small room like a caged bear. The woman no longer helped him dress and came just to bring him something to eat. Where was she? And he wondered where *he* was. And who was that man who always called him some crazy name? He looked down into the brown garden. A black-haired woman sat in a thing like a small house you could see into. Two little kids played with a ball. Why was he locked up? He'd like to play too.

The door opened and he spun.

Mrs. Drew was so astonished to see him on his feet and moving and looking at her with an animated face that she gasped and dropped the tray of food. He took four steps toward her.

"I want out," he said. "I'm *going* out." He strode past her.

"Wait – Mr. Kit–" She hurried after him.

He hesitated at the foot of the stairs and brushed her aside when she tried to detain him. Which way was the garden and the little kids with the ball? He set out through the house to find the back door.

Mrs. Drew bit her lip and then hurried to the surgery. She knocked at the door of the examination room and Dr. Stuart opened it a little way, asking impatiently, "What is it?" When he saw who it was his impatience was replaced with dread. "Is something wrong, Mrs. Drew?"

"I don't know, sir. Mr. Kit told me he was going out – and he did."

Nick's face filled with joy. "Out? Outside? He *told* you? Thank you, God! Mrs. Drew, I can't leave right now. Go outside. Stay with him. If anything untoward happens, come for me at once."

"Yes, sir." In a swirl of gray skirt, she turned and went into the garden to carry out her orders.

She saw Mrs. Stuart sitting in the gazebo, transfixed, staring at the odd scene a few feet away. The tall, blond-haired young man was sitting on the grass with the two children, talking to them. A red ball was tossed from him to Alyce and then rolled to Jamie. Jamie picked up the ball and made his first attempt at throwing. It smacked Mr. Kit in the eye. He let out a yell of anger, picked up the ball, and threw it as hard as he could, sending it sailing into the rosebushes.

Alyce jumped to her feet. "That's my best ball, you big dummy. I wish you'd go away from here!"

Kit got up and glared down at her. "I didn't ask to come here, little girl. I don't even know where I am or who you are. You want me to go away? All right, I will."

"Go!" screamed Alyce. "Go away! Go on! You're not a prince. You're just plain old bad luck."

"Alyce!" scolded her mother.

No one moved for a moment. Then without warning, Kit broke into a run. He went through the gate, past the house, and into a strange woods. His heart pounded and his eyes frantically cast about for something familiar.

Where was he? Where was the river and the crowded, dingy buildings and the alleyways full of starving cats and papers and everything that could be thrown away? Where was the Royal Lion and where was Lizbet? Where was Jonathan – he fell against a tree, gasping. He had dreamed Jonathan was dead. It was a dream because it could not be true.

He ran a little farther. The branches slapped his face and the roots tripped him. He fell to the ground and lay there on a carpet of leaves so sheltered from the sun that they were still damp. He began to cry and buried his face in his arms. He was lost and did not know how to get back to where he should be.

He heard someone's footsteps on the leaves, coming toward him. He sat up and seized a stick that was within reach. If it was that man who had fiddled with him, he would kill him. He started to get up, but his foot slipped on the wet leaves and he fell heavily to the ground.

◻

Nick had left his patients with the barest and quickest of apologies and had run after Kit when Mrs. Drew came in, panicked. She was somewhere behind him, he thought, as he plunged into the woods. He was sick, wondering what he would find, when he came upon Kit just in time to see him fall. He knelt beside him.

"Kit–"

The frightened brown eyes searched his face. "I'm 'Arry. 'Arry Rourke. Why do you keep calling me that? Who are you? Where's this place?"

Nick said softly, "Ki– Harry, I am your friend. I'm a doctor. I'm taking care of you here at my house."

"If Pa finds me here–"

"He can't. He's gone away where he can never bother you or anyone ever again."

"I don't believe you. Where is my brother?"

"He can't be with us just now."

Kit put his hands to his head. "I don't understand at all. Where is Lizbet?"

"Lizbet is away, also. Are you hurt?"

"What d'you care?"

Nick got up and put his hand on Kit's elbow to help him. Kit jerked away. "Get your 'ands off me. I ain't a baby." He clambered to his feet.

"Come along then," said Nick. He was happy that Kit was walking and talking again. But why was he insisting he was Harry? Nick considered taking him home, sitting him down, and explaining everything. Maybe then, with the memories laid out like playing cards in front of him, he would become Kit again. And then he looked at the half-frightened, half-defiant 31-year-old child-man before him. No. Even if it meant he would never have Kit back again, he could never tell him what had happened. If he were to know, it would have to come from inside himself.

Not knowing where this would lead and afraid to speculate, Nick said softly, "Come on, Harry. Let's go home."

"Ain't my 'ome."

"It is for a while." He hesitated and then started through the woods. "Come if you like," he said. "If you want to sleep out here with the snakes and the other creeping things, it's all right with me."

"I ain't afraid of 'em. Let 'em come. I'll make a snake pie, I will."

Nick trudged ahead. In a moment he heard hurrying steps and Kit fell into step with him.

"Don't you lock me up again," he said flatly.

"Very well. But you must give me your word you won't bolt. I can't make you well if you won't stay put and cooperate."

There was silence broken by the sounds of their feet on the leaves. Then, "I won't bolt."

"I will let you eat downstairs with the family if you like."

"With that girl? She's a right little bitch, isn't she."

Nick stopped and faced him. "She is my daughter and you will respect her. Is that understood? You will not use that kind of language anywhere my daughter or my wife or any woman of my house can overhear. Is that also understood?"

Kit mumbled rebellious assent.

Nick wondered what Bronwyn and Alyce would think of the arrangement.

When they arrived at the house, Nick said, "Go upstairs, Harry. Clean yourself for luncheon. I expect clean hands and face and fresh clothes before you come to table."

Kit stamped upstairs louder than was necessary. Nick told Bronwyn the news. She took it in silence and then nodded. "We will try, Nicholas. If it is the means of healing that poor man and sending him into the world again to live his own life, why, then I freely and enthusiastically agree."

When Alyce took her place at the table, she looked angrily at the unwanted guest. Then he smiled at her and with a hand that showed the scratches of thorns, he held out her red ball.

"'Ere's your stupid ball. I got it back," he said. He glanced at Nick, fidgeted, and mumbled, "I'm sorry."

Nick saw them all visibly relax. One hurdle jumped, he thought. Maybe I can sleep tonight.

□

Over the next few days, another problem presented itself: things were disappearing.

Cook complained that food was vanishing from the larder.

Bronwyn found one of her purses open and empty.

The day maid came to him in tears about a gold locket "what was left to me by my mother" missing from her purse.

Nick found his office door open and money missing from his cash box.

There could be but one guilty party.

But how could he accuse him? Later, perhaps, but not now...

More money was missing from his cash box the next day.

He waited until an afternoon when Kit was out in the garden and searched his room. It was all there under the mattress, even the pilfered food, looking the worse for the passage of several days. Nick sighed. Now what?

He watched at dinner that night and saw Kit slip a scone into his pocket. He slipped a second scone into his other pocket. When dinner was ended, Nick said, "K– Harry, I have to speak with you."

The smile was guileless. "But I got to go upstairs."

"Come into my office. Please."

With a sigh, Kit followed him, his hands futilely in front of his bulging pockets.

Without a word, Nick reached into the pockets and removed the scones.

"If you wanted more, why didn't you ask?"

The long-lashed dark eyes lowered and the strong jaw set. "I wanted to put it away for if I go 'ungry."

"You won't go hungry here."

"Says you. Anyway, if Jonathan comes 'e'll need something to eat. We always save for each other."

Nick took Kit's right hand in his, turned it palm upward, and placed the scones on his palm. "They're yours for the asking, Harry. And if Jonathan comes, we'll set another place at table. You needn't steal from us."

The fair skin reddened. He mumbled something and left the room.

The next morning Nick again found that his locked office door had been opened. The missing money was placed neatly on his desk.

He opened his journal.

I want to weep — whether from joy or sorrow, I don't really know. The return of Alyce's ball, the return of the money is proof to me that the real Kit is alive somewhere in the darkened labyrinth of his mind. He has not lost the ethics of a gentleman which St. Denys and his friend Lizbet gave him, but those ethics are buried. And yet they come out — when he is reminded of them. If the ethics are only shallowly buried, then may not his real self also be only shallowly buried? I feel hope and yet I wonder if I should. Perhaps he will always be as he is today. I pray to God that is not the case. Because if it is, what shall I do? What shall I do?

22

Kit's awareness increased little by little, day by day. Questions swarmed in his mind the way gnats swarmed outside in the sunshine. He was at Stuart's home and Stuart was a doctor. His brother was away somewhere but Stuart would not tell him where. Pa supposedly was gone forever; he hoped the sharks got him.

But where were his friends? Where was Lizbet? And the theatre? And the strangest and most puzzling thing of all was himself. Strange and puzzling and frightening.

He sometimes stared at his hands for a long time. They were not his hands; they were too large, with enormous palms and long fingers. Everything was too large. His feet, his entire body. He would spend long minutes staring at his face. It was not the face he knew. It would be rough in the morning and the woman, Mrs. Drew, would shave him. Shave him? Jonathan didn't have to shave; why did he? Grown men shaved, not boys of thirteen. And where had those lines come from across his forehead and at the outside corners of his eyes? His nose looked funny; it had a bump on it.

At times he felt such a fear of the unknown that he would pass two or three days as withdrawn as he had been before. Something was happening or had happened to him; it was like he was looking through someone else's eyes ... Maybe it would be better if he didn't ever know the answer.

He no longer tried to play with Alyce. She bored him. Silly girl, anyway, with her hair ribbons and petticoats. Sometimes he watched her, though, playing with little Jamie. Mrs. Stuart was never far away, mucking about with her flowers. Wistfully, he wondered if he and Jonathan had ever played like that while Ma watched. If they had, he couldn't remember it.

One day Alyce had taken a book outside and then had laid it down to go play with her brother. Kit looked for a long time at the book. For some reason he was half-afraid of it and half-drawn toward it. He picked it up. Lizbet had taught him to read. That, he remembered. But could he remember how to do it? Where was she, anyway? Old Stuart would never answer when he asked.

He glanced around to make sure no one saw him and then, slipping the book into his shirt, he stole into the house and up the stairs. He sat on his bed, his back against the wall, the book propped on his lap, and opened it.

He read it. He read it cover to cover in five minutes and then he read it again. He could feel a grin spreading from one ear to the other. Whatever was wrong with him, at least he could read! Surely Old Stuart would let him try some of his books. He wondered if somewhere he had books that belonged to him.

There was a knock on the door and Old Stuart came in.

"Hello. One of my patients cancelled, so I thought I'd see how you are. I looked outside first and—"

"Thought I'd nipped out of 'ere, didn't you."

"It crossed my mind."

"I told you I wouldn't."

"I know."

"But you think I'm a bloody liar, don't you."

"No. But I know you don't like being confined."

"You don't know nothin' about me."

"I know more about you than you do," Nick said quietly.

Kit was startled but let it pass.

Nick gestured toward the half-hidden book. "Isn't that Alyce's book?"

"She said I could see it." His chin lifted in defiance. "I can read it, too."

Nick wet his lips and asked carefully, hoping against hope, "And do you remember what you read?"

"I ain't stupid."

Nick suppressed a smile. "No. You're not stupid."

Kit rattled off the entire text of the book word for word.

Nick could not stop the soft cry, "My God."

"It's just a stupid story about a rabbit," said Kit, secretly pleased. Then with his sharp gaze on Nick's face he asked the question Nick had prayed to hear and yet dreaded. "What did you mean — you know more about me than me."

"You had a terrible thing happen to you, Harry. It made you very sick for a long time and it made you forget most of your life. Your name isn't—"

Kit jumped to his feet and shouted, "I don't want to 'ear about it!"

"When you're ready, Harry, I'll tell you everything."

Kit looked at Nick, his eyes dark with confusion. "You used t'call me something. What was it?"

"Kit." Saying the name to him brought an almost physical pleasure. "Your name is Kit."

"No." The head of tarnished gold moved back and forth. "No. It's 'Arry."

Nick got up to leave. "Someday you will ask me, Harry. And I will tell you the truth."

"Where is the theatre?" he asked suddenly.

"Theatre?"

"The Royal Lion. Where is Lizbet? I want to see 'er. I mean 'her.' She don't like for me t'leave off me *h*'s. *My h*'s. She's always climbin' me back about it. Speak proper, she says, and folks'll think you're a gentleman born."

"She's right." Nick felt a little thrill of excitement. The door was opening another small crack. Then he had a sudden idea. It might prove to be a terrible idea, might even be dangerous for Kit's recovery and yet instinct told him to try it. "Harry," he said, "you can't go to the Royal Lion and Lizbet is not here. You're not in London anymore."

"Not in Lunnon? Then where the bloody 'ell am I?"

Nick almost said "America" and thought better of it. "Away from the City. But I can take you to a theatre."

The dark eyes brightened. "Would ye do that? Soon? And maybe if I could see some of the books you 'ave, maybe I could try t'read 'em?"

"Of course. I'll bring some up if you like."

"Lizbet says t'always say please and thank you. So ... please if you would bring 'em and thank you for 'em. Just," he added, "don't bring no books about talkin' rabbits."

Nick took some of Alyce's books and Kit devoured them in a day, barely stopping to eat. Nick took poetry and from the New York City Library he borrowed plays, wondering what Kit's reaction would be to them. Whenever Nick saw him the next two weeks he had a book open, reading as if the words were food and he was starving.

One night Nick wrote in his journal:

It is wonderful to see him reading. Especially the plays. He makes no comment about any of them, but he asks for more. I've not given him Shakespeare because it would break my heart for him to reject them. I have an appointment tomorrow to see Mrs. Fiske and Miss Weisberg and Mr. Mulholland. I have an idea that might be the key to unlocking his mind. Today I asked him if he remembered what he had read, some play by Sheridan, and he recited a great chunk of it, correctly I presume. I do not know the play so I cannot attest to that. Then he looked at me with such a cocky, pleased-with-himself expression he almost looked like himself.

I wish I could say certain feelings have vanished. They have not. And as he grows more and more like the Kit I knew those feelings become more insistent. If he continues to follow, as he seems to be doing, a path that is leading him from his childhood forward through his life, he will soon reach the maturity of his teens and

He stopped writing abruptly and read, appalled, what he had just written and knew what he had been about to write. He dipped his pen in the ink and with heavy strokes slashed out the entire unfinished paragraph. Wanting to escape the thoughts, he put away the journal and climbed to the widow's walk, but even there in the cool breeze from the river, he was tormented – Kit as a young man, a hot-blooded youth with physical needs unattached to any emotions – and if his plan worked, Francis Mulholland would be there when Kit needed someone and Mulholland had loved Kit before Nick ever met him–

"My God," he said aloud. "Am I insane? What difference does it make to whom he turns as long as he recovers? And how can I even think of it? I've promised God time and time again – Just make him well and I'll be a monk the rest of my life. Well, you fool, it's almost time to fish or cut bait, as your father-in-law says." He raised one hand to his eyes and cried in soft agony of soul, "But I still love him and I still want him. I wish to God I did not, but I do."

❒

The following afternoon he sat in Mrs. Fiske's hotel parlor and waited for her reaction and that of Francis Mulholland and Rama Weisberg, whom Mrs. Fiske had invited.

Rama dried her eyes. Francis cleared his throat. Mrs. Fiske looked from Nick to Rama to Francis and back at Nick.

"I can't speak for the others, Dr. Stuart, but it would be a privilege to help in any way I can."

"Yes," said Rama in a husky voice. "To think of Kit in the theatre again–!"

"But not as himself," Nick reminded her. "And it might not work."

"But it's worth trying," said Francis. "Anything is worth trying."

"When will you bring him?" Mrs. Fiske asked.

"Tomorrow. I'll bring him in the morning and come fetch him at noon. Mr. Mulholland, if you can supervise him, then, and show him what to do–"

"As a stagehand," said Francis sadly. "The most brilliant actor I've ever seen, a stagehand."

"He will act again," Rama's voice was fierce. "Soon." Turning to Nick she said, "Stuart, I never thought I'd say this, but I'm glad you're around."

He smiled. "Miss Weisberg, I find that an amazing statement."

❐

Kit walked out into the sunshine. It felt good and he stretched like a lazy cat. Where was everyone? He thought the house was empty until he went back inside and found the day girl listlessly dusting.

"Hullo," he said.

She curtseyed and blushed. She had more than one fantasy about the handsome and mysterious houseguest.

"Where is everyone?" he asked.

"The missus and the children are visiting Reverend Carlisle and Dr. Stuart said he had business to tend to."

"Oh." He smiled to himself. A perfect opportunity to explore. A nebulous memory formed, of a huge stone house and acres of emerald grass and trees and of a smaller house – the face of a dark-haired man merged with the memory of the small house and it jarred him. The images faded as fast as they had come. He frowned, but neither the mental picture of the two buildings or the man's face would come again. He shrugged. Wherever he was, it wasn't that big stone house. So he needed to poke about and discover where he was. And Stuart would never know.

He left the fenced garden and walked through a windbreak of poplars and there he found a stable, not a very grand one, not nearly as fine as the one at St. Denys Hill. He stopped, once again shaken by a half-formed memory. What was St. Denys Hill? It seemed important that he remember but like the stone house, the cottage, and the man's face, the image would not return.

A fair-haired young man was grooming a black filly out in the sunlight. His sleeves were rolled up and muscles played in his forearm as he stroked the horse's ebony coat. Kit stopped and let his eyes travel over the man's body. Something tingled and sparked in his groin and he felt his breath quicken. The man's slightly bowed legs were sturdy and his arse was firm.

"Hullo," Kit said.

The boy looked up. "Hello, Mr. St. Denys."

St. Denys? *St. Denys Hill.* The name burst into his conscious mind. "Why do you call me that?"

The boy looked confused. "Well, Dr. Stuart told us all that you was ill and was coming to stay and he wanted our help if he needed it."

His breath was like a knot in his chest. "You ... think you know who I am?"

The boy grinned. "I get it. It's a game. Sure I know. You're famous. I've even seen your picture on a theatre sign in the city. 'Kit St. Denys,' it said in big black letters." He looked at Kit then resumed brushing the horse, his hand moving slowly. Offhandedly he said, "You look better in person."

Kit was not listening. The name was running around in his brain like a crazed squirrel. Kit St. Denys. Kit. St. Denys. KitStDenys, KitStDenys. *Kit.* That was what Nick called him—

He was suddenly aware the boy had spoken. "Are you all right, sir? You look like you seen a ghost."

"Maybe I have," he whispered. "I'm — I'm feeling rather light-headed. Do you have somewhere I could sit down?"

The boy nodded and took him into his own quarters in the stable. It was hot in there but at least it was out of the sun. Kit sat down on the cot and looked up at the boy.

"Do you know what Dr. Stuart's first name is?" His mouth was dry; his tongue felt as if it were glued to the roof of his mouth as he waited for the answer, somehow knowing what it would be.

"It's Nicholas, I think."

Nick. Nickie. Kit. St. Denys Hill. Names began to batter him until he could scarcely think. *Rawdon. Xavier. Hamlet. Romeo. Rama. Francis.* What were these names? He got up and walked from the stable. The boy watched him go.

How had he known what Stuart's name was? he wondered, feeling almost dazed. Why did the name "Nickie" seem as natural as breathing? He broke into a run as he neared the house. Stuart had said anytime he wanted to know the answers he would be told. He wanted to. He wanted to know *now!* Stuart better make good on his promise or else.

He was panting and disheveled when he burst into Nick's office, where Nick was berating the day girl for letting Kit go out unattended. She was almost in tears. Nick heard a panic-stricken voice behind him.

"Stuart, you said you'd tell me everything. Tell me. Tell me now."

Nick jerked about. The inflection and clear pronunciation were Kit's, not Harry's. The face he saw was anguished. He said to the girl, "Susan, I ought not have been so hard on you. No harm was done. Leave us."

She sniffled and shut the door behind her. The two men stood face-to-face. Nick's heart raced with hope. Was the nightmare over at last?

"Talk," Kit demanded, and his eyes dared Nick to make sense of his life.

Nick nodded. "Sit down."

"I don't want to sit down."

"As you wish. But it's a long story." Kit sat down. Nick poured each of them a glass of wine. "We may need this before it's over."

Nick told him everything he knew about his father's abuse, Lizbet and the theatre, and his brother's death.

Tears filled Kit's eyes. "Why can't I remember any of this? I dreamed Jonathan was dead – but it was no dream, was it."

"No. I'm sorry." He continued. He told of the adoption by St. Denys and the work in the theatre. He told him of the night they met, when Kit hurt his arm on the sword. He went no further, afraid Kit's hold on reality was too fragile to hear the rest. He was taken by surprise when Kit stared at him as if drawing secrets from his soul.

"What were you to me?" he asked.

Nick was not prepared for the question. He stammered, "A – a friend."

"Just a friend?"

"Of course. What else?"

"I don't know. But in my mind this afternoon I kept hearing the name 'Nickie.' And somehow I know it was you. And there is something trying to be remembered. About you or someone else I don't know. Nickie. Why would I call you that?"

"You, uh, said it sometimes when you were feeling ... silly. Like a – a joke."

Kit thought about it, then asked suddenly, "You said something happened to me that made me lose my memory. What happened?"

"I'm your doctor as well as your friend, Kit. I think we've opened enough new doors for one night."

Kit looked tempted to pursue it and then to Nick's relief seemed to put it aside. "Kit." He said his own name aloud, trying it as he would a new suit of clothing. "Kit. Not Harry Rourke. Kit St. Denys." He leaned back and closed his eyes. "I think you're right. I've heard about all I can take in today. New name, new ... everything. How will I get used to it all?"

Nick hesitated, then said, "I have an idea that may help you get well even faster." He told him then of his visit that afternoon to the theatre. He did not tell him the theatre belonged to him, but only that people who had known him before were going to do everything they could to bring him back to normal.

"So then I will find out who I really am." Kit's forehead wrinkled. "I think I'm afraid to find out. I think maybe I'm a criminal or something."

"You needn't be afraid. You're a well-respected man, a consummate professional of incredible talent."

The skeptical look on Kit's face said without words, "I don't believe you." Aloud he said, "Those people you just told me about ... Rama, Francis. I thought those names this afternoon. They are real people, not just my imagination?"

"Very real. They're your good friends. As is Mrs. Fiske, a great lady."

"And I am to work in that theatre?"

"Yes, behind the scenes, learning it all over again. Maybe hearing the sounds and smelling the smells and watching the actors will open the door for you all the way."

"And I will remember everything?"

"It's my earnest prayer."

Kit rubbed his temple. "I am so confused! And I still think you are one of the biggest mysteries in all this."

"Hardly. There are no mysteries to me at all."

Kit did not smile.

◻

The next morning Nick cancelled his first appointments and took Kit to the ferryboat for the ride across the river.

"You have crossed this river several times," said Nick. "But you don't remember."

"No."

Kit said nothing else. He was conscious of his heart beating erratically the nearer they came to the city. He bit his thumbnail, his anxious gaze fixed on the city beyond. Maybe he shouldn't try to remember anything. Maybe he would be better off never to know.

He turned his head to look at Stuart's clean profile and the black hair sifting over his forehead in the breeze. He had an unaccountable urge to reach out and touch Stuart's hand.

Nickie, he said to himself. Nickie. It felt so right. Why?

23

Kit had a dream once when he was a child, of being in a dark alleyway with things snatching at him from the blackness and of there being a door someplace nearby if he could just find it. He felt that way as he walked into the theatre with Nick.

He had stopped outside and studied the playbills for Mrs. Fiske's production of *A Doll's House*. Nick had told him he knew her, but the face on the playbill meant nothing. They went into the theatre where a rehearsal was under way. He saw the red-haired woman. She and a man were on the stage and she exited, shutting a door. After the door was shut there came a loud bang.

He heard the laughter of invisible people somewhere behind the curtains. The red-haired woman came back out on the stage, laughing. "Richard, if you do that tonight your head will roll."

One of the invisible voices said, "Well, that slam is so important I just wanted to give it all the drama it deserved."

"As I said, Richard dear, your head will roll. Let me try it again. I wasn't happy with that last scene the way I did it last night."

As they sat halfway back, Nick watched Kit, who was not behaving as Nick had expected. Instead of watching the stage and the actors, he fidgeted, shifting in his seat, crossing and uncrossing his legs. Suddenly he stood up.

"I want to go."

"But why? Don't you want to meet your old friends?"

"I want to go!" He gripped Nick's arm and Nick was surprised to find that Kit's hand was trembling. Nick nodded and followed him from the auditorium to the street. Out in the sunlight he saw that Kit's face was ashen and a patina of sweat gleamed on his skin.

"Kit, what's wrong?"

"I don't know, I don't know. Something bad."

"What do you mean?"

"I told you I don't *know!* It felt so cold in there. Something bad happened in that place. I can feel it."

Nick was unnerved by Kit's reaction to the theatre. He had made not the slightest hint about Rourke's death. Kit had guessed somehow. Or was it a sixth-sense revelation? Kit had told him about hearing a woman scream the night Lizbet Porter was murdered and the story had made Nick shiver. If he told Kit the truth now, would it do more harm than good? He had no way of knowing or even guessing with any degree of intelligence, but he had to do something. Kit was pacing up and down in front of him, imploring him to take him back to the house.

If he did the wrong thing, Nick feared Kit would retreat again into his shell and never come out. On the other hand, if he did not face the theatre now he might never face it.

"Kit, listen to me."

"I want to leave. Now."

"You were right. Something bad did happen there. Something terrible. And what happened is what made you sick."

Kit made a wild gesture. "I don't want to hear about it. Get me away from here now or I'm going to puke all over the sidewalk."

Please let this be the right thing to do, Nick prayed and hoped God heard him. "No. Kit, I think you have to face it. Your father, Tom Rourke, died in this place."

—black-bearded face brutal hands hateful voice knife blood—

Kit's eyes had a crazed look to them as he took a step backward and then another. For one instant, like a startled cat, he froze and then, like the cat, shot into movement and was gone.

"Kit—" Nick ran after him, shoving people aside. He lost him in the crowd. "Damn, oh damn me for a fool—"

He searched as long as he dared and saw no sign of him. A baker remembered seeing a tall, fair-haired man run by his window. A woman with a baby in a pram remembered being almost knocked to the ground by such a man. A policeman said someone had reported a man of that description running and reported him because he might be a thief even though he looked like a gentleman.

"Oh, God," Nick prayed, "keep him safe until I find him."

He continued looking until twilight and then, exhausted, he went to the police to report Kit's disappearance. The officer behind the desk looked at him as if he were crazy.

"He hasn't been missing long enough to be worried about it," he said.

"I'm his doctor. I told you. He's been very, very sick. He was in an asylum for several months and has since been under my care. He doesn't know how to live in the outside world yet and something frightened him."

The officer's eyes narrowed. "A lunatic? You let a lunatic loose on the people in this city?"

"He's not dangerous. I just want him found and returned to my care. Please. He hasn't committed any crime."

"Yet." The officer read off the description Nick had given to him. Then he frowned. "Sounds familiar." He glanced again at the name and his eyebrows shot up. "St. Denys! The actor who murdered his old man?"

Nick flinched. "It was self-defense."

"Some self-defense," the policeman snorted. "He stabbed him a hundred times."

"Just find him," snapped Nick. He wrote out his address. "Please send me a telegram at once, to this address on Long Island. I'll pay a reward if that's what it takes."

With a sardonic smile the officer took the slip of paper.

❑

Kit ran without direction until his breath burned in his lungs. When he could go no further he slumped with his shoulder against a wall and gulped air into his lungs. A thousand people flowed by in a blur of colors and a cacophony of screeching voices.

Then a gentleman stopped and said, "Are you ill?"

He looked beseechingly into the man's eyes because he could not answer. The man gripped his elbow and guided him into the dark interior of a saloon. He had hazy memories of being in saloons as a child, of getting beer in a bucket for his pa. Pa. At the word he whimpered.

The brown-haired man made him sit down and loosened his collar for him. The next thing he knew there was a small glass of whiskey in front of him. He downed it in one swallow and choked. The man said with sympathy, "You'll be all right," and lightly patted his back as he spluttered and coughed.

"No," gasped Kit. "I won't be. I want to die."

The man laughed. "Nonsense. Big, handsome fellow like you with everything to live for. Why, for someone like you the world is a pearl-bearing oyster. Would you like me to take you home?"

"I don't have a home. No place to go."

"But I do," the man said in a low voice. Under the table he squeezed Kit's knee. "My apartment is not far from here."

Kit stared at the face and then at the man's other hand as it lay on the table. A man's hand. Square-tipped, manicured fingers. Dark hair. —*small stone house a dark-haired man named Rawdon*— Something sent a flood of heat through him. "All right," he said.

The man continued to smile. "You know, you look a lot like St. Denys, the actor. Amazing resemblance. His face was all over the newspapers a year or so ago."

"I'm—" —*justifiable homicide homicide homicide disordered mind confined confined homicide thud of a gavel*— "I'm not ... him."

The man laughed. "I didn't suppose you were. He's locked away somewhere. Crazy as a bedbug."

I should leave alone, Kit told himself. *He says I'm crazy. I probably am.* He looked at the black window; it was night outside. There was a ghost waiting for him out there.

He looked into the man's face. "If you take me home, can I sleep there all night?"

The man's eyes darted around in alarm. "Lower your voice, for godsake," he hissed. "You don't know who's listening. Of course you can stay. Come on."

The man hired a cab which took them to a brownstone and an apartment in the brownstone and a bed in the apartment and another glass of whiskey in the bedroom. Kit was befuddled and offered neither protest nor help when the man undressed him and then himself. Within minutes they were on the bed and the man's hands swarmed all over him. He himself was awkward and ignorant, knowing nothing of what he was to do. But within a very few minutes Kit was aroused; his mind went on holiday while his body directed its own actions. There was pain that somehow became an electrifying pleasure. In the moment of coming he cried a name: "Rawdon!" ...*the Dower House and Rawdon McPherson teaching him what he wanted to know while Papa St. Denys was away*...

The man, having accomplished what he had taken Kit there for, left the bed, pulled on a dressing gown, and went to the water closet. When he returned he counted out several bills and held them out.

"What is that for?" Kit asked.

"Your act," chuckled the man. "It was good. Maybe you should be an actor like the real St. Denys."

"What act?"

He laughed. "The virgin act. It was almost convincing. You're a little old to be in that line of work but you're good. I wouldn't mind getting with you again in a few days." He put the money in Kit's hand.

Puzzled, Kit took it, picked his trousers up off the floor and shoved the money into the pocket, then tossed them on the floor again and returned to bed.

"Hey, what do you think you're doing?" the man demanded.

"I ... you said I could stay all night."

"Well, you didn't think I meant it, surely! What would I do with you? If you think you could make another twenty dollars tonight you're mistaken. I couldn't get it up again if my life depended on it. Now get your clothes on and get out."

"It's dark outside."

"I don't give a damn. Out." He peeled off more money. "Here. This is as much as I have; just keep your mouth shut about it."

Kit dressed slowly. It was terribly dark outside and the phantoms were still there. If he could have stayed here they could not find him.

He took the extra money and walked toward the bedroom door, wondering where he would go. As he reached for the handle another scene from his past flashed across his mind — *a girl named Helen on her back in the alley with her skirt up and a man on top of her, putting his thing inside her and when they got up he paid her and said she was a—*

Kit spun around and cried, "You think I'm a man's whore, don't you!"

"Is there a different term for it now?" the man sneered.

Kit swung his fist and felt a solid thud as he connected with the man's jaw. The man fell back on the bed, senseless, his mouth open. Kit stuffed the money in the gaping mouth. Then he ran from the room and from the brownstone. He ran pursued by daemons until he found a deserted carriage house behind a once-grand house and there he stayed until morning, huddled, shivering, in a corner, kicking at the rats that came near.

When it was light out he left again, with no place to go and no one to turn to. Hungry, he wished he had kept the money the man had given him. He paused at a bakery and when the baker's attention was elsewhere, he stole two hot buns. It pleased him to think he hadn't lost his touch.

Although he had no direction he found himself once again at the theatre where Stuart had taken him the day before. And again, as if they held the answers to his mysteries, he studied the playbills.

LAST WEEK

MRS. FISKE

in

A DOLL'S HOUSE

There was a picture of the red-haired woman he had seen on stage when he was there with Stuart.

"Kit!"

The soft woman's voice beside him made him jump. He turned his head to see Mrs. Fiske, her delicate, ordinary-looking face transfigured by a beautiful smile. "Kit! We've all been worried sick about you!" She put her small hand on his arm. "We expected you yesterday."

"Ex-expected me?" he stammered, confused. He had no concept of how wild and unkempt he looked to her. "S-something happened."

"Dear boy, what is wrong? You don't look well."

"Nothing's wrong. Nothing." *...justifiable homicide disordered mind confined danger to society confined until...*

"You do remember me, don't you?" she asked.

"Stuart told me you are one of my friends."

"He spoke the truth. Come in." Then she smiled. "Listen to me! Inviting you into your own theatre."

He gaped at her. *"My theatre?"*

"Of course, dear. Did he not tell you that? Look."

She drew him back a few steps and pointed to the elegant words on a carved golden sign: ST. DENYS THEATRE. His jaw dropped and he blinked. "My theatre. Mine. It is not possible."

Her voice was soft with affection and pity as she said, "I have a key. We're in rehearsal for our last week of performances. I'll give you my key." She exhaled gustily. "I'm ready for a rest!"

She unlocked the door and walked ahead of him, sensing his need for space and silence. When she turned to him, she said, "I have a few things to see to in my dressing room. If you need me, I will be there."

"I don't know where the dressing rooms are."

"Then I'll show you." He followed her through the exit, down the hallway to the corridor onto which the dressing rooms opened.

The walls bulged toward him and they were wet with something red. He was only half-aware of her face turned toward him, her mouth open and moving. The corridor stank like blood. Sweat poured from him, soaking his shirt. His eyes were riveted on one door out of the many. One door. He reached for the doorknob, his hand shaking so violently he could hardly open the door. All the evil he had ever felt was coalesced into that room. Whatever the bad thing was it had happened there. He knew it. He heard her voice and could not understand what she said. He opened the door.

He stood on the threshold for an eternity, staring at the spot where a faint brownish stain marred the floor. Violent images raged in his mind. He gasped, fighting for breath. He felt her hand on his arm and he shook her off. He took a step into the room and reeled from the shock, reaching out to steady himself against the wall.

"It happened here," he cried. "Pa was here. He attacked me. I killed him. He fell there." He knelt and touched his fingers to the brown stain. "That is his blood. I had a knife. He was dead. But I stabbed him over. And over. I am a killer." His eyes were stark and terrible. "They're right. I am mad. I am a murderer." Slowly he stood up, unable to wrench his tortured gaze from the stain. "I am crazy and I will be locked up again—"

Minnie made him look at her. "No, you won't. We won't let that happen. What happened here was dreadful but you had no choice in the matter. It was your life or his. Kit, you're distraught. Please come back to my suite. Harrison and I would love to have you stay with us for a few days. Then you can come to the theatre with me and—"

"Leave me alone!" he shouted. "You, Stuart, everyone! Leave me alone!"

He walked away from her, feeling he could not get away fast enough.

"Kit!" she called imploringly. He quickened his pace. She did not know what to do. Her instinct was to notify Stuart at once. And yet maybe Kit was right. Maybe what he needed most was to be left alone.

❏

Across the river, Nick was trying not to pace the floor. Events were out of his hands. The city was too large. The police would have to find Kit. Time and again he cursed both himself and God – himself for being such a fool as to tell Kit the terrible truth and God for allowing him to do it. The clock struck with a single chime for twelve-thirty. He had not planned to see patients this day, but Mrs. Webster was having what he was sure was false labor and he had agreed to see her. She was to be there at one o'clock. And Mrs. Murdoch had called, frightened by "funny things" her heart was doing; he suspected Mrs. Murdoch was again doctoring herself with Danish Heart Regulator. He had no choice but to see them. It was just as well. He needed something to take his mind off Kit. Damn it, Kit could be in terrible trouble and he would not know it until it was too late.

He gave a start when Alyce came in, looking glum.

"What's wrong, sweetheart?"

She sighed. "Nothing."

"You look like a thundercloud. What is it?"

"I ... oh, you're busy, Papa."

"I know I've been too busy for a while, Alyce. But I promise you, as soon as Uncle Kit is cured I'll make it up to you. Now tell me what's wrong."

She sighed again. "You forgot my birthday yesterday."

Dismayed, he sat down and drew her to him to sit on his knee. "I didn't, did I? Oh, sweetheart, I'm sorry. I've been so..." He couldn't look into her eyes and give her an excuse. "Alyce. Saturday why don't I have Cook fix us a picnic hamper and you and I and Mama will go to the amusement park."

She looked hopefully at him. "Alone? Or will *he* go with us?"

"He? Jamie? He's too young."

"No. Mr. St. Denys."

He licked his lips, trying not to show how much he hoped Kit would be back, safe and sound, long before Saturday. "No, sweetheart. He's – visiting friends across the river. I don't believe he'll be here."

"Good," she said, pleased. Her eyes danced, her gloom was forgotten. "Can I ride–"

"May I."

"May I ride the Ferris wheel and the roller coaster and the merry-go-round? And eat popcorn and get a flavored ice?"

"All that and more," he said. "We'll ride the roller coaster and eat popcorn and ices till we're sick and Mama is cross. Now you have to run along. I have to get ready to see a patient."

"Who? Mrs. Murdoch? I heard Mrs. Flemisch tell Mama that Mrs. Jackson told her there's nothing wrong with Mrs. Murdoch, that she just has her cap set for you since Mr. Murdoch went to his reward."

He gave her a severe look. "Alyce, that is simpleminded gossip and you know how I feel about that." Then he smiled. "Anyway, Mrs. Murdoch could set ten caps for me and it would do her no good. I'm already taken."

Alyce skipped from the room, the sash on the back of her frock and the large bow in her hair bouncing. She was getting so grown-up, he thought. So tall. Ten years old now. Almost a young lady. Before too many years passed young bucks would be wanting to court her. He frowned. Who was in charge of telling little girls about being women, and warning them about men? He'd have to ask Bronwyn, hoping she would say, "It's my job, of course, and I've already taken care of it."

⌐

Kit wandered distraught, alone, surrounded by the milling throngs of the city. He was dizzy from hunger and unable to focus his thoughts on stealing. Once he stepped into the path of an ale wagon and was roundly cursed. He numbly watched it go on its way, wishing he had not jumped out of the way. He would be better off if he had been trampled to death.

He wandered on, a wild-eyed stranger, unshaven and dirty; mothers held their children a little closer when he passed by. The sunlight made something in the gutter shine and he pounced, coming up triumphant with two coins. They bought him a thick pretzel and a glass of beer at a nearby tavern. When he emerged from the tavern, he saw people lining up on either side of the street, watching up the street with laughter and squeals of delight. Curious, he joined them.

Coming toward them, with flags flying and gold trim gleaming and plumed horses prancing and clowns tumbling and costumed characters from storybooks on floats, came the circus parade. There were huge gray animals he knew he should recognize but did not. There were dozens of matched horses and horse-drawn cages with lions and tigers and leopards. At the end of the parade a calliope screeched and whistled and hooted. A small number of ordinary men walked behind the calliope and from time to time the man at

•289•

their head would leave them and approach the crowd, sometimes rejoining them with another man. Kit was startled when the fellow came to him.

"Hey, you. Wanta work? A dollar when you're done and a free ticket to the circus."

A dollar — that would buy enough food to satisfy him for a while. He nodded and followed the circus man, falling in with the others. They walked until they came to Madison Square Garden and there Kit was handed a bucket of sawdust and a shovel. The air was alive with the sounds of voices, hammering, metal hitting metal, an occasional animal sound.

"Hey, you, roustabout. You ain't bein' paid to gawk. Get that sawdust down."

While dumping and spreading his fifth heavy bucketful inside and on the perimeter of the performance rings, Kit asked a man working beside him, "What's it for?"

"Oh, they'll tell you a lot of things, but mostly it's for shit. Makes it easier to clean up."

"Shit?"

"Elephant, horse ... circus puts out a lot of it."

Elephant. Now Kit remembered. That was what the enormous gray animal was. He'd ridden one once on a dare and remembered the sharp ridge of its spine and the stiff wirelike hairs. The friend who dared him refused to pay since he hadn't ridden in the nude. So he did. And regretted it for days afterward.

He was given his ticket and was paid his dollar and immediately spent it on a dinner of pork chops and potatoes and pie and beer. He tried to eat it all, but it left him slightly sick.

He returned to the circus at performance time, but he was less interested in the acts than he was in watching the audience. There were a lot of wallets in pockets, a lot of lady's purses secured by nothing but a thin string. Many a man left a gold watch exposed like an apple on a tree when he raised his hands to applaud. Kit was pleased to find that his hands, though larger, were still skillful. Slowly, without drawing attention to himself, he edged toward the exit.

Suddenly he heard a voice shout, "Thief! Thief! Stop him! He has my watch!"

Kit panicked and ran into a security guard as stout as a brick wall. He staggered back. Another guard ran over and they dragged

Kit outside. The first guard hit him in the belly with his fist. While he was gasping for air the guards emptied the swag from his pockets and put it in theirs. Then they hit him a couple of more times and left him in the dirt.

Kit slowly picked himself up. Thrown out. Humiliated. And he hadn't even seen the elephant act. It was getting chilly and night was falling. He did not know where to go or what to do. If he could find that theatre again he could break in and stay there, but he was not sure of its location. If he could find the tavern where he met the man the other night, maybe he could find him again. And if not him, then someone like him. And this time he'd keep the money.

Passing a store window by a street lamp, he stopped and stared at his reflection, aghast. Who would want him now except for a target in a Wild West show? He was filthy. He found a horse trough and washed his face and hands, finger-combed his damp hair, and brushed off as much dirt as he could. Then he wandered from tavern to tavern, hoping to see his rescuer again. He'd apologize for hitting him, promise him anything. He stood for several minutes outside a place that seemed familiar. The smells of the drink and the food lured him. He went in and stood just inside the door until his eyes adjusted. There were few women inside.

A slim young man with a nervous, ferrety way of moving, came toward him and then sat at the bar. He turned his head, looked at Kit, looked away to order a drink, and then looked at him again. He smiled and beckoned Kit over.

"D'you have any idea who you look like?" the ferret-man asked. "Of course you don't. You look kind of like an actor who used to be around here a couple of years ago. Name of St. Denys."

Kit felt a tremor inside. "I never heard of him. My name's, uh, Harry."

"Well, Harry, even given the beard and the crooked nose the resemblance is uncanny." He continued to stare at Kit in silence.

Finally Kit burst out, "I don't have any money and no place to go. Give me a place to sleep and something to eat and I'll do anything."

The young man's eyebrows lifted. "Anything?"

"Anything. I – I'd strip and paint myself green if I had to."

"Well," came the answer with a chuckle, "you needn't go so far as to paint yourself. As for the other ... I have a kind of private little business maybe you could help me with. I find young gentlemen willin' to be friendly to older gentlemen, if you get my drift. You're not young enough to be a regular, but there's gentlemen in this town who would pay plenty to believe they were with Kit St. Denys."

Kit swallowed. "Where is the real St. Denys?"

"Oh, who knows? Who cares? He's crazy, locked up somewhere. Well, if you're game to work for me, order some dinner and I'll pay. Then we'll go back to my place. If you clean up as good as I think you will, we might have a real profitable thing here. Amazing, the resemblance between you and that St. Denys." He laughed again. "You'll be worth your weight in gold." He punched Kit's shoulder. "Fifty-fifty."

24

T wo days and nights dragged on with no word from or about Kit. Nick grew more worried by the minute. He tried to telephone Mrs. Fiske but was unable to reach her.

Saturday morning arrived clear and bright, the brooding clouds of the past few days just a memory. He wished he had not promised Alyce the picnic and trip to the amusement park, for he was not only distressed but had for days been ignoring a cobwebby feeling of malaise. Instead of the park he wanted to go back to the city and try again to find Kit. But a promise is a promise even if one's heart is not in it.

He was in his room changing into old tweeds suitable for roller-coaster riding when there was a discreet knock at his door. Bronwyn stood there, also in casual dress, with few ruffles and frills, and a flat sailor hat on her piled-up hair. She handed him a telegram. Curious, she stood there waiting for him to open it.

"Ready to go, Papa," said Alyce, coming from the nursery. Nanny had pulled the girl's hair back in tight braids so her hair would not whip into her eyes during a screaming descent. She was almost dancing with excitement. "Cook has fixed the most fabulous picnic!"

Nick ripped the telegram open and Bronwyn asked, "Nicholas, what is it? Bad news?"

He scanned the small sheet of paper and whispered, "Thank God. He's been found." Even so, the message was disturbing.

St. Denys in custody. Come get him before he's charged.
Sgt. Dennis Malone, NYPD

"I'll be back as soon as I can," he said to Bronwyn. *Charged?* he wondered. *Charged with what?* It was too frightening to speculate about.

"Where are you going?" she asked, her voice strained.

He was aware of Alyce staring at him, her face white.

"I have to go to the city."

"Now?" demanded Bronwyn. "Why?"

"He's in trouble. I don't know what to expect." He went past Alyce, then turned. "Sweetheart, we'll go tomorrow. Or – or the next day." He reached out to touch her cheek and she slapped his hand away.

"I hate you!" she screamed. "I hate you! I want my real father back and I wish you were dead instead!"

"Alyce–," he cried.

Bronwyn's look was fierce. "Go, Nicholas. Do what you have to do. I'll see to my daughter."

For a moment he wavered. Then he plunged down the stairs. He would make it up to Alyce and Bronwyn as soon as he could.

❒

The police sergeant looked Nick over as if suspecting him of some crime. "You're Stuart, eh? You here to get your friend, I assume."

"Yes. But your wire said something about charges. I don't understand. What kind of charges?"

The sergeant snorted. "Morals, what else. He was picked up in a raid along with some other fairies. He's lucky he's not bein' charged with assault. The rest of 'em just screamed and pranced along quiet-like, but that one thought he had to fight all the way to the station. One of my men's got a black eye and another one's got a split lip. They had to bust a baton on his head to subdue him."

"He's sick," Nick protested.

"He's lucky he ain't dead. Sign here." He shoved a paper across the desk. "Sergeant Jackson said you told him something about a reward...?" he added under his breath after making sure no one was near enough to hear.

Nick nodded and counted out several bills.

"There's *two* of us involved, Dr. Stuart."

Nick counted out a few more bills.

"And I wonder what folks would say if they knew about him bein' a fairy? And while we're on the subject, it's kinda suspicious, for a respectable doctor like yourself t'be so worried about one of *them,* ain't it? Folks might just have their own thoughts about that if they found out."

Nick's lips tightened. He emptied his wallet, keeping just enough for transportation. The sergeant nodded in satisfaction and gave orders for St. Denys to be released.

•294•

Looking battered but defiant, Kit was brought out by an officer who had a firm grip on his arm. Kit succeeded in jerking his arm from the officer's grasp.

"Come along," said Nick. "You're free."

Kit glowered at the officer. At the door he turned and made an obscene gesture. Nick grabbed him. "Let's get away from here before they throw us both in." Out on the dusty street Nick glanced at him. "Are you all right?"

"No, I'm not all right," Kit snarled. "I have a lump on the back of my head that hurts like bloody hell."

"I'll look at it."

"I'm hungry."

"You'll have to wait. I had to pay through the nose to get your arse out of jail."

Kit mumbled, "I suppose I ought to thank you."

"It would be a sign of civility."

"Thank you."

Nick wanted to know what had happened to him, where he had disappeared to, but he waited until they were home. Nick took him into the surgery and examined his head. "It's nasty but not fatal," he said, and took a brown bottle of disinfectant from the cabinet. "This will sting a little."

Kit flinched, but did not complain as Nick dabbed it on.

"Why did you fight them?" Nick asked.

"I didn't like what they were calling me. I didn't like being shoved. And I didn't want to go with them. Three good reasons, the way I see it."

"The sergeant said it was a raid...?"

Kit ignored the question and looked sullenly down at his hands.

"Kit, why won't you talk to me?"

"I wish you'd leave me alone. I didn't ask you to meddle, did I." He wished Stuart would stop talking. If he kept on badgering, sooner or later he would find out what Kit had been doing for two days. Stuart was the closest thing to a friend he had; he didn't want him to turn away.

"I've been so worried about you," said Nick. "You can't just — vanish like that."

"Why not?" The words were defiant; the tone was bitter. "Everyone'd be better off if I disappeared forever."

"Stop it." Nick's voice rose without his realizing it. "Stop it. I didn't spend two years bringing you out of limbo just to have you talk that way."

Kit's voice was low. "Why don't you leave me alone," he said again. "I'm no good. Just leave me alone."

❐

Nick went with him upstairs. As soon as they reached Kit's room Kit lay down and closed his eyes.

Nick said, "If you get an extremely bad headache let me know at once."

"No. Just leave me alone."

"Head injuries can—"

"It's nothing. Leave me alone."

With a sigh, Nick went to the door.

"Are you going to lock the door?" Kit asked in a dead voice.

"No," said Nick. "I won't lock you in. There's no need. There's nothing wrong with you that time won't cure."

Kit gave a sharp bark of laughter. "Oh, Stuart. You think you know so much about me and you haven't a clue."

"We'll talk tomorrow."

He left Kit's room and went to the nursery. He bent over Jamie's bed to touch his lips to the soft cheek, aching with love for the baby. Alyce had the curtains drawn on her new four-poster "grown-up" bed. He paused. Those drawn curtains meant "Leave me alone." He hurt inside, knowing how he had disappointed her, and had been disappointing her for months.

His last stop was Bronwyn's room. He halted outside the door, then knocked, expecting no answer.

"Come in," came the quiet voice of his wife.

He entered. She was sitting beside the window, rocking. "I saw you come home," she said. "With him."

He made a helpless gesture. "He's sick, Bronwyn. I don't know what else to tell you." He wished she would rant and rave at him. Rage would be easier to take than the accusing calm. He took a step toward her. She said one word:

"Don't."

"Bronwyn, I'm sorry about what happened today. You'd understand, and so would Alyce, if I had to go out to a woman in labor.

Why can't you see that it's the same thing? I have a sick patient who needed me. I had to go."

"It isn't just today, Nicholas. It's yesterday. And last week. And last month. And last *year*. You are tearing this family apart with neglect because of that man and I don't understand it. Before he came here I would have sworn you loved me and the children. Now I don't know what you feel."

"You know I love my family!"

She raised one hand to her eyes. "I don't know what I know. Please leave me, Nicholas."

"Bronwyn—"

"Please."

Later, in his own bed he tossed restlessly. How could one man try so hard to make so many people happy and end up making them all miserable?

◻

The house was silent except for the ticking of the clocks as Kit stole downstairs to Nick's office. He picked the lock with ease as he had done before, and then opened the liquor cabinet, pushing aside the bottles of sherry and light claret. Far at the back he found the whiskey he was looking for. Then he unlocked the secretary and pulled out the inside drawer he had seen on one of his earlier explorations and removed the small pistol. He shut the drawer and went outside.

◻

Nick was unable to sleep at all. He got up, dressed, and went down to the office. If he couldn't sleep he could at least read some of the medical journals that had accumulated. As he passed the open kitchen door he noticed that the back door was ajar. There was a ghostly white blur in the moon-shadowed gazebo and he watched a moment before realizing it was not just an illusion. The white blur separated into an arm and lifted. Nick saw a glitter of moonlight on glass or metal. The figure left the gazebo and the moonlight turned his hair to a mane of silver.

Then Nick could see that in Kit's left hand he held a bottle and in his right hand he held a gun.

"Kit—!" he breathed and went outside. Kit did not see him. He turned the bottle upside down and the contents splattered at his feet.

Nick approached with caution. The gun, Kit's fragile hold on reality − anything could happen. He called Kit's name softly. Kit stiffened but did not turn.

"Leave me alone," he snarled, shifting the gun to his left hand. He turned, then, taking aim at Nick, his hand steady. "I'll blow your brains out." His face was wet.

"Kit, come back into the house."

"Go to hell."

"You're drunk. You don't know what you're doing."

"No. I'm not. I'm sober as a judge and I just wasted your whiskey."

"Give me the gun."

"Go to hell."

Nick reached for it and saw Kit thumb back the hammer. "Kit, what do you think you're doing?"

"What does it look like, you bloody fool?" The unnaturally bright eyes never left Nick's face. "I'm going to walk through that gate and go into the woods and blow my brains out. And if you try to stop me I'll blow yours out too."

"Why?"

"Why?" He broke into cracked, hysterical laughter. "I'm not fit to live, that's why. I killed my old man. I know that now. I didn't just kill him once − I stabbed and stabbed and stabbed − blood, so much blood, oceans of blood− At the theatre I remembered every bit of it. Why didn't you tell me? Why did you let me find out like that?"

Nick moved closer. "I thought I was doing the best thing. I thought there was time."

"Well, you were wrong."

"Please give me the gun. Let's go inside and talk. Or − or talk out here, I don't care. Just give me the gun."

"I told you what I'm going to do."

"You can't."

Kit snorted. "Oh, yes, I can. I checked. It's loaded."

"Kit, you can't throw your life away."

"Give me one reason."

"You just can't."

"That's no reason."

"Your father deserved to die."

"So do I."

"No. No, you don't. Give me the gun."

"You haven't given me a reason yet."

"You would be breaking the heart of someone who loves you."

Kit laughed, a harsh ugly sound. "To be sure. No one I know of. Give me a name. Just one. You can't, can you."

"Yes, I can." Nick took a step nearer. "I love you, Kit."

Kit spat on the ground and steadied the aim of the gun. "Don't come closer."

"Listen to me. We were lovers, you and I." Nick saw confusion sweep Kit's face. "'Nickie.' Doesn't that sound familiar? That's what you called me. That's why I knew so much about you. I knew things no one but a lover could know. Give me the gun. We can be lovers again. We'll find a way. Just give me the gun. Don't hurt yourself. Don't hurt either of us."

The gun wavered. "We were lovers? You and someone like me?"

"For more than a year. And it would have been longer but something happened. Perhaps we would never have gotten separated—"

... "something happened" ... St. Denys Hill ... himself and Rawdon on the steps, Rawdon's hands on him, and he loving every minute of it and Nick had seen...

Kit licked his lips. Nick saw his uncertainty grow. "We wouldn't have separated if I hadn't acted like a whore? Is that what you mean?"

"You remember what happened?"

Kit laughed again, that cracked, hysterical laugh. "If *that* little scene upset you—! Do you know where I was for two days?"

"I don't want to hear—"

Kit's voice rose. "A male whorehouse, Nickie. I had more men than I can count — I was had by more men than I can count — so help me God I don't know if I was a whore or one of the users and it didn't matter. I'd still be there if the owner'd remembered to pay the police this month! And that's what the fine, upstanding young doctor, pillar of the community, says he loves!"

"It doesn't matter to me. Give me the gun."

"It matters to me. Papa St. Denys once told me he took me out of the gutter and he was sorry he had. He shouldn't have bothered. It's in my blood, the gutter is. Thief, killer, whore. You can't love me, nobody can." His voice broke. Tears spilled over.

Nick grabbed for the gun. Kit gasped. They grappled. The gun went off. They both froze for an instant. Neither was hurt. Then Nick easily took the gun and laid it in an urn. He drew Kit into his arms and held him, his throat tight.

"Yes, I can love you," he said softly. "And I do. Kit, Kit, you've been through such torment, you're hurting so much, don't turn me away." Kit wrapped his arms around him as if he were his only salvation. "Now let's go back in and get some rest," said Nick. "We'll talk later, decide what to do."

◻

Bronwyn, awakened by the gunshot, had jumped from her bed and hurried to the window, her heart pounding. She saw the fore-shortened figures across the garden. Then she gasped. Mr. St. Denys had a gun. She was rooted to the floor by shock and fear. That madman would kill Nicholas and her children and herself— She seized the fireplace poker and was poised to run downstairs and out to the garden when silence fell. She ran back to the window. The gun was visible, lying in the urn that held a half-dead plant. The two men were just standing there. Nicholas was speaking. And then – then an incredible thing happened – Nicholas held out his arms and suddenly Mr. St. Denys and her husband were close together, and it appeared to be an embrace.

She sank down upon the chair, her mouth dry. She did not know the meaning of what she had just seen, but terrible fear invaded her entire body. Fear that there was some – some unholy alliance between them. No. No. It was all right. Did she not embrace Virginia and Chastity when they met and parted? It was friendship, nothing more. Then her own words came back to her: "You are tearing this family apart because of this man. I used to believe you loved us..." She squeezed her eyes shut. Unholy alliance, she thought, dazed. Her father had used those words in a sermon about Sodom and Gomorrah.

"Unholy alliance," she whimpered.

She shook her head, determined not to judge without knowing. Even so, as she crawled back into bed to spend a sleepless, shivering night, her teeth chattered and nausea racked her.

She heard their steps coming up the stairs, going down the corridor, and up the other stairs that led to the room where Mr. St. Denys stayed. She prayed with everything in her that she would hear Nicholas's steps returning soon, though what it would signify if they didn't, she did not know.

In only a few minutes she heard Nick's steps pass her door and a moment later his own door closed. She went limp with relief. Perhaps she should tell her father about this frightening night, tell him everything. She had kept her father in the dark since Mr. St. Denys first came there, telling him as little as possible. Tomorrow she would go to him. He was a godly man; he would know what to tell her to do.

But ... her father had never liked Nicholas. If he were not a man of God she would think he hated her husband. No. She could not seek advice from her father. She could seek advice from no one. Whatever was wrong with her marriage could be fixed. She just had to try harder.

❐

Early in the morning, Nick went upstairs to Kit's room to see how he was. He was not there. Nick picked up a note that lay on the bed.

> I am going back to the theatre. If there is any salvation for me it is there. Let us both forget what was said in the garden. I know my presence is stressful for your wife and I do not wish to burden her further. Whatever may have been between us in the past is over. Do not seek me. I can never repay you for your kindness and care.
>
> K St. D

Nick stood there for a long time, reading it over and over. This was the letter of a lucid man. One who knew what he was doing. One who had made a decision. His vision blurred. He must have been mad to think they could have it just the way it had been before.

He was suddenly aware of being almost too tired to blink.

His head was aching and dull; he decided to lie down again for only a few minutes...

Nick did not leave his bed that day or the next and then he stopped counting. All he wanted was sleep.

He was vaguely aware of Bronwyn hovering over him and of young Dr. Galvin poking at him. He was aware of hurting in every bone and of being thirsty. He was aware of speaking but did not hear himself.

Bronwyn looked helplessly down at her husband. She was still stunned at the suddenness of his illness, although when she cast her mind back on it she knew she should have seen the signs of strain and overwork. It was the fault of Mr. St. Denys. Nicholas had spent so much time worrying about him and looking after him he had had no time left to look after himself.

And Dr. Galvin had not been much help. "I think it's simple exhaustion," he said. "Keep him cool. Get liquids into him as much as you can. Let him rest. I'll look back in tomorrow." He heard his patient's voice and bent a little closer. "I can't understand what he's saying. Can you?"

"No," said Bronwyn, her voice clipped. She lied. She knew what he was saying. He was saying the name she hated most in all the world.

"Kit ... Is Kit all right? ... Where is he...?"

Even on his sickbed he could not stop worrying about that horrible man!

❒

Kit absently looked at the books on the bookshelves in the apartment over the theatre. The books, like the apartment itself, still seemed to belong to someone else, just as the theatre itself was a foreign country to him even though his name was over the door. He had not gone back to the dressing room, though he had ventured backstage. And for some reason he did not understand he was reluctant to sleep in his bed, and had slept every night on the couch, uncomfortable though it was.

Each night he had taken a different young man to the apartment, young men whose names he did not ask and whose faces he forgot at once. The hurried couplings had taken place on the couch or on blankets laid on the floor, much to the annoyance of the young men, who had expected more comfort.

There hadn't been much joy in it, Kit thought. None of them had been worth the bother. Perhaps he wouldn't go out tonight.

Nick Stuart had said, "We were lovers."

"Then why can't I remember that part of it?" Kit asked aloud. "Why can I remember fucking Rawdon and that servant and others, but Nick is no part of it. Why can I remember that last quarrel Nick and I had before he left, but I can't remember ever sleeping with him? He said it was for 'more than a year.' Damn it. Why can't I remember?" Then something occurred to him. "Maybe I can't remember it because it never happened. He lied. He was trying to get me to give in and give him the gun. He would have said anything."

This new knowledge cut, and the pain was deep. He had wanted to believe that someone as fine as Nick Stuart could have been his lover. More fool he.

His brows drew together. "Well, damn him to hell. I don't need him. This city is full of men who would want me, I warrant. If not for love then for money."

And there was much money. At least Nick had told him the truth about that. Mrs. Fiske had gone with him to the theatre manager's office and to his solicitor's office, and he had over the past few days learned that he had a great deal of money.

It still startled him when he was recognized on the street. Strangers spoke to him, wishing him well and expressing hope he would soon be acting again.

From the wings he had watched the final performances of Mrs. Fiske's play. And she had been right that the smells and the sounds and the sights would stir his memory. But they stirred nothing else. There was no burning desire to be on stage, no impatience to get back into harness. It were as though he was watching through a layman's eyes.

He was tired of inspecting the half-familiar books and decided to go down into the theatre once more. Perhaps he would even force himself to confront the dressing room again, though the very thought made his guts twist. He was at the back door of the theatre, ready to unlock it, when a messenger in the uniform of the telegraph company approached.

"Mr. St. Denys?" the boy asked.

Kit eyed him. Not too bad-looking. Wilde, as he recalled, had lost his freedom over his penchant for telegraph boys. "Yes," he said, "I'm St. Denys."

"Message, sir."

Kit tipped him, took the telegram, and tore it open. The boy touched his cap and disappeared.

Mr. SD, Nicholas is quite ill and asks to see you.
                                            Mrs. NS

Nick – ill? Why, Nick had the constitution of a horse. He was never sick. Kit's eyes widened. "Constitution of a horse"? "Never sick"? How had he known that unless Nick had told the truth?

He put the key back into his pocket and left, the theatre and the dressing room forgotten. If he hurried he could catch the three o'clock ferry.

And it was on the ferry ride that he was almost overwhelmed by the memories for which he had been rummaging in his mind. "Lovers," Nick had said. And the memories told him Nick had not lied.

Despite his worry, Kit smiled.

No. Nick had not lied.

Nickie. Lover.

25

Bronwyn twisted the strings of her purse as she waited on the front porch of the most notorious woman on Long Island. Mrs. Murray was not received. It was worth one's reputation to be seen speaking to Mrs. Murray socially. Mrs. Murray was known to have been divorced, she was not allowed into the church for that reason, and, to make matters worse, it was rumored that she even smoked cigars and was an advocate of Votes for Women. She was unacceptable as much for one reason as for the others.

Bronwyn had spoken to her many times in the days before Jamie's birth when she was one of the directresses of the orphanage, for Mrs. Murray had been generous with both time and money. But even Bronwyn's enlightened attitudes did not extend so far as to offer friendship to the woman. But now she needed the kind of help that only someone like Mrs. Murray could give her.

For two days Bronwyn had stood forgotten in her husband's bedroom and watched her enemy minister to him, doing the things she longed to do to prove her love. He held water to Nicholas's dry lips. He bathed Nicholas's feverish face and body with cool water — much more awkwardly than *she* would have done. He talked to Nicholas and made him smile and sometimes laugh weakly. When Nicholas could sit up, her enemy spoon-fed him his first coddled egg. And they had laughed together like idiots when part of it slipped from the spoon to splat against Nicholas's nightshirt.

Before her eyes — and, she thought bitterly, at her invitation! — her enemy was winning. She knew she had to find a way to prove to Nicholas how strong her opposition was to that man, show him in unarguable terms what he stood to lose if he did not cast that man aside. She could not ask her father; she was still reluctant to expose Nicholas to her father's enmity. No, she had to find another source.

And then, like an answer to a question, she had caught a glimpse of the outlawed Mrs. Murray coming from the milliner's shop.

"Mrs. Murray," she called with a bright smile.

Mrs. Murray stopped, her eyebrows shooting up in surprise when she saw who had hailed her. "Mrs. Stuart," she said with a pleasant but wary smile. "I haven't seen you for several months at the orphanage."

"No, I – I haven't been there since my son was born. I wanted to devote myself to him."

Mrs. Murray waited.

"Mrs. Murray, I wonder if I might speak to you in private someday soon. I need your help."

The pretty face showed surprise. "By all means. Call upon me this afternoon and I will try to help, though I confess you have taken me by surprise." With a nod of her head she walked away, leaving Bronwyn standing there feeling foolish.

So it was that she now stood on the porch and wished she were somewhere else.

Mrs. Murray opened her own door and smiled. It occurred to Bronwyn that she had never seen Mrs. Murray without a hat. Her hair was a soft, pale graying blonde and she looked younger. She invited Bronwyn in and hung her lightweight coat on the coatrack in the spotless hall.

"I don't have lady callers," Mrs. Murray said. "But I suppose you know that." She took Bronwyn into a cozy parlor where a silver tea service, cups for two, and tea cakes were waiting. "Now then," she said. "How may I help you?"

Tea with Mrs. Murray! thought Bronwyn. Mr. St. Denys had indeed driven her to desperation. At once shame washed over her. How could she sit here in the woman's own home, beneath the steady gaze of light blue eyes, and think such a thing?

"Mrs. Murray, I need advice and I – I didn't know who else I could turn to – I mean, I don't know anyone else who–" She stopped, flustered.

Mrs. Murray straightened and the warmth of her face faded. "Advice, Mrs. Stuart? From me?"

"I don't wish to offend you, but I have heard that your life has ... been different ... oh, I'm not putting this well, I know..."

Mrs. Murray smiled a distant smile. "Why don't you just tell me what's wrong."

And then Bronwyn poured out the whole story, stopping often to dry her eyes, hating the tears but unable to stop them. Her marriage had been perfect, she said, until St. Denys came along. She told her about the endless months he had lived there, a silent ghost draining the life from her marriage. She took a deep breath and told her about the scene in the garden, and at last told her about the past few days as she watched St. Denys usurp her place. "I don't know what to do," she said.

Mrs. Murray spoke softly. "Mrs. Stuart, my life, as you say, has been different. I read a great deal because–" She gave a small, self-deprecating smile. "–what else have I to do? I'm not invited to tea parties. Tell me, Mrs. Stuart, have you ever heard the word 'homosexual'?"

Bronwyn shook her head.

"Well, whether it's even a word or not is a matter of some controversy. But that's neither here nor there. A Hungarian doctor by the name of Benkert invented it as a way of describing a condition of mind..."

Bronwyn knotted and unknotted her sodden handkerchief. "Mrs. Murray, please, what has this to do with me?"

"He was describing men such as your husband."

"What do you mean?"

"He invented the word to describe men who love other men. And by extension, women who love other women."

Something squeezed Bronwyn's heart. "What do you ... mean?"

"You've heard the Bible verses, I know, since you are a minister's daughter and faithful churchgoer." There was mockery in her voice. "The Bible condemns such a condition, just as it condemns divorced women. I am twice condemned, you see." Her pale eyes were challenging, daring Bronwyn to damn her. "I, like your husband, am drawn by my own sex."

"No..." Bronwyn felt faint. Such a thing was not even possible.

"Mrs. Stuart, are you all right?"

Bronwyn steadied and hastily put down her teacup. The motion was not lost upon her hostess.

"It isn't contagious, Mrs. Stuart," she said dryly. "You came here for advice. What advice do you want from me?"

"I want to save my marriage and I – I thought if I threatened my husband with – with divorce papers – he would cast St. Denys out of – his life – our life – but I didn't know where to go."

"Oh. Simple matter. You need an attorney. The papers can be drawn up, you can show them to him, and ... maybe it will work.

Mrs. Stuart, I'm sure you're uneasy just now, so perhaps you should go. Come back tomorrow and I will introduce you to my attorney. He helped me with my divorce. Will you return or are you afraid of me now?"

Bronwyn's answer was fierce. "I'll do anything to win my husband back."

She returned the next day, fearful but determined. Mrs. Murray introduced her to the attorney and left them alone to talk. The attorney showed her a divorce petition and explained it to her. Bronwyn left two hours later, having paid the attorney and taken the petition, telling him she had to think the matter over for a few days. The horrible word "divorce" stood before her as her only means of scaring Nicholas into coming to heel. But even though it was just an empty threat, it was an ugly word.

❐

When Nick was on his way to recovery, Kit went back to his apartment. He now could sleep in the bed; it no longer threatened him. He could lie there and be with Nick in his mind if not in body, knowing that as soon as Nick's health was normal, he would be there in that bed.

With most of the pieces of his life now in place he braved the dressing room again a few days later. The terror returned, but not as strong, and he made himself stay there and stand toe to toe with the hobgoblins that inhabited the room. They battered him with bloody visions and he stood his ground. When he walked from the room he was drenched with sweat, but he was a free man.

That same day he made another decision and went to the *Dramatic Mirror* to set it in motion.

Harrison Fiske welcomed him with open arms and a shout of happiness when he said, "I'm going to start rehearsal for a play. I want to place a casting call in your paper."

"Thank God!" Fiske said, pumping Kit's hand up and down. "Thank God! This calls for a celebration. Minnie and I want you to join us for dinner and bring your best lady friend. Rama Weisberg, perhaps? Minnie always did feel that you two were destined to walk down the aisle."

Kit smiled. "I don't think so, but bringing her is a good idea." He had not seen Rama since his recovery. Did not, in fact, know how to find her. But he would. He would need her and Francis Mulholland both if he was going to burst once more upon the New York theatre scene.

Harrison Fiske wrote the ad and had it in the next edition of the paper:

ST. DENYS CASTING CALL
ACTORS & ACTRESSES TAKE NOTE
KIT ST. DENYS IS BACK AND LOADED FOR BEAR
NOW CASTING HAMLET

Kit read it and laughed. He had never heard the American phrase "loaded for bear" but he liked it.

☐

Nick read the copy Kit sent him and smiled with eagerness. To see Kit perform again! He had thought it would never happen. He would have to find a way to see him alone. Soon.

Bronwyn was seated across the table from him when he read it. She saw his happy smile. "What is in the paper that brightens your day so much?" she asked, smiling in return. "You look like a canary-eating cat."

He folded the paper and showed her. "Isn't it wonderful? I didn't think ever to see that."

Her smile froze. "Yes," she managed to say. "It's wonderful."

Since her talk with the attorney, she had done everything possible to make their marriage work without resorting to that last desperate measure. She had fired Cook and had taken to preparing all meals herself. She had cleaned and polished until everything in the house shone. She agreed with everything he said even when she disagreed. She had gone against her own nature and been self-effacing and subservient, the way the Bible said wives should be. She had dressed in clinging silken nightdresses and had gone into his room. And it was all just so much treading water, she thought now. He never noticed any of it. And yet his face shone from within over that stupid announcement in that stupid paper. But her smile was fixed and did not give her away.

☐

The play was cast in record time. Rama was the first one to respond and she and Kit had hugged until Rama thought her back would break. There was never any question of who would play the queen,

•309•

just as there was no question of who would play Hamlet. Francis Mulholland, now sporting a full beard and having grown to Falstaffian proportions, was hired as stage manager.

The night that casting was complete, Nick, using his resumed hospital schedule as an excuse to stay in the city, spent the night at the apartment.

With Nick, Kit found the joy that had been missing. They made love, bathed, slept, and woke to make love again, and as the sun rose, yet again.

Nick knew now that his promises to God had been a sham. He hoped God didn't know it yet.

❐

Photographs were taken of the new cast, and Kit gave Nick a photograph of himself as Hamlet. Nick remembered the one he had torn to shreds and thrown into the sea when he left England. This one was even more magnetic. The brooding eyes cast a challenge at the viewer; the crooked nose added to the sense of simmering passion. It was the most powerful picture Nick had ever seen of him. He took it home and hid it in his locked desk.

They fell into a routine over the next few weeks. Nick stayed there on Mondays and Fridays. "I'm on call at the hospital," he explained to Bronwyn, and no longer stopped to ponder the absence of guilt. After all, she was not being hurt. She did not even know. There were times in life when ignorance was indeed bliss, he thought. He bought her gifts, and gifts for the children, to make up for the times he was gone.

The only thing that seemed odd to him was that Kit did not talk about the play. Whenever Nick asked him, he changed the subject. Nick was too happy to suspect anything was wrong.

Until opening night.

A light snow fell that night. Nick attended with Bronwyn, who, much to his dismay had insisted upon going though she refused to buy a new dress for the occasion. He was proud to see a long queue of people outside the theatre and when they went in he heard someone say that many of those outside would have to be turned away.

❐

Something isn't right, thought Kit as he examined Yorick's skull and said the words appropriate to the scene. None of it had been right.

The evening seemed interminable. *Something isn't right,* he thought again with growing desperation as he recited words, phrases, sentences. *What am I doing wrong?* He could hear noises from the audience — coughing, shifting, rattling of programs. This should not happen. This never happened! The last scene mercifully ended the torture.

There was applause, but it was tentative, almost puzzled.

There was only one curtain call.

The cast tried to pretend it had been a wonderful performance. He stopped their enthusiastic words with, "You were all fine. I stunk like a three-day-dead fish and I don't know why."

Nick, too, had been aware of the restlessness of the audience, and had been almost as panic-stricken as Kit. He wanted to stand up and shout for them to be still. He was puzzled by Bronwyn's odd smile of satisfaction as they left the theatre.

The critics the next day were unmerciful. "Boring." "An audience subjected to four hours of boredom." "A great drama turned into verbal pudding." "Somnambulistic performance by St. Denys." "Excellent supporting cast drowns in the tide of ineptitude of the star." "In kindness one can but hope that Mr. St. Denys's long illness has not ruined his stellar career."

There was no queue for the second night. The reviews were worse than for opening night.

The third night there was standing room to spare.

The fourth night there were people scattered in the balcony, which had previously been filled.

The fifth night there were seats left on the main floor.

The sixth and seventh nights they played to a handful of people.

And each night Kit knew the critics were right: he was boring. And he didn't understand it.

The eighth night, a few people arrived to buy tickets and found signs across the playbills: CANCELLED.

There was no jubilant cast party. Kit paid the cast, and thanked them for their excellent work against all odds. Not even Rama and Francis were invited to stay behind.

He went upstairs to think, to analyze, to figure out.

When Nick came to him next, after the run had been cancelled, and started to protest that the production had been outstanding, Kit said, "Nickie, don't. It isn't necessary."

"But you—"

"Let's not talk for a while. Let's go to bed. I need to do something I'm good at."

There was a bitter edge to their intimacy that night, and when it was over, Kit said without warning, "Nick, I'm going home. To England."

Nick was aghast. "What! My God – why?"

"Something's wrong. The play ... Nick, I was dead in it. The fire wasn't there. And without the fire the words mean nothing. An oyster could have performed as well."

"You're out of practice, that's all! That's no reason to run away." He sat up and looked down at Kit. Kit had never looked more vulnerable. "You can't go."

"I have to."

"What will I do without you? Haven't you even thought about me?"

"Thought and thought. But I have to go. Maybe there, where my acting began, I can find it again. And maybe not."

"You *can't* go."

"I can, I *must,* and I will. I already have the ticket."

Nick got up and pulled on his clothes with jerky, angry motions. "I sacrificed my life and my family's life for two years to save you, and this is the thanks I get. Desertion."

"That's a fine word, coming from you!"

"You can't leave me. *You're* the one who said we were bound by that unbreakable cord, remember?"

Kit's voice was low. "I remember. Maybe I was wrong."

Nick sat down on the bed and as if he were blind and seeing with his fingertips he touched Kit's shoulders and arms and chest. "I need you," he whispered. "We need each other."

Kit's arms went around Nick's neck and he pulled him down to lie on top of him. "I won't leave until December. After all, there's the theatre to sell and other things to see to. I'm here now," he said. His eyes were sad, but he smiled. "And I'm loaded for bear."

❏

Nick went through the motions of seeing his patients, and doing his daily routine. He played with Jamie, took Alyce and Bronwyn out in the new sleigh on the first early snow that coated the roads enough. But he could not keep away the thought that before Christmas Kit would be gone.

He began staying more nights in town.

Bronwyn's desperation grew day by day. He did not see it.

He was surprised when she entered the office early one morning.

"Nicholas, may I have a few minutes of your time?" she asked. There was something in her voice that made him look up and put aside his account book.

"Yes, dearest?"

"Nicholas, I love you."

"And I you." Odd that she should be saying that this time of day and with such a strange expression.

"But there comes a time," she went on, "when ... well, if the house were on fire I would go into the flames to save my children, or you. I guess I did that recently."

"What are you talking about? It's not like you to talk in riddles."

"No. I suppose not." She laid an envelope before him. "This is the answer to the riddle. Read it. Please."

Nick took out the long document that was in the envelope. His jaw dropped. "Bronwyn! A petition for a divorce? What is the meaning of this? You can't be serious."

"But I am. Nicholas, I can't bear it anymore. You've shut me out of your life. He has taken my place and I won't be second to him, I just won't!" She clasped her fingers together to keep them from trembling. She was determined not to show weakness, but oh! it was hard. "You will have to choose between that man and your family."

He threw the paper aside with contempt. "You can't make a demand like that! Am I not allowed to have friends?"

"You have no friends. Only that man. I don't know what he is to you. I don't want to know. There is not room for both of us in your life." She was shaking and sick inside, but outwardly she was firm as steel. "Choose, Nicholas. If you choose him, then all you need do is affix your signature to that paper." She turned on her heel and left. With dignity she walked up the stairs to her room, where she locked the door and wept. She hadn't thought it would go this far.

◻

He stared after her. She meant it. She *meant* it! Dear God! In order to get some kind of bizarre revenge on Kit she was willing to face the disgrace that society heaped upon a divorced woman. Why? There was no way she could know the truth about them.

He frantically scanned the document. Kit was not named, thank God. The grounds were Nicholas Stuart's "unmoral, indecent, and flagrant sexual misconduct with a person known to the petitioner."

"Oh, my God," he said, in horrified realization. "She does know."

The terms of the divorce petition were merciless: he would not be allowed to see the children until they were twenty-one and then only if the children asked to see him.

"Oh, God," he said again. Then he broke into harsh laughter. "Oh, God, You are getting even, aren't You? You don't let a broken promise go unnoticed! My children. You can't let her take away my children."

A small voice spoke: "But she isn't, is she? She said it was left to you. If you don't sign it, if you give up Kit, you will not lose the children. And isn't Kit leaving anyway? Are you not being separated again, this time through Kit's decision?"

Damn them! Damn them both, Kit and Bronwyn. He wished he'd never set eyes on either of them.

He leaped up, grabbed his coat and a few small items, and bolted from the house. "Tell Mrs. Stuart I will be away for a few days," he told the day girl as he hurried from the house, with a little bundle under one arm.

He had to get away from the house, from her, from Kit, from the children. He had to think things through.

❐

Kit was shaving, dressed only in trousers and shoes, when someone knocked on the door. Thinking it was Francis, who was supposed to come there this morning, he went to the door with a towel around his bare neck, lather on his face, and a razor in his hand. He was taken aback to see Mrs. Stuart.

Hastily he wiped off the lather. "Uh – Mrs. Stuart, would you, uh, like to come in?"

She stepped in and he loped to the bedroom to pull on a shirt and coat.

"Won't you, uh, won't you sit down?" he asked, when he returned in a few minutes, his collar open and his sleeve buttons undone. She was still standing beside the door, her parasol gripped like a weapon.

"No. Mr. St. Denys, I have come to tell you that you have lost the battle."

"What battle?"

"Nicholas is my husband. You can't take him away from me."

"My dear lady, that never entered my mind." He thought about telling her she didn't know what she was talking about, but he suddenly knew that, somehow, she did.

"I don't know why you felt compelled to hurt me and my children, but—"

"I never intended to hurt you or the children. Mrs. Stuart, I have nothing but admiration for you as a woman and a mother, neither of which, I'm sure, is easy. And I have a heart full of gratitude. You took me in when I had no other place to go except a madhouse."

"I didn't take you in," she said through stiff lips. "He did."

"You're not making any of this very easy, Mrs. Stuart."

"Why should I?"

"Do you think I make a practice of injuring wives, ma'am? I assure you, I do not."

"I came here for one reason, Mr. St. Denys. Leave my husband alone. He has been given an ultimatum that he will have to accept. I want you to leave our lives alone. I demand that you never see him again under any circumstances."

It was on Kit's tongue to tell her it was a moot point, that he was leaving. Then he said, "Isn't that his decision? If he never wants to see me again, then I'll abide by that. But he has the right to decide what he wants to do. It's his life."

"No. It isn't. When he wed me and accepted the responsibility of Alyce and then sired Jamie—" Looking oddly triumphant, she said, "And that's why you've lost, Mr. St. Denys. You can't give him children. His life is not his own; it's part and parcel of ours and you have no place in it. I am not a person who hates easily, Mr. St. Denys. In fact, I don't believe I have ever hated in my life. Until now. You preyed upon my innocent Nicholas, though I don't know how or why and—"

"I didn't 'prey' upon him, Mrs. Stuart," he said coldly. "He was more than willing."

She choked, "If I had a gun I would shoot you, Mr. St. Denys."

Kit shut the door behind her. He was tired of fighting. Himself, his memories, the world, Nick's wife. St. Denys Hill was a lighthouse in the midst of a hurricane. He wished he could go that very day.

□

In an ugly rented room in New Jersey, Nick paced the floor, stopping from time to time to stare intently at the four things he had brought with him from home.

The divorce petition.

The photograph of himself, Bronwyn, and the children, all looking stiff and unnatural, but forever united as a family on the heavy paper.

The photograph of Kit as Hamlet.

Shakespeare's sonnets.

In times past he would have prayed to God for guidance. Now he knew there was no point in it. He had to make the decision alone.

Throughout the night he continued pacing, occasionally picking up one or another of the objects, and putting it down, often with tears in his eyes.

Give up Jamie? Never see him go to school, put on his first pair of long pants, go to university, bring home an apple-cheeked girl for his parents to meet? Never again feel those chubby little arms around his neck or feel a sloppy baby-kiss on his own lips?

And what of Alyce? Not the child of his body but still his daughter. Not see her complete her metamorphosis from child into woman with a good brain and the will to use it? Not see her also go to university and someday become a bride?

And Bronwyn, what of her? A good woman with strength and intelligence, and such love for him that she was willing to fight for him?

And last, what of Kit? Kit, who had looked so vulnerable. Kit, who lit his life in a way no one else ever had or ever would. He picked up the book of sonnets and though he did not need to read the words written partly in Kit's hand and partly in his, he read them aloud.

"'Without the sanction of Society, Without the sanction of the Church, Without the sanction of God, Without the sanction even of yourself, I love you.'" The words seemed to become part of the air he breathed.

It was almost dawn. He went home on the next boat. His decision was made.

26

Bronwyn was sewing a button on one of Alyce's frocks while Alyce sprawled on the nursery floor reading to Jamie. Nick watched them, unnoticed. Bronwyn laughed at something Alyce read. How long had it been? he wondered, since he had heard her laugh? She looked up and saw him standing there, rumpled and unshaven. She rose, and put the frock aside.

"Alyce, I'm going to talk to your father for a few minutes. Nanny is outside. You can watch Jamie, can't you?"

"Of course, Mama." She rolled her eyes and grinned at her father, who had long since been forgiven. He smiled at her.

Jamie came walking toward him, intense concentration on his little face. Reaching Nick, he leaned against his legs and clutched the fabric of his trousers as if intending to scale the height.

"Up," he demanded. Nick scooped him up and cuddled him.

"My son," he said against the tiny ear. "My sweet little son."

Then he put Jamie down, and followed Bronwyn to the sitting room adjacent to her bedroom. Her back was straight. When she turned to face him, she was smiling slightly and her face was serene.

"Have you made your decision?" she asked.

"Yes." Slowly he handed her the divorce petition. His signature was at the bottom, assenting to everything.

She gasped, and paled. He helped her to her blue velvet chair.

"But why?" she cried, tears welling up. "I was so sure – I thought you would see – *why?*"

He knelt in front of her and took her hands in his. "Dearest girl, it was the most difficult thing I have ever done and I know I will regret it a thousand times."

"I thought you cared – about me, about us–"

"I did. I do. I always will."

"Then tell me why! For the love of God, Nicholas, tell me why! Tell me what I did wrong!"

He was stricken by her words. "You did nothing wrong. Nothing."

"But I couldn't make you happy." Her voice was thick with grief. "I tried. I should have tried harder."

He pressed his lips against the palms of her hands. "No. No. Listen to me. Listen to me. Bronwyn, there could not be a better wife and mother than you. There could not be better children than ours. You gave me peace, something I never really knew before. You gave me contentment. But..." How, he wondered not for the first time, does one explain the unexplainable?

She jerked her hands from his grasp and in frustrated rage beat at his face and shoulders until she stopped, weeping. "I don't want to lose you, Nicholas. Please, please, change your mind. I'll tear the paper up. You said I gave you peace and contentment. Can *he* do the same?"

"No," he said quietly. "He won't bring me peace. He'll give me sleepless nights and unease. It will be like living in the open in the midst of a lightning storm. But I..." His voice trailed off. Explanations were useless. "I love him," he said.

"More than you love us."

"No. Not more. Perhaps I even love you more. But I am *in* love with him and that's ... different altogether." Again he took her hands and looked into her eyes, pleading with her to understand what he himself did not. "Without him I am incomplete. For good or ill, he is the other part of me. I don't know how else to say it."

Her head lowered. Her shoulders shook and she sucked in deep sobbing breaths in an attempt to stop crying. Nick took his handkerchief and gently blotted at her wet face.

"The house is yours, of course. You will want for nothing and neither will the children. I will take whatever steps are necessary to provide for their education. I want..." He stopped and then went on. "I want you to remarry, Bronwyn. Give my children a better father than I have been. Promise me."

"But I want you."

He could not answer and so he put his arms around her. Hers went around his neck and her soft cheek touched his scratchy one.

"All I ask," he said past the tightness in his throat, "is that you write me and let me know how you and the children are; tell me what they're doing; send a photograph once in a while."

With a raw gasp she said, "I didn't know that I could hurt so much a second time. I thought when Alyce's father died I could never hurt that way again. But this is worse. He had no choice. You do."

He brushed her hair back and kissed her. "No, my darling, I don't. And if it's any comfort, he may not even want me. He's going home to England. The ship leaves this afternoon."

He felt like a monster when he saw hope in her eyes. "Then you will come back to us!"

"No. I made the decision. I can't go back on it. It would be no good for any of us." He kissed her again, went to his room, and packed his clothes. He could send for his medical books later. He paused outside the nursery but knew if he went in he was lost. He stopped by the surgery to pick up his medical bag and instruments. Then he walked from the house and did not let himself look back.

❐

The whistle of the steamer *Plantagenet* split the air as the crew cast off from the dock. Gulls swooped and squawked overhead as if trying to hurry the ship along. Kit looked up at them, wishing he were one of them. No cares in life except eating and avoiding being eaten. A short life but a merry one. The deck was crowded at times with people, many of whom would, within a few hours, be in their cabins wishing they were dead. He'd never been seasick but he felt sorry for those who were. He paid no attention to those who passed him or those who stopped beside him and tried to engage him in conversation; they never stayed long because he did not answer them.

Someone else came to stand beside him. Whoever it was neither moved nor spoke and Kit wished he would go away. He glanced at him from the corner of his eye and then turned toward him in astonishment.

"Nickie! What are you doing here?"

"The same as you. Going home."

The people still thronged about them. Kit had to content himself with just a look, across a gulf of a few inches.

"How did you get on? When? Why?"

Nick smiled, but his eyes were melancholy. "The 'why' I would as soon not talk about yet. As to how and when, I paid some young sport twice what his ticket cost him. You're an expensive addiction, St. Denys."

Kit grinned. "Especially to someone as tight with a dollar as you are." He hoped Nick's sadness would not be there forever.

"At least I'm not a spendthrift. I remember a certain Egyptian vase you bought once for an outlandish sum of money that turned out—"

"—to have been made the year before by a genius at copying artifacts. I know, I know. And you never even knew about the *faux* Rembrandt. You would have been hysterical."

Nick laughed a little. "I can't believe you could be fooled by a fake Rembrandt."

"Ah, but it was a good one." He saw Nick look over his shoulder in the direction of the city that was soon going to be out of sight.

"Don't look back, Nickie. As you once said, it's salt in a wound. Don't look back."

The haunted look came again. "Damn the past, full speed ahead? I don't think I can do that, Kit. I'm not sure I even want to."

"Well, love, whatever you want of me for however long you want it, it's yours."

"Forever, St. Denys. I don't want to ever go through this again."

"Forever is a long time."

"I don't care." He swallowed. "You said it yourself; I need a nest."

"St. Denys Hill will make a fine, big nest." He looked at Nick. "Are you sure you know what you're doing? You know we're going to fall on our faces more than once."

"I know. But if we're there to pick each other up, it won't matter."

Kit's voice was soft. "You know I'll make you angry."

"I know that, too. And I suppose there's some slight, very slight, chance I'll annoy you from time to time."

"Very, very slight. I am so blessed."

Nick moved closer. To hell with what the other passengers might think. They'd been through too much to worry about it. His elbow touched Kit's as it rested on the railing. His left hand sought Kit's right. They turned their faces toward the open sea. Their hands were palm to palm and their fingers were linked, warm in spite of the wintry air.

A gull flew a noisy loop in front of them.

Kit made a face at the bird. "Did anyone ask for your opinion?" he said.

The bird flew away in a dudgeon.

The gray sea rolled on beneath the homebound ship.